SNOOPY™

COWABUNGA!

SNOOPY™
COWABUNGA!

CHARLES M. SCHULZ

**Andrews McMeel
Publishing, LLC**
Kansas City • Sydney • London

Andrews McMeel Publishing, LLC
an Andrews McMeel Universal company
1130 Walnut Street, Kansas City, Missouri 64106

www.andrewsmcmeel.com

www.peanuts.com

13 14 15 16 17 SDB 10 9 8 7 6 5 4 3 2

ISBN: 978-1-4494-5079-3

Library of Congress Control Number: 2013940278

Made by:
Shenzhen Donnelley Printing Company Ltd.
Address and location of manufacturer:
No. 47, Wuhe Nan Road, Bantian Ind. Zone,
Shenzhen China, 518129
2nd Printing – 8/26/13

ATTENTION: SCHOOLS AND BUSINESSES

Andrews McMeel books are available at quantity discounts with bulk purchase for educational, business, or sales promotional use. For information, please e-mail the Andrews McMeel Publishing Special Sales Department:
specialsales@amuniversal.com

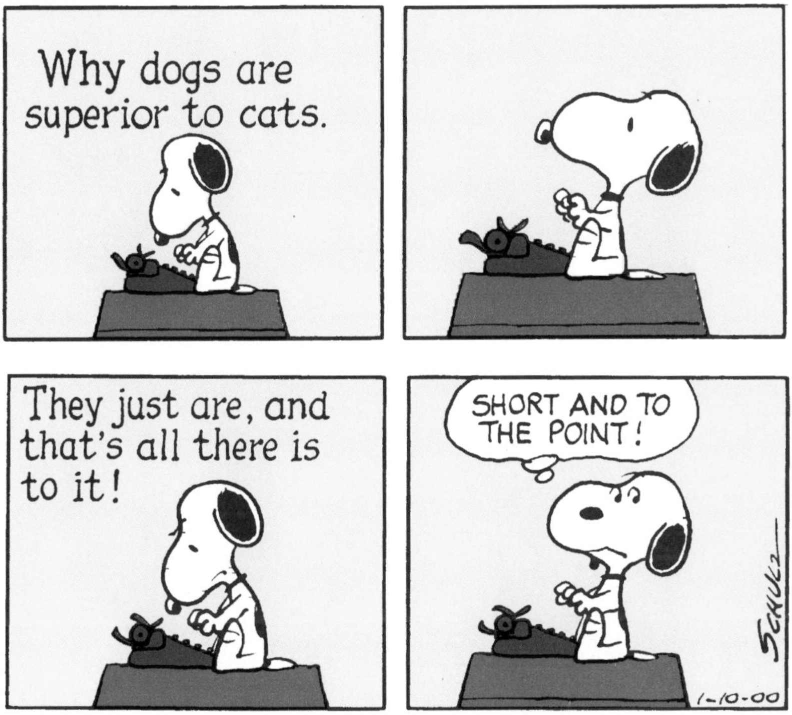
Why dogs are superior to cats.
They just are, and that's all there is to it!
SHORT AND TO THE POINT!
SCHULZ
1-10-00

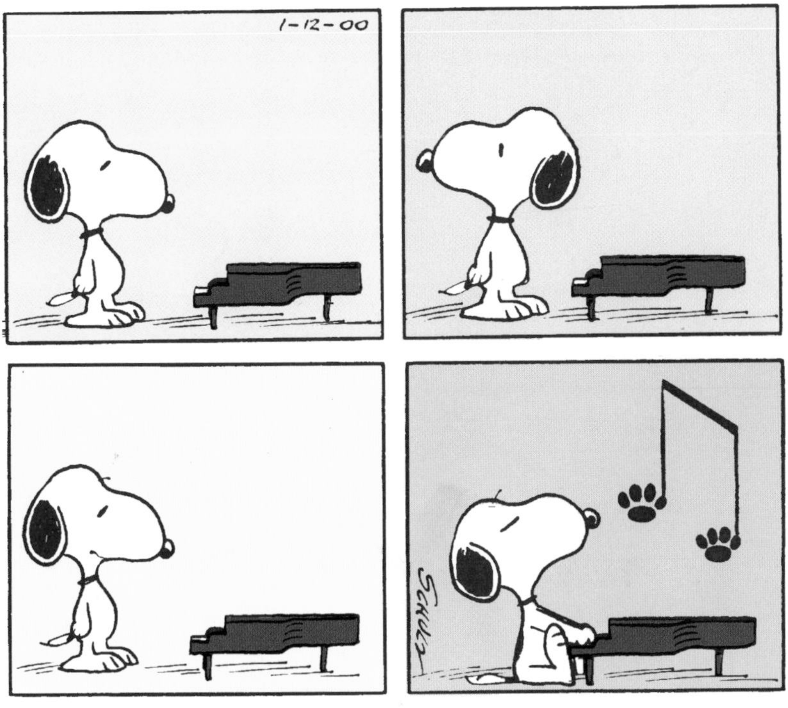
1-12-00
SCHULZ

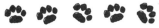

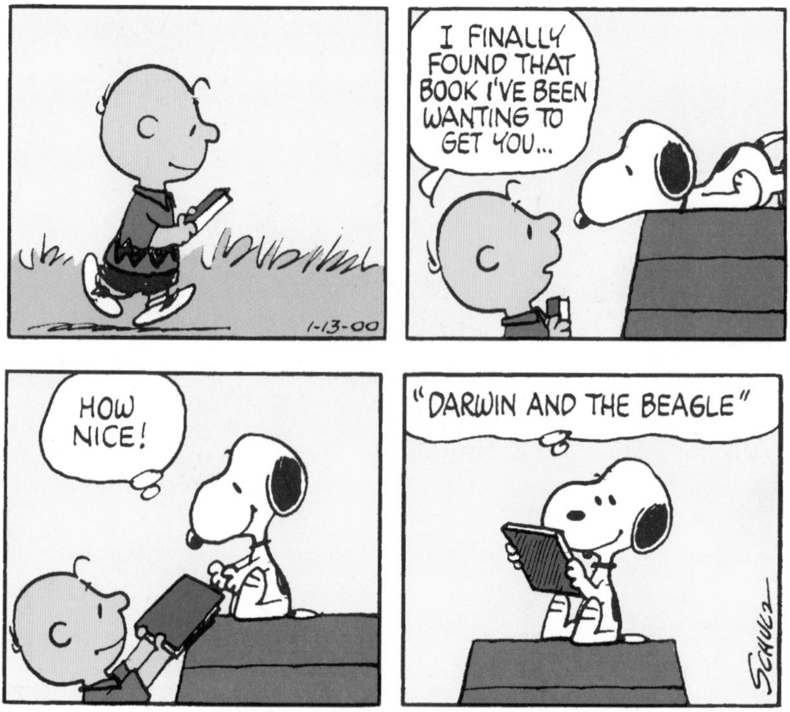
1-13-00
I FINALLY FOUND THAT BOOK I'VE BEEN WANTING TO GET YOU...
HOW NICE!
"DARWIN AND THE BEAGLE"
SCHULZ

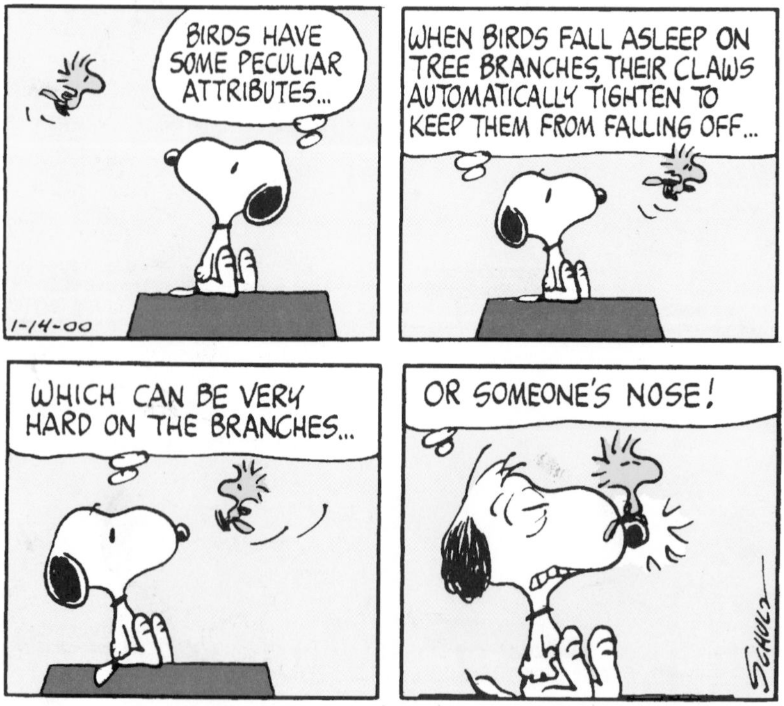
BIRDS HAVE SOME PECULIAR ATTRIBUTES...
1-14-00
WHEN BIRDS FALL ASLEEP ON TREE BRANCHES, THEIR CLAWS AUTOMATICALLY TIGHTEN TO KEEP THEM FROM FALLING OFF...
WHICH CAN BE VERY HARD ON THE BRANCHES...
OR SOMEONE'S NOSE!
SCHULZ

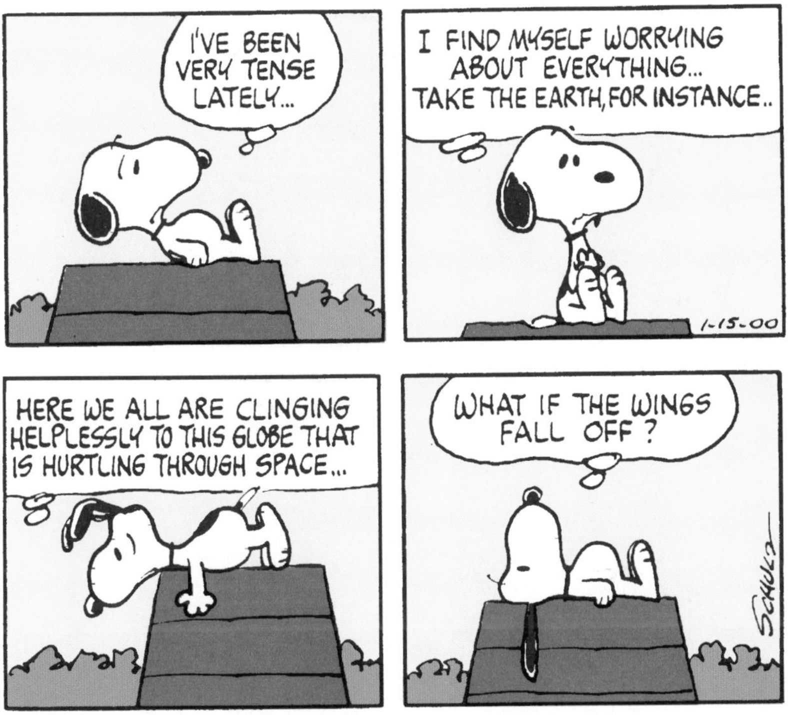
I'VE BEEN VERY TENSE LATELY...
I FIND MYSELF WORRYING ABOUT EVERYTHING... TAKE THE EARTH, FOR INSTANCE..
1-15-00
HERE WE ALL ARE CLINGING HELPLESSLY TO THIS GLOBE THAT IS HURTLING THROUGH SPACE...
WHAT IF THE WINGS FALL OFF ?
SCHULZ

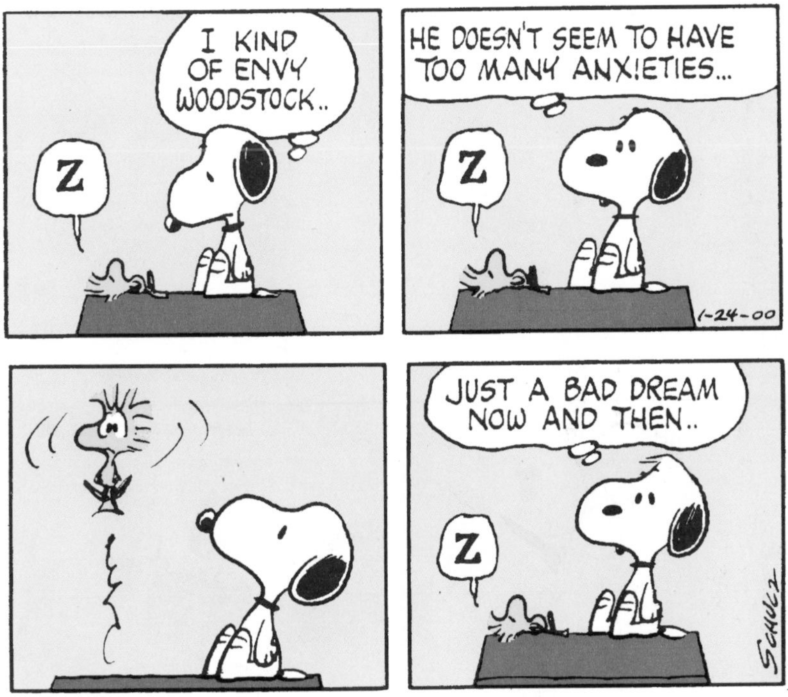
I KIND OF ENVY WOODSTOCK..
Z
HE DOESN'T SEEM TO HAVE TOO MANY ANXIETIES...
Z
1-24-00
JUST A BAD DREAM NOW AND THEN..
Z
SCHULZ

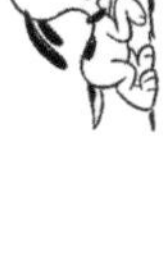

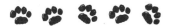

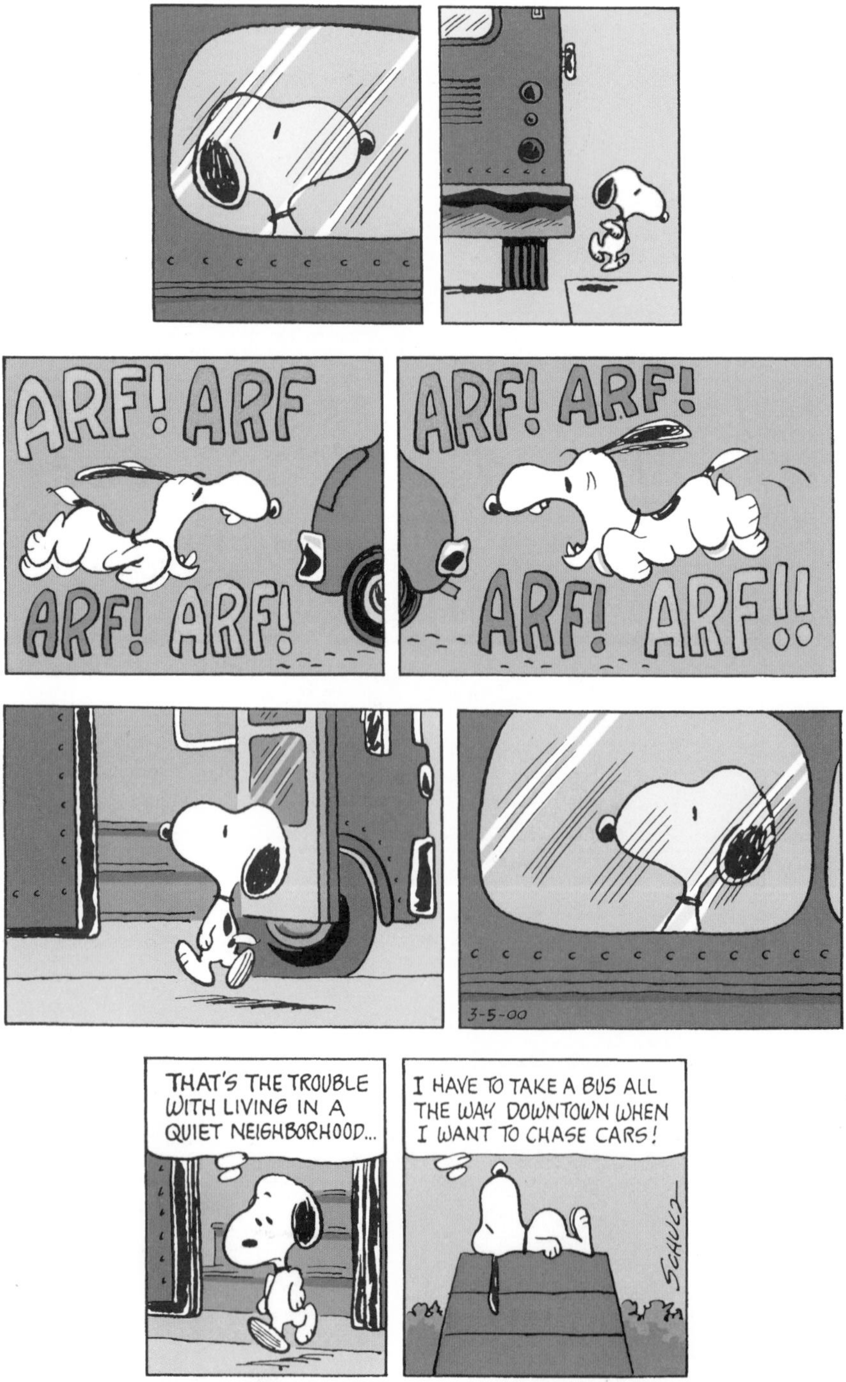
ARF! ARF
ARF! ARF!
ARF! ARF!
ARF! ARF!!
3-5-00
THAT'S THE TROUBLE WITH LIVING IN A QUIET NEIGHBORHOOD...
I HAVE TO TAKE A BUS ALL THE WAY DOWNTOWN WHEN I WANT TO CHASE CARS!
SCHULZ

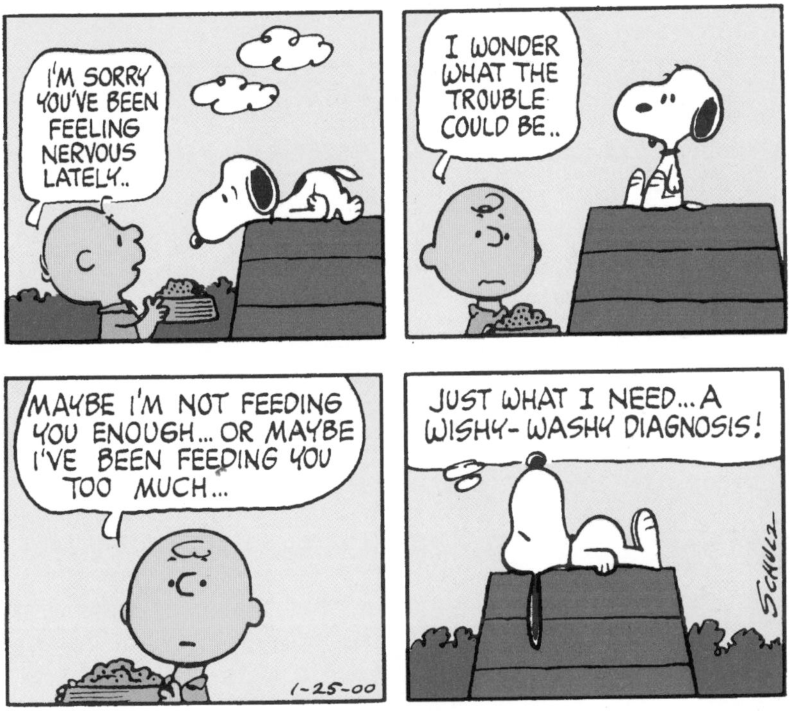
I'M SORRY YOU'VE BEEN FEELING NERVOUS LATELY..
I WONDER WHAT THE TROUBLE COULD BE..
MAYBE I'M NOT FEEDING YOU ENOUGH... OR MAYBE I'VE BEEN FEEDING YOU TOO MUCH...
1-25-00
JUST WHAT I NEED... A WISHY-WASHY DIAGNOSIS!
SCHULZ

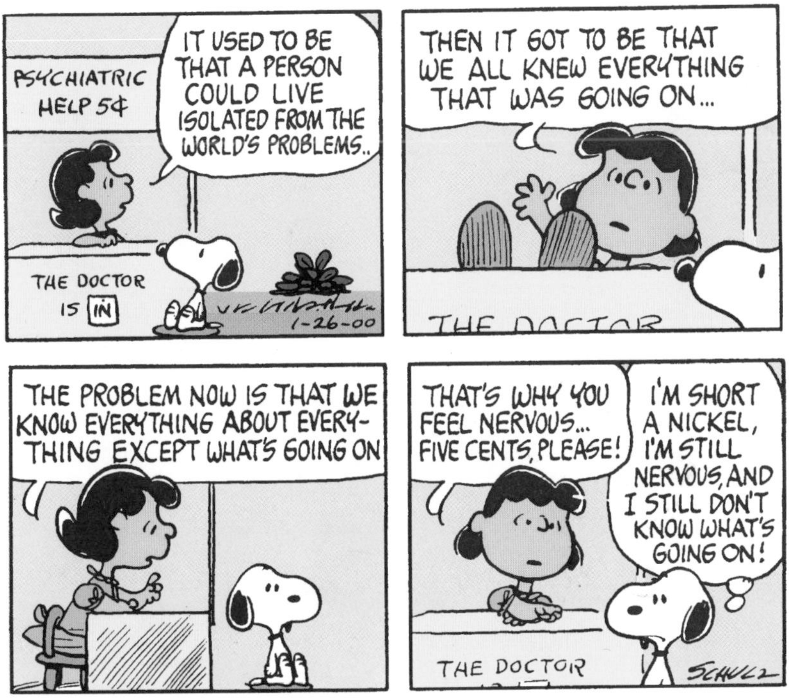
PSYCHIATRIC HELP 5¢
IT USED TO BE THAT A PERSON COULD LIVE ISOLATED FROM THE WORLD'S PROBLEMS..
THE DOCTOR IS IN
1-26-00
THEN IT GOT TO BE THAT WE ALL KNEW EVERYTHING THAT WAS GOING ON...
THE PROBLEM NOW IS THAT WE KNOW EVERYTHING ABOUT EVERYTHING EXCEPT WHAT'S GOING ON
THAT'S WHY YOU FEEL NERVOUS... FIVE CENTS, PLEASE!
I'M SHORT A NICKEL, I'M STILL NERVOUS, AND I STILL DON'T KNOW WHAT'S GOING ON!
THE DOCTOR
SCHULZ

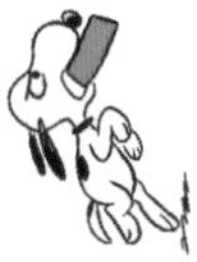

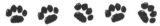

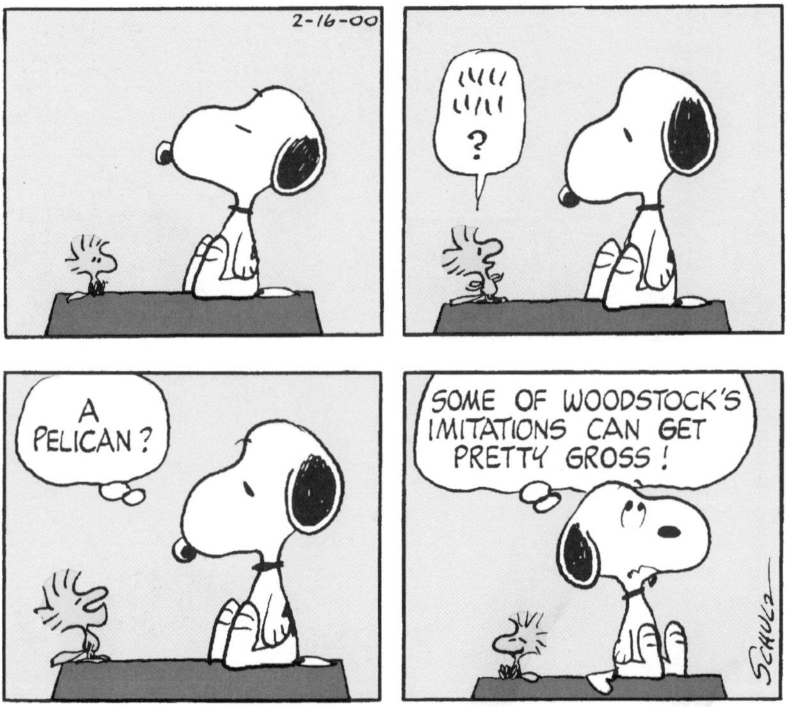
2-16-00
?
A PELICAN?
SOME OF WOODSTOCK'S IMITATIONS CAN GET PRETTY GROSS!
SCHULZ

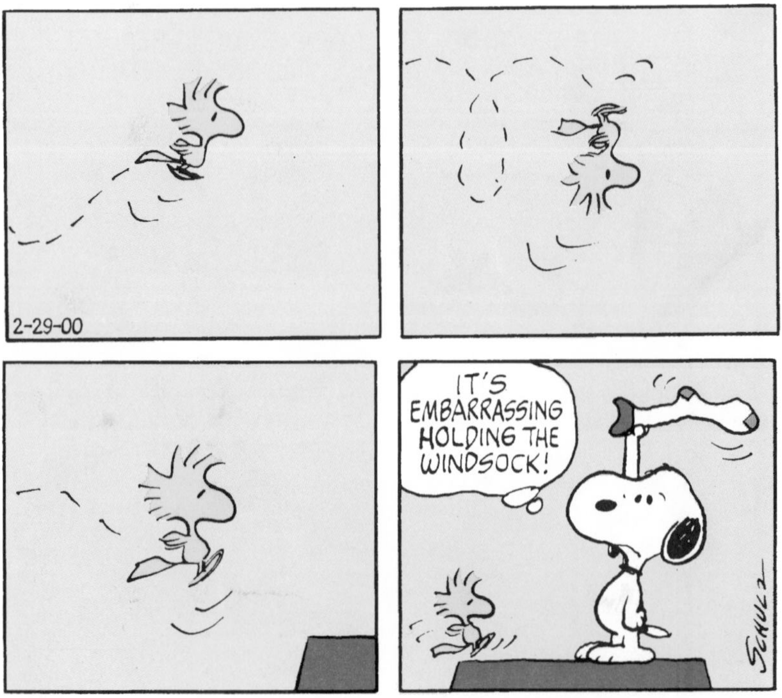
2-29-00
IT'S EMBARRASSING HOLDING THE WINDSOCK!
SCHULZ

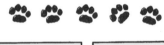

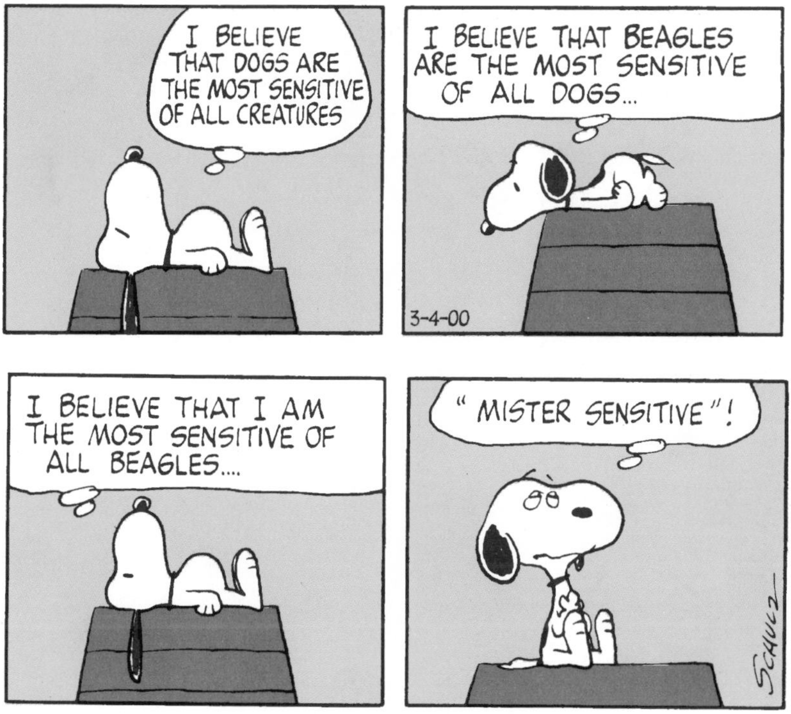
I BELIEVE THAT DOGS ARE THE MOST SENSITIVE OF ALL CREATURES
I BELIEVE THAT BEAGLES ARE THE MOST SENSITIVE OF ALL DOGS...
3-4-00
I BELIEVE THAT I AM THE MOST SENSITIVE OF ALL BEAGLES....
"MISTER SENSITIVE"!
SCHULZ

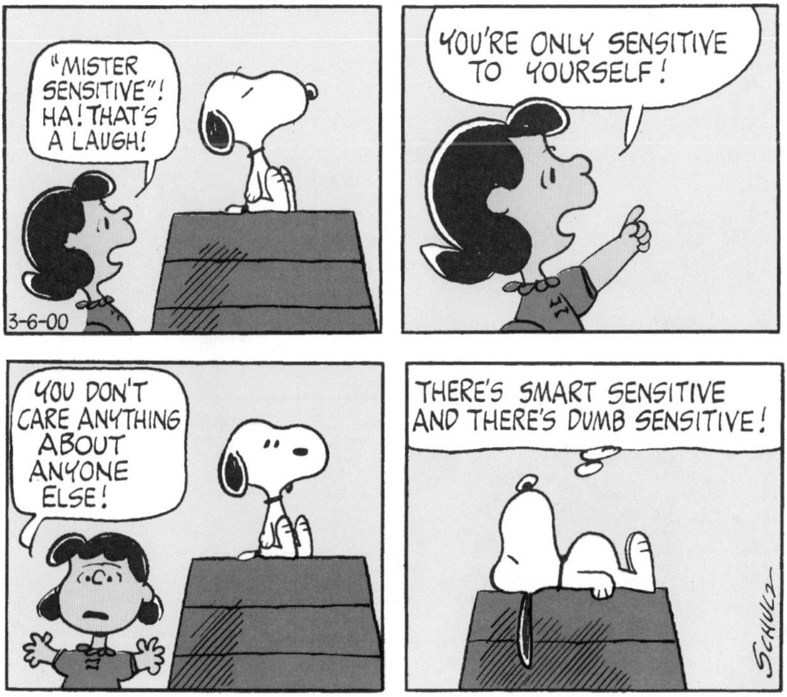
"MISTER SENSITIVE"! HA! THAT'S A LAUGH!
3-6-00
YOU'RE ONLY SENSITIVE TO YOURSELF!
YOU DON'T CARE ANYTHING ABOUT ANYONE ELSE!
THERE'S SMART SENSITIVE AND THERE'S DUMB SENSITIVE!
SCHULZ

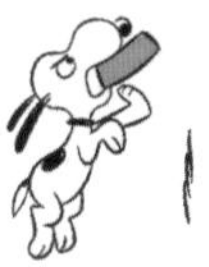

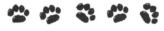

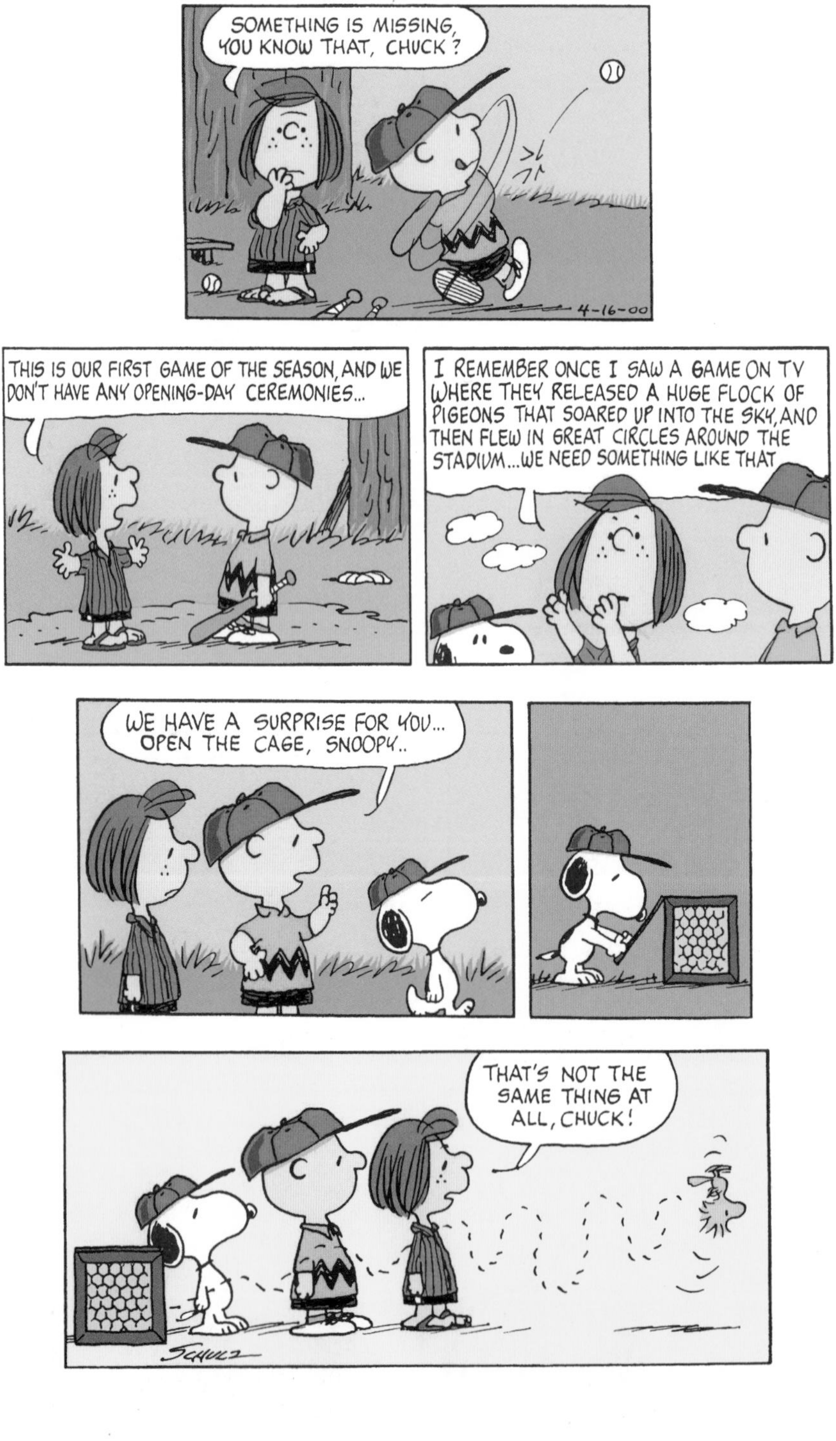
SOMETHING IS MISSING, YOU KNOW THAT, CHUCK?
4-16-00
THIS IS OUR FIRST GAME OF THE SEASON, AND WE DON'T HAVE ANY OPENING-DAY CEREMONIES...
I REMEMBER ONCE I SAW A GAME ON TV WHERE THEY RELEASED A HUGE FLOCK OF PIGEONS THAT SOARED UP INTO THE SKY, AND THEN FLEW IN GREAT CIRCLES AROUND THE STADIUM...WE NEED SOMETHING LIKE THAT
WE HAVE A SURPRISE FOR YOU... OPEN THE CAGE, SNOOPY..
THAT'S NOT THE SAME THING AT ALL, CHUCK!
SCHULZ

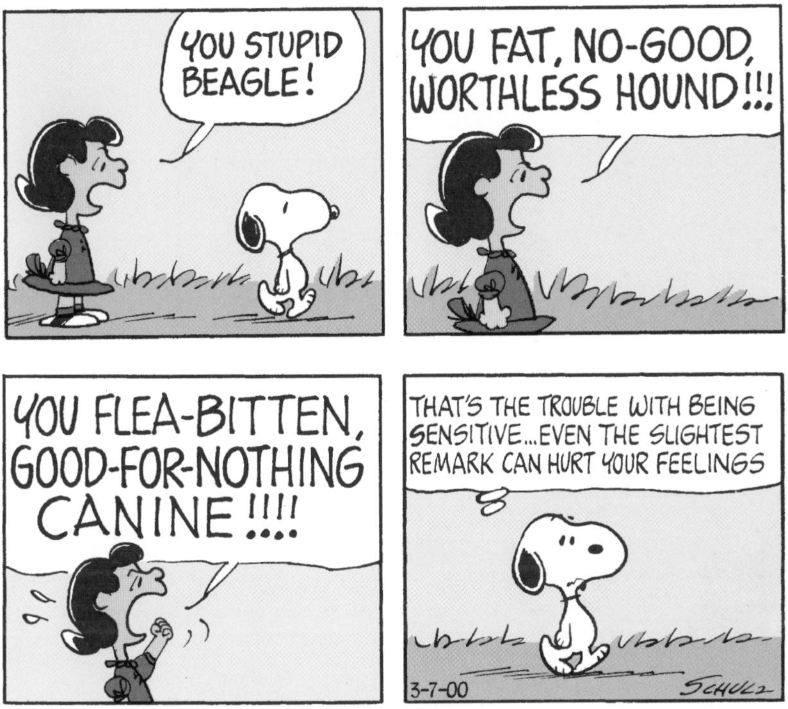
YOU STUPID BEAGLE!
YOU FAT, NO-GOOD, WORTHLESS HOUND!!!
YOU FLEA-BITTEN, GOOD-FOR-NOTHING CANINE!!!!
THAT'S THE TROUBLE WITH BEING SENSITIVE...EVEN THE SLIGHTEST REMARK CAN HURT YOUR FEELINGS
3-7-00
SCHULZ

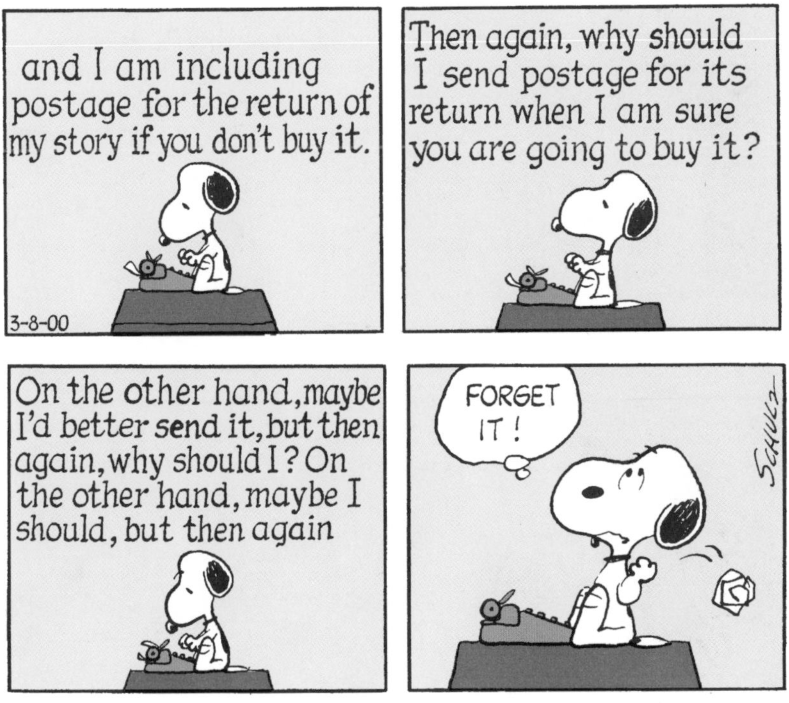
and I am including postage for the return of my story if you don't buy it.
3-8-00
Then again, why should I send postage for its return when I am sure you are going to buy it?
On the other hand, maybe I'd better send it, but then again, why should I? On the other hand, maybe I should, but then again
FORGET IT!
SCHULZ

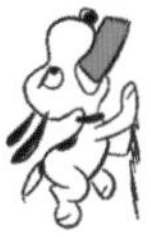

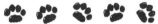

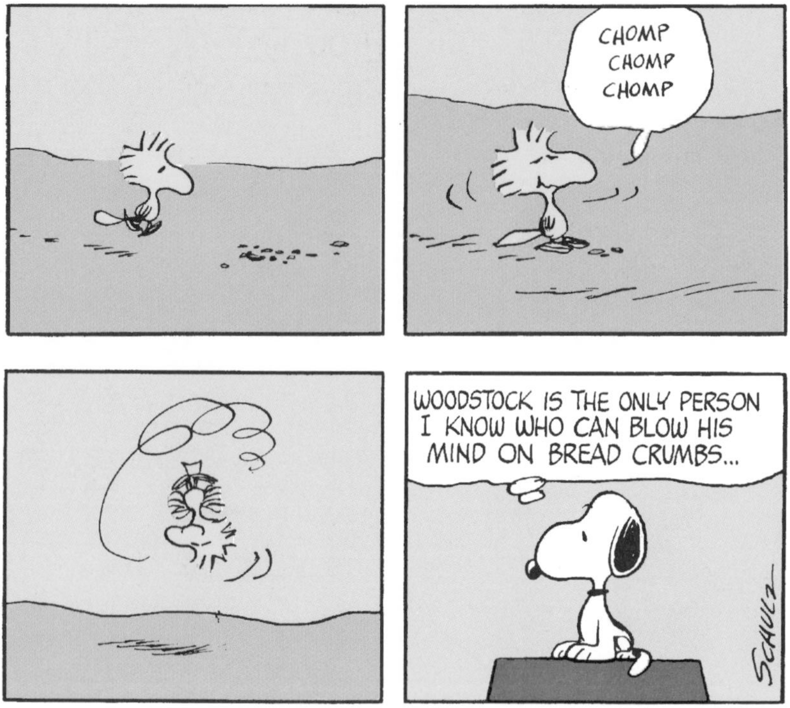
CHOMP
CHOMP
CHOMP
WOODSTOCK IS THE ONLY PERSON I KNOW WHO CAN BLOW HIS MIND ON BREAD CRUMBS...
SCHULZ

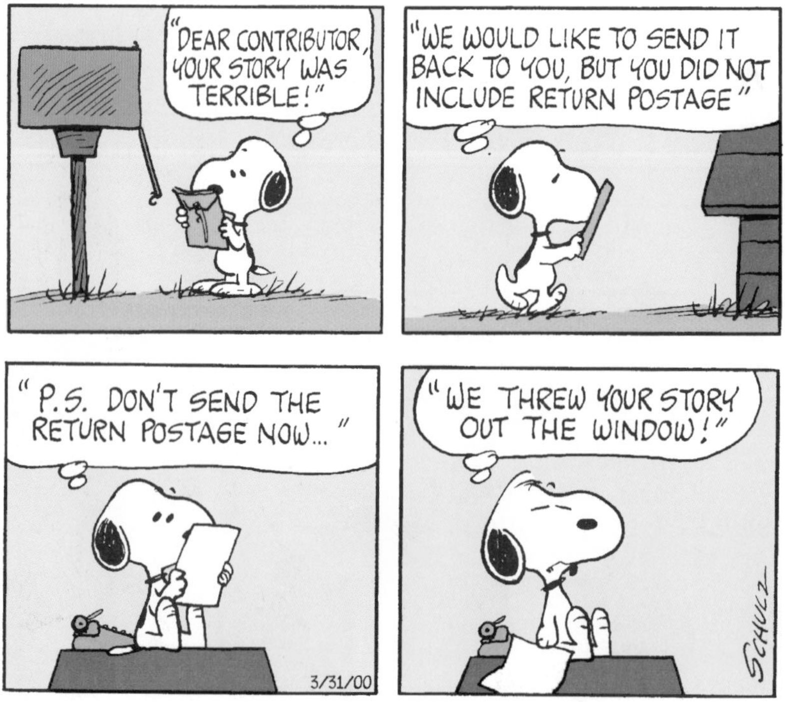
"DEAR CONTRIBUTOR, YOUR STORY WAS TERRIBLE!"
"WE WOULD LIKE TO SEND IT BACK TO YOU, BUT YOU DID NOT INCLUDE RETURN POSTAGE"
"P.S. DON'T SEND THE RETURN POSTAGE NOW..."
3/31/00
"WE THREW YOUR STORY OUT THE WINDOW!"
SCHULZ

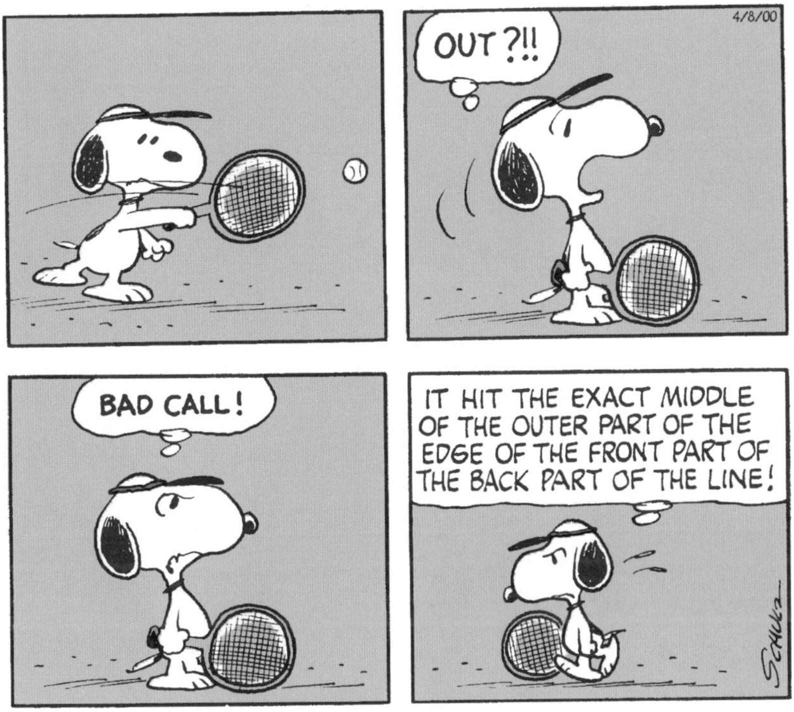
4/8/00
OUT?!!
BAD CALL!
IT HIT THE EXACT MIDDLE OF THE OUTER PART OF THE EDGE OF THE FRONT PART OF THE BACK PART OF THE LINE!
SCHULZ

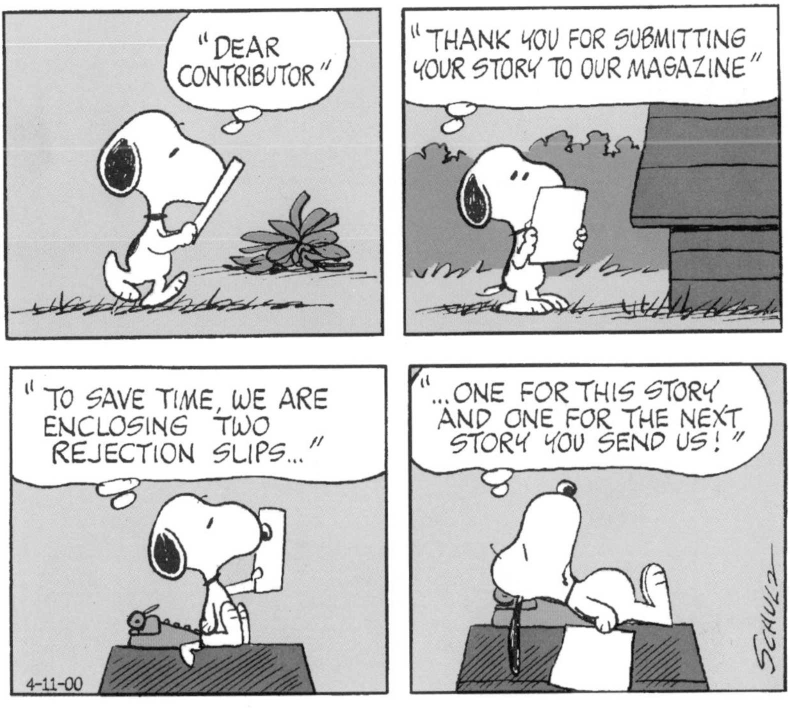
"DEAR CONTRIBUTOR"
"THANK YOU FOR SUBMITTING YOUR STORY TO OUR MAGAZINE"
"TO SAVE TIME, WE ARE ENCLOSING TWO REJECTION SLIPS..."
"...ONE FOR THIS STORY AND ONE FOR THE NEXT STORY YOU SEND US!"
4-11-00
SCHULZ

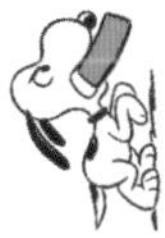

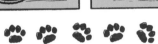

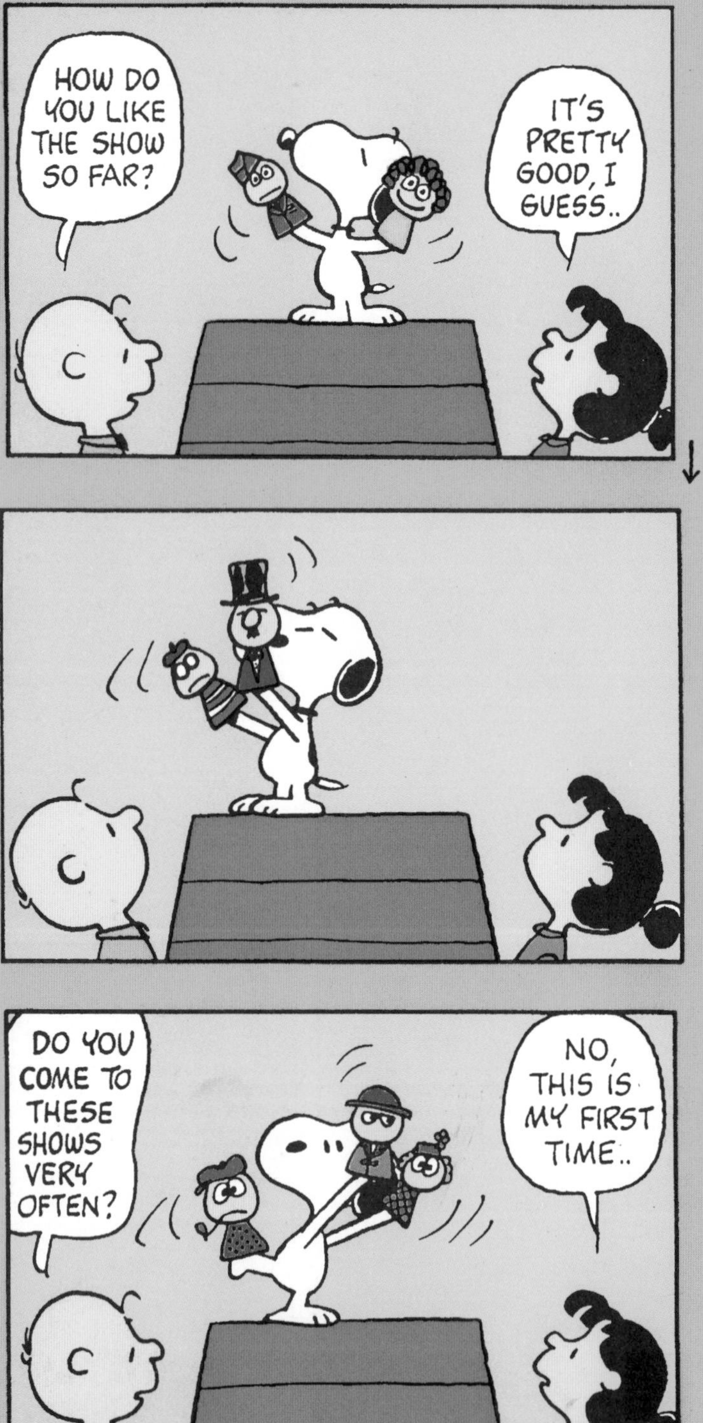
HOW DO YOU LIKE THE SHOW SO FAR?
IT'S PRETTY GOOD, I GUESS..
DO YOU COME TO THESE SHOWS VERY OFTEN?
NO, THIS IS MY FIRST TIME..

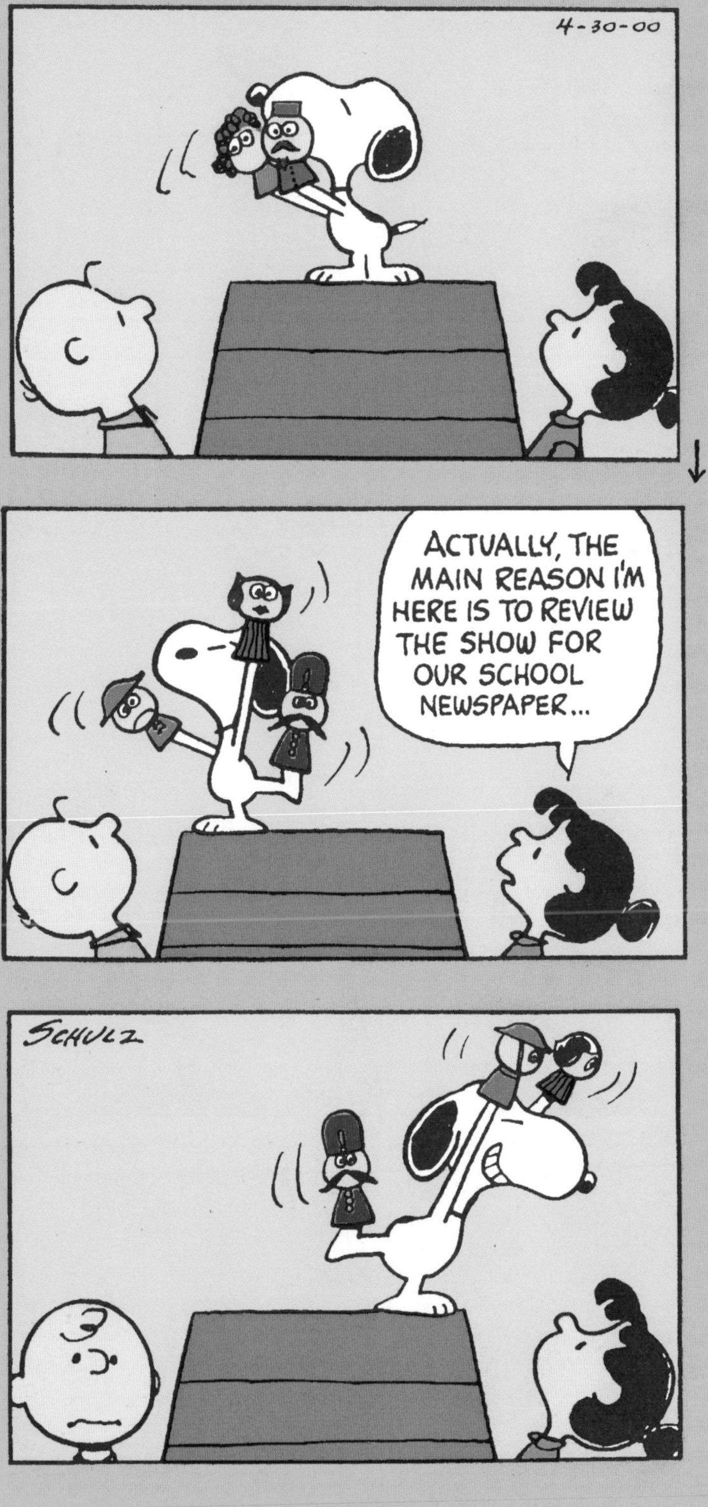
4-30-00
ACTUALLY, THE MAIN REASON I'M HERE IS TO REVIEW THE SHOW FOR OUR SCHOOL NEWSPAPER...
SCHULZ

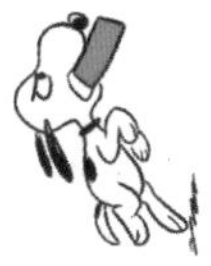

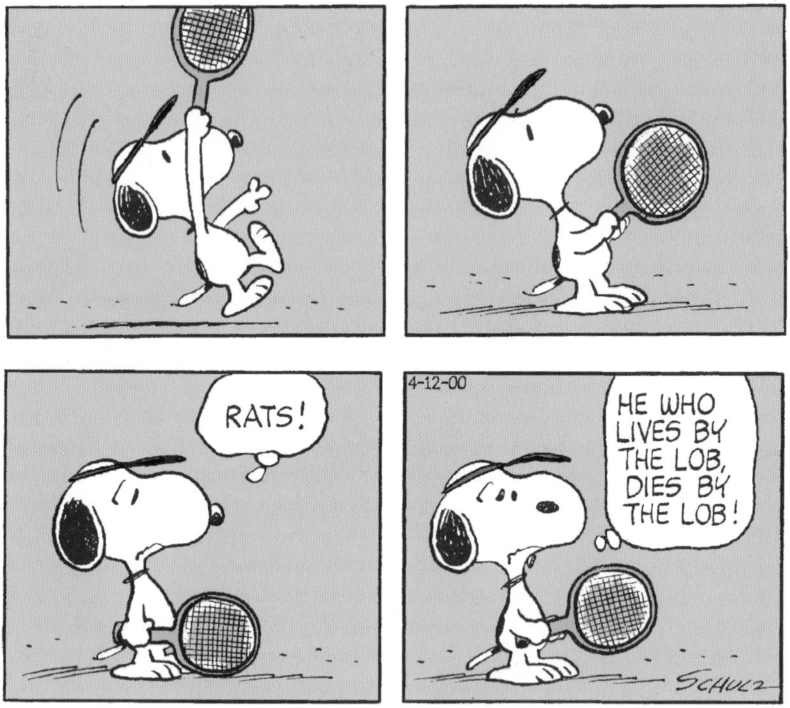
4-12-00
RATS!
HE WHO LIVES BY THE LOB, DIES BY THE LOB!
SCHULZ

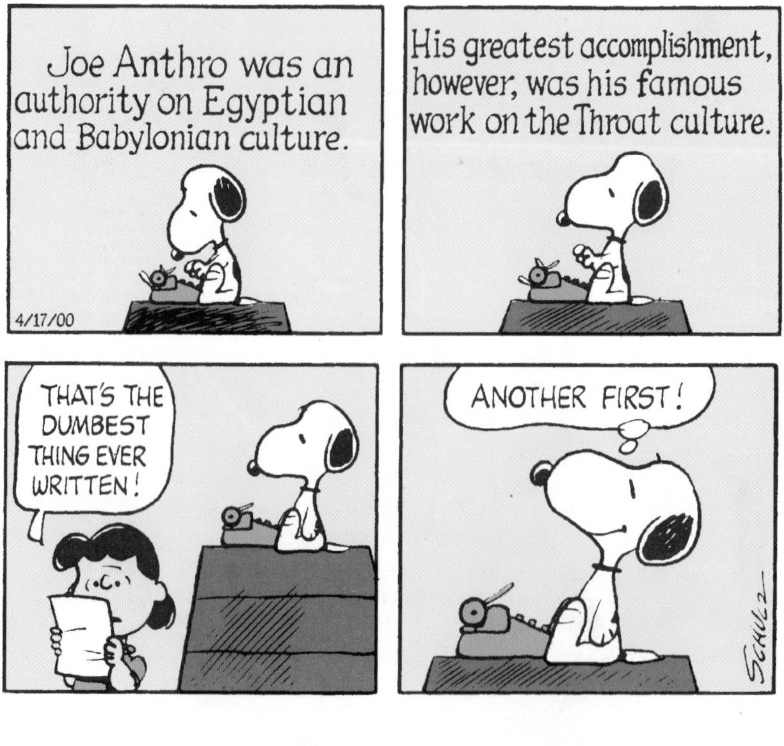
Joe Anthro was an authority on Egyptian and Babylonian culture.
4/17/00
His greatest accomplishment, however, was his famous work on the Throat culture.
THAT'S THE DUMBEST THING EVER WRITTEN!
ANOTHER FIRST!
SCHULZ

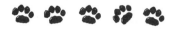

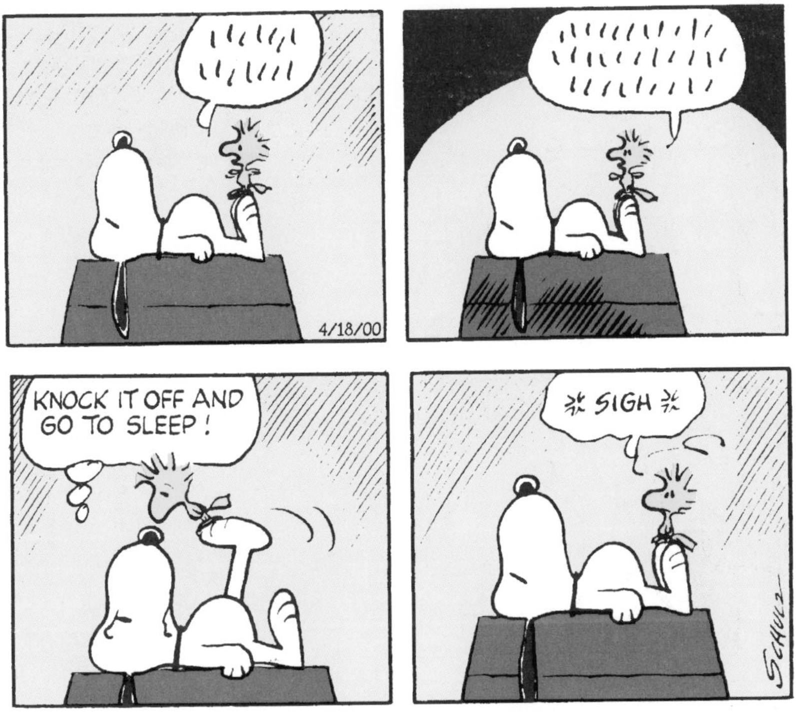
4/18/00
KNOCK IT OFF AND GO TO SLEEP!
SIGH
SCHULZ

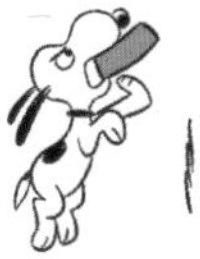

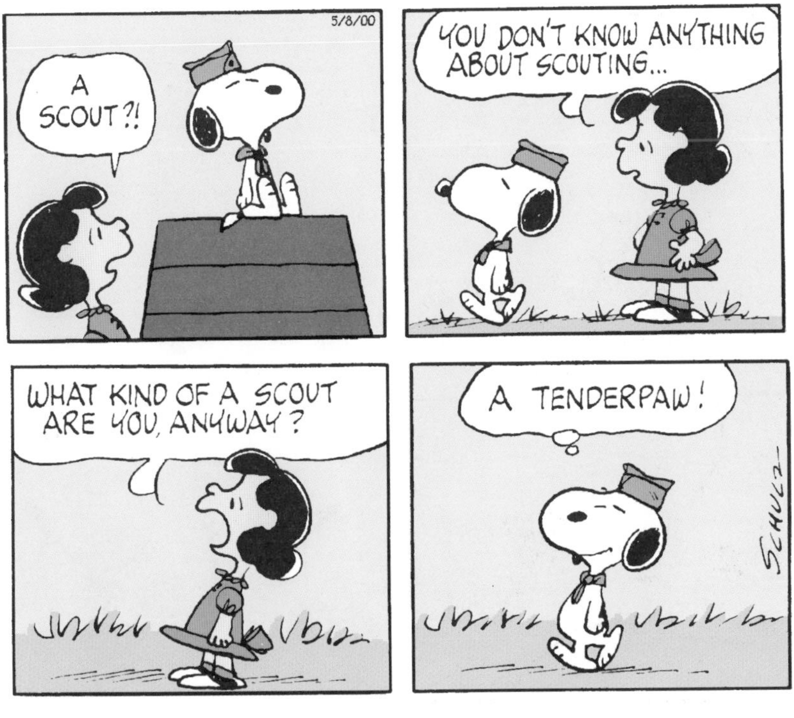
5/8/00
A SCOUT?!
YOU DON'T KNOW ANYTHING ABOUT SCOUTING...
WHAT KIND OF A SCOUT ARE YOU, ANYWAY?
A TENDERPAW!
SCHULZ

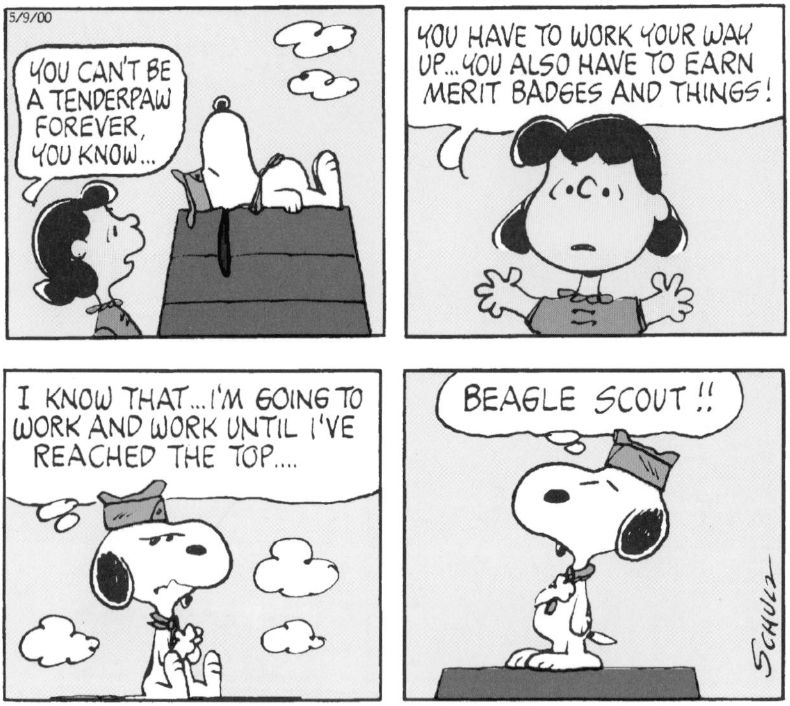
5/9/00
YOU CAN'T BE A TENDERPAW FOREVER, YOU KNOW...
YOU HAVE TO WORK YOUR WAY UP...YOU ALSO HAVE TO EARN MERIT BADGES AND THINGS!
I KNOW THAT...I'M GOING TO WORK AND WORK UNTIL I'VE REACHED THE TOP....
BEAGLE SCOUT!!
SCHULZ

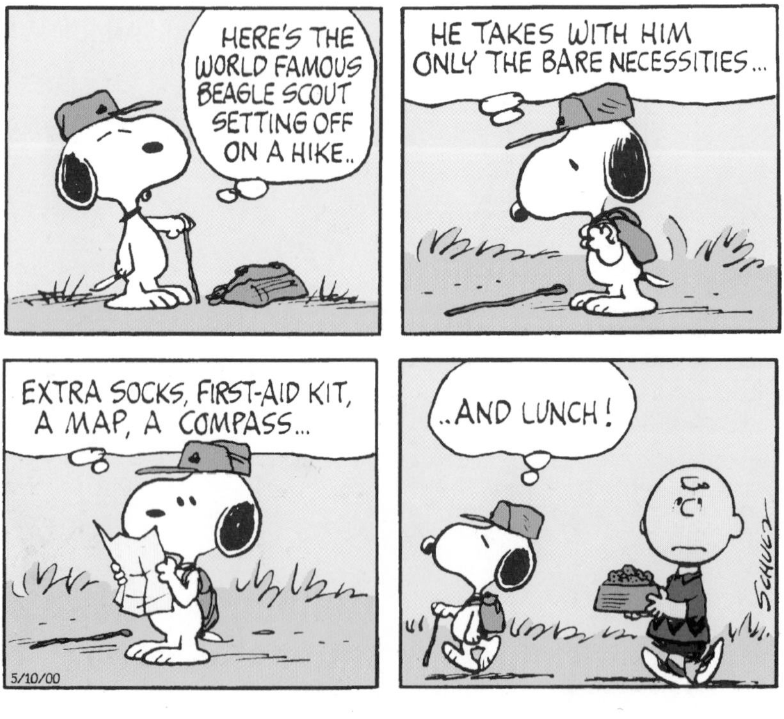
HERE'S THE WORLD FAMOUS BEAGLE SCOUT SETTING OFF ON A HIKE..
HE TAKES WITH HIM ONLY THE BARE NECESSITIES...
EXTRA SOCKS, FIRST-AID KIT, A MAP, A COMPASS...
..AND LUNCH!
SCHULZ
5/10/00

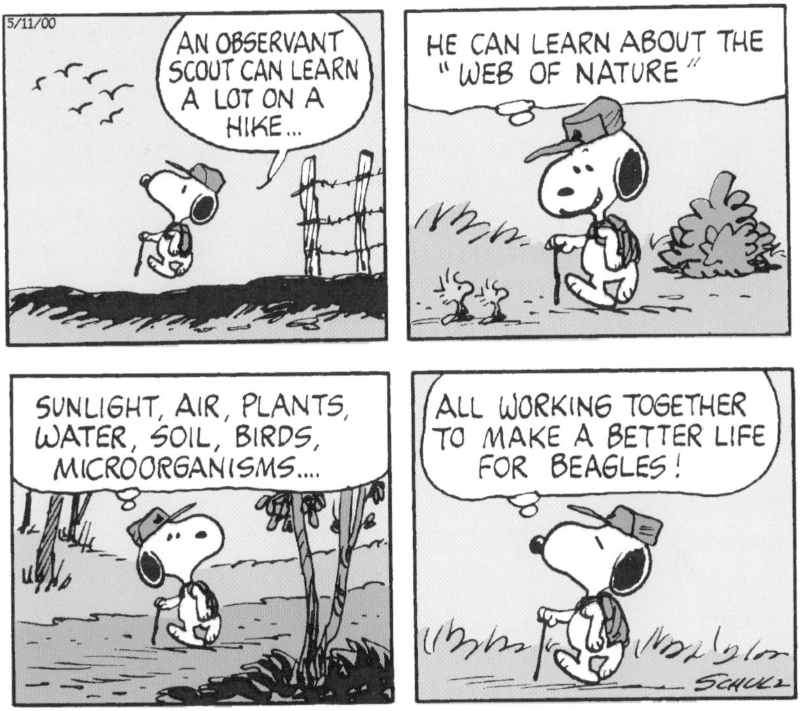
5/11/00
AN OBSERVANT SCOUT CAN LEARN A LOT ON A HIKE...
HE CAN LEARN ABOUT THE "WEB OF NATURE"
SUNLIGHT, AIR, PLANTS, WATER, SOIL, BIRDS, MICROORGANISMS....
ALL WORKING TOGETHER TO MAKE A BETTER LIFE FOR BEAGLES!
SCHULZ

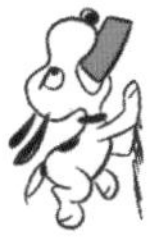

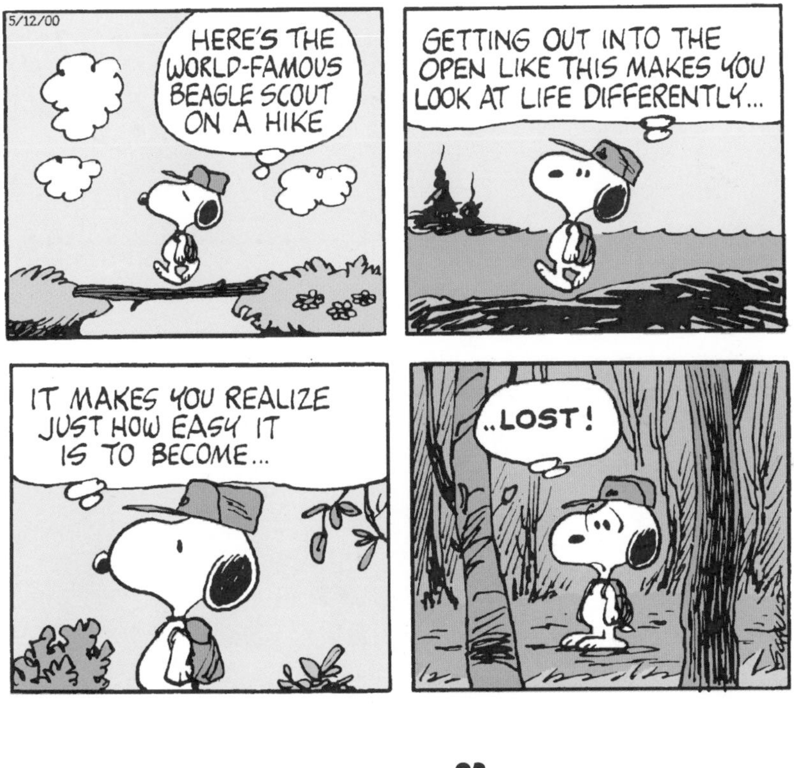
5/12/00
HERE'S THE WORLD-FAMOUS BEAGLE SCOUT ON A HIKE
GETTING OUT INTO THE OPEN LIKE THIS MAKES YOU LOOK AT LIFE DIFFERENTLY...
IT MAKES YOU REALIZE JUST HOW EASY IT IS TO BECOME...
..LOST!
SCHULZ

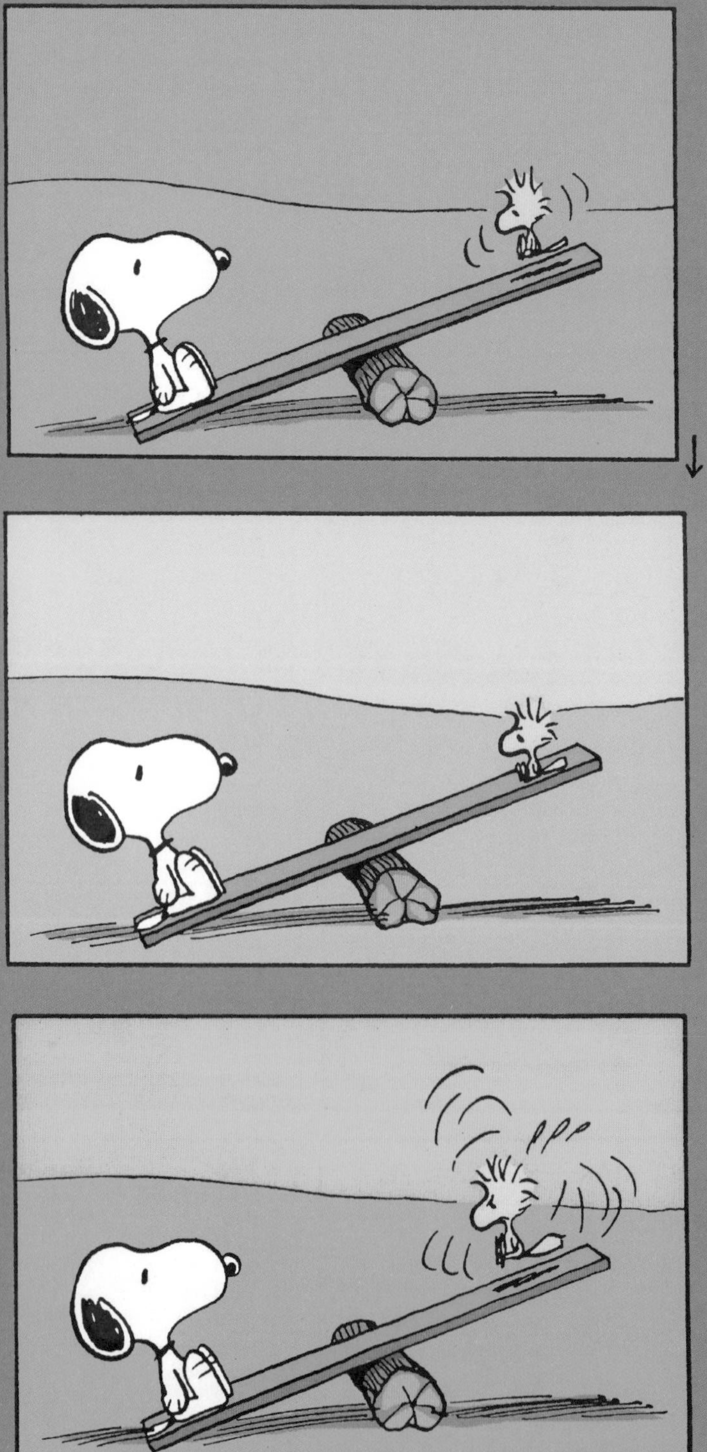

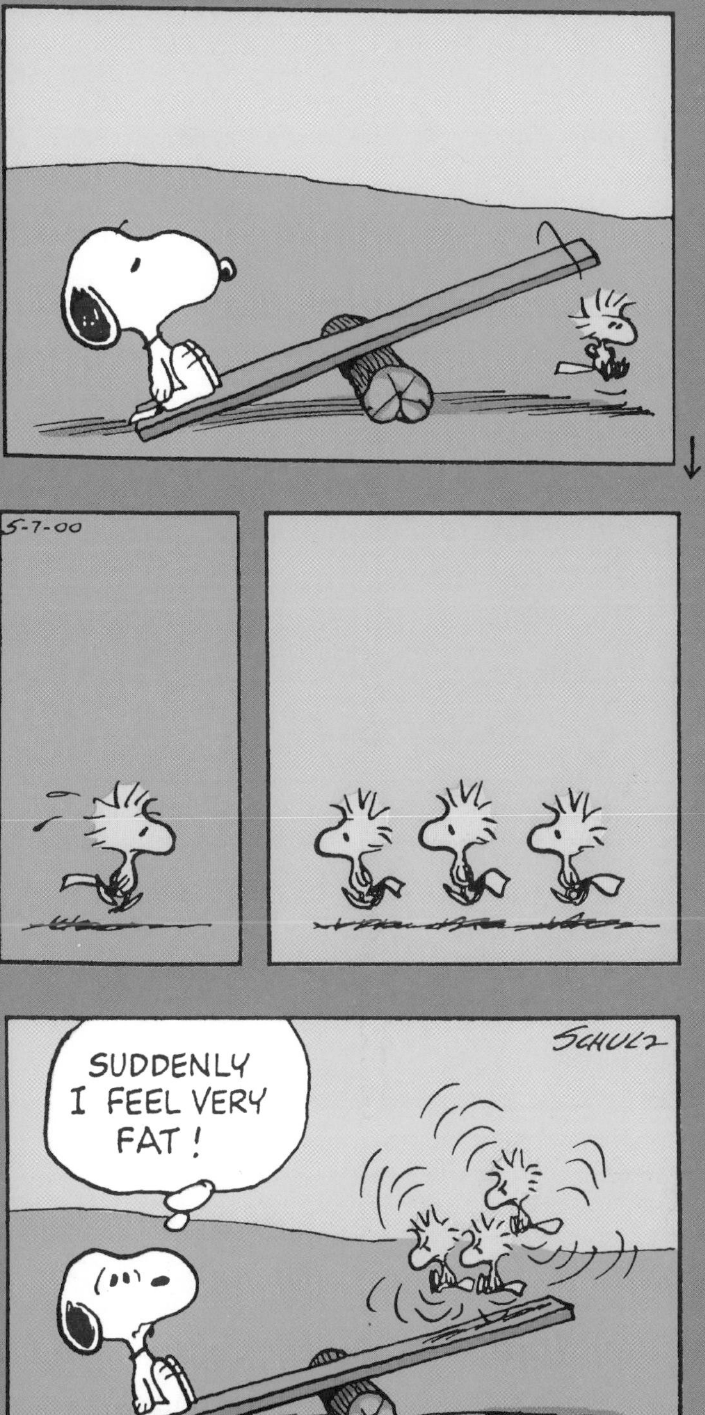
5-7-00
SUDDENLY I FEEL VERY FAT!
SCHULZ

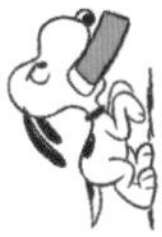

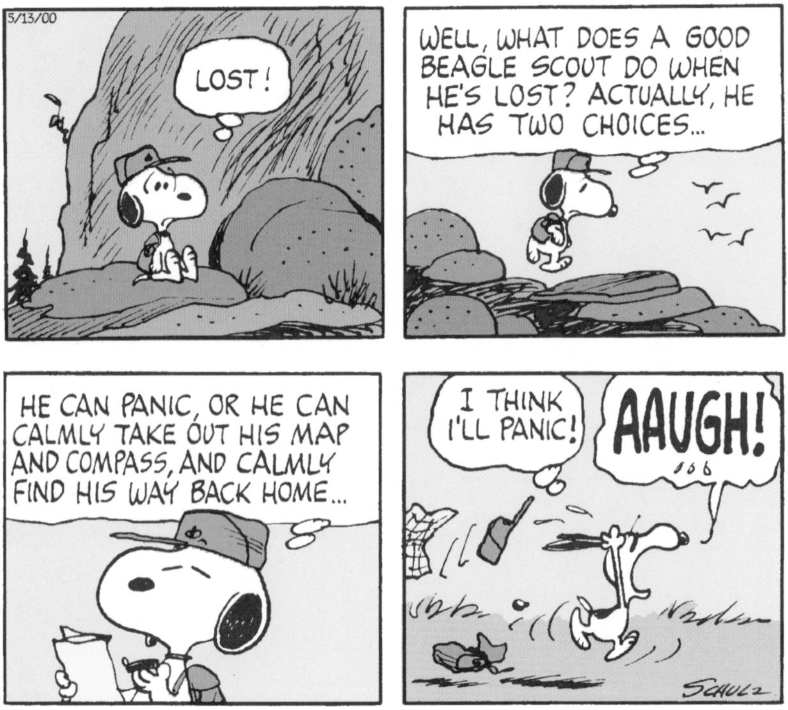
5/13/00
LOST!
WELL, WHAT DOES A GOOD BEAGLE SCOUT DO WHEN HE'S LOST? ACTUALLY, HE HAS TWO CHOICES...
HE CAN PANIC, OR HE CAN CALMLY TAKE OUT HIS MAP AND COMPASS, AND CALMLY FIND HIS WAY BACK HOME...
I THINK I'LL PANIC!
AAUGH!
SCHULZ

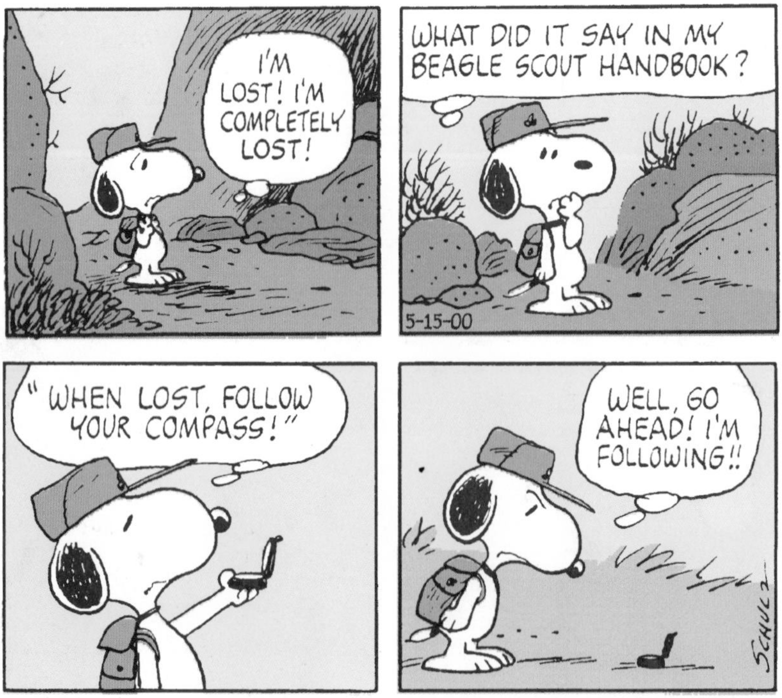
I'M LOST! I'M COMPLETELY LOST!
WHAT DID IT SAY IN MY BEAGLE SCOUT HANDBOOK?
5-15-00
"WHEN LOST, FOLLOW YOUR COMPASS!"
WELL, GO AHEAD! I'M FOLLOWING!!
SCHULZ

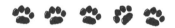

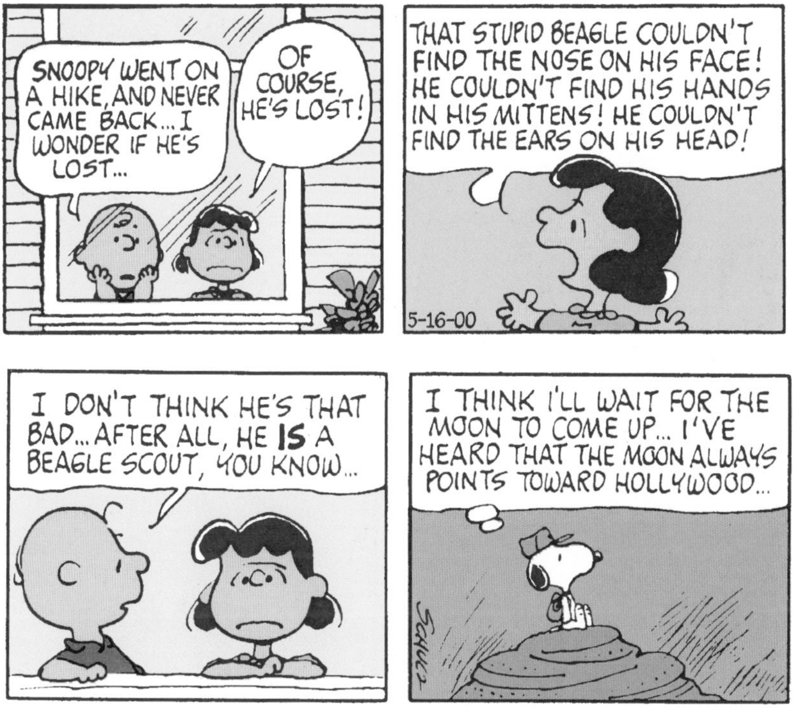
SNOOPY WENT ON A HIKE, AND NEVER CAME BACK... I WONDER IF HE'S LOST...
OF COURSE, HE'S LOST!
THAT STUPID BEAGLE COULDN'T FIND THE NOSE ON HIS FACE! HE COULDN'T FIND HIS HANDS IN HIS MITTENS! HE COULDN'T FIND THE EARS ON HIS HEAD!
5-16-00
I DON'T THINK HE'S THAT BAD... AFTER ALL, HE **IS** A BEAGLE SCOUT, YOU KNOW...
I THINK I'LL WAIT FOR THE MOON TO COME UP... I'VE HEARD THAT THE MOON ALWAYS POINTS TOWARD HOLLYWOOD...
SCHULZ

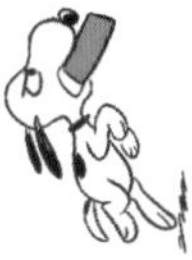

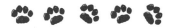

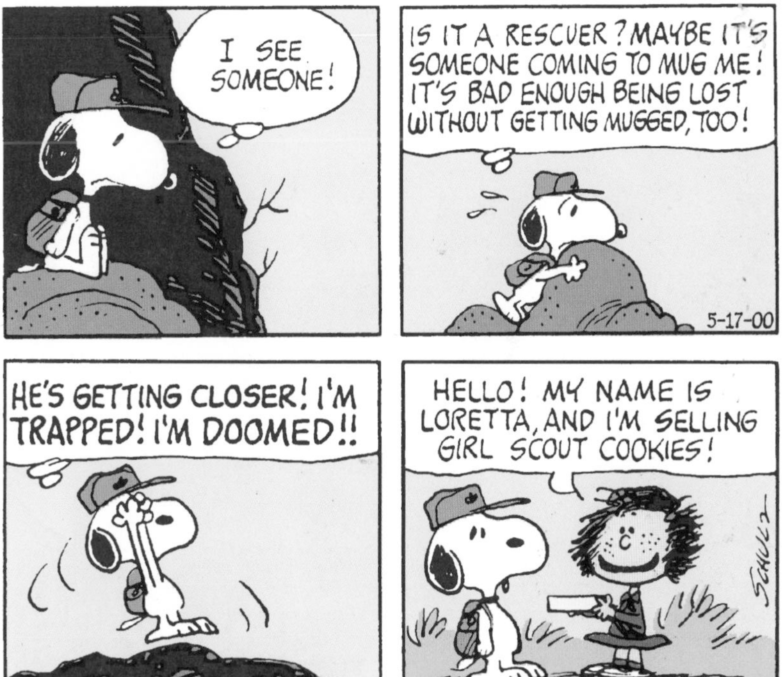
I SEE SOMEONE!
IS IT A RESCUER? MAYBE IT'S SOMEONE COMING TO MUG ME! IT'S BAD ENOUGH BEING LOST WITHOUT GETTING MUGGED, TOO!
5-17-00
HE'S GETTING CLOSER! I'M TRAPPED! I'M DOOMED!!
HELLO! MY NAME IS LORETTA, AND I'M SELLING GIRL SCOUT COOKIES!
SCHULZ

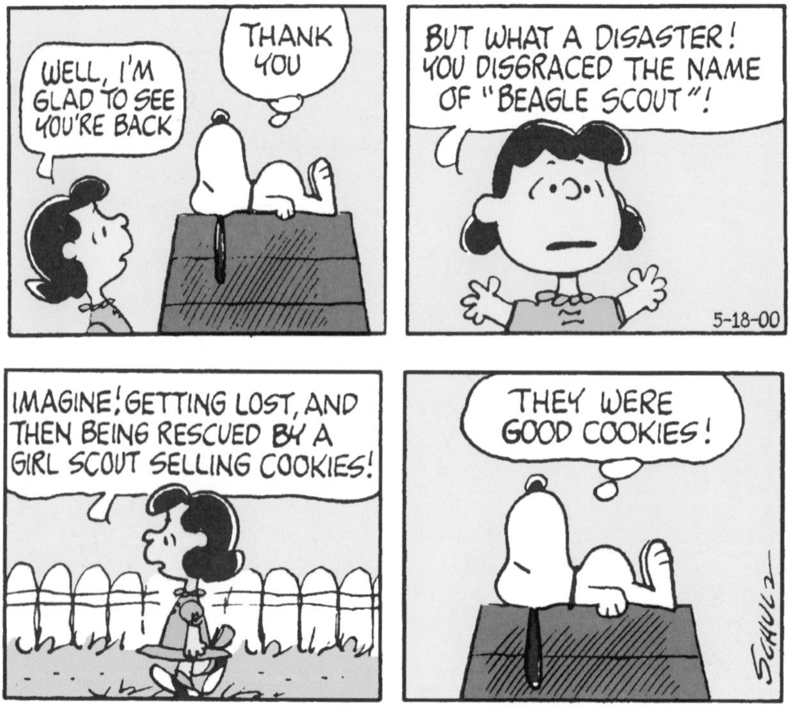
WELL, I'M GLAD TO SEE YOU'RE BACK
THANK YOU
BUT WHAT A DISASTER! YOU DISGRACED THE NAME OF "BEAGLE SCOUT"!
5-18-00
IMAGINE! GETTING LOST, AND THEN BEING RESCUED BY A GIRL SCOUT SELLING COOKIES!
THEY WERE GOOD COOKIES!
SCHULZ

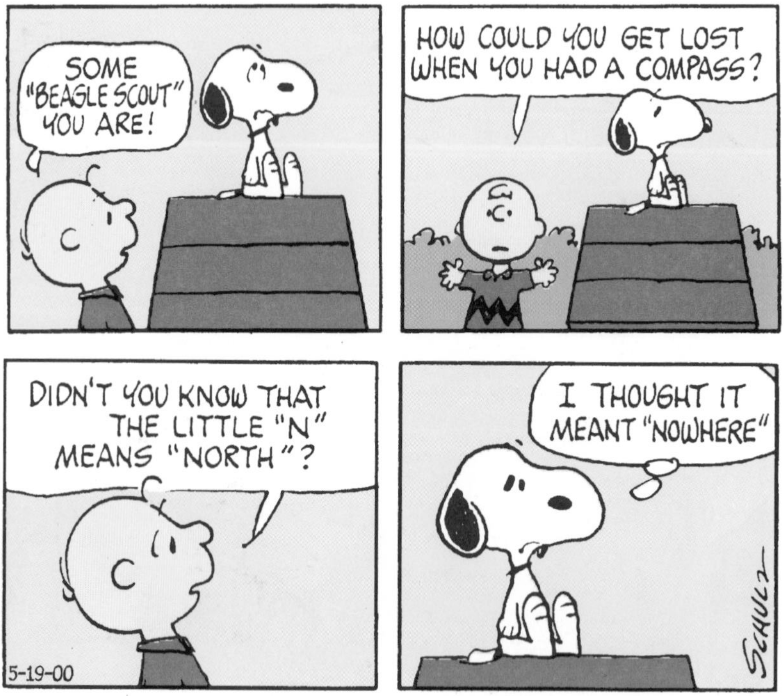
SOME "BEAGLE SCOUT" YOU ARE!
HOW COULD YOU GET LOST WHEN YOU HAD A COMPASS?
DIDN'T YOU KNOW THAT THE LITTLE "N" MEANS "NORTH"?
5-19-00
I THOUGHT IT MEANT "NOWHERE"
SCHULZ

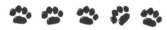

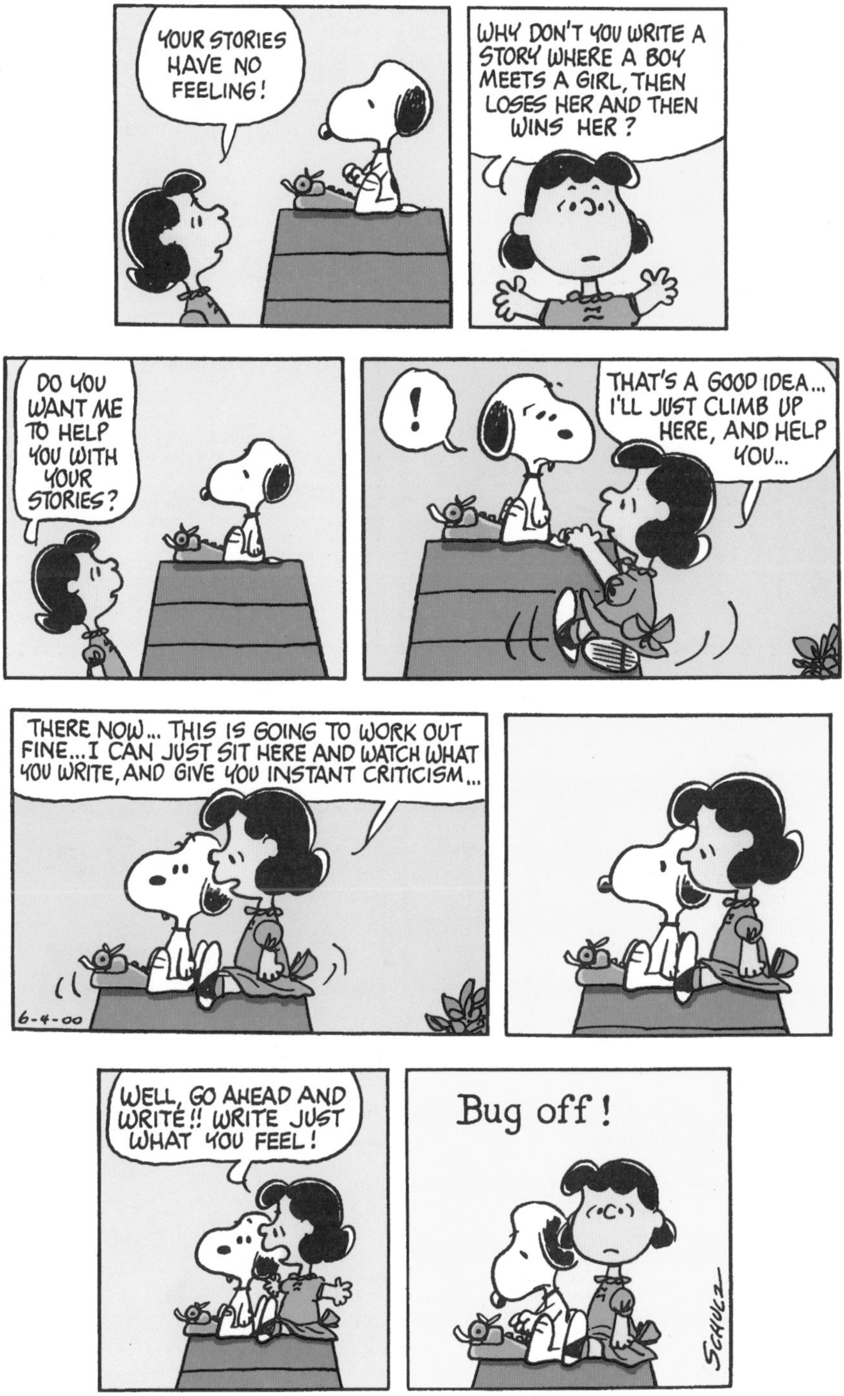
YOUR STORIES HAVE NO FEELING!
WHY DON'T YOU WRITE A STORY WHERE A BOY MEETS A GIRL, THEN LOSES HER AND THEN WINS HER?
DO YOU WANT ME TO HELP YOU WITH YOUR STORIES?
!
THAT'S A GOOD IDEA... I'LL JUST CLIMB UP HERE, AND HELP YOU...
THERE NOW... THIS IS GOING TO WORK OUT FINE... I CAN JUST SIT HERE AND WATCH WHAT YOU WRITE, AND GIVE YOU INSTANT CRITICISM...
6-4-00
WELL, GO AHEAD AND WRITE!! WRITE JUST WHAT YOU FEEL!
Bug off!
SCHULZ

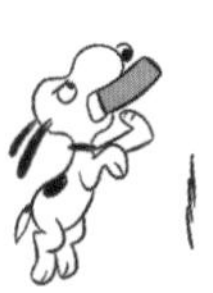

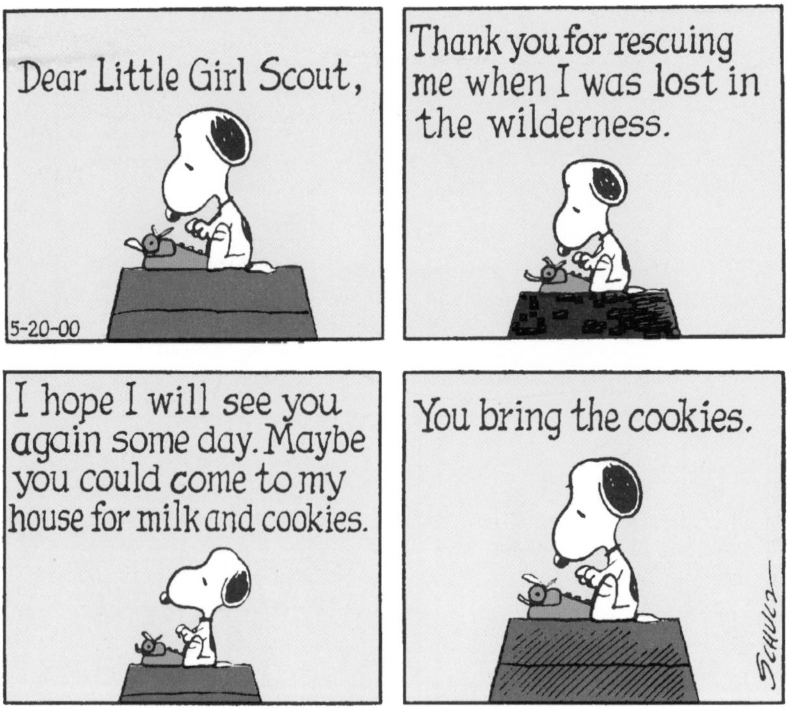
Dear Little Girl Scout,
5-20-00
Thank you for rescuing me when I was lost in the wilderness.
I hope I will see you again some day. Maybe you could come to my house for milk and cookies.
You bring the cookies.
SCHULZ

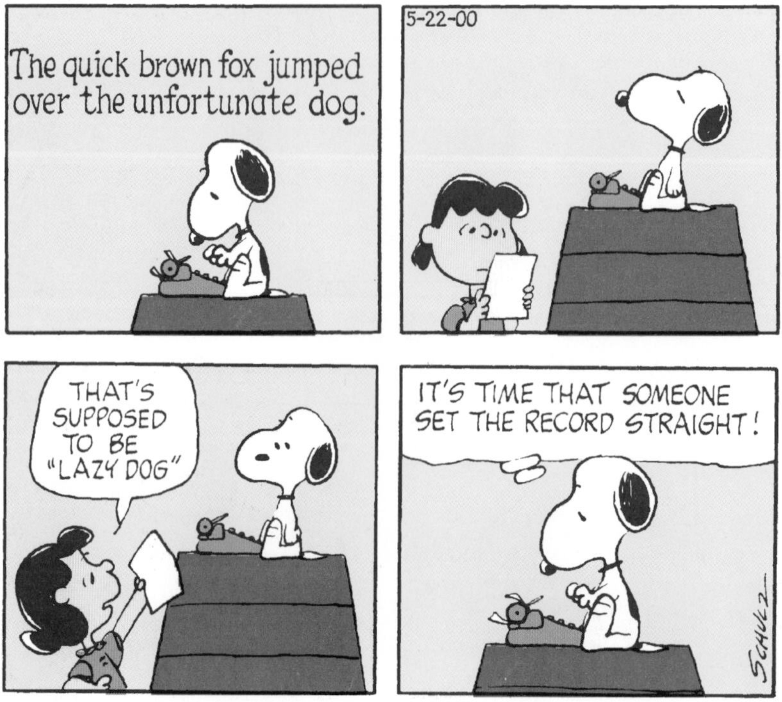
The quick brown fox jumped over the unfortunate dog.
5-22-00
THAT'S SUPPOSED TO BE "LAZY DOG"
IT'S TIME THAT SOMEONE SET THE RECORD STRAIGHT!
SCHULZ

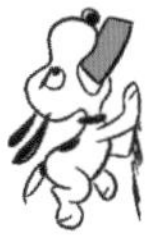

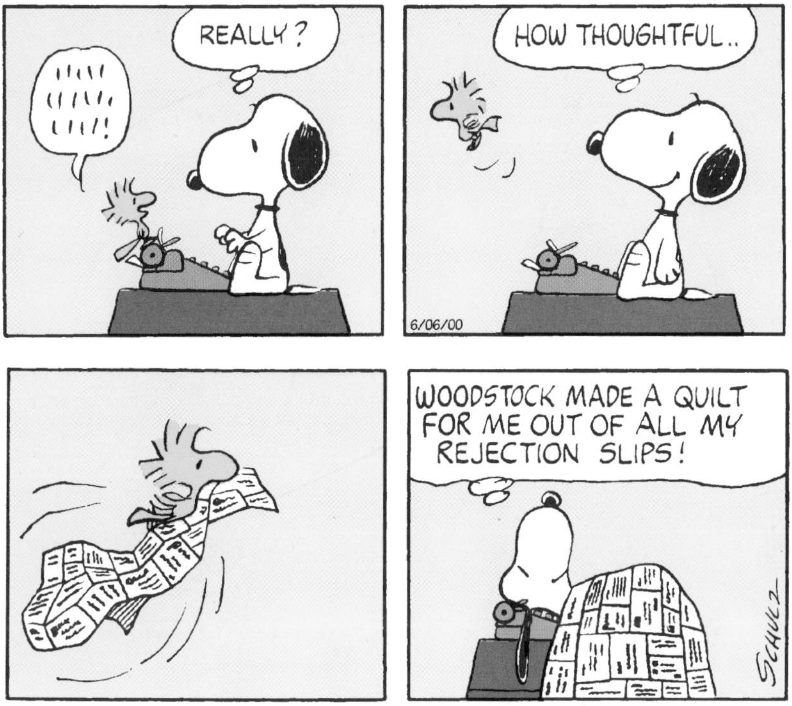
REALLY?
HOW THOUGHTFUL..
6/06/00
WOODSTOCK MADE A QUILT FOR ME OUT OF ALL MY REJECTION SLIPS!
SCHULZ

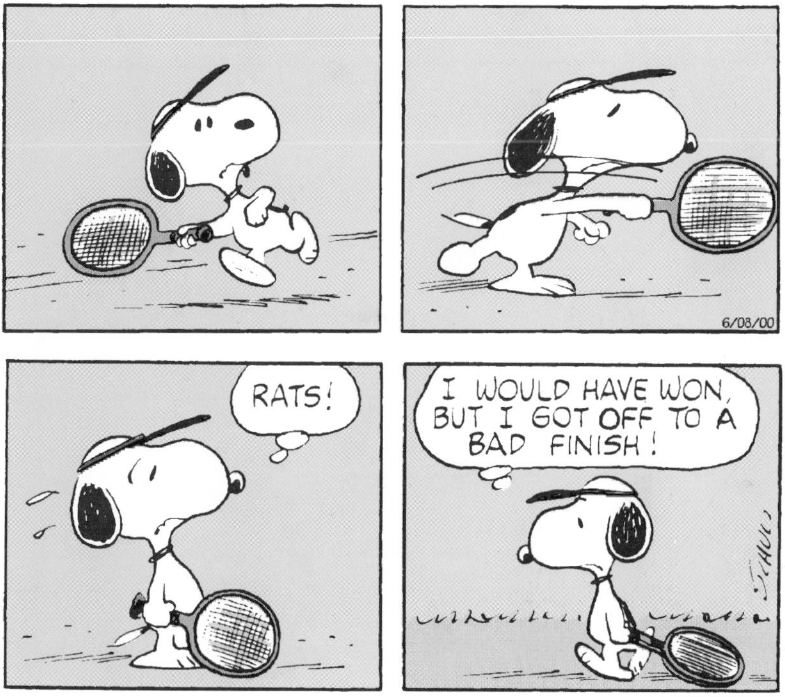
6/08/00
RATS!
I WOULD HAVE WON, BUT I GOT OFF TO A BAD FINISH!
SCHULZ

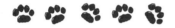

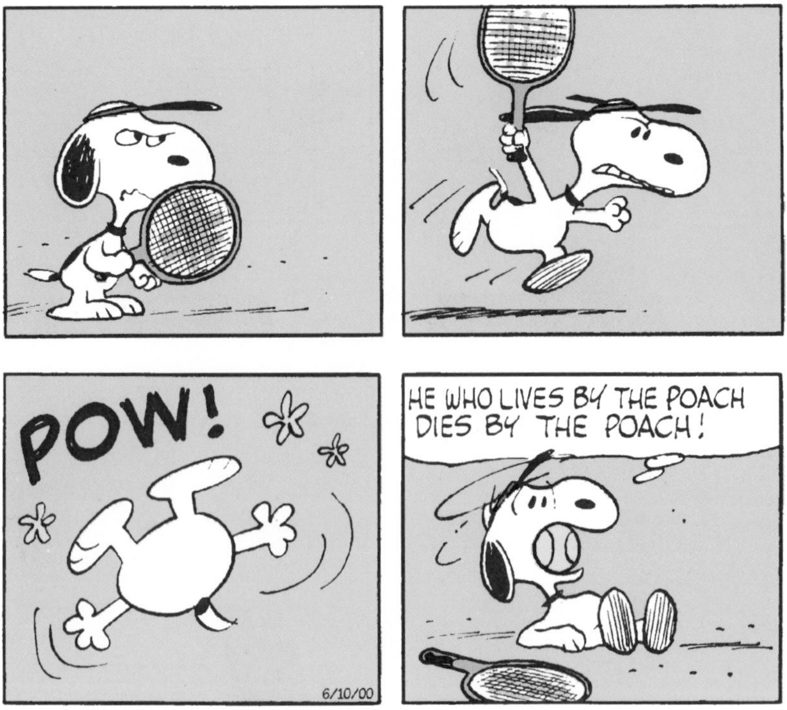
POW!
HE WHO LIVES BY THE POACH DIES BY THE POACH!
6/10/00

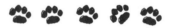

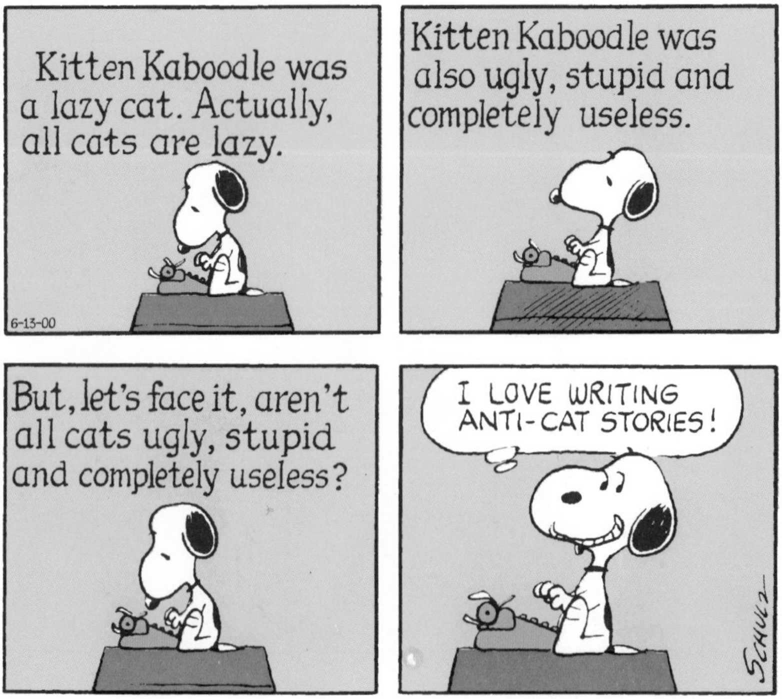
Kitten Kaboodle was a lazy cat. Actually, all cats are lazy.
6-13-00
Kitten Kaboodle was also ugly, stupid and completely useless.
But, let's face it, aren't all cats ugly, stupid and completely useless?
I LOVE WRITING ANTI-CAT STORIES!
SCHULZ

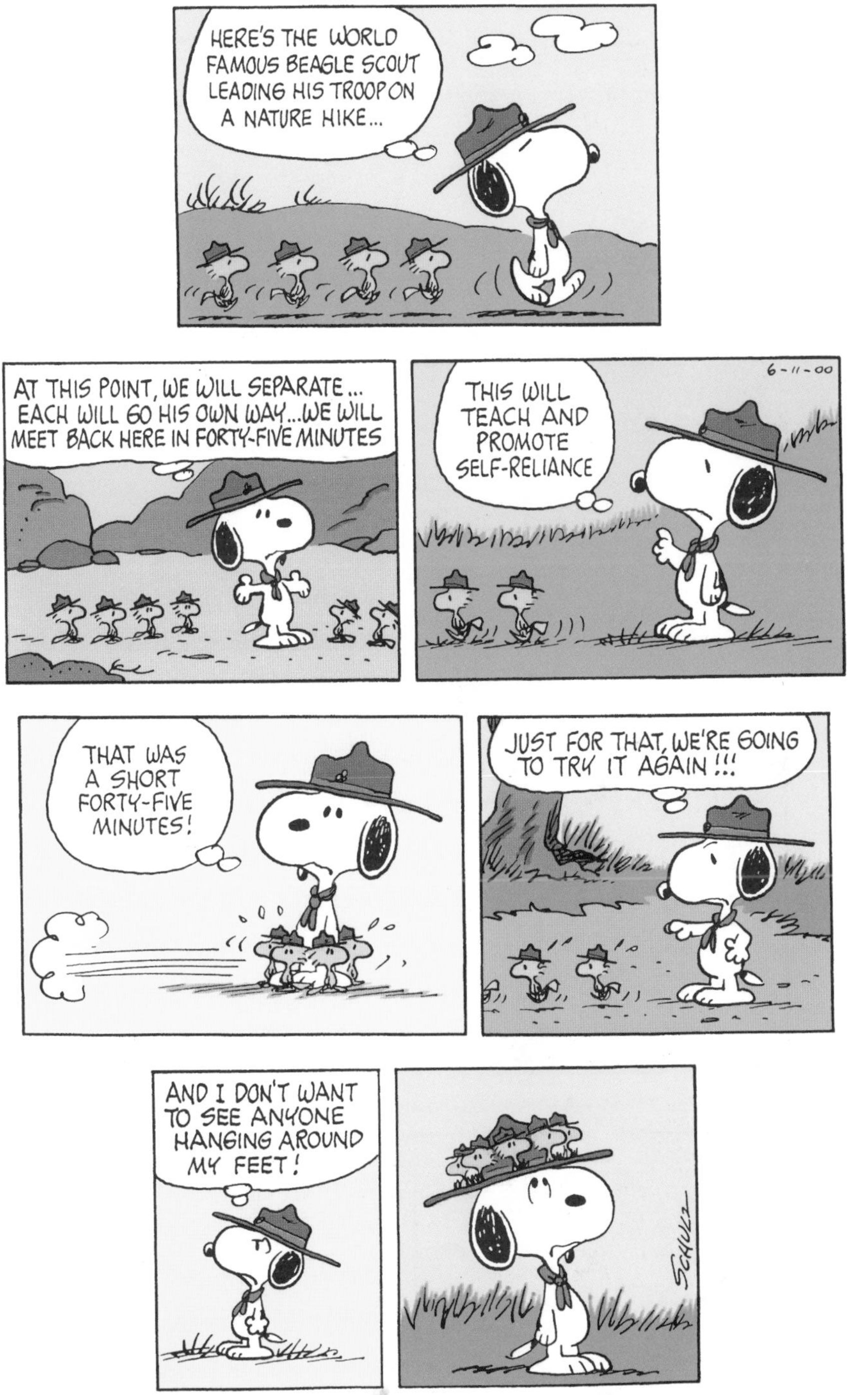
HERE'S THE WORLD FAMOUS BEAGLE SCOUT LEADING HIS TROOP ON A NATURE HIKE...
AT THIS POINT, WE WILL SEPARATE... EACH WILL GO HIS OWN WAY...WE WILL MEET BACK HERE IN FORTY-FIVE MINUTES
6-11-00
THIS WILL TEACH AND PROMOTE SELF-RELIANCE
THAT WAS A SHORT FORTY-FIVE MINUTES!
JUST FOR THAT, WE'RE GOING TO TRY IT AGAIN!!!
AND I DON'T WANT TO SEE ANYONE HANGING AROUND MY FEET!
SCHULZ

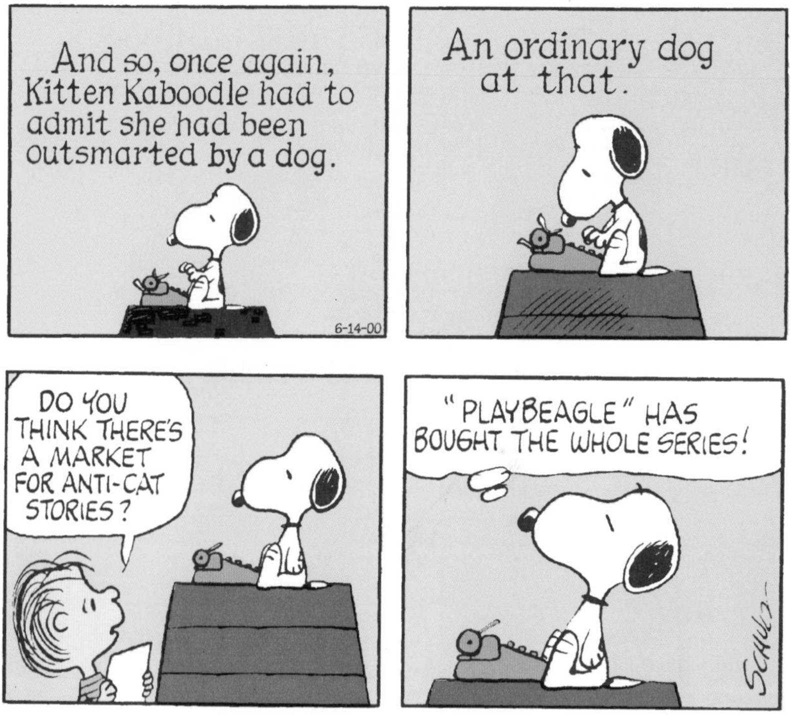

And so, once again, Kitten Kaboodle had to admit she had been outsmarted by a dog.
6-14-00
An ordinary dog at that.
DO YOU THINK THERE'S A MARKET FOR ANTI-CAT STORIES?
"PLAYBEAGLE" HAS BOUGHT THE WHOLE SERIES!

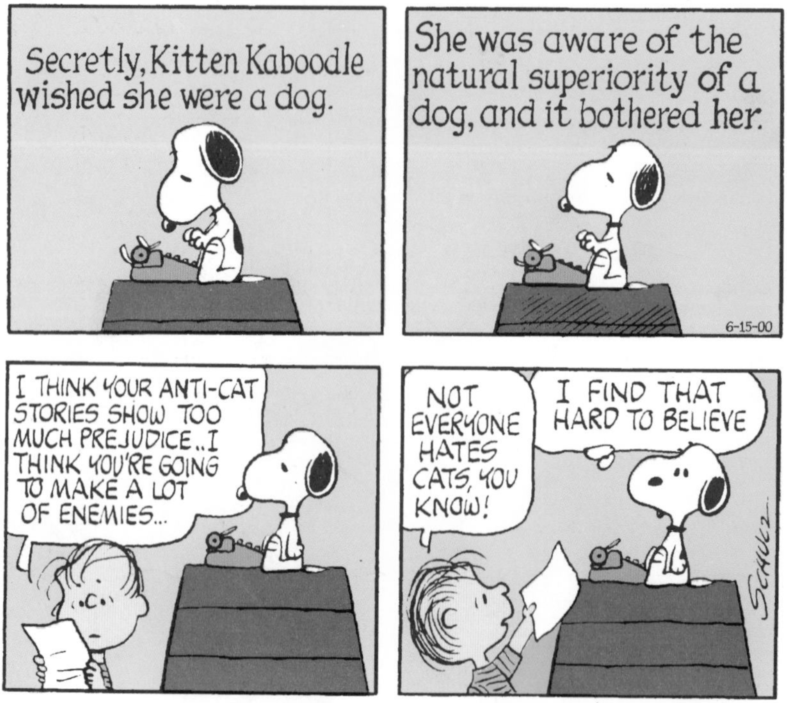

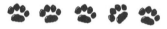

Secretly, Kitten Kaboodle wished she were a dog.
She was aware of the natural superiority of a dog, and it bothered her.
6-15-00
I THINK YOUR ANTI-CAT STORIES SHOW TOO MUCH PREJUDICE..I THINK YOU'RE GOING TO MAKE A LOT OF ENEMIES...
NOT EVERYONE HATES CATS, YOU KNOW!
I FIND THAT HARD TO BELIEVE

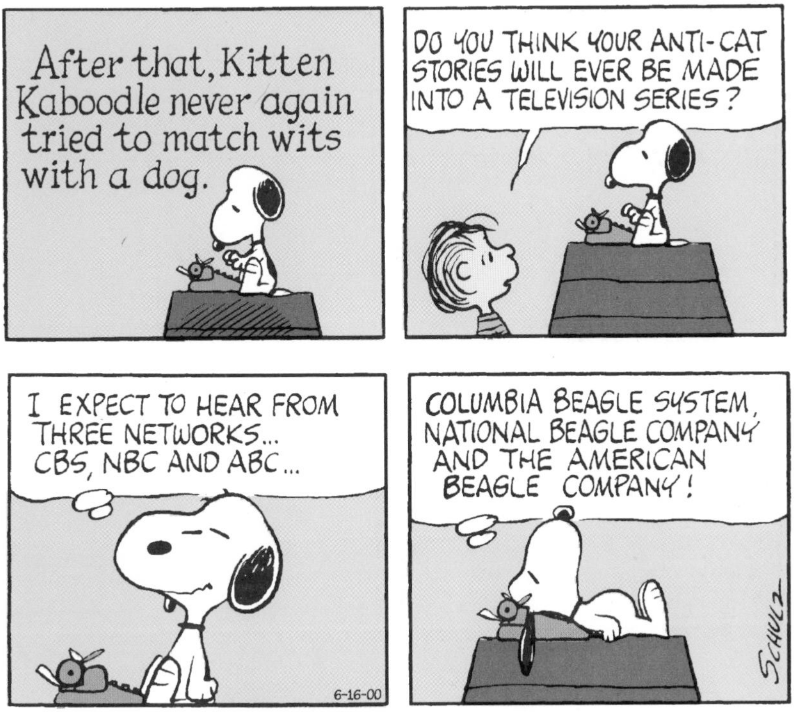
After that, Kitten Kaboodle never again tried to match wits with a dog.
DO YOU THINK YOUR ANTI-CAT STORIES WILL EVER BE MADE INTO A TELEVISION SERIES?
I EXPECT TO HEAR FROM THREE NETWORKS... CBS, NBC AND ABC...
6-16-00
COLUMBIA BEAGLE SYSTEM, NATIONAL BEAGLE COMPANY AND THE AMERICAN BEAGLE COMPANY!
SCHULZ

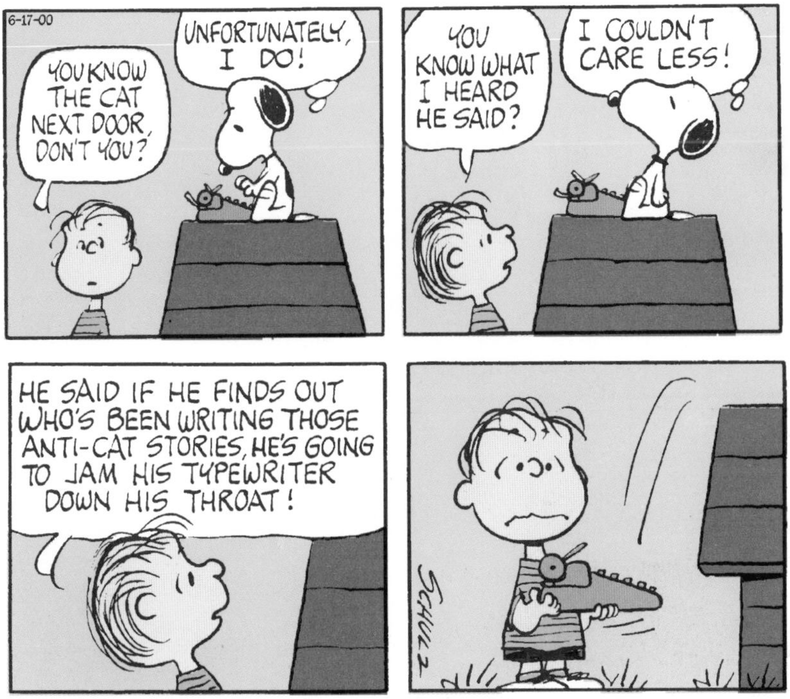
6-17-00
YOU KNOW THE CAT NEXT DOOR, DON'T YOU?
UNFORTUNATELY, I DO!
YOU KNOW WHAT I HEARD HE SAID?
I COULDN'T CARE LESS!
HE SAID IF HE FINDS OUT WHO'S BEEN WRITING THOSE ANTI-CAT STORIES, HE'S GOING TO JAM HIS TYPEWRITER DOWN HIS THROAT!
SCHULZ

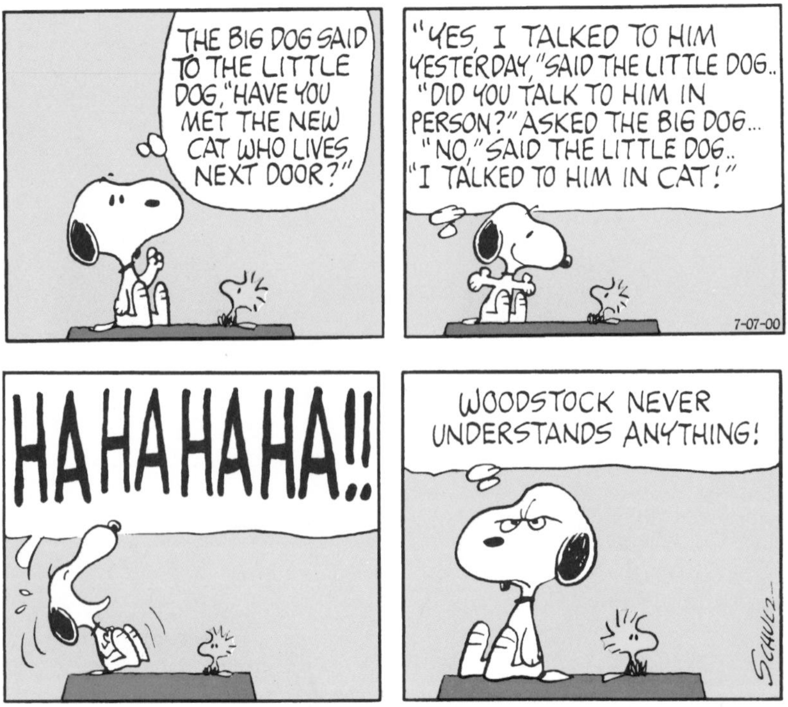
THE BIG DOG SAID TO THE LITTLE DOG, "HAVE YOU MET THE NEW CAT WHO LIVES NEXT DOOR?"
"YES, I TALKED TO HIM YESTERDAY," SAID THE LITTLE DOG.. "DID YOU TALK TO HIM IN PERSON?" ASKED THE BIG DOG... "NO," SAID THE LITTLE DOG.. "I TALKED TO HIM IN CAT!"
7-07-00
HAHAHAHA!!
WOODSTOCK NEVER UNDERSTANDS ANYTHING!
SCHULZ

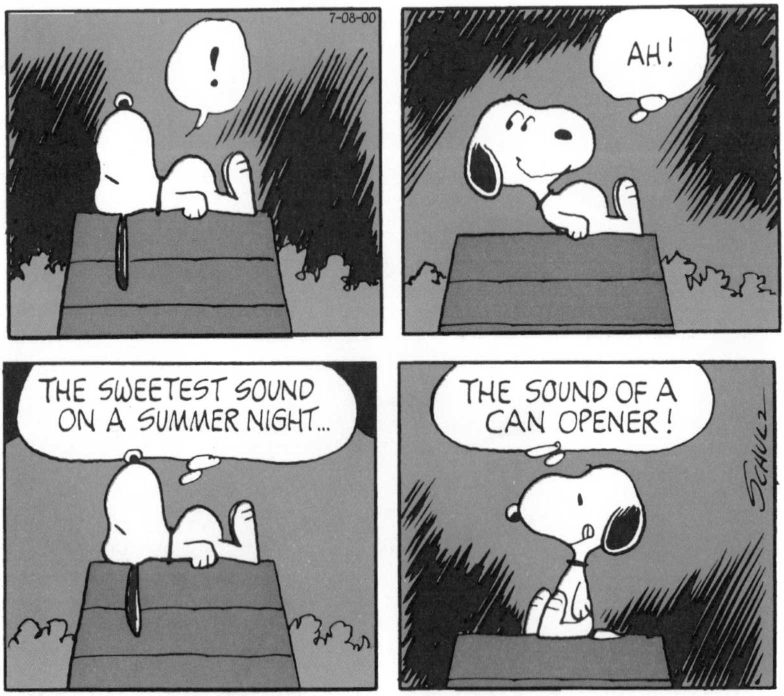
7-08-00
!
AH!
THE SWEETEST SOUND ON A SUMMER NIGHT...
THE SOUND OF A CAN OPENER!
SCHULZ

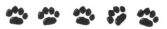

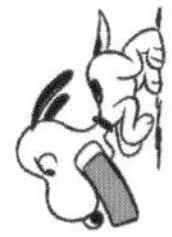

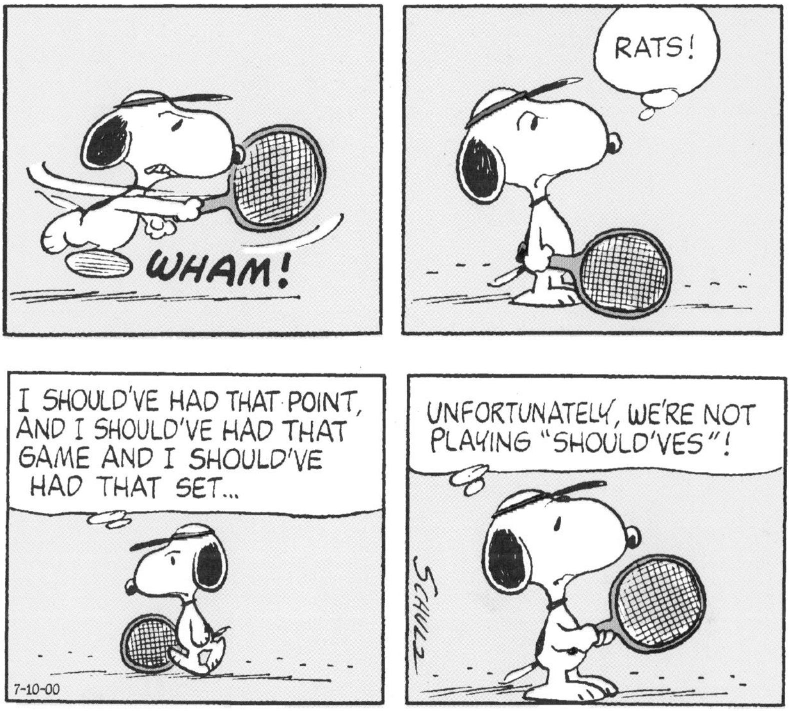
WHAM!
RATS!
I SHOULD'VE HAD THAT POINT, AND I SHOULD'VE HAD THAT GAME AND I SHOULD'VE HAD THAT SET...
7-10-00
UNFORTUNATELY, WE'RE NOT PLAYING "SHOULD'VES"!
SCHULZ

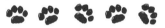

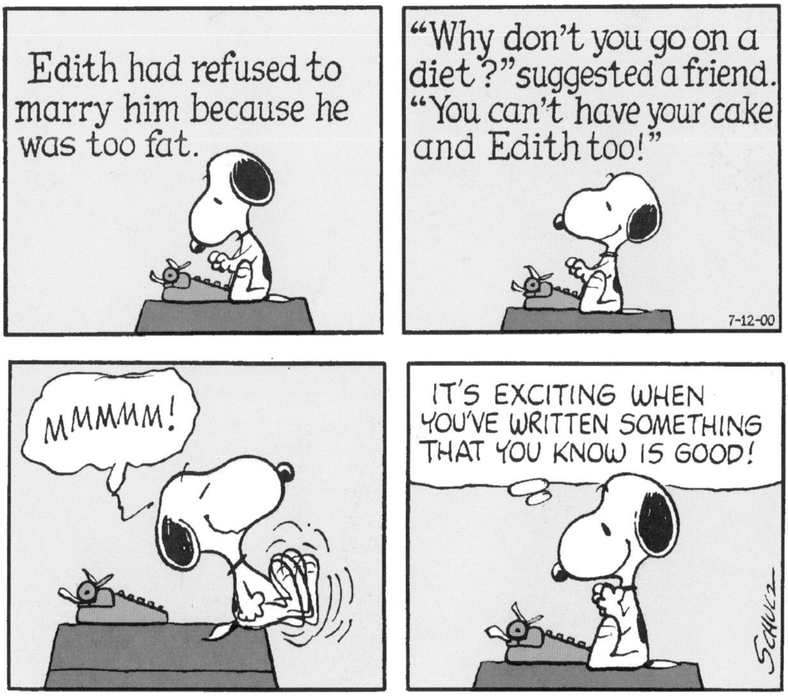
Edith had refused to marry him because he was too fat.
"Why don't you go on a diet?" suggested a friend. "You can't have your cake and Edith too!"
7-12-00
MMMMM!
IT'S EXCITING WHEN YOU'VE WRITTEN SOMETHING THAT YOU KNOW IS GOOD!
SCHULZ

6-25-00

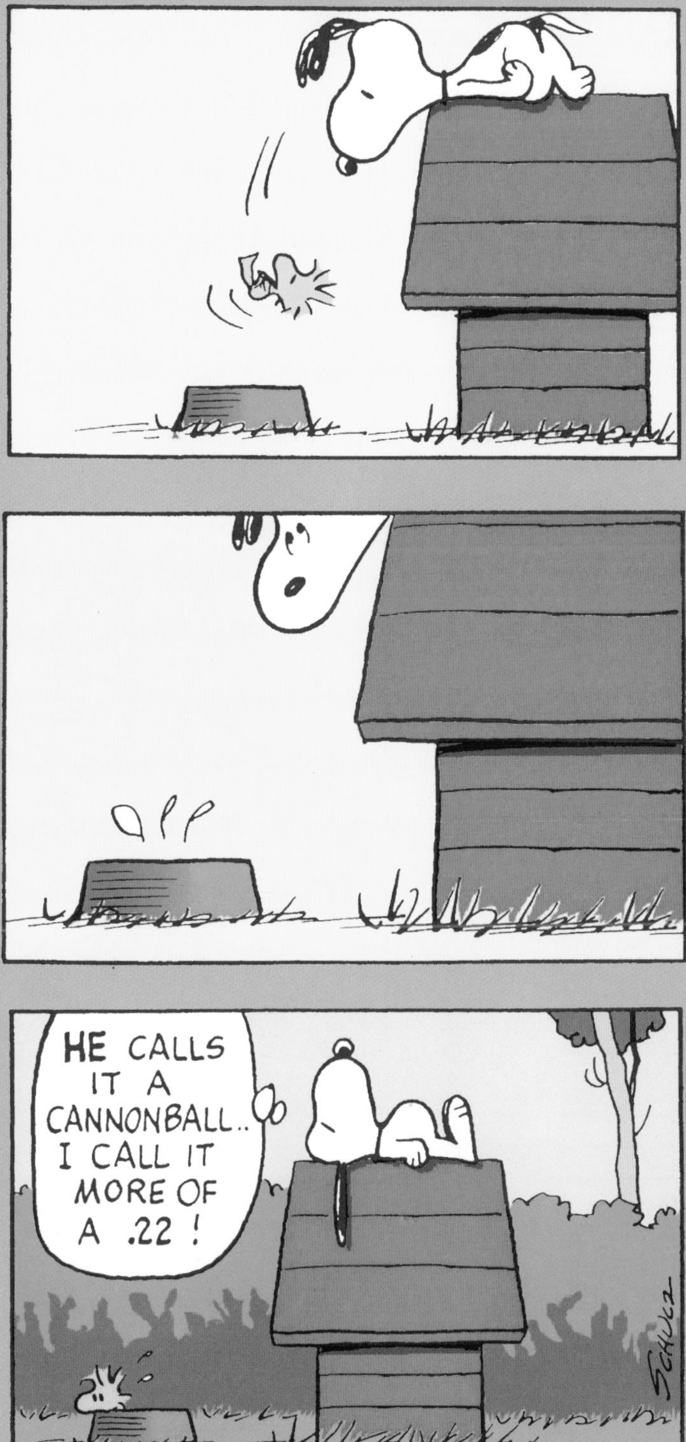
HE CALLS IT A CANNONBALL.. I CALL IT MORE OF A .22 !
SCHULZ

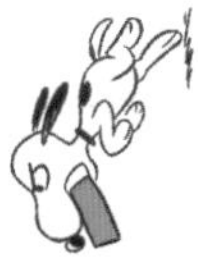

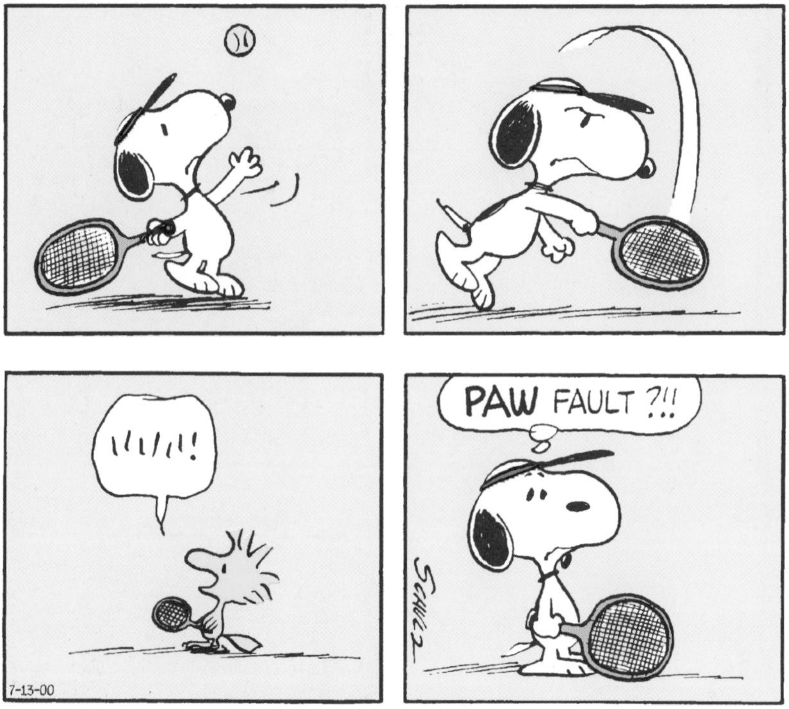
PAW FAULT ?!!
SCHULZ
7-13-00

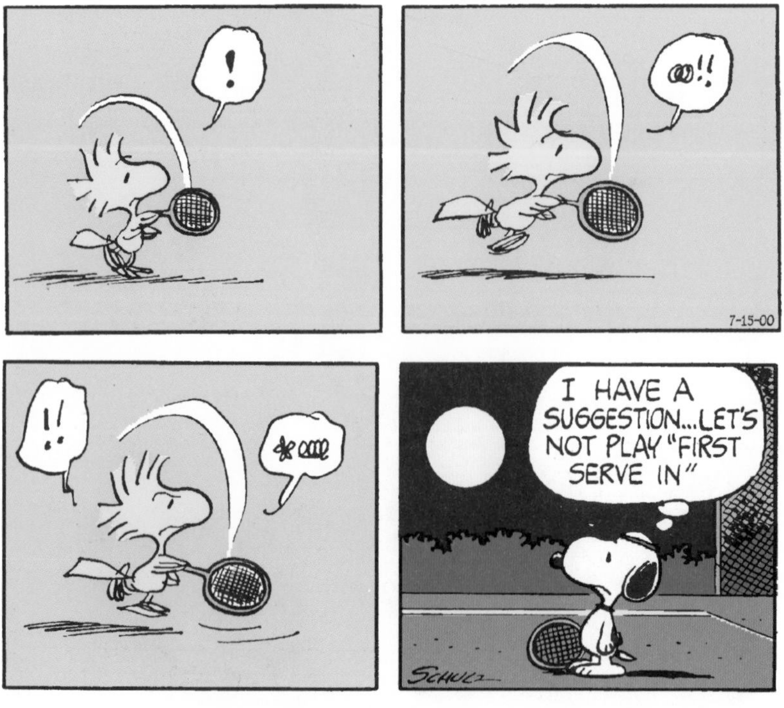
!
7-15-00
!!
I HAVE A SUGGESTION...LET'S NOT PLAY "FIRST SERVE IN"
SCHULZ

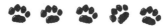

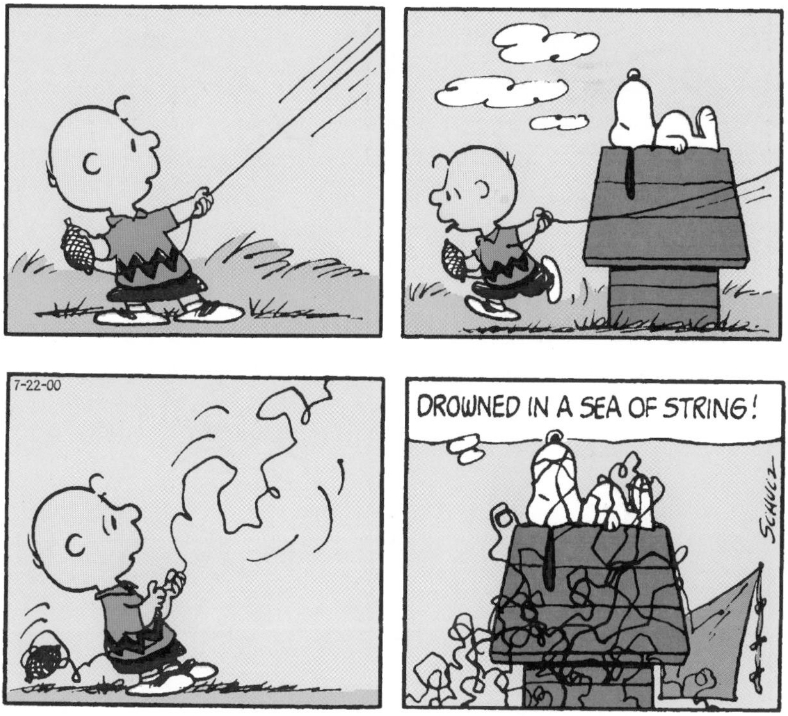
7-22-00
DROWNED IN A SEA OF STRING!
SCHULZ

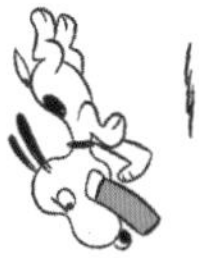

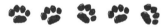

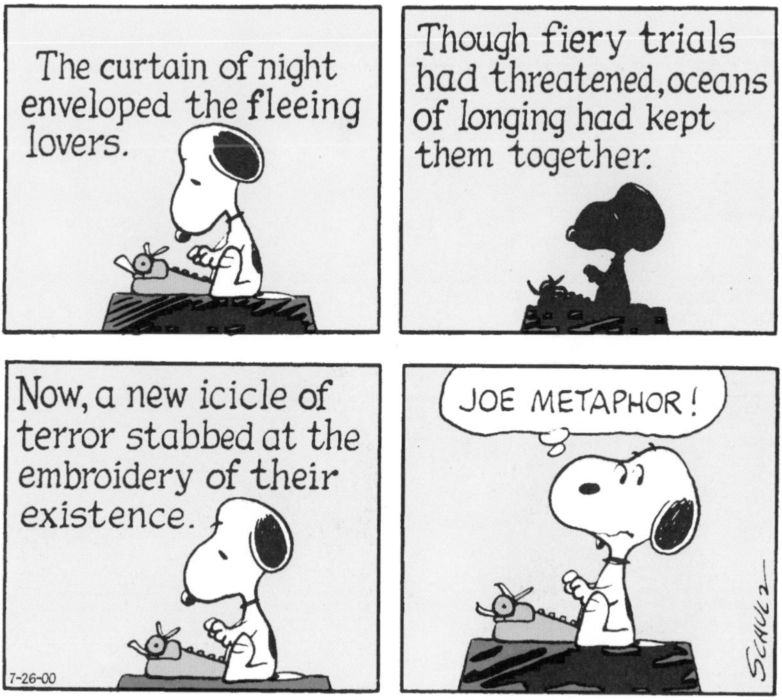
The curtain of night enveloped the fleeing lovers.
Though fiery trials had threatened, oceans of longing had kept them together.
Now, a new icicle of terror stabbed at the embroidery of their existence.
7-26-00
JOE METAPHOR!
SCHULZ

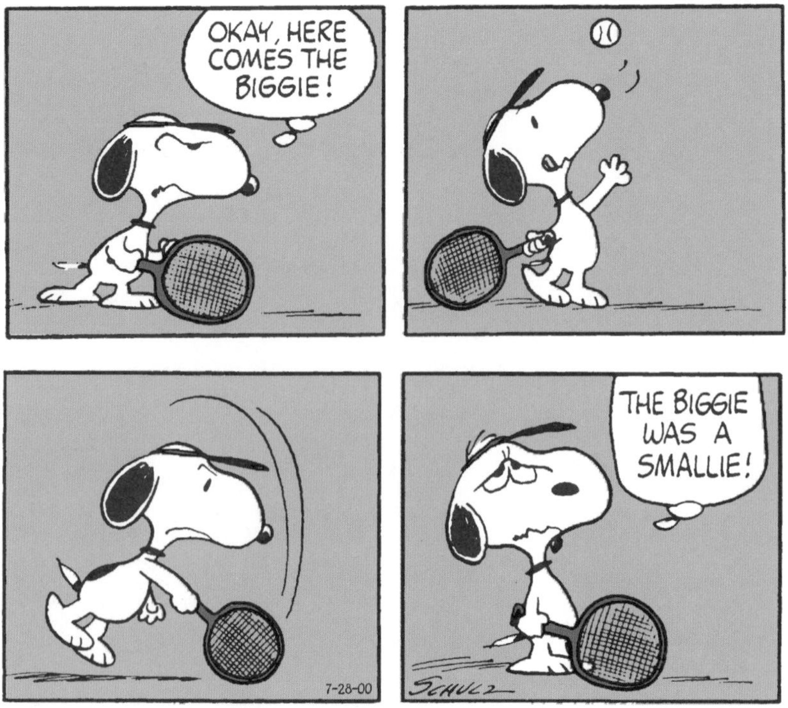
OKAY, HERE COMES THE BIGGIE!
THE BIGGIE WAS A SMALLIE!
7-28-00
SCHULZ

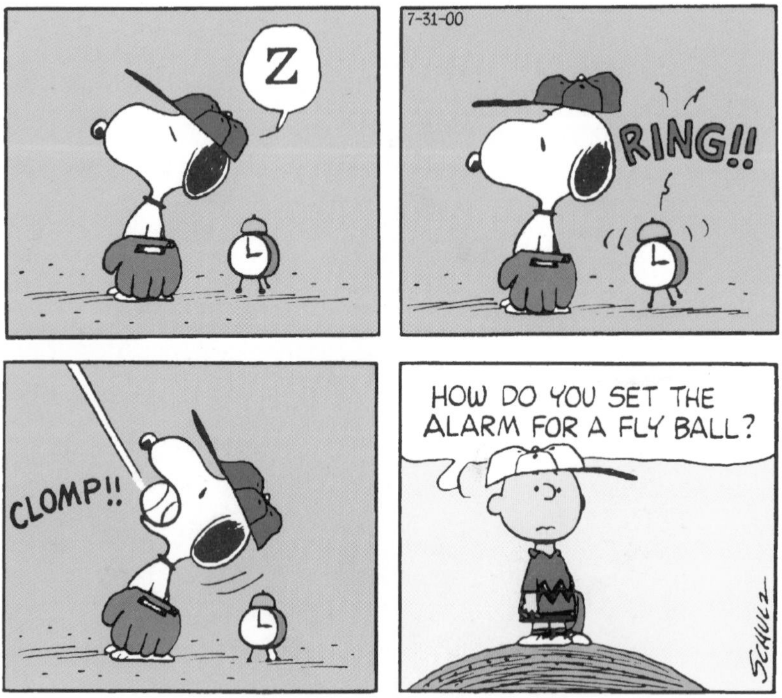
Z
7-31-00
RING!!
CLOMP!!
HOW DO YOU SET THE ALARM FOR A FLY BALL?
SCHULZ

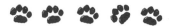

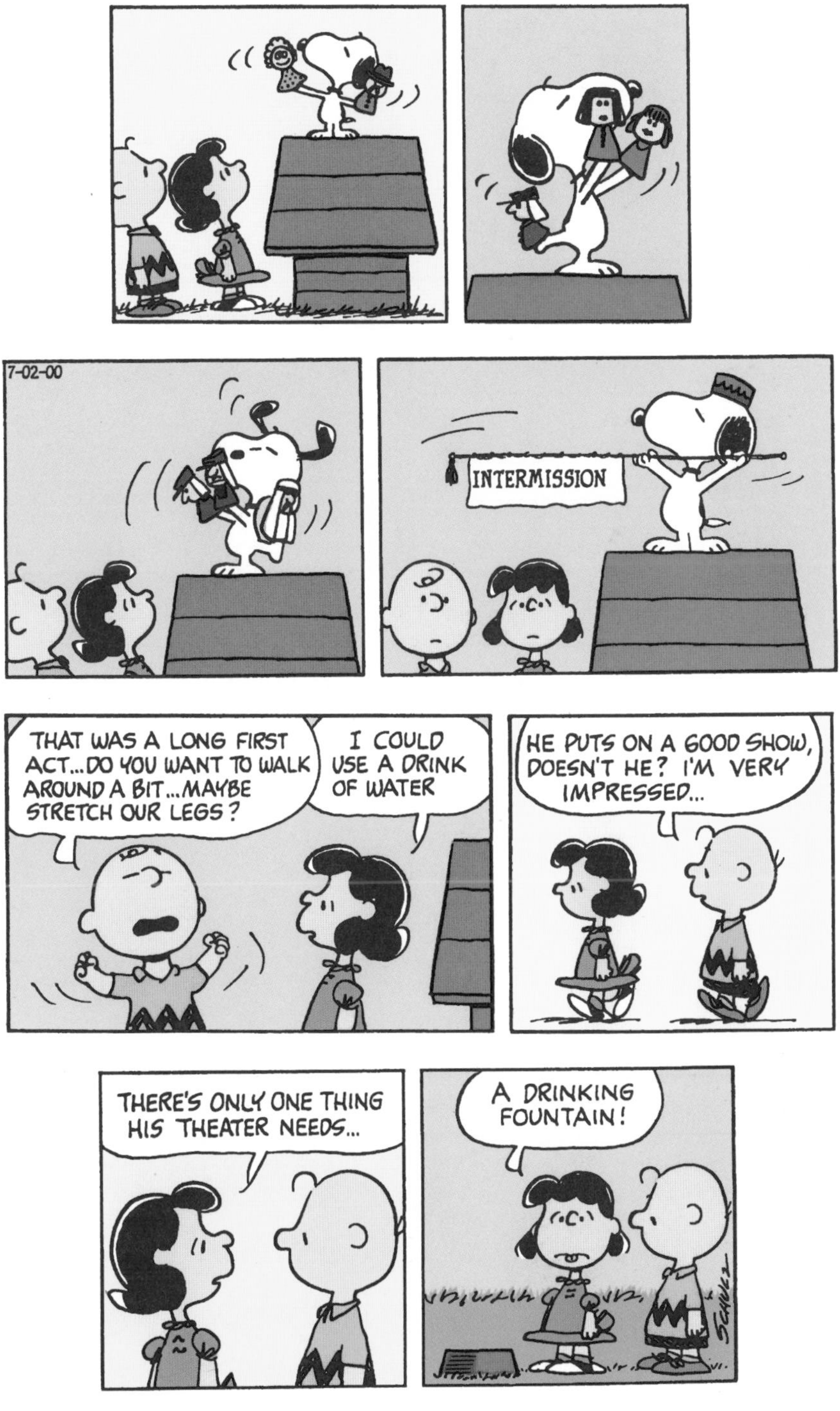
7-02-00
INTERMISSION
THAT WAS A LONG FIRST ACT...DO YOU WANT TO WALK AROUND A BIT...MAYBE STRETCH OUR LEGS?
I COULD USE A DRINK OF WATER
HE PUTS ON A GOOD SHOW, DOESN'T HE? I'M VERY IMPRESSED...
THERE'S ONLY ONE THING HIS THEATER NEEDS...
A DRINKING FOUNTAIN!
SCHULZ

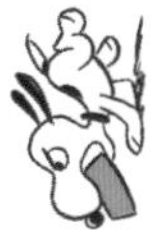

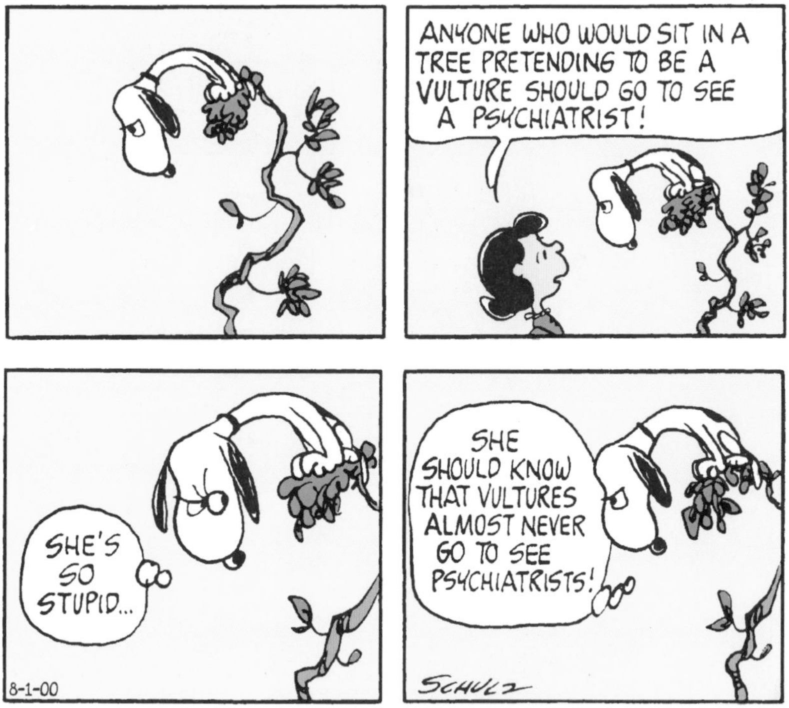
ANYONE WHO WOULD SIT IN A TREE PRETENDING TO BE A VULTURE SHOULD GO TO SEE A PSYCHIATRIST!
SHE'S SO STUPID...
SHE SHOULD KNOW THAT VULTURES ALMOST NEVER GO TO SEE PSYCHIATRISTS!
8-1-00
SCHULZ

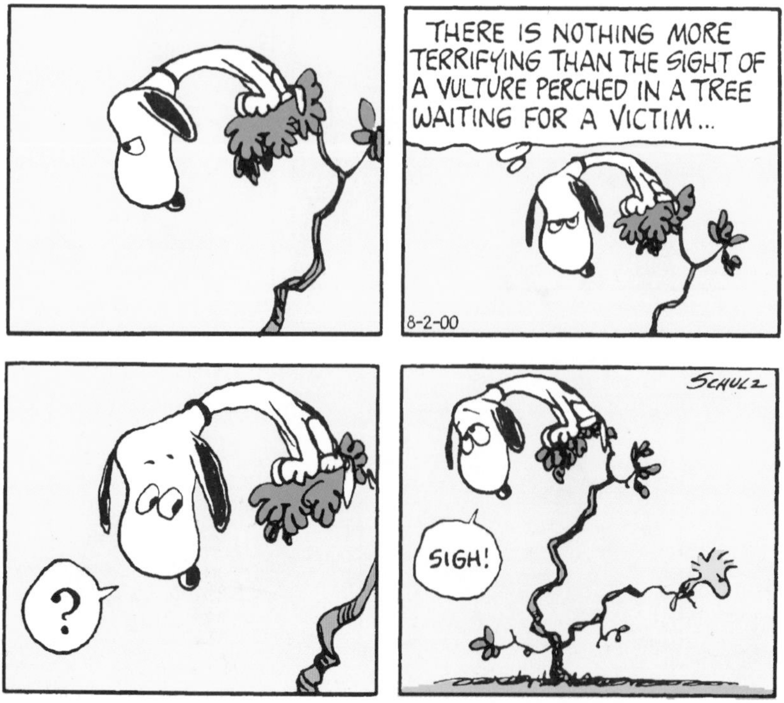
THERE IS NOTHING MORE TERRIFYING THAN THE SIGHT OF A VULTURE PERCHED IN A TREE WAITING FOR A VICTIM...
8-2-00
?
SCHULZ
SIGH!

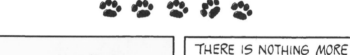

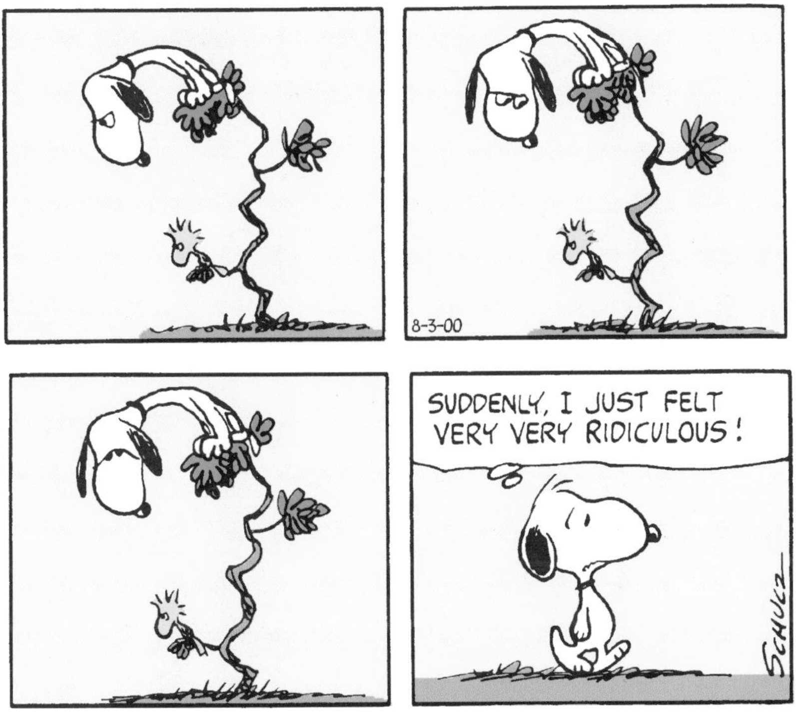
8-3-00
SUDDENLY, I JUST FELT VERY VERY RIDICULOUS!
SCHULZ

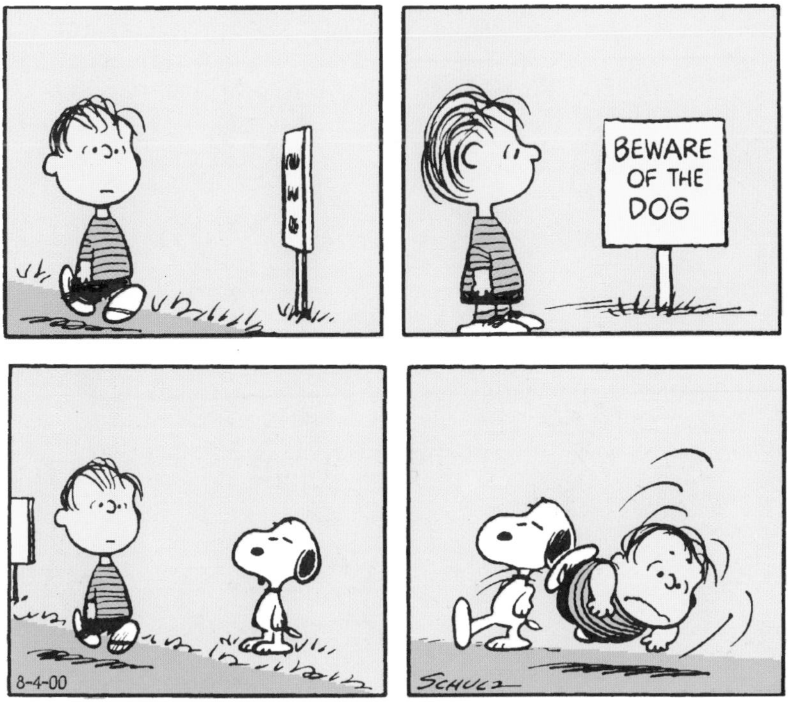
BEWARE OF THE DOG
8-4-00
SCHULZ

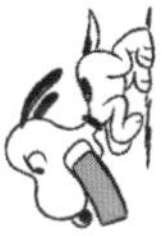

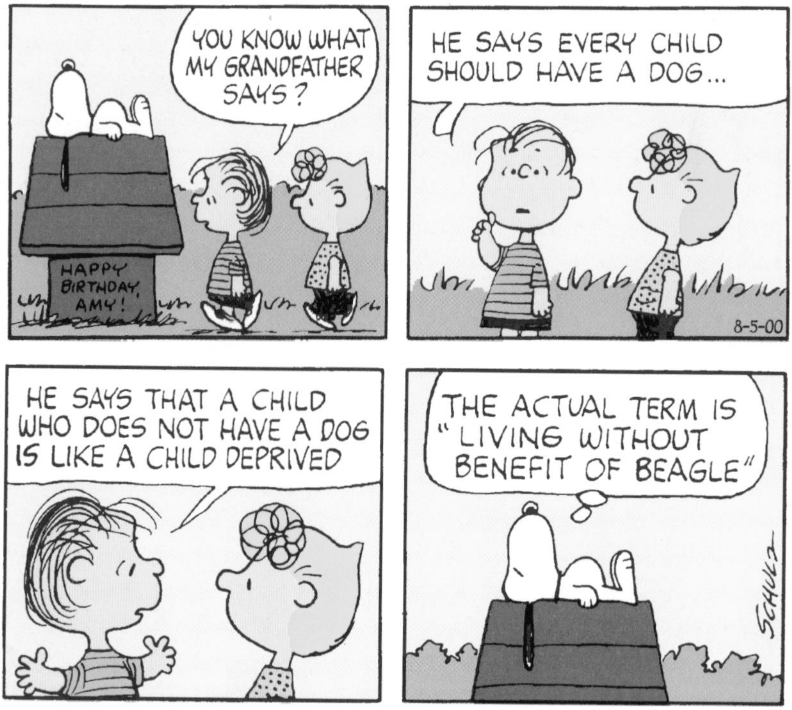
YOU KNOW WHAT MY GRANDFATHER SAYS?
HAPPY BIRTHDAY, AMY!
HE SAYS EVERY CHILD SHOULD HAVE A DOG...
8-5-00
HE SAYS THAT A CHILD WHO DOES NOT HAVE A DOG IS LIKE A CHILD DEPRIVED
THE ACTUAL TERM IS "LIVING WITHOUT BENEFIT OF BEAGLE"
SCHULZ

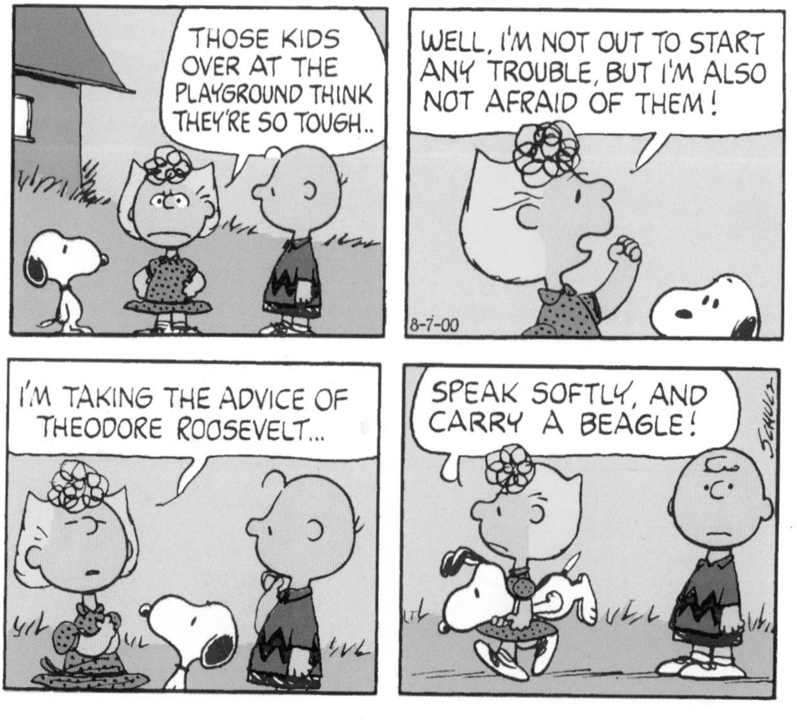
THOSE KIDS OVER AT THE PLAYGROUND THINK THEY'RE SO TOUGH..
WELL, I'M NOT OUT TO START ANY TROUBLE, BUT I'M ALSO NOT AFRAID OF THEM!
8-7-00
I'M TAKING THE ADVICE OF THEODORE ROOSEVELT...
SPEAK SOFTLY, AND CARRY A BEAGLE!
SCHULZ

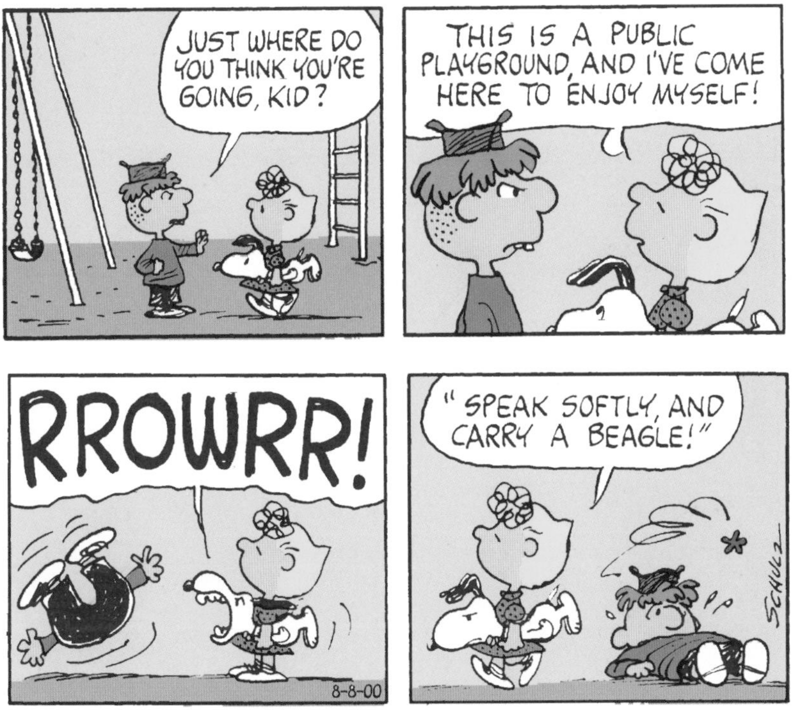
JUST WHERE DO YOU THINK YOU'RE GOING, KID?
THIS IS A PUBLIC PLAYGROUND, AND I'VE COME HERE TO ENJOY MYSELF!
RROWRR!
8-8-00
"SPEAK SOFTLY, AND CARRY A BEAGLE!"
SCHULZ

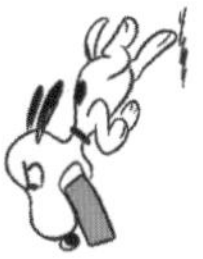

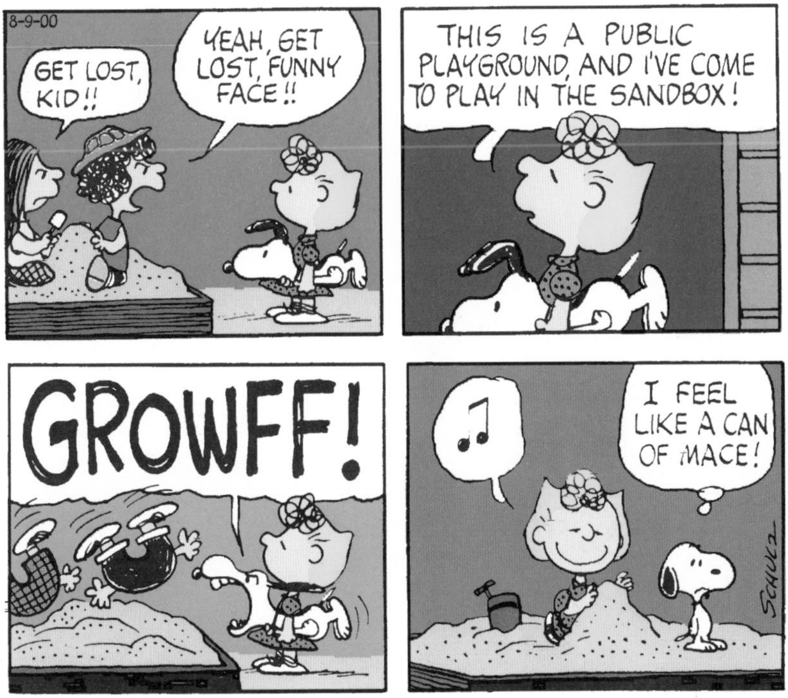
8-9-00
GET LOST, KID!!
YEAH, GET LOST, FUNNY FACE!!
THIS IS A PUBLIC PLAYGROUND, AND I'VE COME TO PLAY IN THE SANDBOX!
GROWFF!
I FEEL LIKE A CAN OF MACE!
SCHULZ

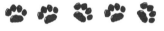

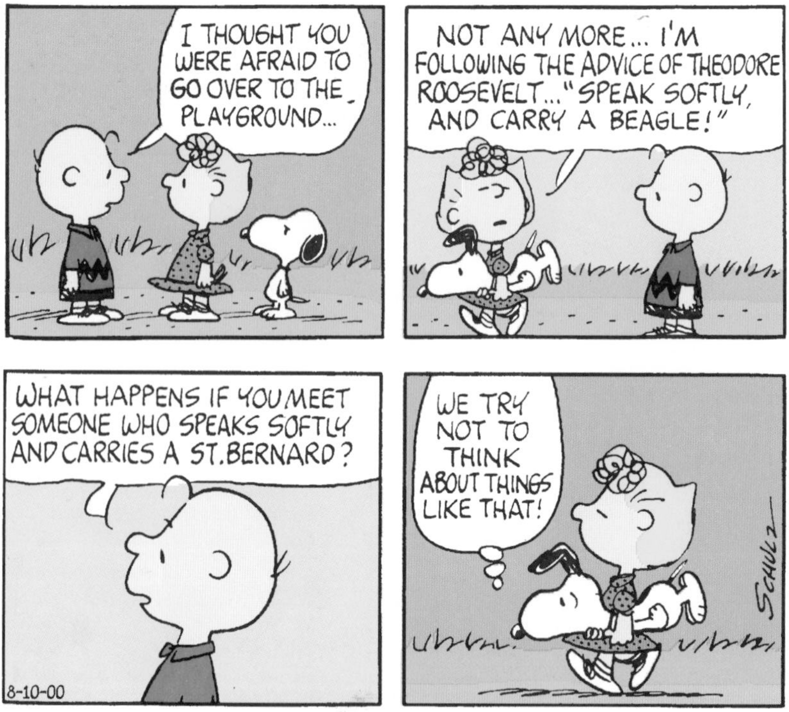
I THOUGHT YOU WERE AFRAID TO GO OVER TO THE PLAYGROUND...
NOT ANY MORE... I'M FOLLOWING THE ADVICE OF THEODORE ROOSEVELT..."SPEAK SOFTLY, AND CARRY A BEAGLE!"
WHAT HAPPENS IF YOU MEET SOMEONE WHO SPEAKS SOFTLY AND CARRIES A ST. BERNARD?
8-10-00
WE TRY NOT TO THINK ABOUT THINGS LIKE THAT!
SCHULZ

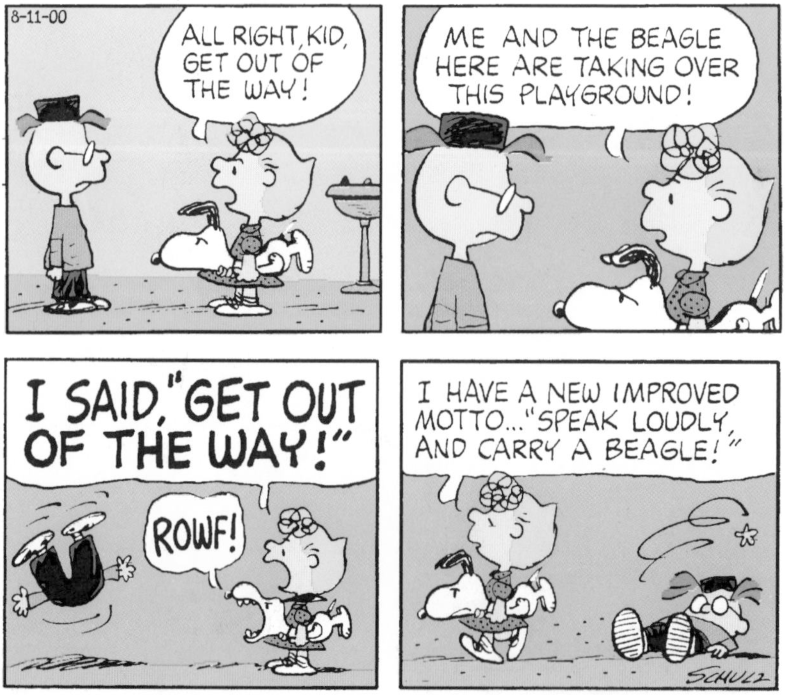
8-11-00
ALL RIGHT, KID, GET OUT OF THE WAY!
ME AND THE BEAGLE HERE ARE TAKING OVER THIS PLAYGROUND!
I SAID, "GET OUT OF THE WAY!"
ROWF!
I HAVE A NEW IMPROVED MOTTO..."SPEAK LOUDLY, AND CARRY A BEAGLE!"
SCHULZ

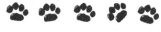

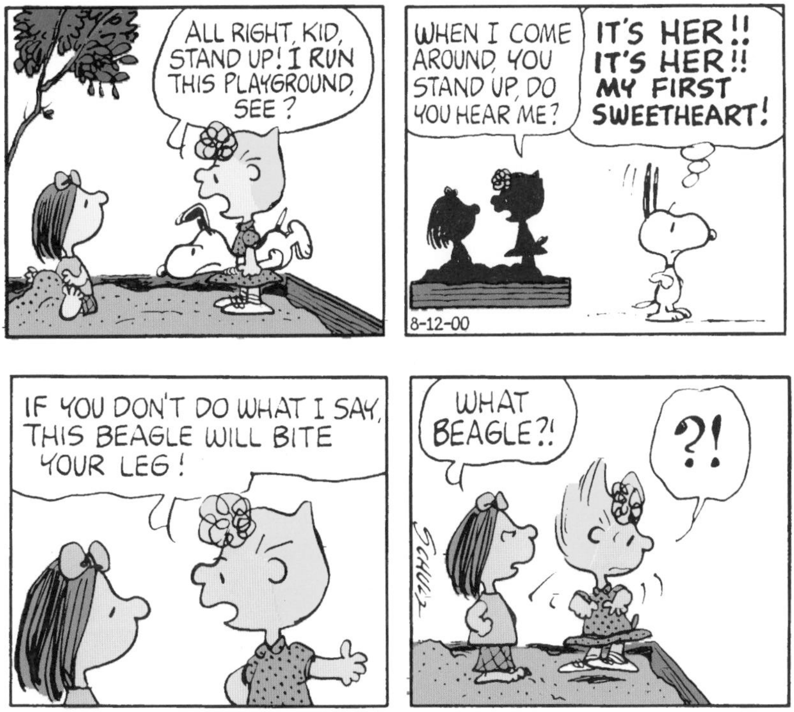
ALL RIGHT, KID, STAND UP! I RUN THIS PLAYGROUND, SEE?
WHEN I COME AROUND, YOU STAND UP, DO YOU HEAR ME?
IT'S HER!! IT'S HER!! MY FIRST SWEETHEART!
8-12-00
IF YOU DON'T DO WHAT I SAY, THIS BEAGLE WILL BITE YOUR LEG!
WHAT BEAGLE?!
?!
SCHULZ

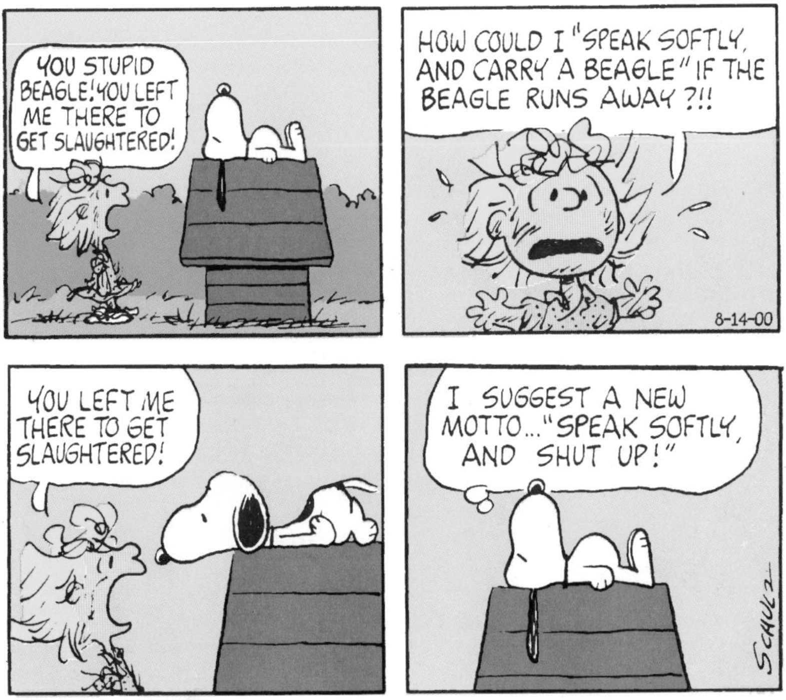
YOU STUPID BEAGLE! YOU LEFT ME THERE TO GET SLAUGHTERED!
HOW COULD I "SPEAK SOFTLY, AND CARRY A BEAGLE" IF THE BEAGLE RUNS AWAY?!!
8-14-00
YOU LEFT ME THERE TO GET SLAUGHTERED!
I SUGGEST A NEW MOTTO..."SPEAK SOFTLY, AND SHUT UP!"
SCHULZ

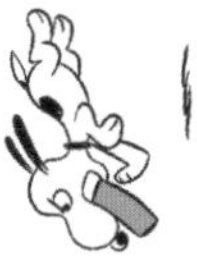

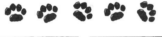

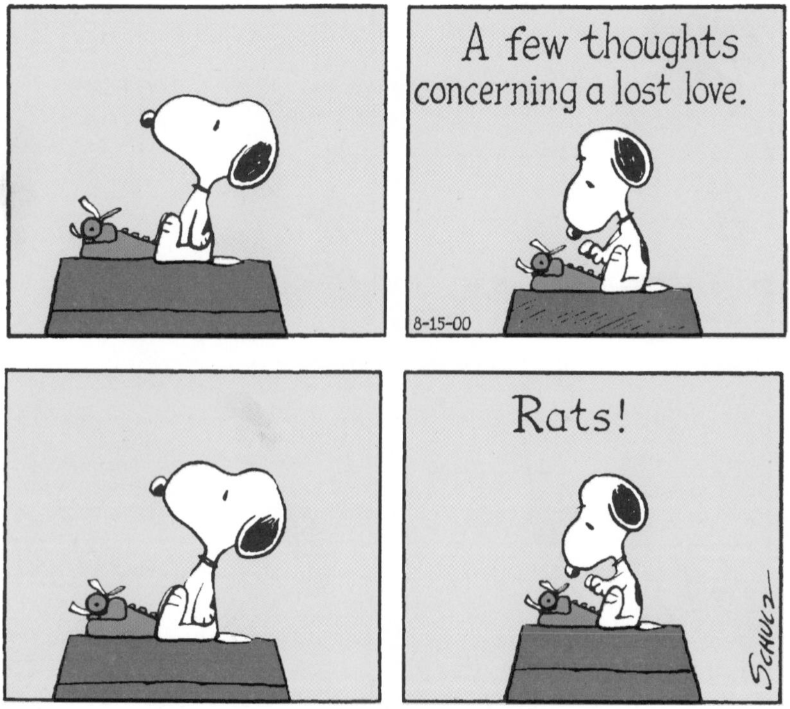
A few thoughts concerning a lost love.
8-15-00
Rats!

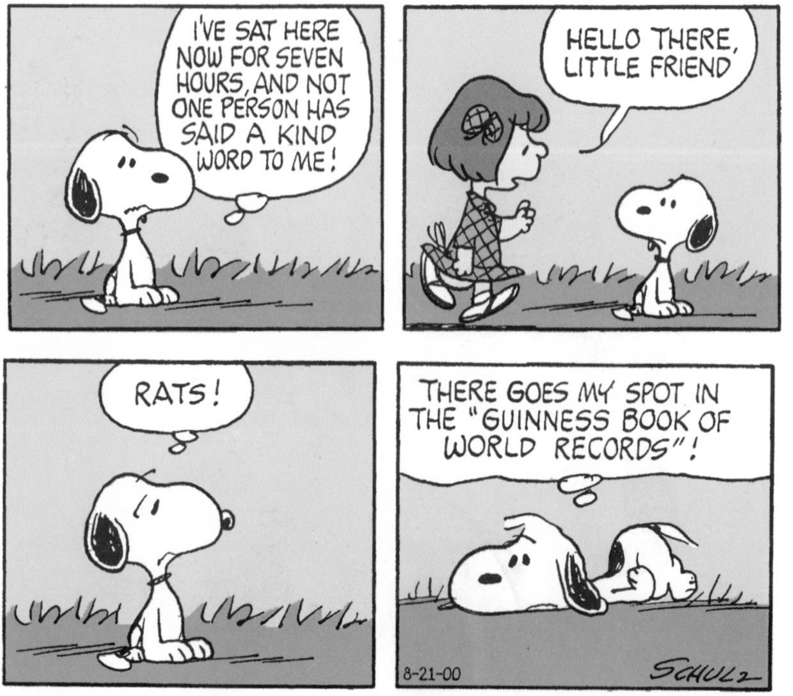
I'VE SAT HERE NOW FOR SEVEN HOURS, AND NOT ONE PERSON HAS SAID A KIND WORD TO ME!
HELLO THERE, LITTLE FRIEND
RATS!
THERE GOES MY SPOT IN THE "GUINNESS BOOK OF WORLD RECORDS"!
8-21-00

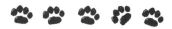

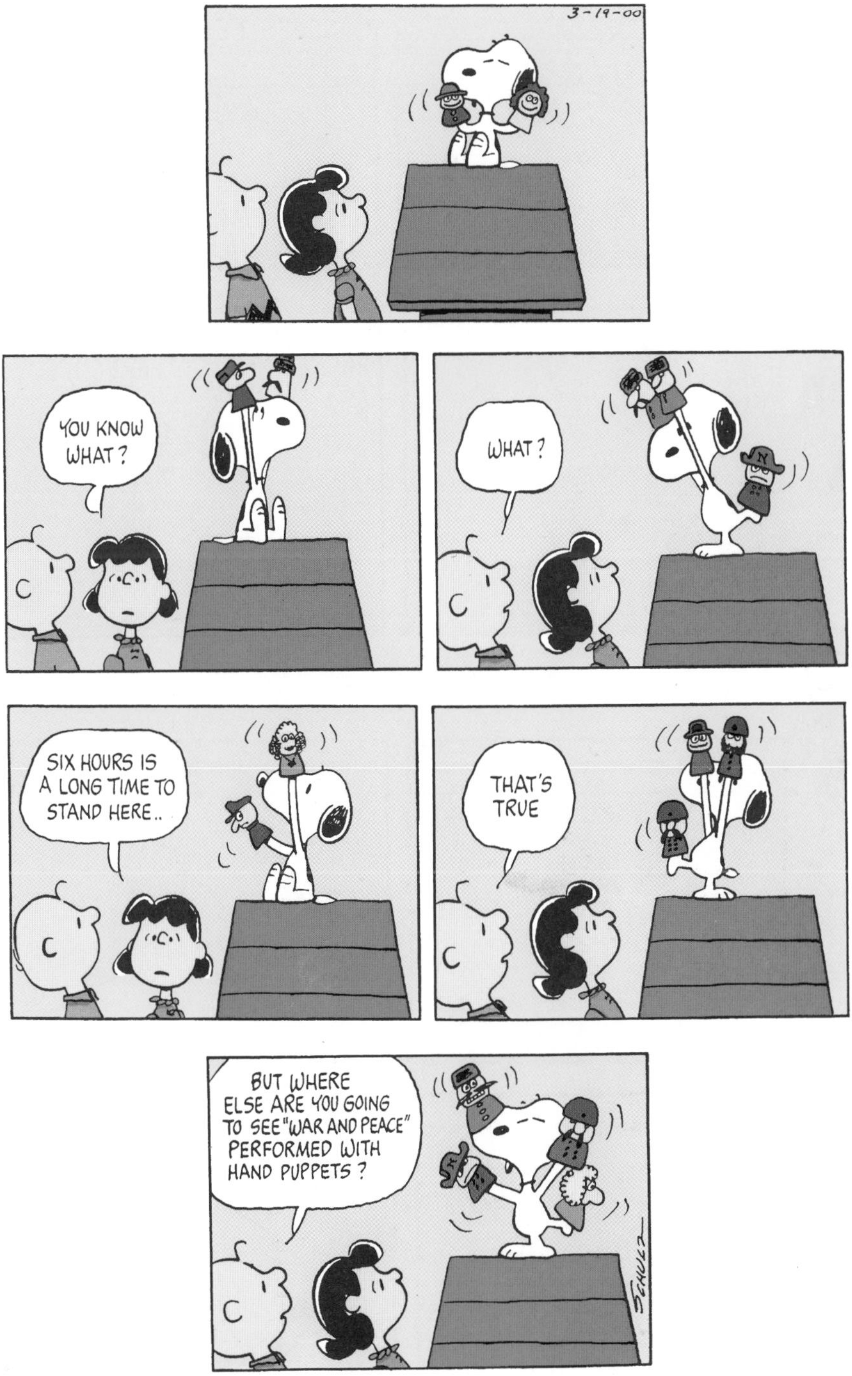
3-19-00
YOU KNOW WHAT?
WHAT?
SIX HOURS IS A LONG TIME TO STAND HERE..
THAT'S TRUE
BUT WHERE ELSE ARE YOU GOING TO SEE "WAR AND PEACE" PERFORMED WITH HAND PUPPETS?
SCHULZ

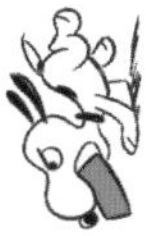

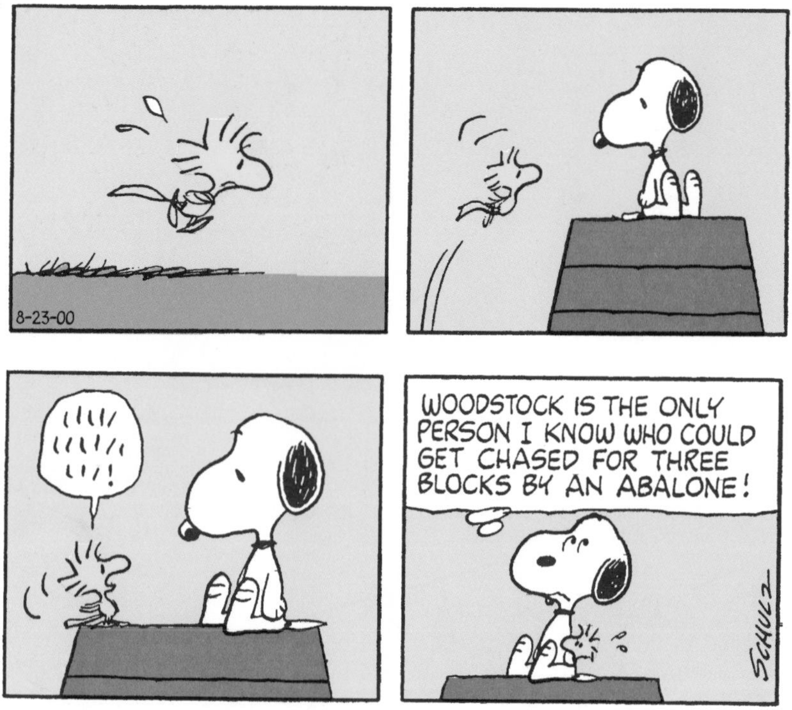
8-23-00
WOODSTOCK IS THE ONLY PERSON I KNOW WHO COULD GET CHASED FOR THREE BLOCKS BY AN ABALONE!
SCHULZ

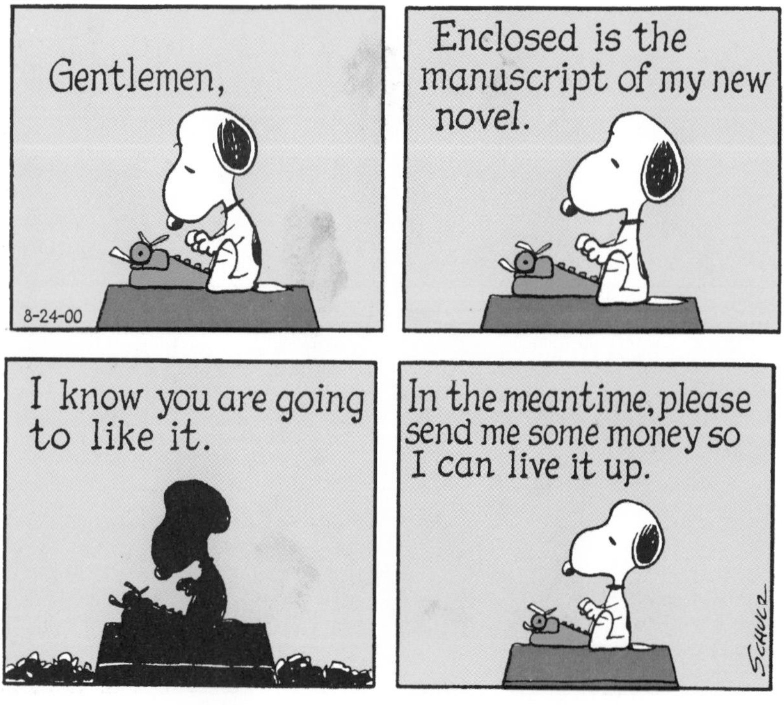
Gentlemen,
8-24-00
Enclosed is the manuscript of my new novel.
I know you are going to like it.
In the meantime, please send me some money so I can live it up.
SCHULZ

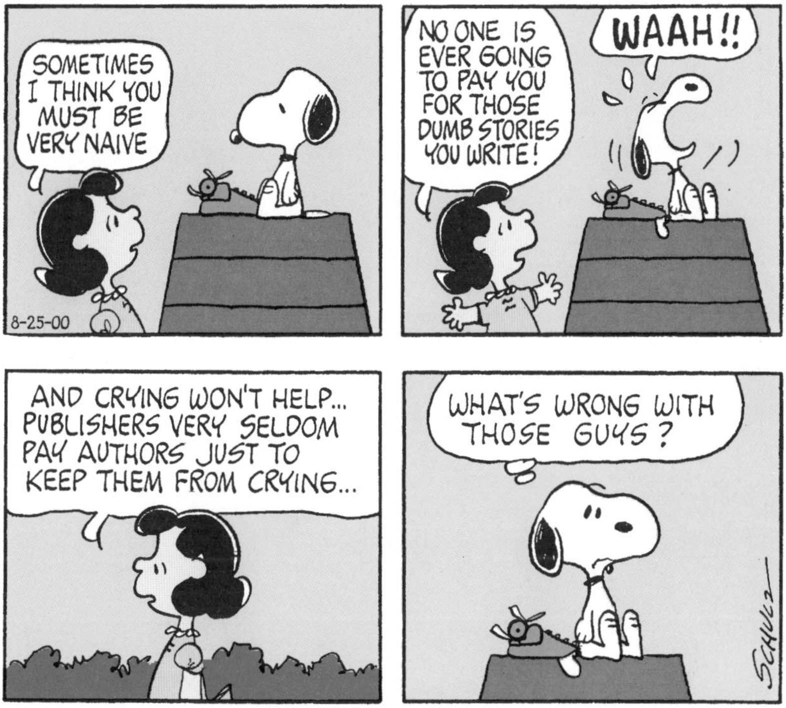
SOMETIMES I THINK YOU MUST BE VERY NAIVE
8-25-00
NO ONE IS EVER GOING TO PAY YOU FOR THOSE DUMB STORIES YOU WRITE!
WAAH!!
AND CRYING WON'T HELP... PUBLISHERS VERY SELDOM PAY AUTHORS JUST TO KEEP THEM FROM CRYING...
WHAT'S WRONG WITH THOSE GUYS?
SCHULZ

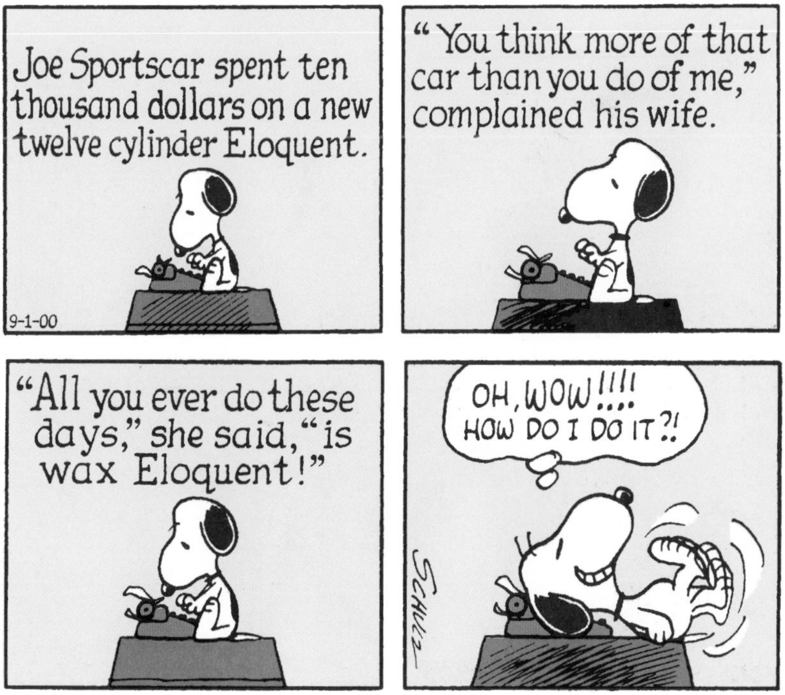
Joe Sportscar spent ten thousand dollars on a new twelve cylinder Eloquent.
9-1-00
"You think more of that car than you do of me," complained his wife.
"All you ever do these days," she said, "is wax Eloquent!"
OH, WOW!!!!.... HOW DO I DO IT?!
SCHULZ

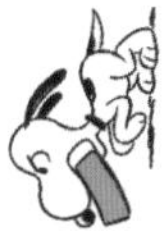

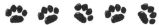

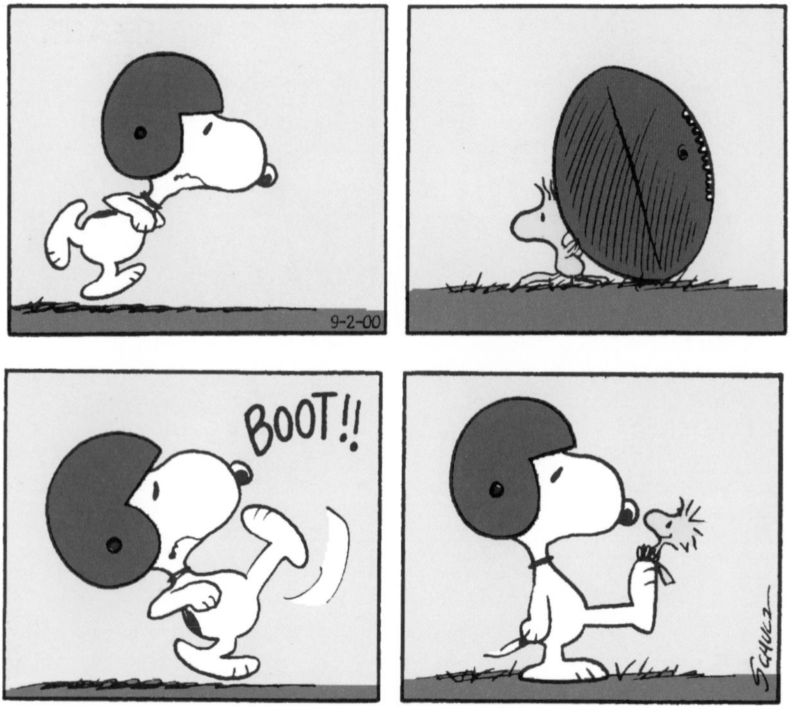
9-2-00
BOOT!!

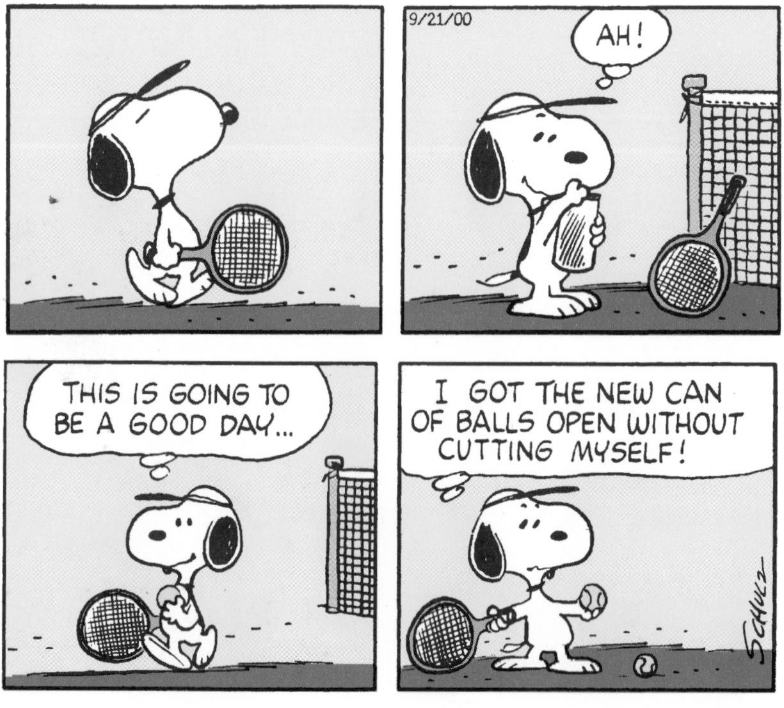
9/21/00
AH!
THIS IS GOING TO BE A GOOD DAY...
I GOT THE NEW CAN OF BALLS OPEN WITHOUT CUTTING MYSELF!

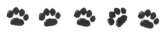

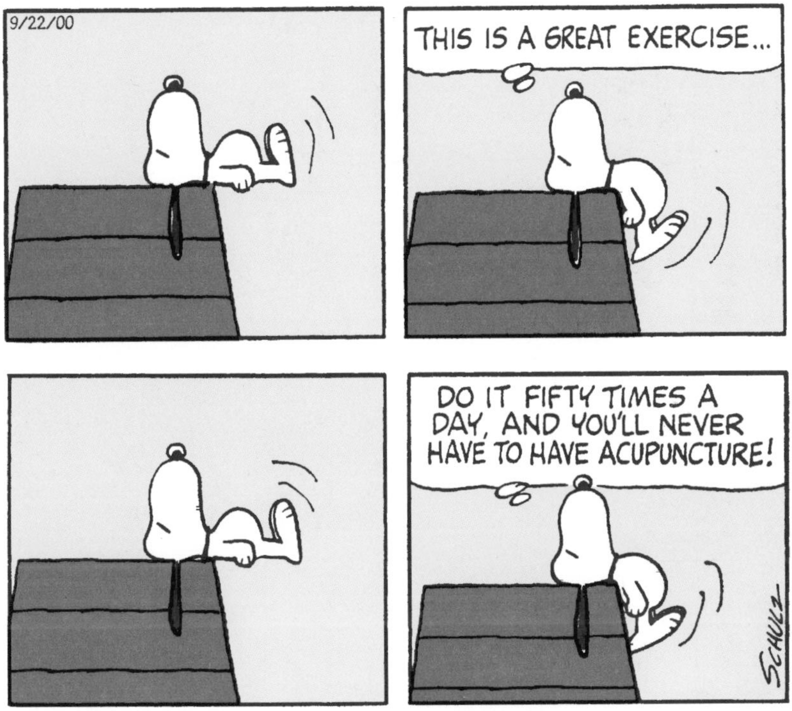
9/22/00
THIS IS A GREAT EXERCISE...
DO IT FIFTY TIMES A DAY, AND YOU'LL NEVER HAVE TO HAVE ACUPUNCTURE!
SCHULZ

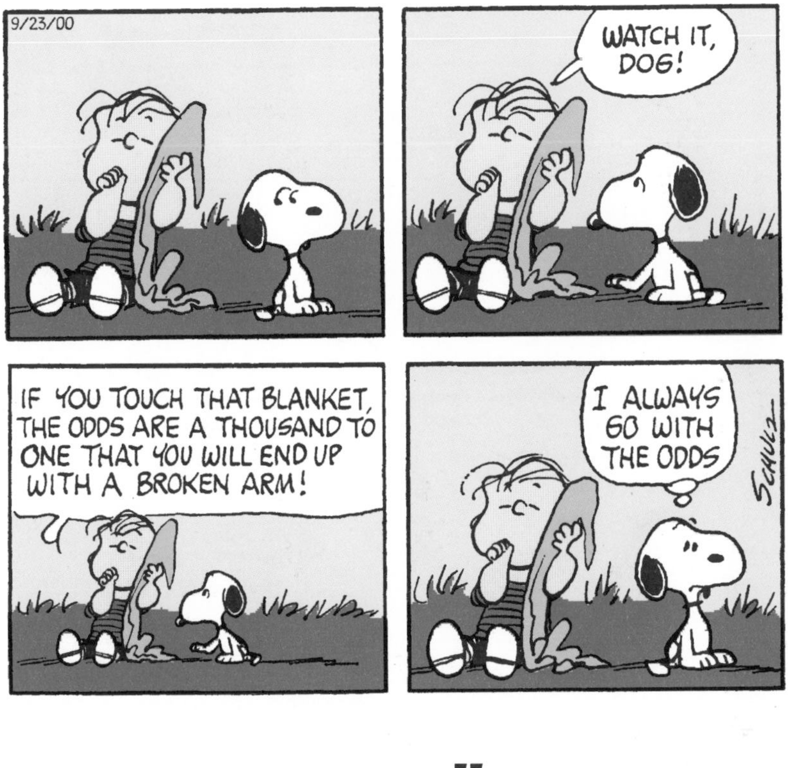
9/23/00
WATCH IT, DOG!
IF YOU TOUCH THAT BLANKET, THE ODDS ARE A THOUSAND TO ONE THAT YOU WILL END UP WITH A BROKEN ARM!
I ALWAYS GO WITH THE ODDS
SCHULZ

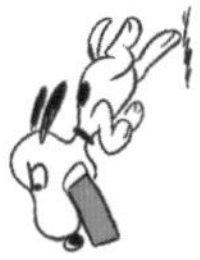

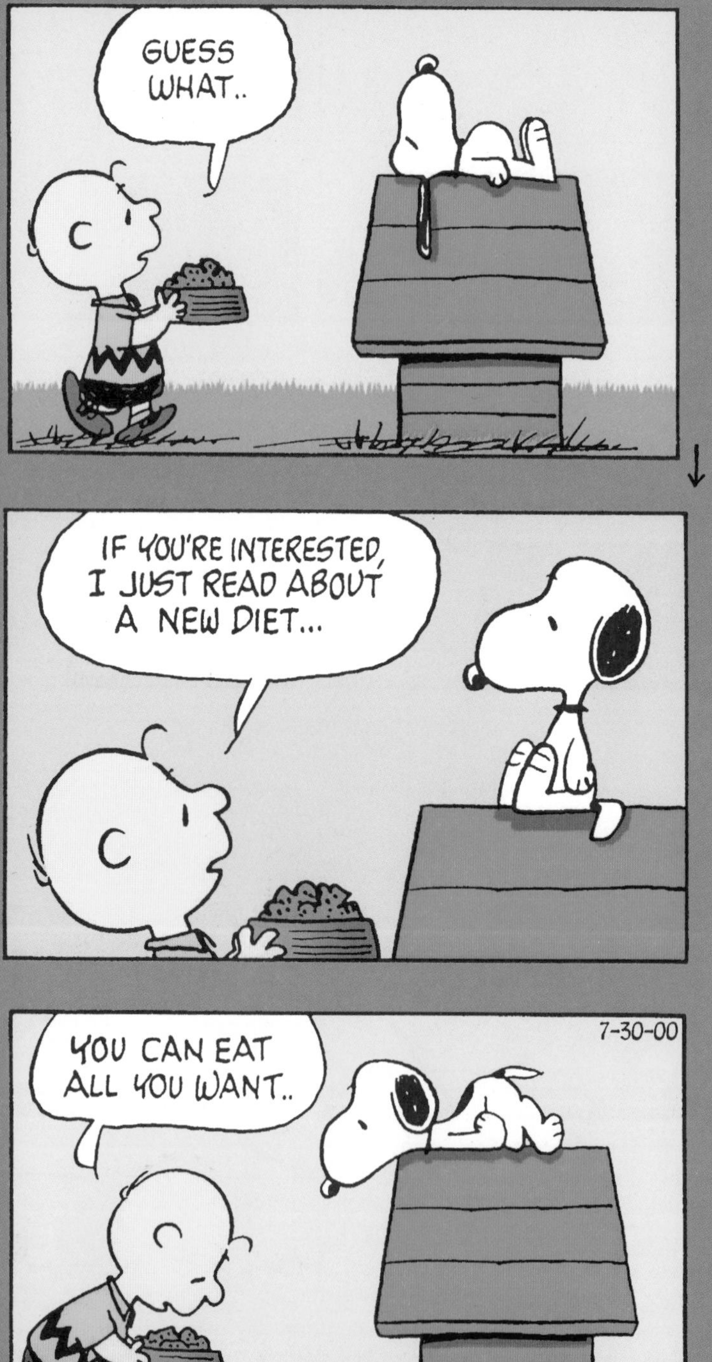
GUESS WHAT..
IF YOU'RE INTERESTED, I JUST READ ABOUT A NEW DIET...
YOU CAN EAT ALL YOU WANT..
7-30-00

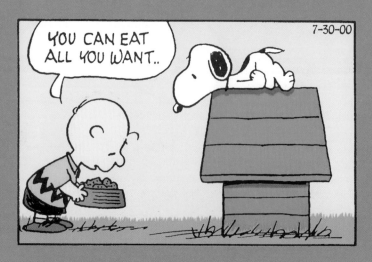

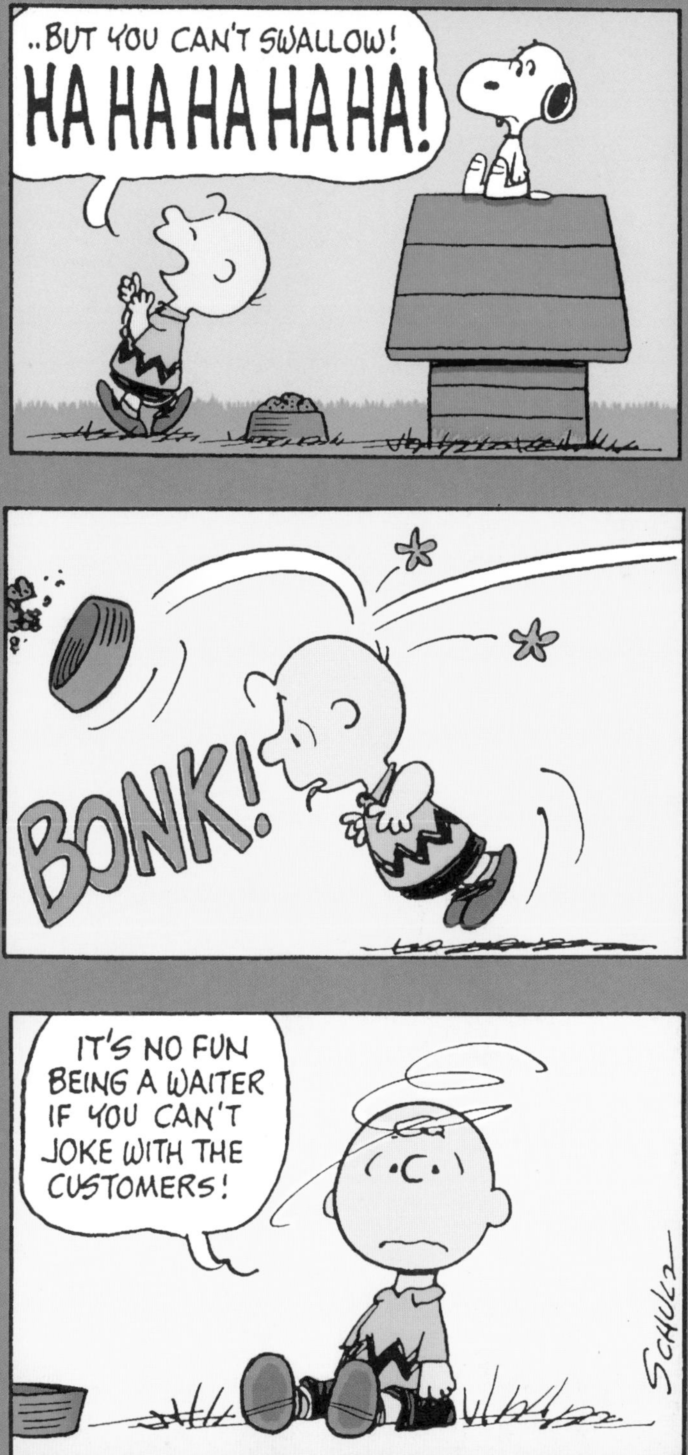
..BUT YOU CAN'T SWALLOW! HA HA HA HA HA HA!
BONK!
IT'S NO FUN BEING A WAITER IF YOU CAN'T JOKE WITH THE CUSTOMERS!
SCHULZ

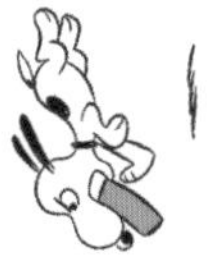

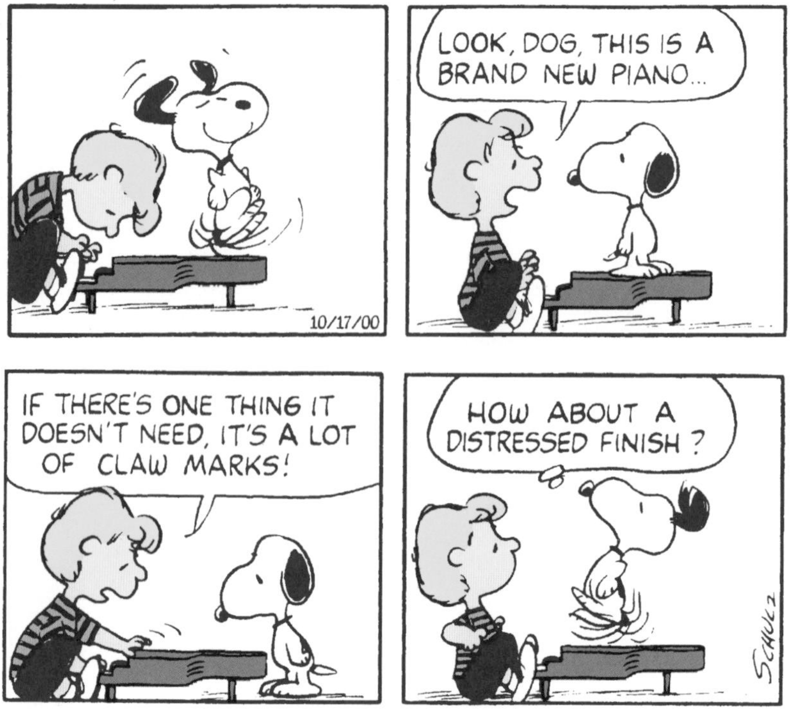
10/17/00
LOOK, DOG, THIS IS A BRAND NEW PIANO...
IF THERE'S ONE THING IT DOESN'T NEED, IT'S A LOT OF CLAW MARKS!
HOW ABOUT A DISTRESSED FINISH ?
SCHULZ

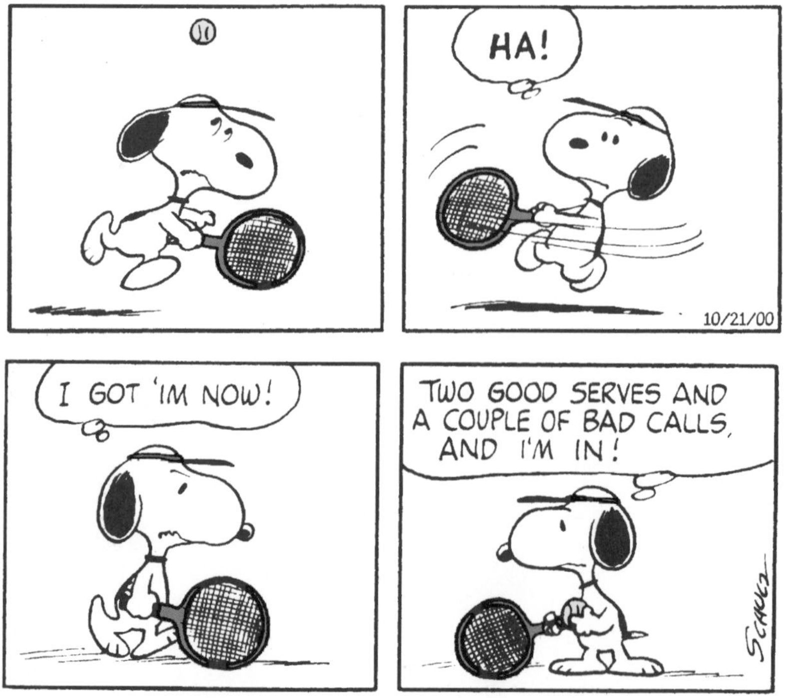
HA!
10/21/00
I GOT 'IM NOW!
TWO GOOD SERVES AND A COUPLE OF BAD CALLS, AND I'M IN!
SCHULZ

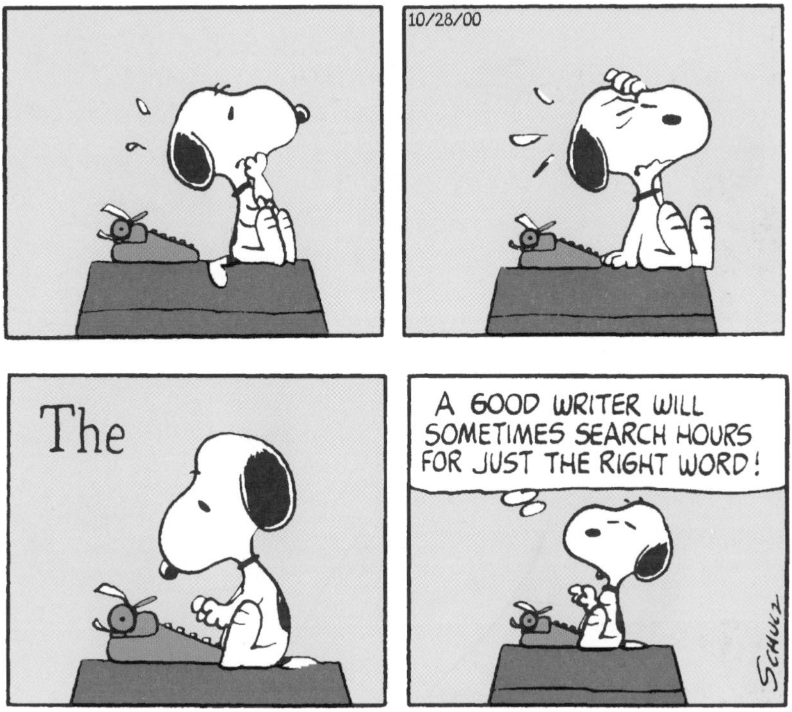
10/28/00
The
A GOOD WRITER WILL SOMETIMES SEARCH HOURS FOR JUST THE RIGHT WORD!
SCHULZ

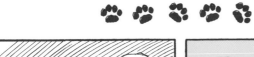

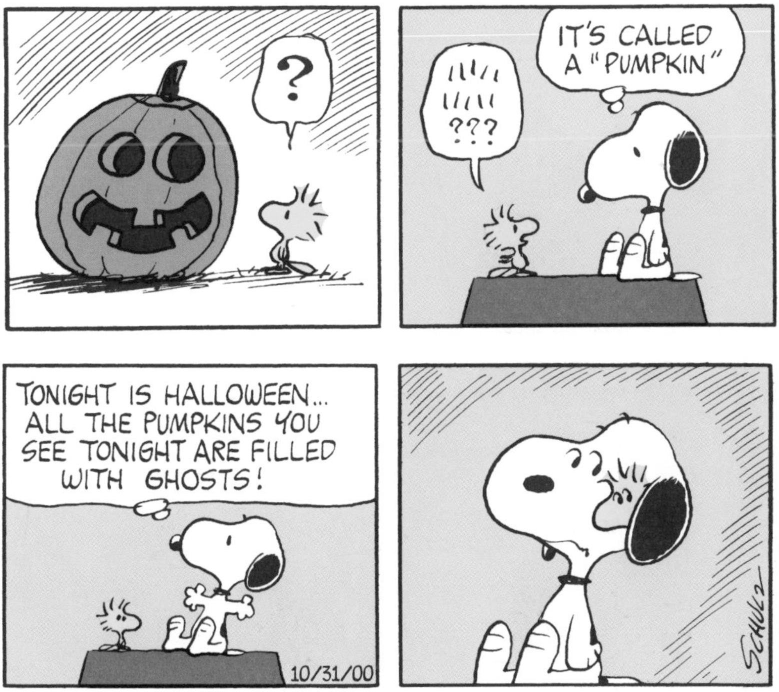
?
???
IT'S CALLED A "PUMPKIN"
TONIGHT IS HALLOWEEN... ALL THE PUMPKINS YOU SEE TONIGHT ARE FILLED WITH GHOSTS!
10/31/00
SCHULZ

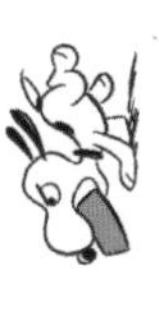

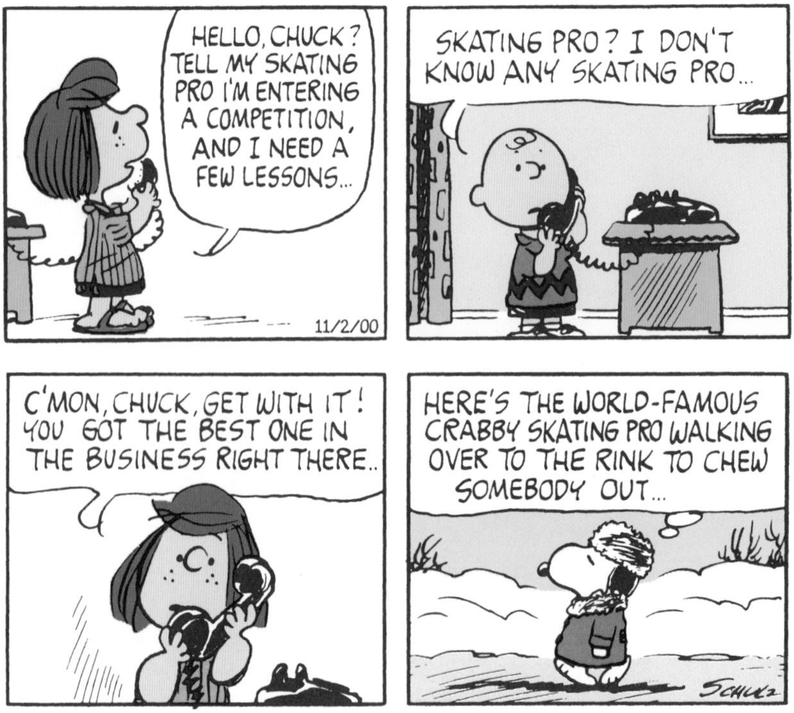
HELLO, CHUCK? TELL MY SKATING PRO I'M ENTERING A COMPETITION, AND I NEED A FEW LESSONS...
11/2/00
SKATING PRO? I DON'T KNOW ANY SKATING PRO...
C'MON, CHUCK, GET WITH IT! YOU GOT THE BEST ONE IN THE BUSINESS RIGHT THERE..
HERE'S THE WORLD-FAMOUS CRABBY SKATING PRO WALKING OVER TO THE RINK TO CHEW SOMEBODY OUT...

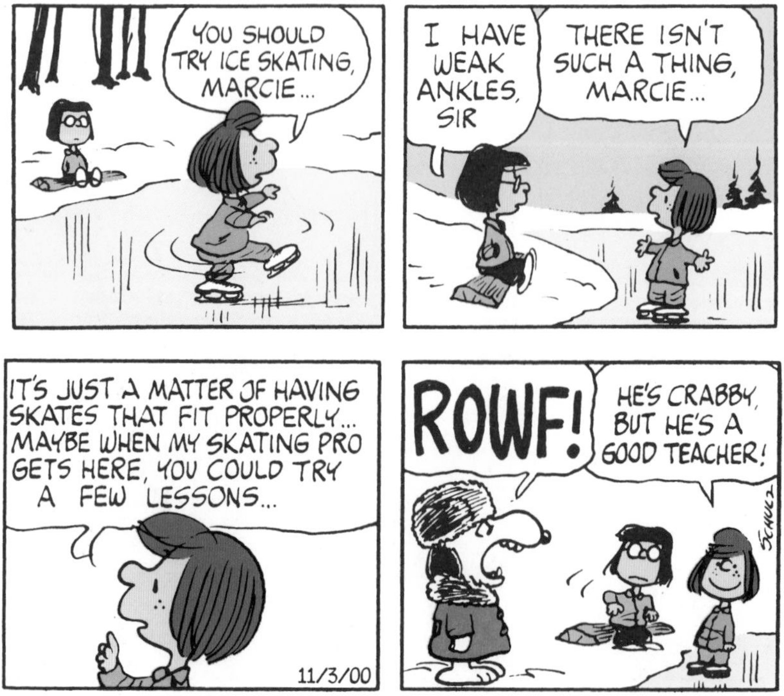
YOU SHOULD TRY ICE SKATING, MARCIE...
I HAVE WEAK ANKLES, SIR
THERE ISN'T SUCH A THING, MARCIE...
IT'S JUST A MATTER OF HAVING SKATES THAT FIT PROPERLY... MAYBE WHEN MY SKATING PRO GETS HERE, YOU COULD TRY A FEW LESSONS...
11/3/00
ROWF!
HE'S CRABBY, BUT HE'S A GOOD TEACHER!

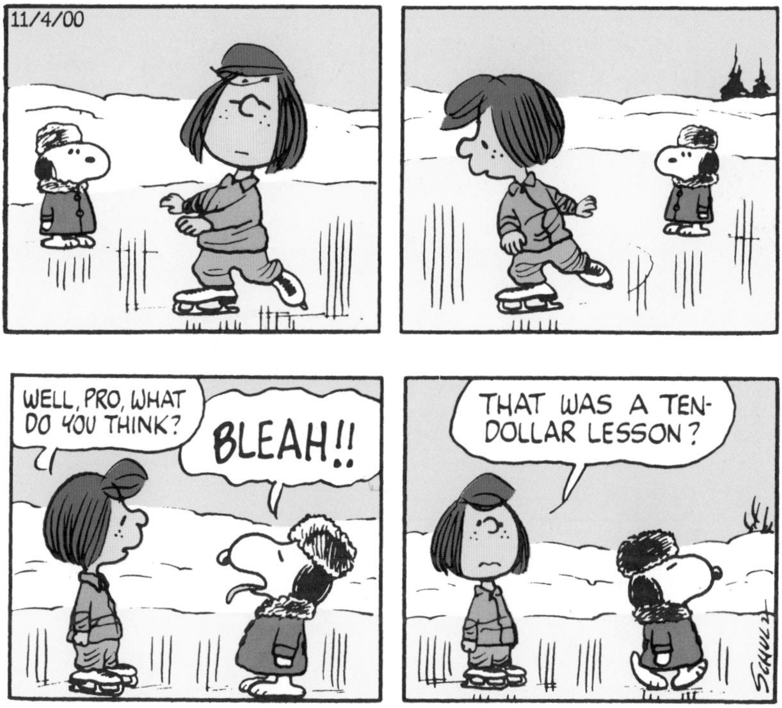
11/4/00
WELL, PRO, WHAT DO YOU THINK?
BLEAH!!
THAT WAS A TEN-DOLLAR LESSON?
SCHULZ

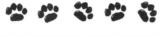

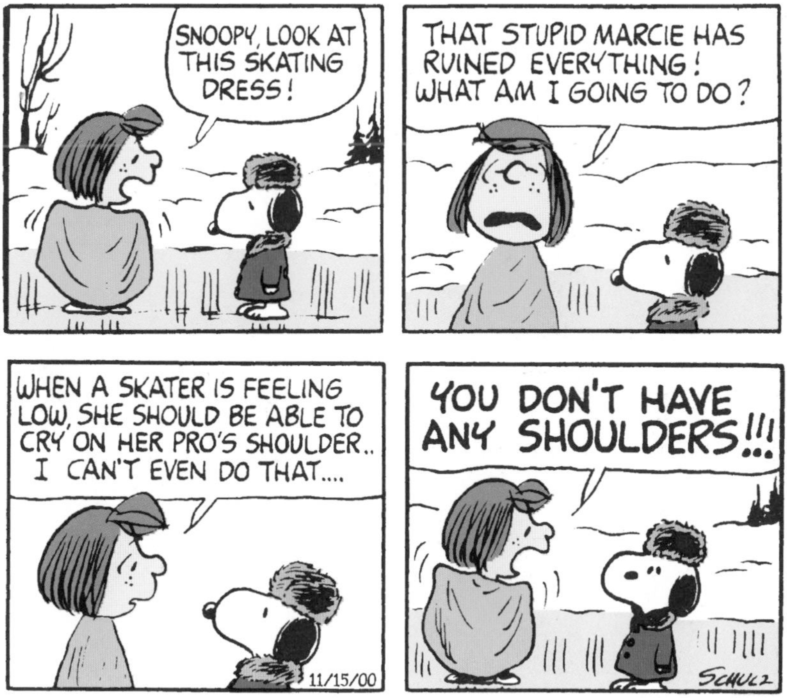
SNOOPY, LOOK AT THIS SKATING DRESS!
THAT STUPID MARCIE HAS RUINED EVERYTHING! WHAT AM I GOING TO DO?
WHEN A SKATER IS FEELING LOW, SHE SHOULD BE ABLE TO CRY ON HER PRO'S SHOULDER.. I CAN'T EVEN DO THAT....
11/15/00
YOU DON'T HAVE ANY SHOULDERS!!!
SCHULZ

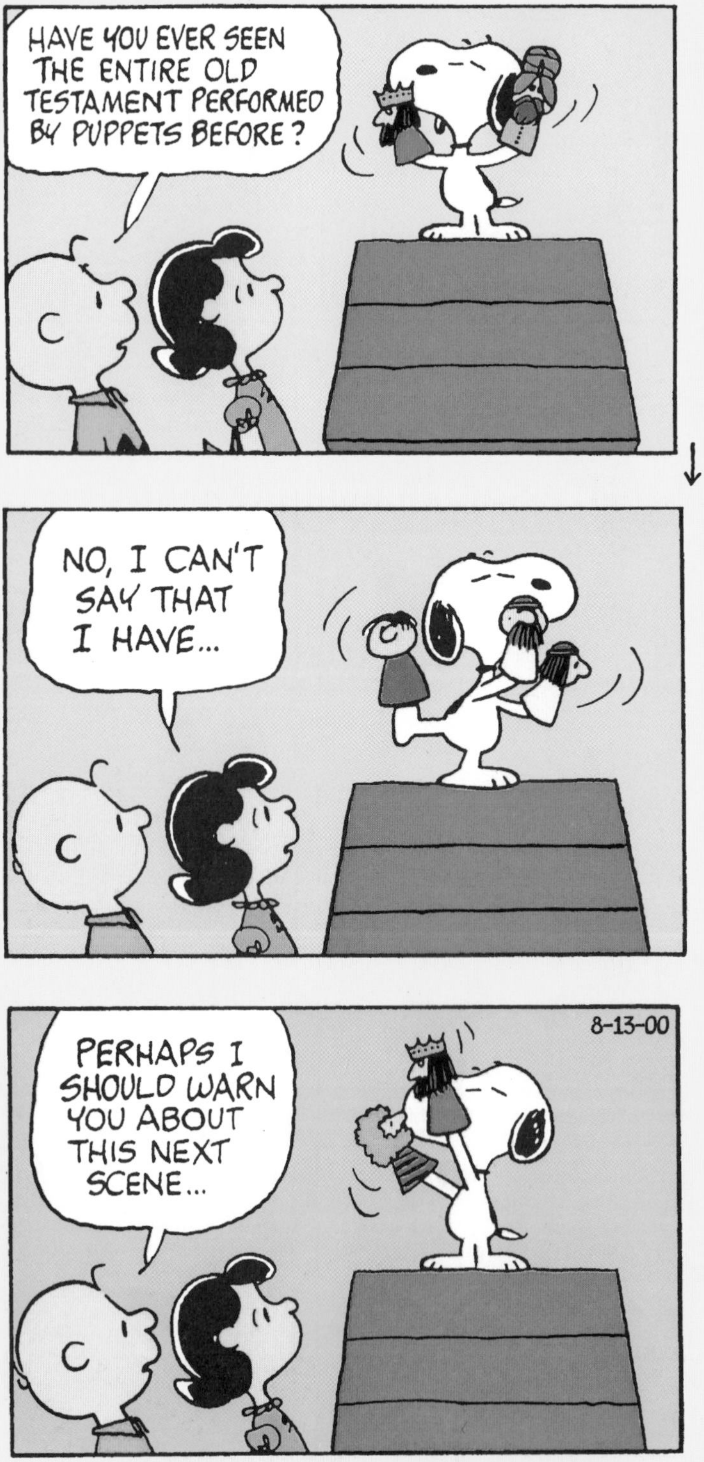
HAVE YOU EVER SEEN THE ENTIRE OLD TESTAMENT PERFORMED BY PUPPETS BEFORE?
NO, I CAN'T SAY THAT I HAVE...
8-13-00
PERHAPS I SHOULD WARN YOU ABOUT THIS NEXT SCENE...

WHAT NEXT SCENE?
SPLASH!
THE PARTING OF THE RED SEA!
SCHULZ

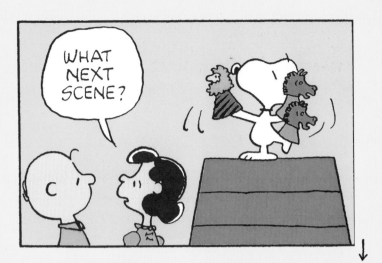

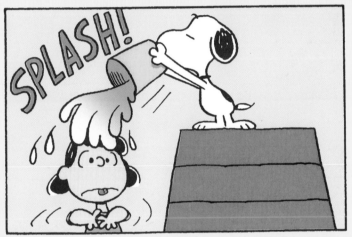

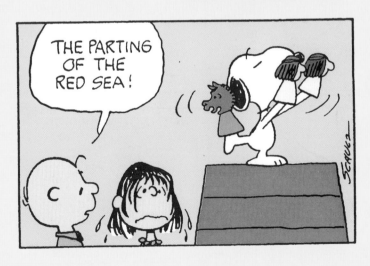

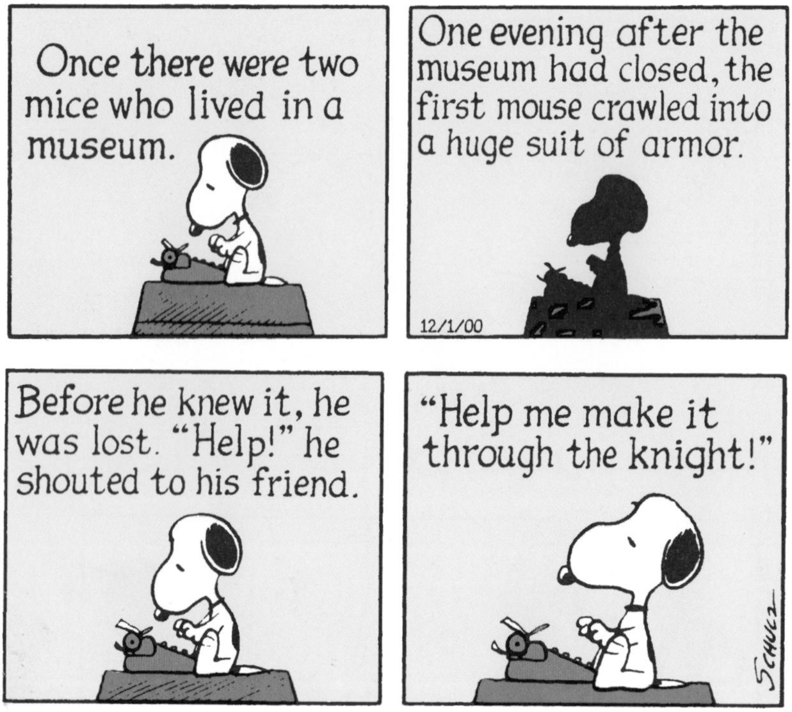
Once there were two mice who lived in a museum.
One evening after the museum had closed, the first mouse crawled into a huge suit of armor.
12/1/00
Before he knew it, he was lost. "Help!" he shouted to his friend.
"Help me make it through the knight!"
SCHULZ

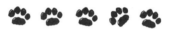

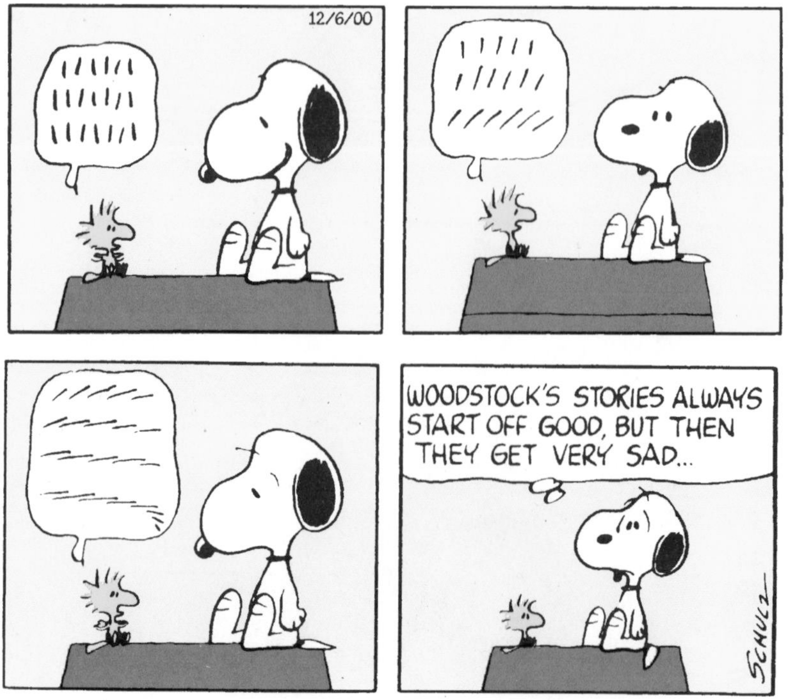
12/6/00
WOODSTOCK'S STORIES ALWAYS START OFF GOOD, BUT THEN THEY GET VERY SAD...
SCHULZ

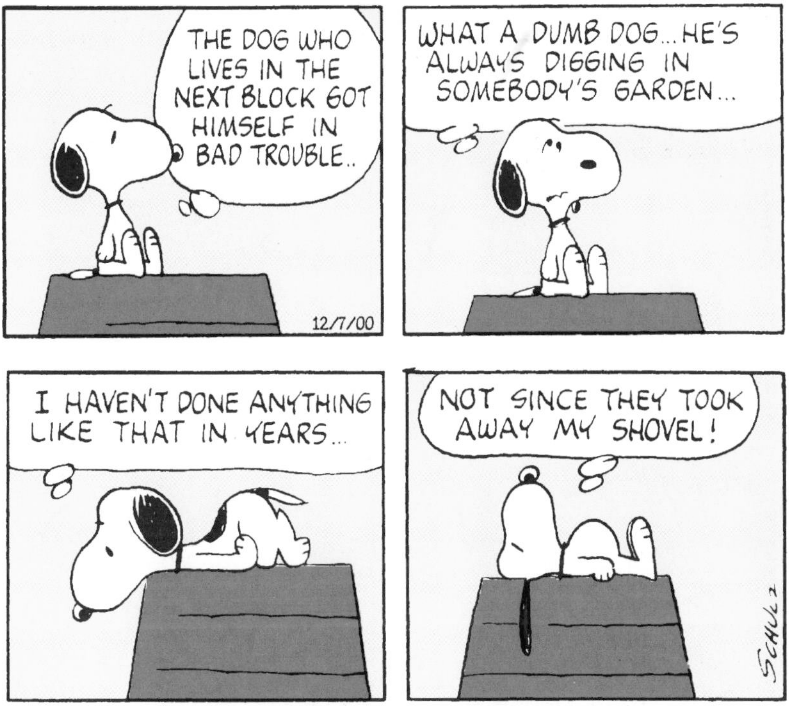
THE DOG WHO LIVES IN THE NEXT BLOCK GOT HIMSELF IN BAD TROUBLE..
12/7/00
WHAT A DUMB DOG... HE'S ALWAYS DIGGING IN SOMEBODY'S GARDEN...
I HAVEN'T DONE ANYTHING LIKE THAT IN YEARS...
NOT SINCE THEY TOOK AWAY MY SHOVEL!
SCHULZ

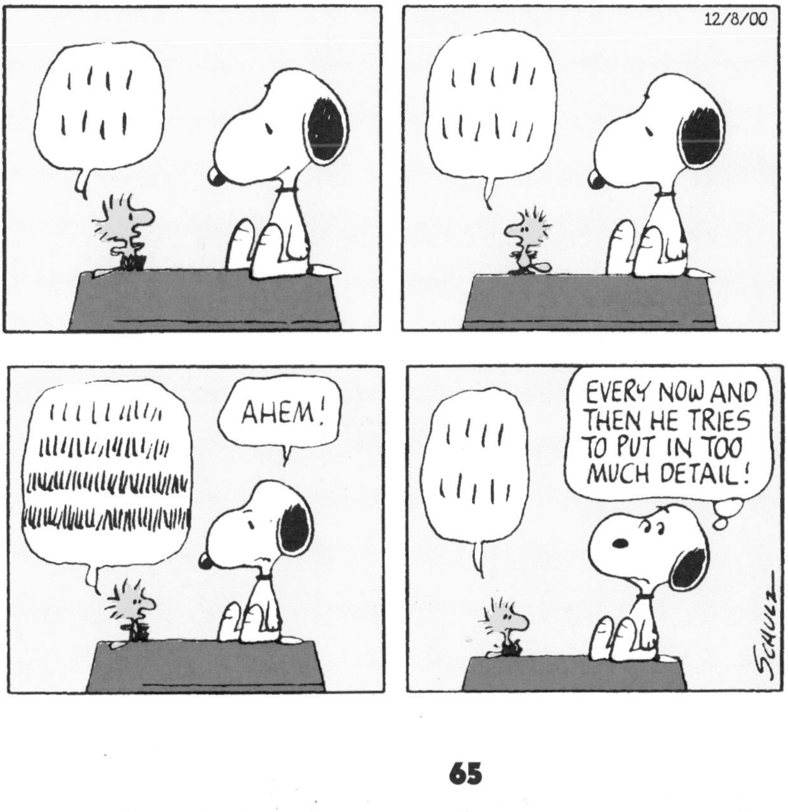
12/8/00
AHEM!
EVERY NOW AND THEN HE TRIES TO PUT IN TOO MUCH DETAIL!
SCHULZ

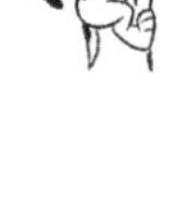

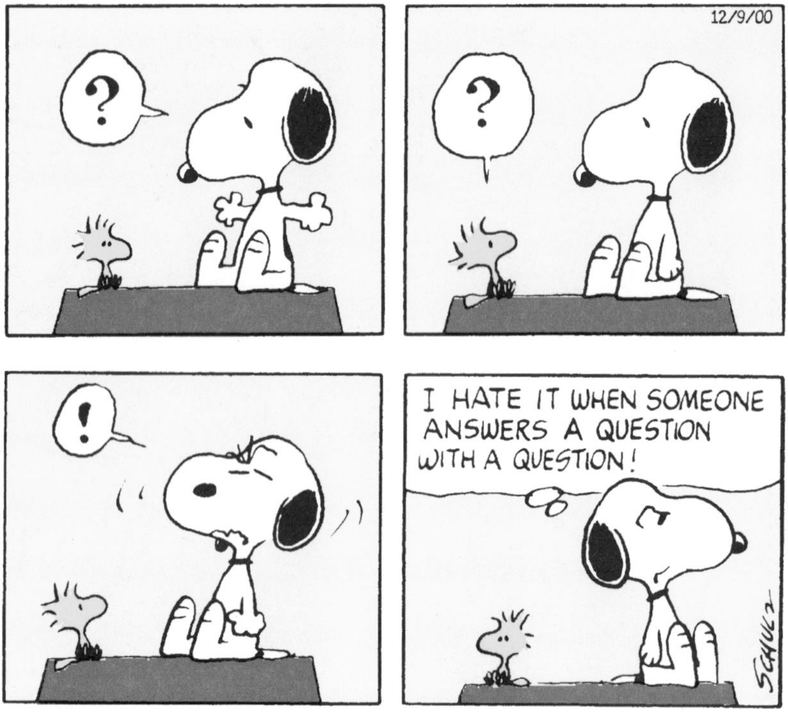
12/9/00
?
?
!
I HATE IT WHEN SOMEONE ANSWERS A QUESTION WITH A QUESTION!
SCHULZ

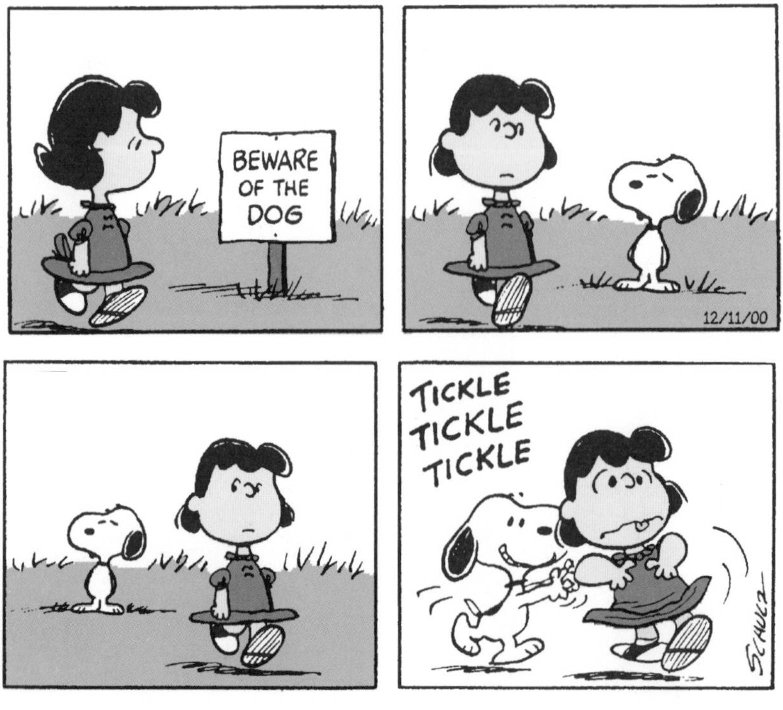
BEWARE OF THE DOG
12/11/00
TICKLE TICKLE TICKLE
SCHULZ

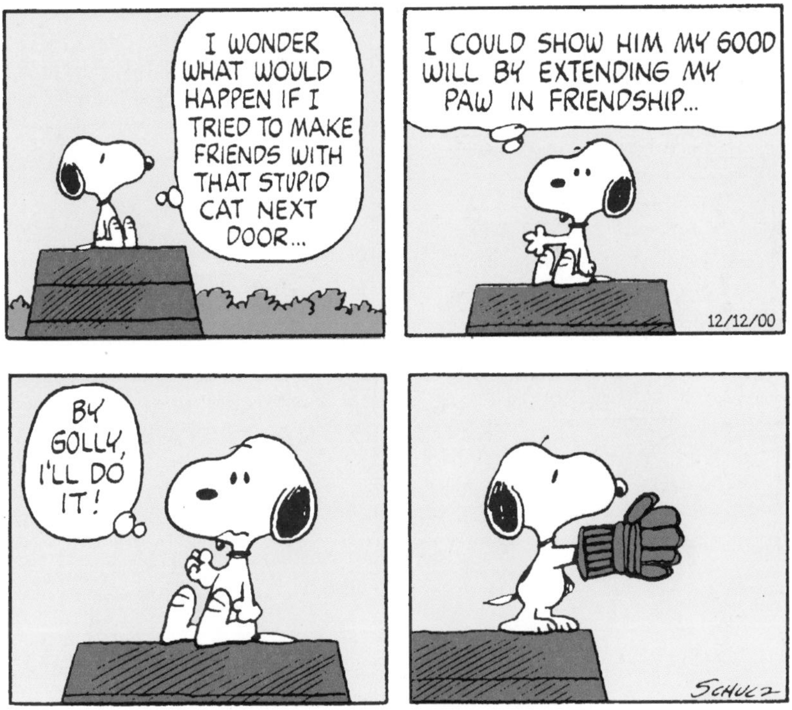
I WONDER WHAT WOULD HAPPEN IF I TRIED TO MAKE FRIENDS WITH THAT STUPID CAT NEXT DOOR...
I COULD SHOW HIM MY GOOD WILL BY EXTENDING MY PAW IN FRIENDSHIP...
12/12/00
BY GOLLY, I'LL DO IT!
SCHULZ

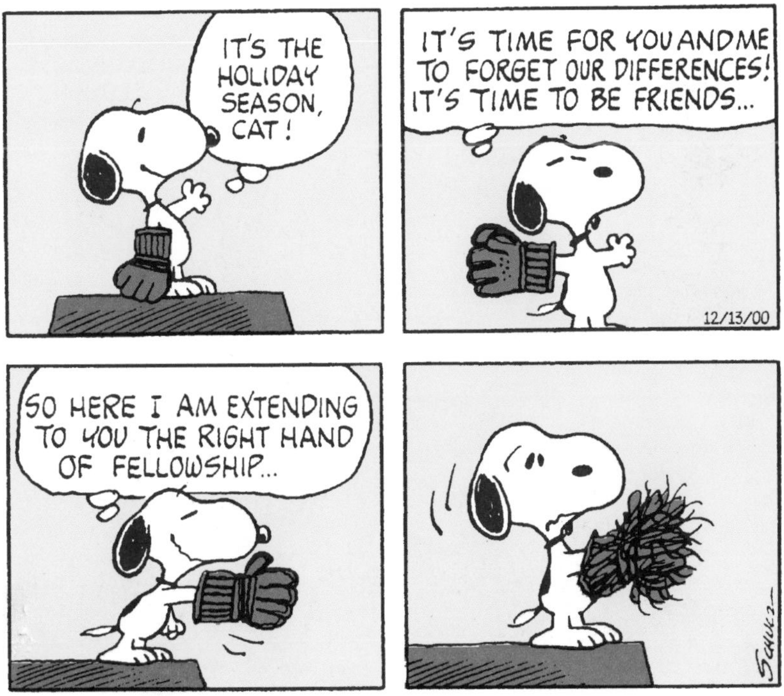
IT'S THE HOLIDAY SEASON, CAT!
IT'S TIME FOR YOU AND ME TO FORGET OUR DIFFERENCES! IT'S TIME TO BE FRIENDS...
12/13/00
SO HERE I AM EXTENDING TO YOU THE RIGHT HAND OF FELLOWSHIP...
SCHULZ

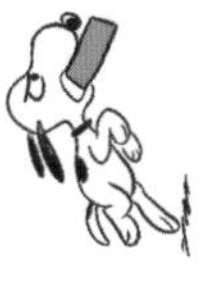

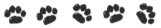

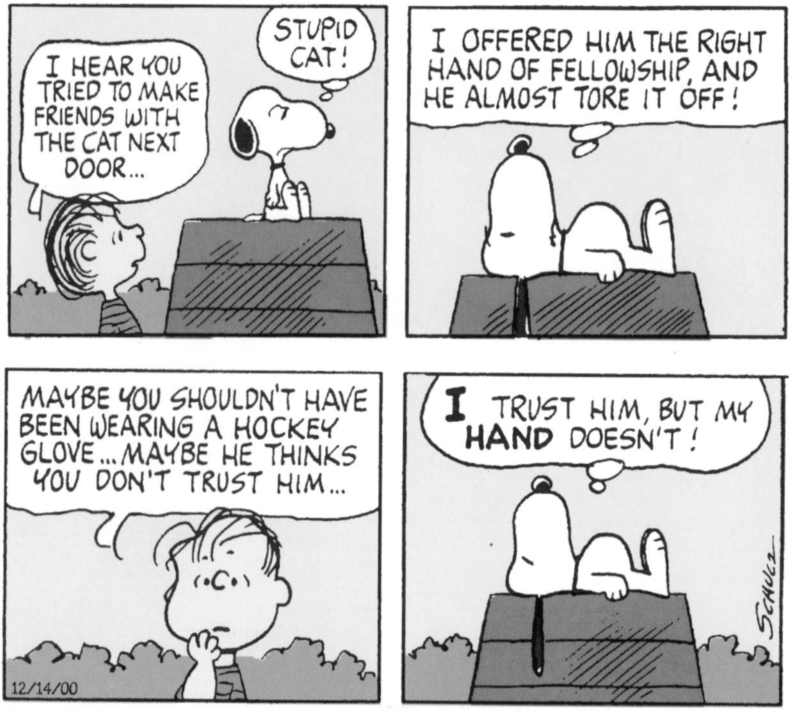
I HEAR YOU TRIED TO MAKE FRIENDS WITH THE CAT NEXT DOOR...
STUPID CAT!
I OFFERED HIM THE RIGHT HAND OF FELLOWSHIP, AND HE ALMOST TORE IT OFF!
MAYBE YOU SHOULDN'T HAVE BEEN WEARING A HOCKEY GLOVE...MAYBE HE THINKS YOU DON'T TRUST HIM...
12/14/00
I TRUST HIM, BUT MY **HAND** DOESN'T!
SCHULZ

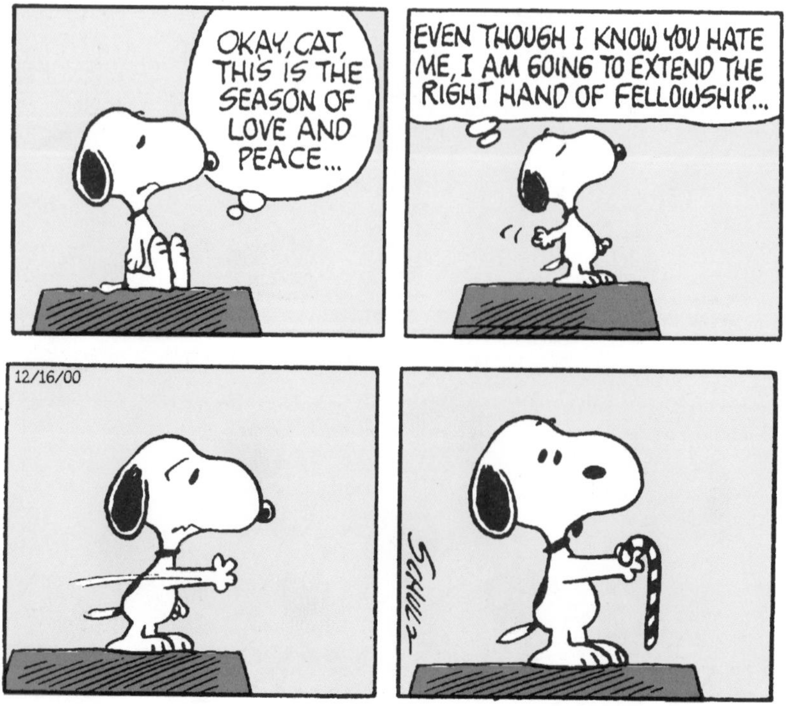
OKAY, CAT, THIS IS THE SEASON OF LOVE AND PEACE...
EVEN THOUGH I KNOW YOU HATE ME, I AM GOING TO EXTEND THE RIGHT HAND OF FELLOWSHIP...
12/16/00
SCHULZ

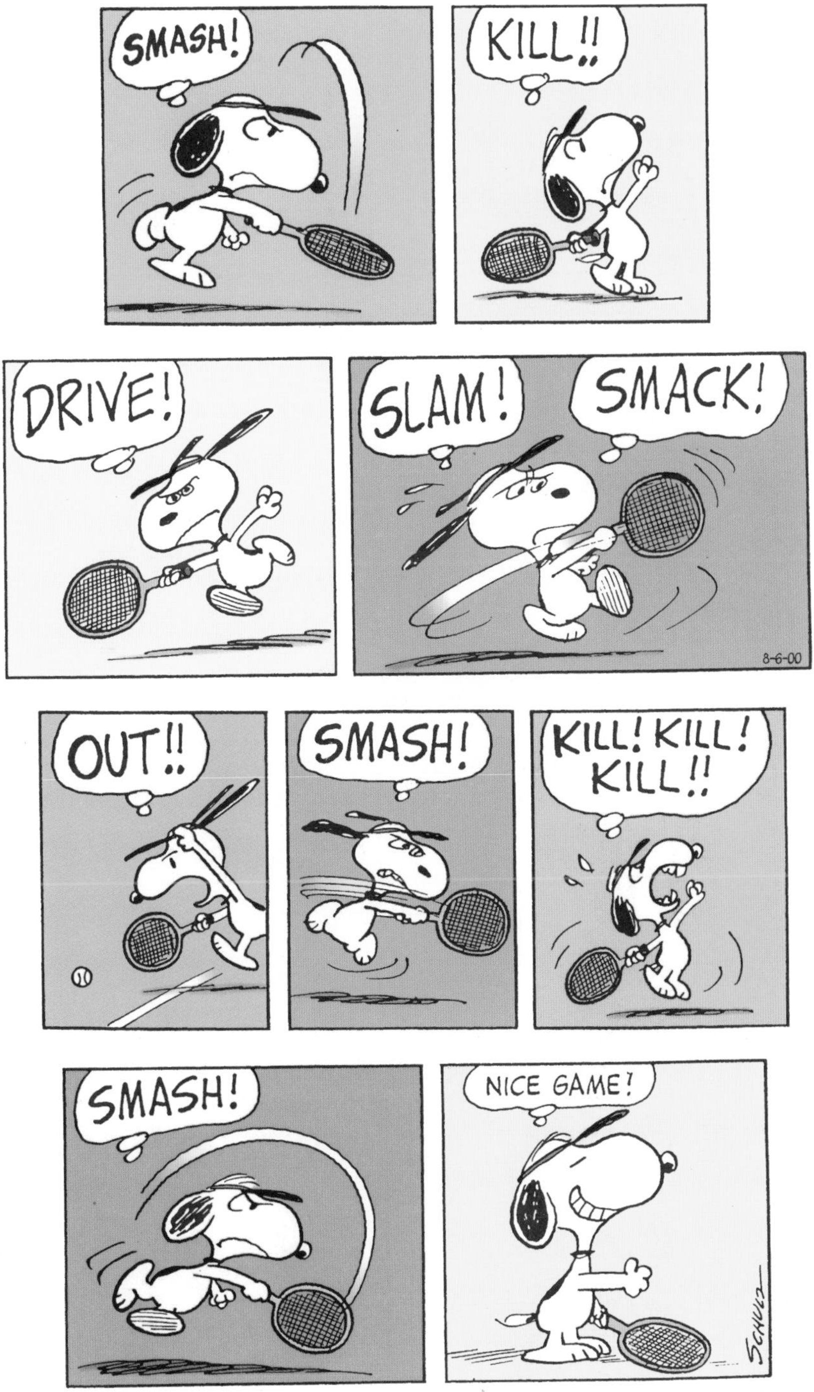
SMASH!
KILL!!
DRIVE!
SLAM!
SMACK!
8-6-00
OUT!!
SMASH!
KILL! KILL!
KILL!!
SMASH!
NICE GAME!
SCHULZ

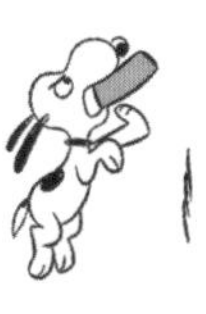

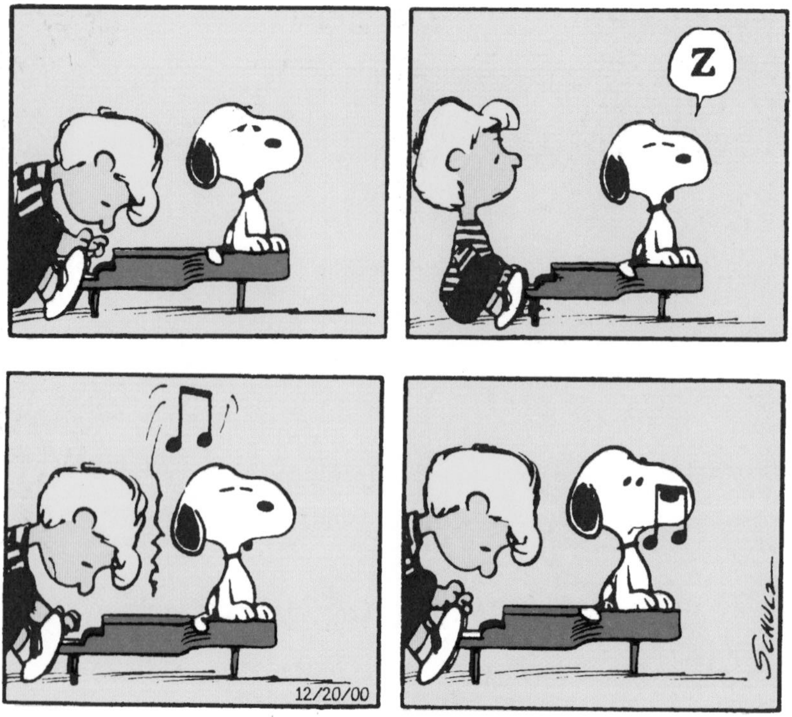
Z
12/20/00

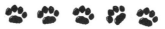

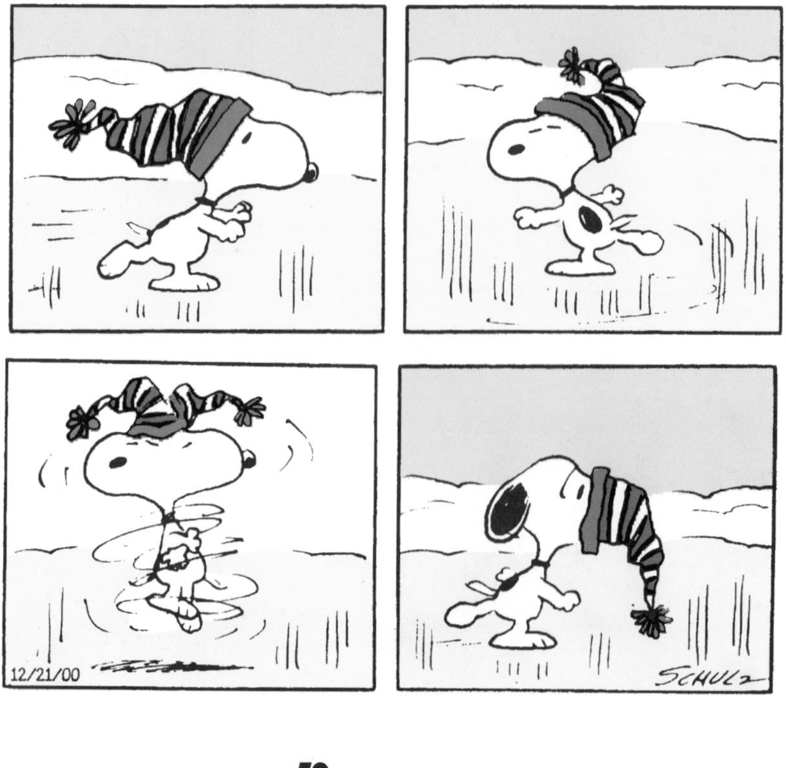
12/21/00

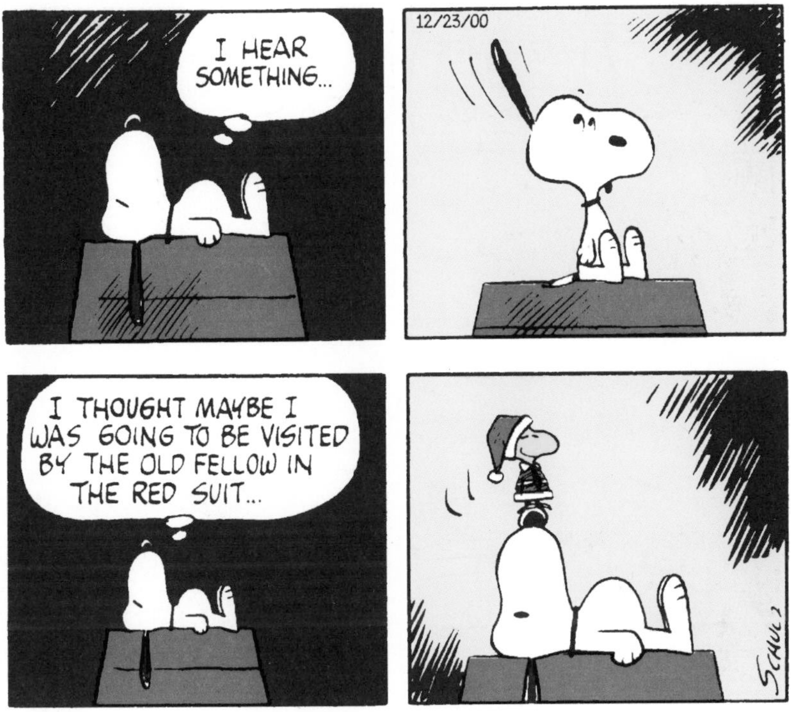
12/23/00
I HEAR SOMETHING...
I THOUGHT MAYBE I WAS GOING TO BE VISITED BY THE OLD FELLOW IN THE RED SUIT...
SCHULZ

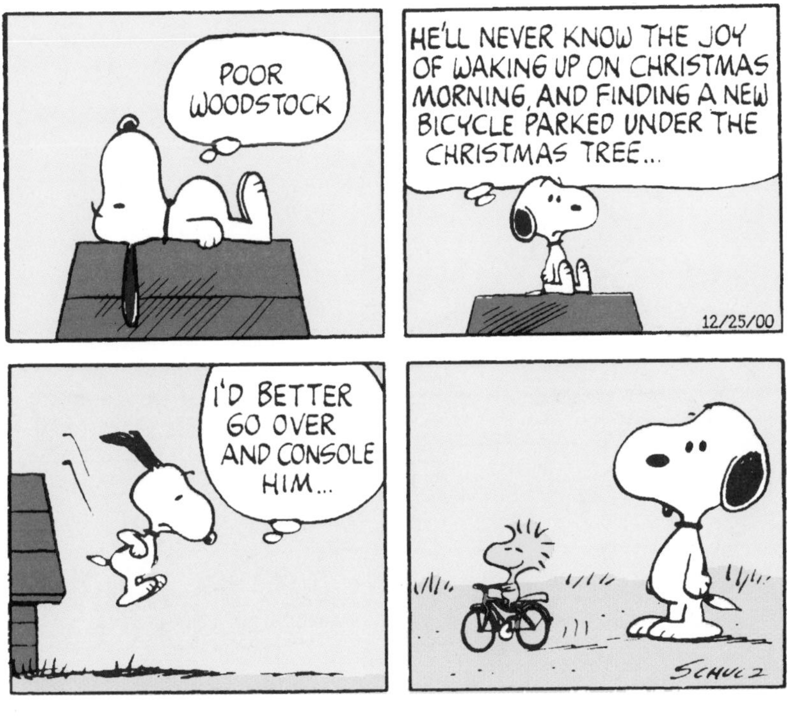
POOR WOODSTOCK
HE'LL NEVER KNOW THE JOY OF WAKING UP ON CHRISTMAS MORNING, AND FINDING A NEW BICYCLE PARKED UNDER THE CHRISTMAS TREE...
12/25/00
I'D BETTER GO OVER AND CONSOLE HIM...
SCHULZ

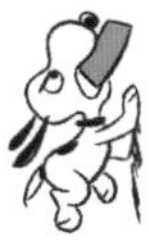

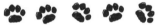

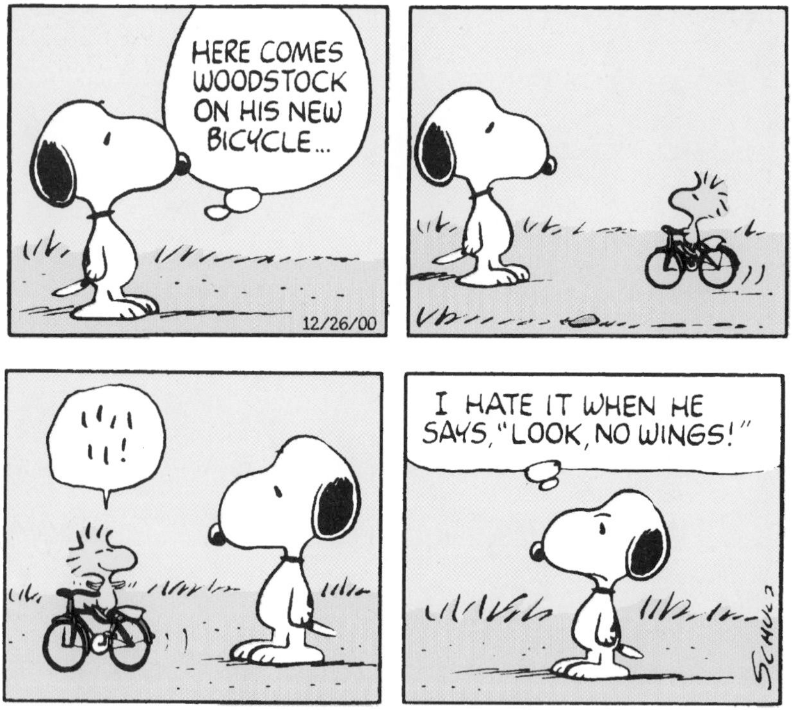
HERE COMES WOODSTOCK ON HIS NEW BICYCLE...
12/26/00
I HATE IT WHEN HE SAYS, "LOOK, NO WINGS!"
SCHULZ

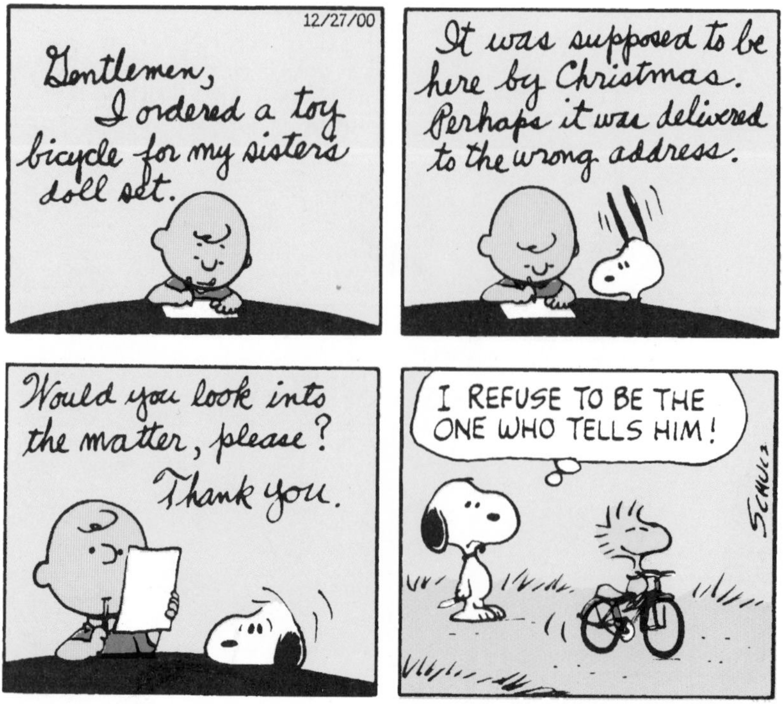
12/27/00
Gentlemen,
I ordered a toy bicycle for my sister's doll set.
It was supposed to be here by Christmas. Perhaps it was delivered to the wrong address.
Would you look into the matter, please?
Thank you.
I REFUSE TO BE THE ONE WHO TELLS HIM!
SCHULZ

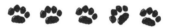

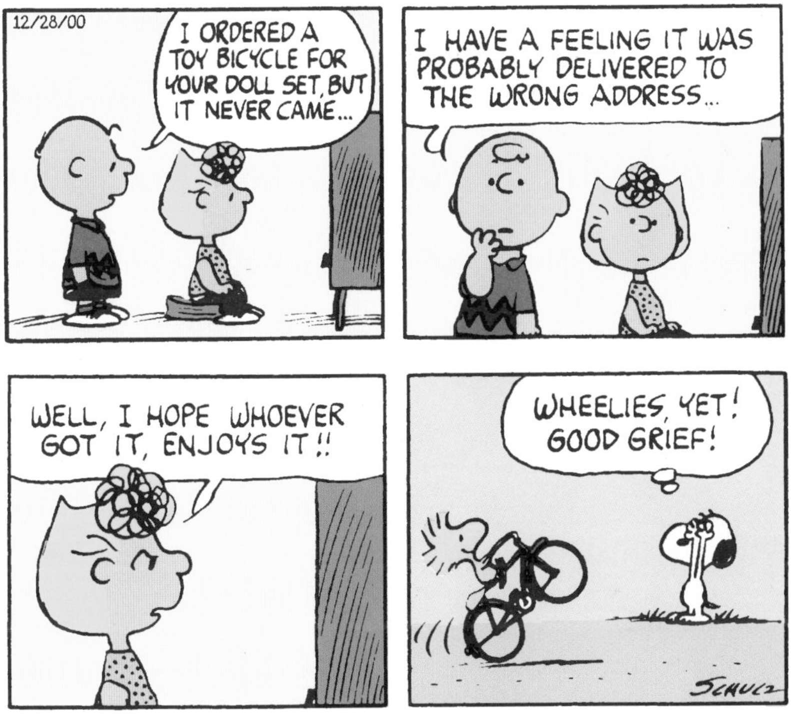
12/28/00
I ORDERED A TOY BICYCLE FOR YOUR DOLL SET, BUT IT NEVER CAME...
I HAVE A FEELING IT WAS PROBABLY DELIVERED TO THE WRONG ADDRESS...
WELL, I HOPE WHOEVER GOT IT, ENJOYS IT!!
WHEELIES, YET! GOOD GRIEF!
SCHULZ

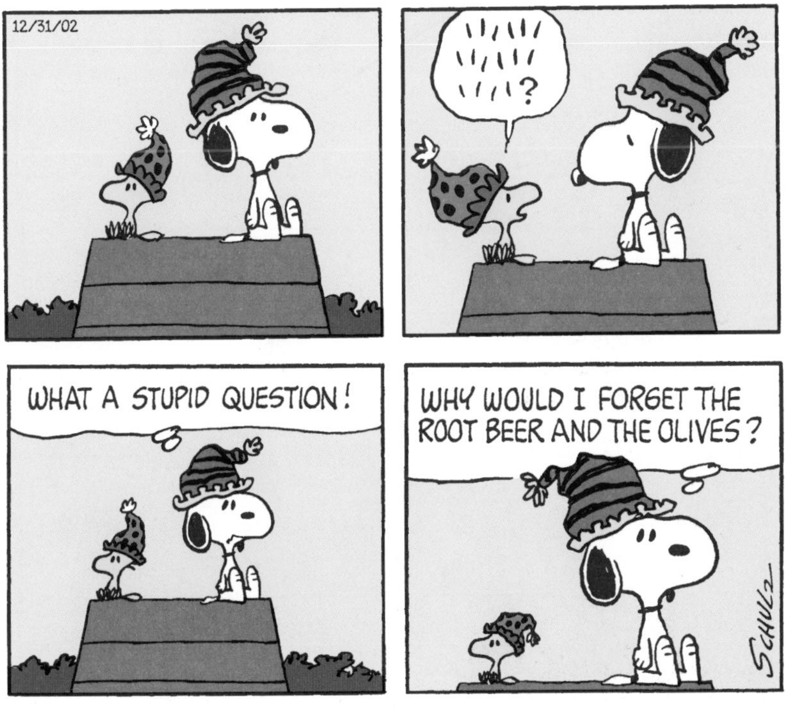
12/31/02
?
WHAT A STUPID QUESTION!
WHY WOULD I FORGET THE ROOT BEER AND THE OLIVES?
SCHULZ

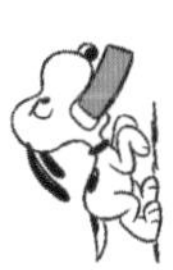

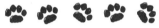

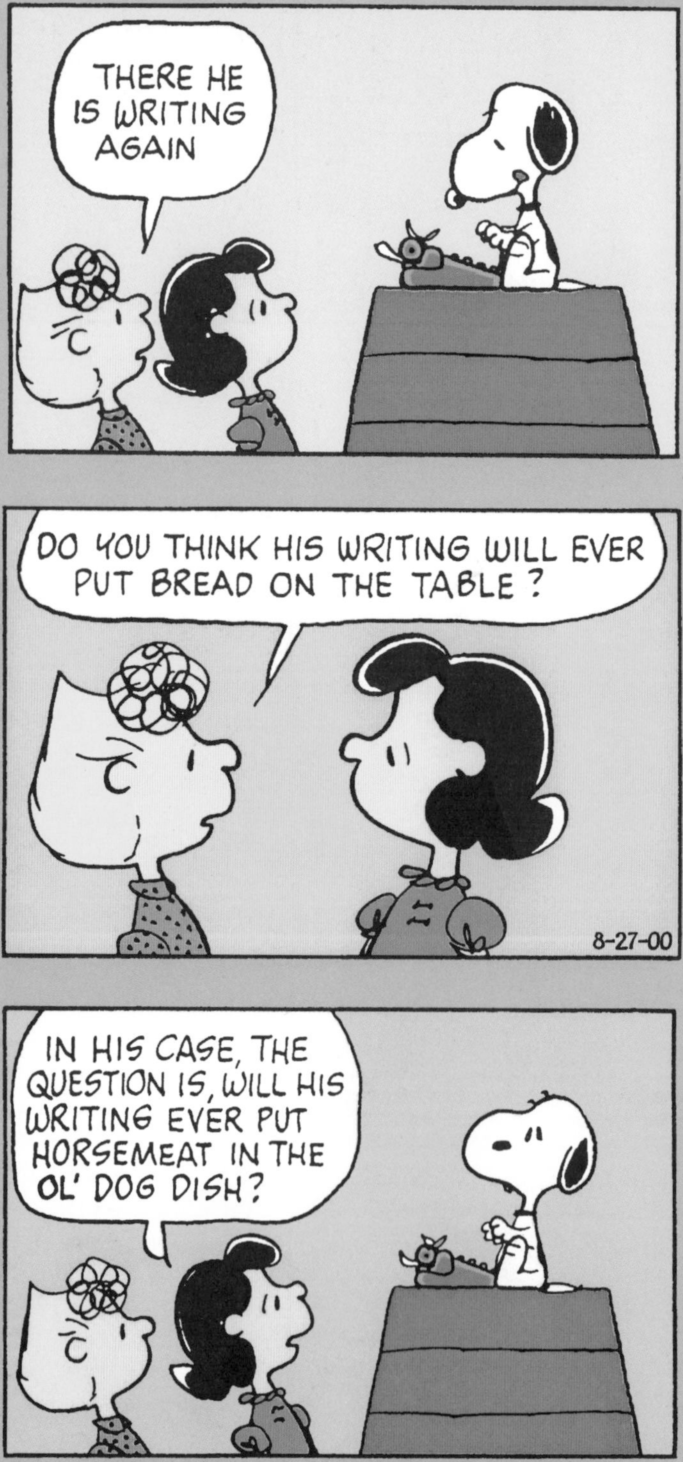
THERE HE IS WRITING AGAIN
DO YOU THINK HIS WRITING WILL EVER PUT BREAD ON THE TABLE?
8-27-00
IN HIS CASE, THE QUESTION IS, WILL HIS WRITING EVER PUT HORSEMEAT IN THE OL' DOG DISH?

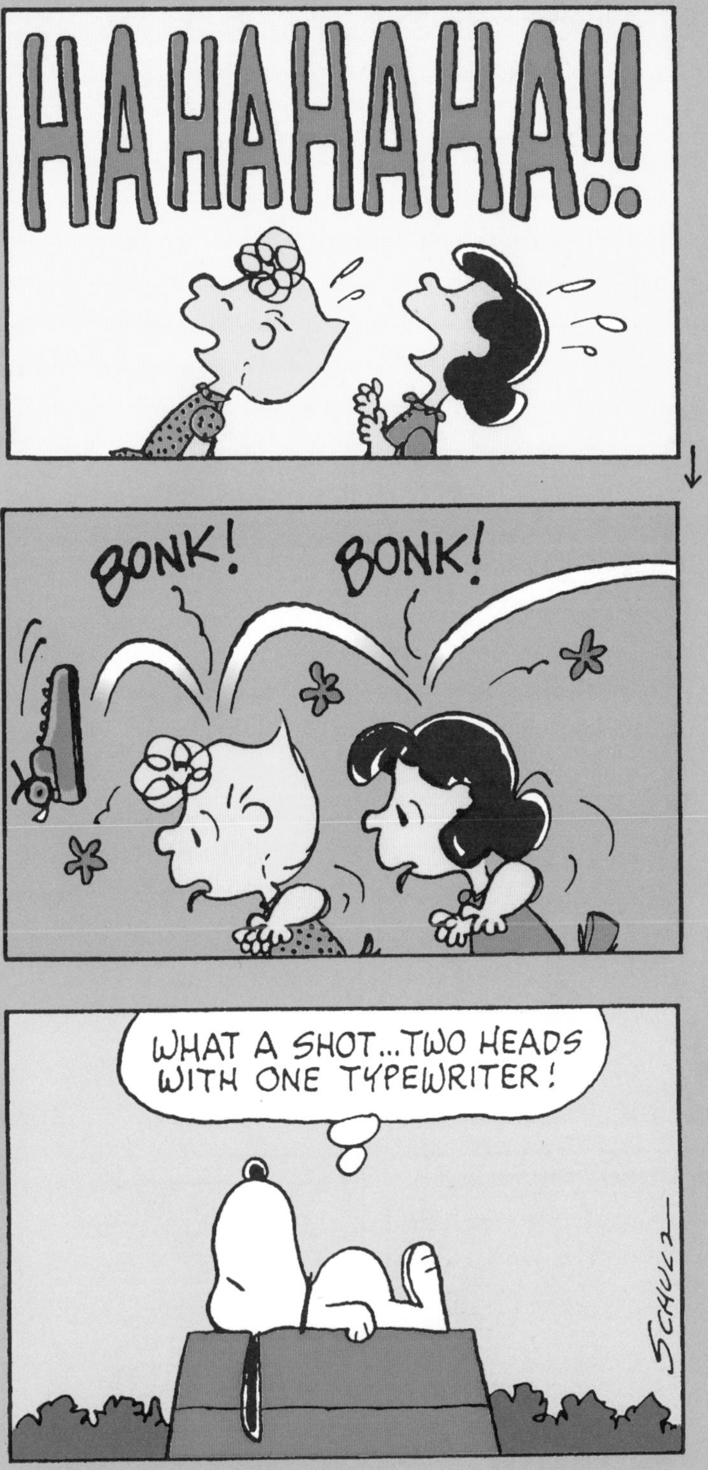
HAHAHAHA!!
BONK!
BONK!
WHAT A SHOT...TWO HEADS WITH ONE TYPEWRITER!
SCHULZ

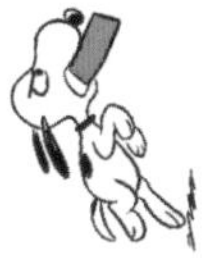

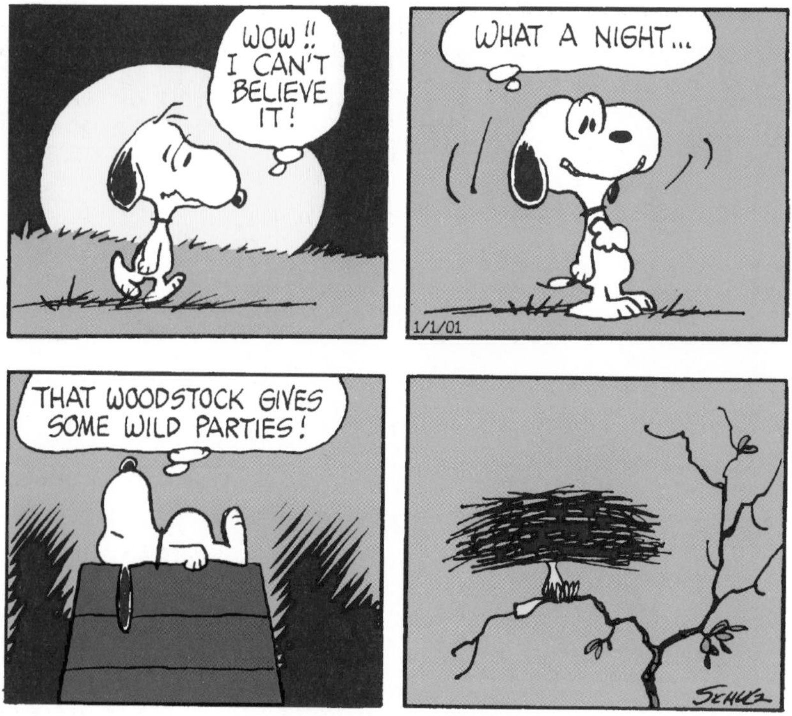
WOW !! I CAN'T BELIEVE IT !
WHAT A NIGHT...
1/1/01
THAT WOODSTOCK GIVES SOME WILD PARTIES !

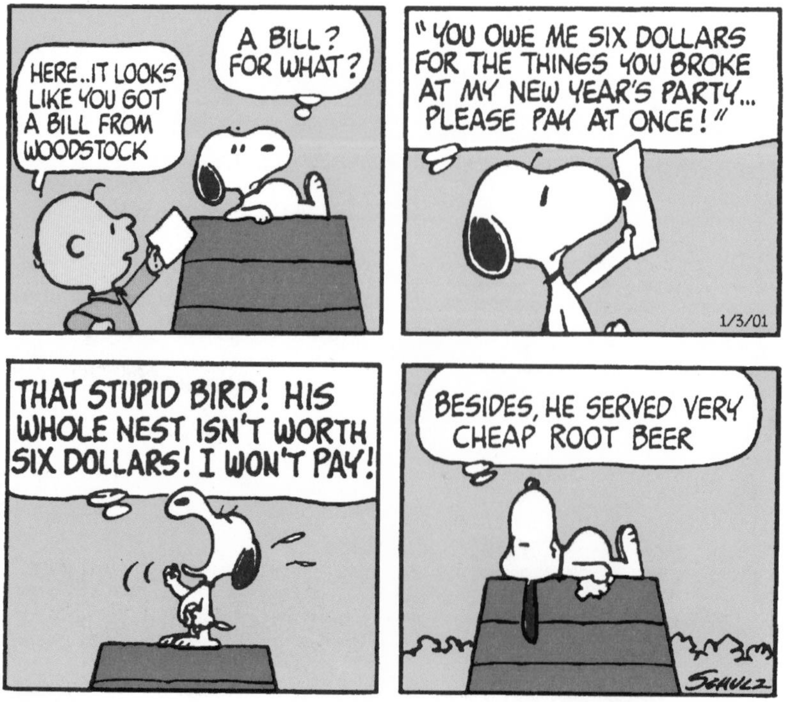
HERE..IT LOOKS LIKE YOU GOT A BILL FROM WOODSTOCK
A BILL ? FOR WHAT ?
"YOU OWE ME SIX DOLLARS FOR THE THINGS YOU BROKE AT MY NEW YEAR'S PARTY... PLEASE PAY AT ONCE !"
1/3/01
THAT STUPID BIRD! HIS WHOLE NEST ISN'T WORTH SIX DOLLARS! I WON'T PAY!
BESIDES, HE SERVED VERY CHEAP ROOT BEER

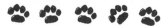

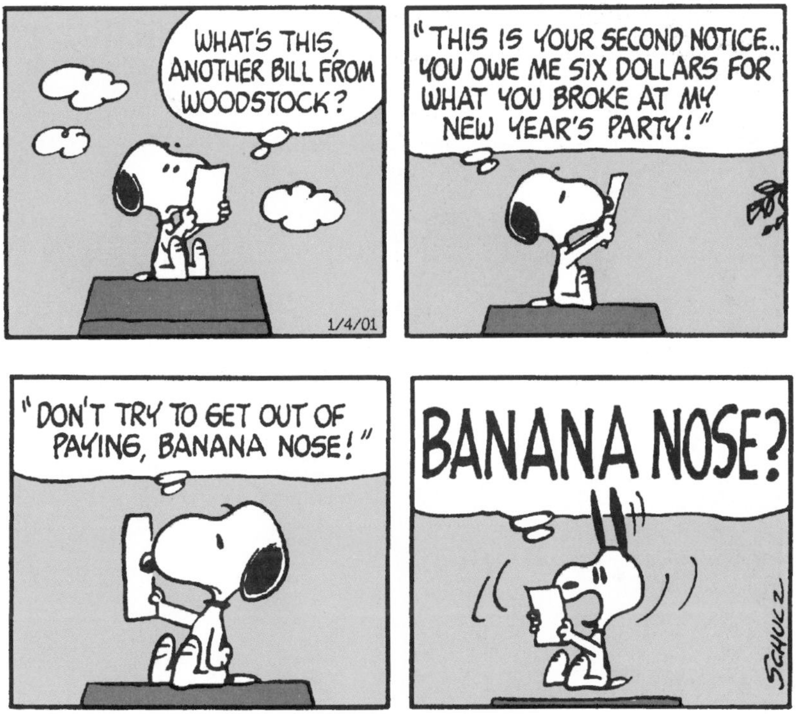
WHAT'S THIS, ANOTHER BILL FROM WOODSTOCK?
1/4/01
"THIS IS YOUR SECOND NOTICE.. YOU OWE ME SIX DOLLARS FOR WHAT YOU BROKE AT MY NEW YEAR'S PARTY!"
"DON'T TRY TO GET OUT OF PAYING, BANANA NOSE!"
BANANA NOSE?

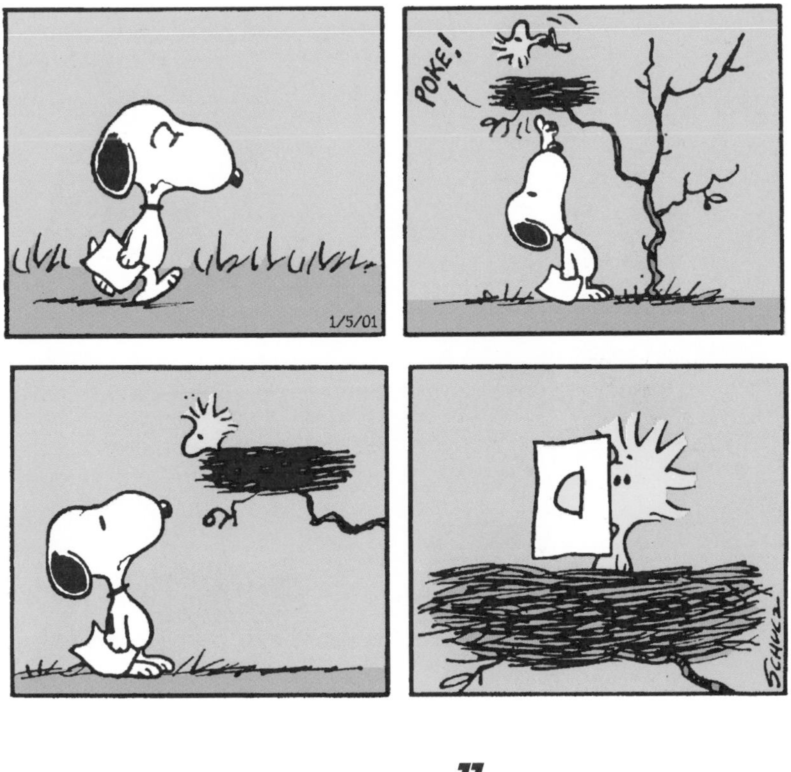
1/5/01
POKE!

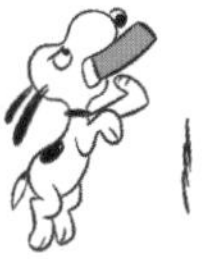

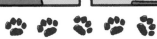

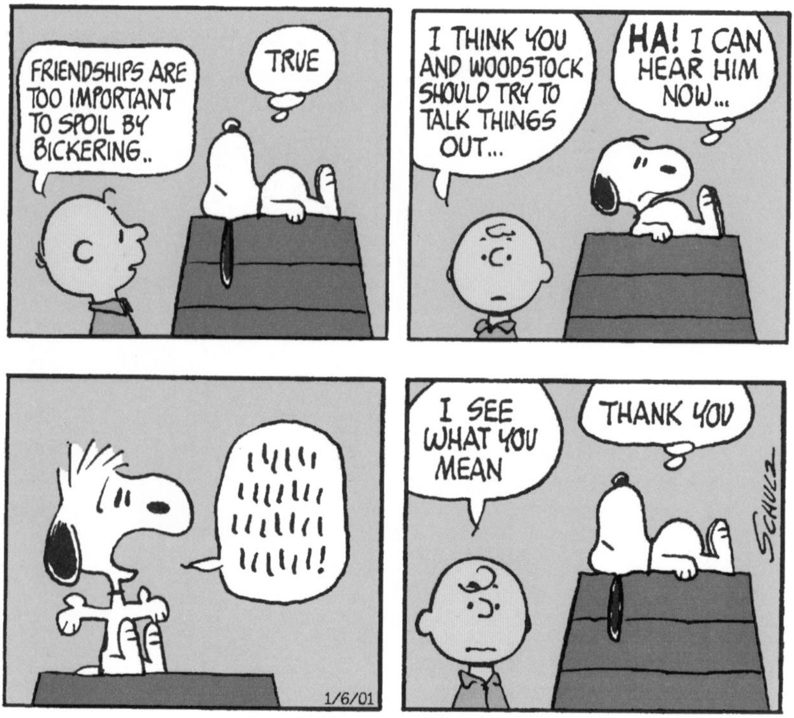
FRIENDSHIPS ARE TOO IMPORTANT TO SPOIL BY BICKERING..
TRUE
I THINK YOU AND WOODSTOCK SHOULD TRY TO TALK THINGS OUT...
HA! I CAN HEAR HIM NOW...
1/6/01
I SEE WHAT YOU MEAN
THANK YOU
SCHULZ

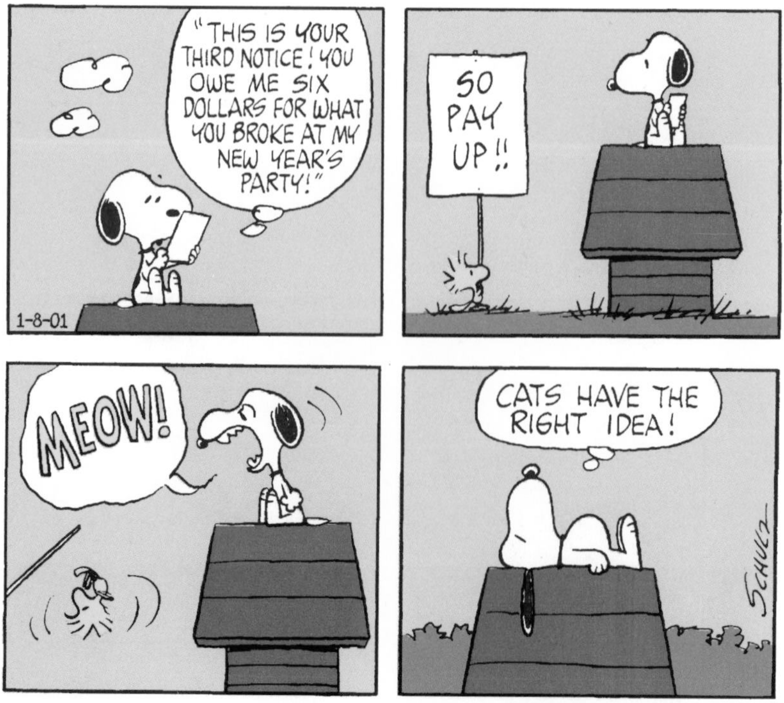
"THIS IS YOUR THIRD NOTICE! YOU OWE ME SIX DOLLARS FOR WHAT YOU BROKE AT MY NEW YEAR'S PARTY!"
1-8-01
SO PAY UP!!
MEOW!
CATS HAVE THE RIGHT IDEA!
SCHULZ

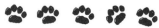

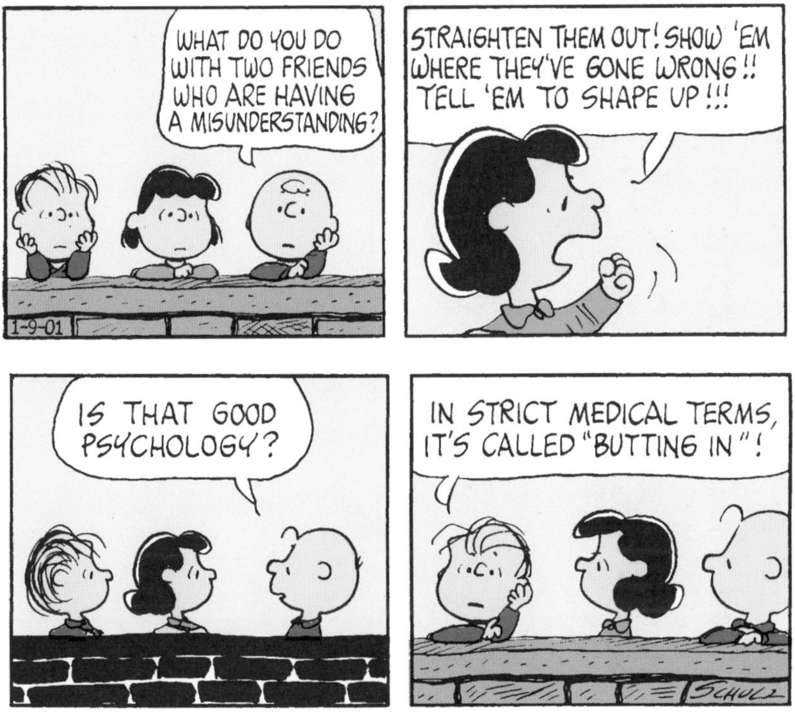
WHAT DO YOU DO WITH TWO FRIENDS WHO ARE HAVING A MISUNDERSTANDING?
STRAIGHTEN THEM OUT! SHOW 'EM WHERE THEY'VE GONE WRONG!! TELL 'EM TO SHAPE UP!!!
IS THAT GOOD PSYCHOLOGY?
IN STRICT MEDICAL TERMS, IT'S CALLED "BUTTING IN"!
1-9-01
SCHULZ

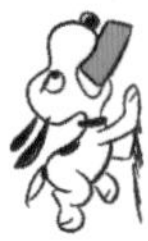

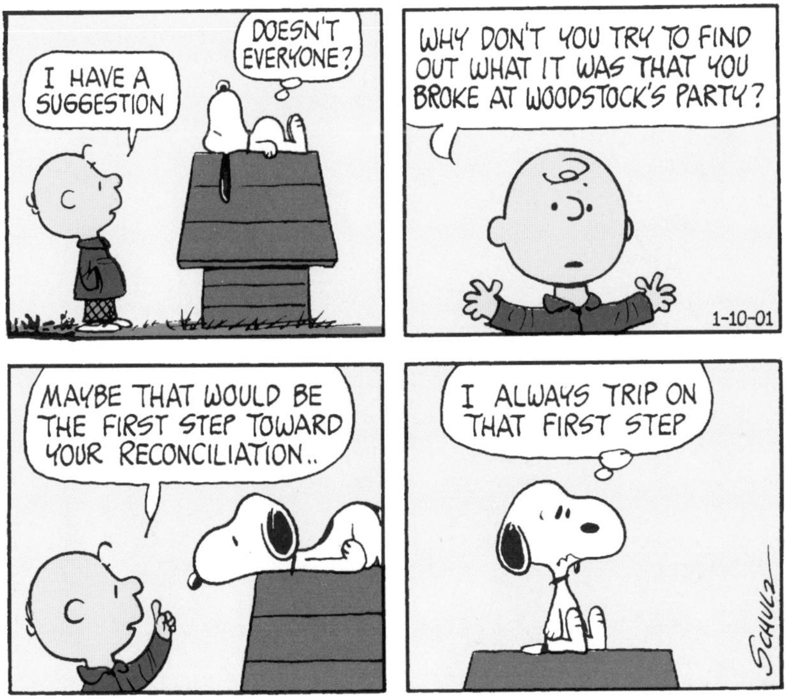
I HAVE A SUGGESTION
DOESN'T EVERYONE?
WHY DON'T YOU TRY TO FIND OUT WHAT IT WAS THAT YOU BROKE AT WOODSTOCK'S PARTY?
1-10-01
MAYBE THAT WOULD BE THE FIRST STEP TOWARD YOUR RECONCILIATION..
I ALWAYS TRIP ON THAT FIRST STEP
SCHULZ

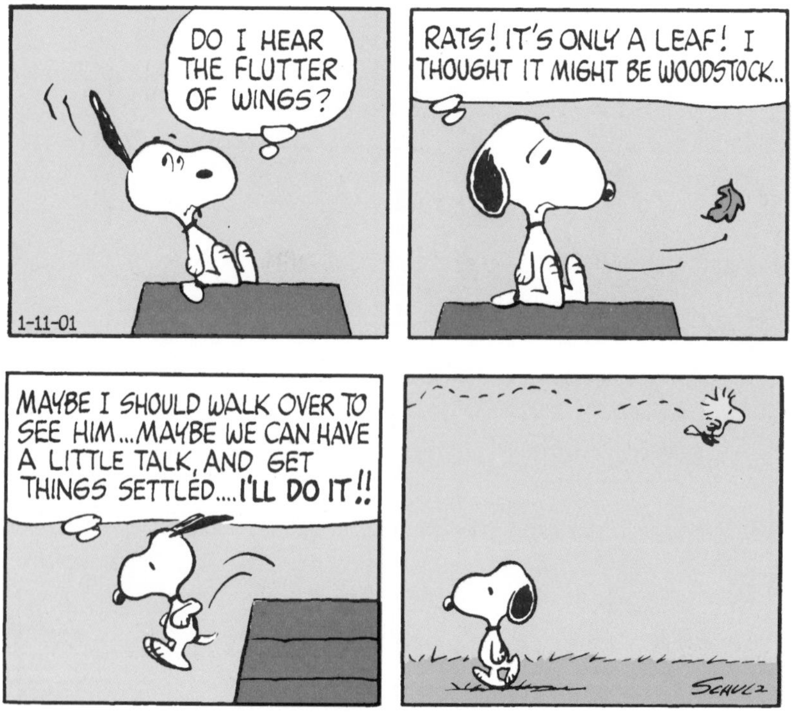
DO I HEAR THE FLUTTER OF WINGS?
1-11-01
RATS! IT'S ONLY A LEAF! I THOUGHT IT MIGHT BE WOODSTOCK..
MAYBE I SHOULD WALK OVER TO SEE HIM...MAYBE WE CAN HAVE A LITTLE TALK, AND GET THINGS SETTLED....I'LL DO IT!!
SCHULZ

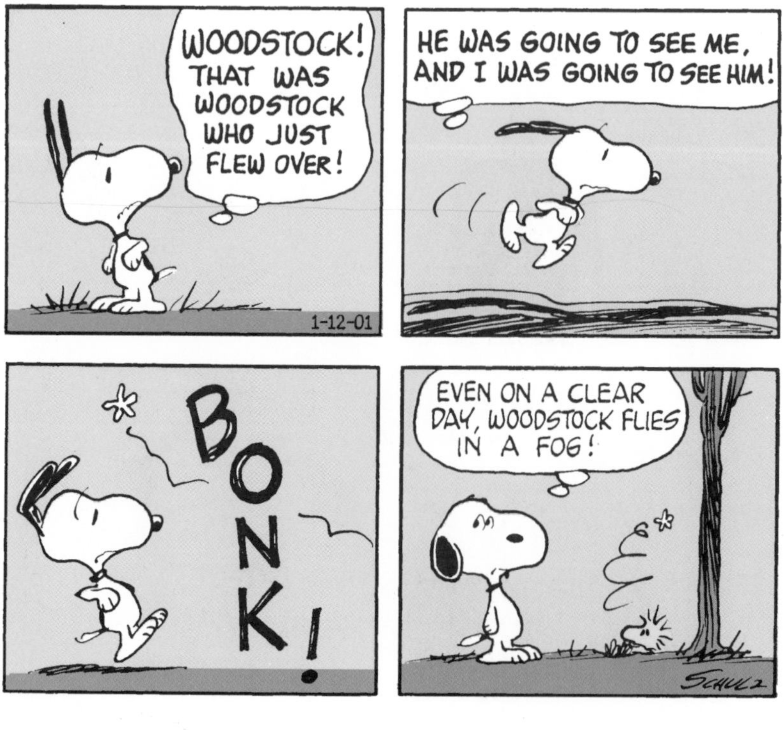
WOODSTOCK! THAT WAS WOODSTOCK WHO JUST FLEW OVER!
1-12-01
HE WAS GOING TO SEE ME, AND I WAS GOING TO SEE HIM!
BONK!
EVEN ON A CLEAR DAY, WOODSTOCK FLIES IN A FOG!
SCHULZ

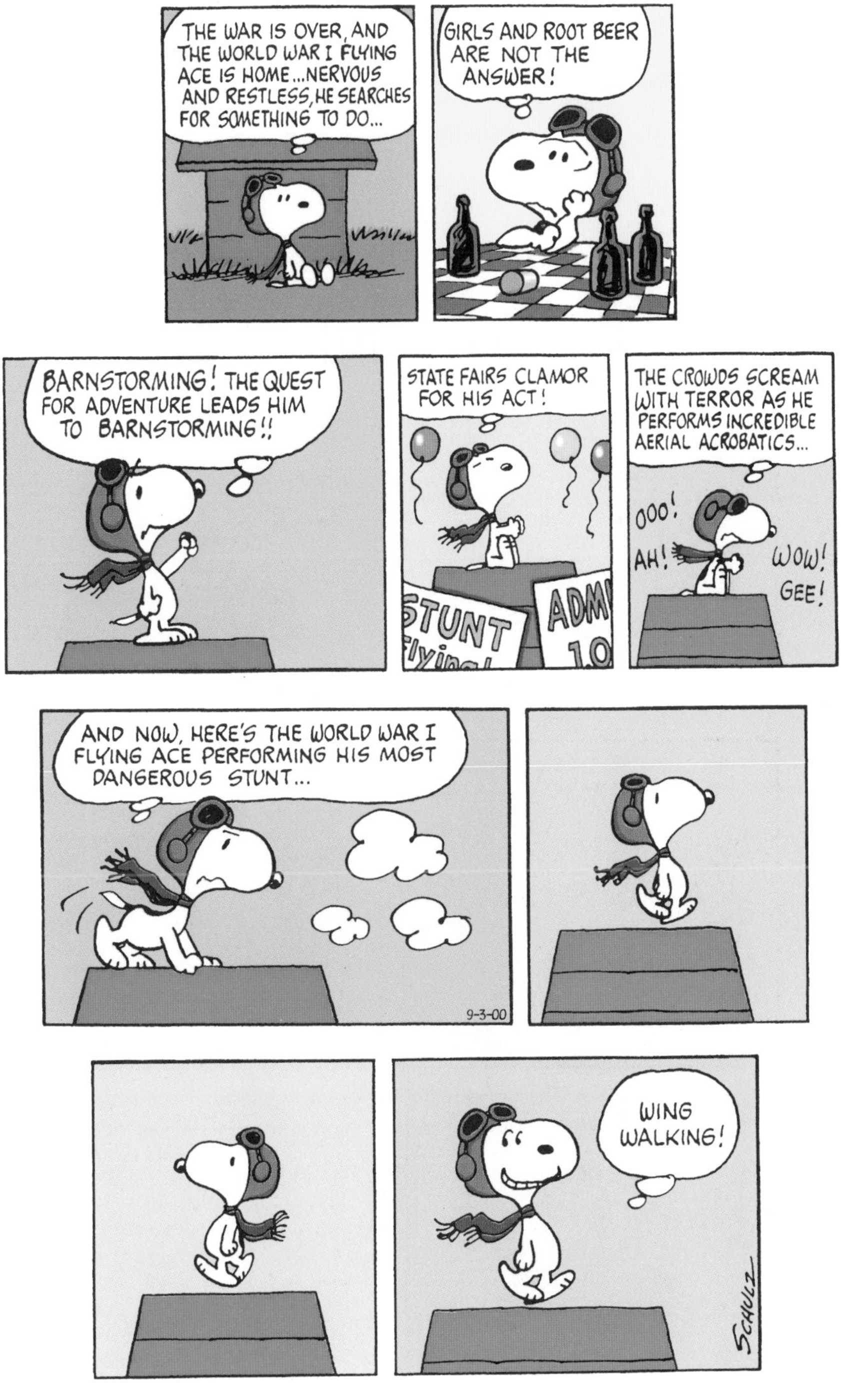
THE WAR IS OVER, AND THE WORLD WAR I FLYING ACE IS HOME...NERVOUS AND RESTLESS, HE SEARCHES FOR SOMETHING TO DO...
GIRLS AND ROOT BEER ARE NOT THE ANSWER!
BARNSTORMING! THE QUEST FOR ADVENTURE LEADS HIM TO BARNSTORMING!!
STATE FAIRS CLAMOR FOR HIS ACT!
STUNT
THE CROWDS SCREAM WITH TERROR AS HE PERFORMS INCREDIBLE AERIAL ACROBATICS...
OOO!
AH!
WOW!
GEE!
AND NOW, HERE'S THE WORLD WAR I FLYING ACE PERFORMING HIS MOST DANGEROUS STUNT...
9-3-00
WING WALKING!
SCHULZ

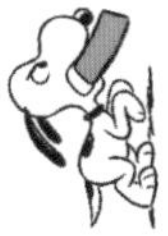

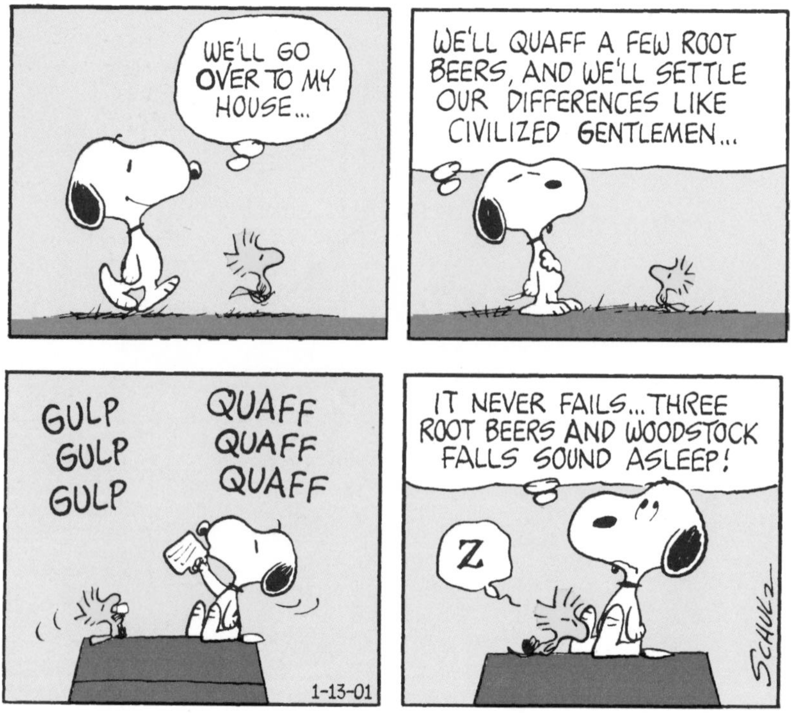
WE'LL GO OVER TO MY HOUSE...
WE'LL QUAFF A FEW ROOT BEERS, AND WE'LL SETTLE OUR DIFFERENCES LIKE CIVILIZED GENTLEMEN...
GULP GULP GULP
QUAFF QUAFF QUAFF
1-13-01
IT NEVER FAILS...THREE ROOT BEERS AND WOODSTOCK FALLS SOUND ASLEEP!
Z
SCHULZ

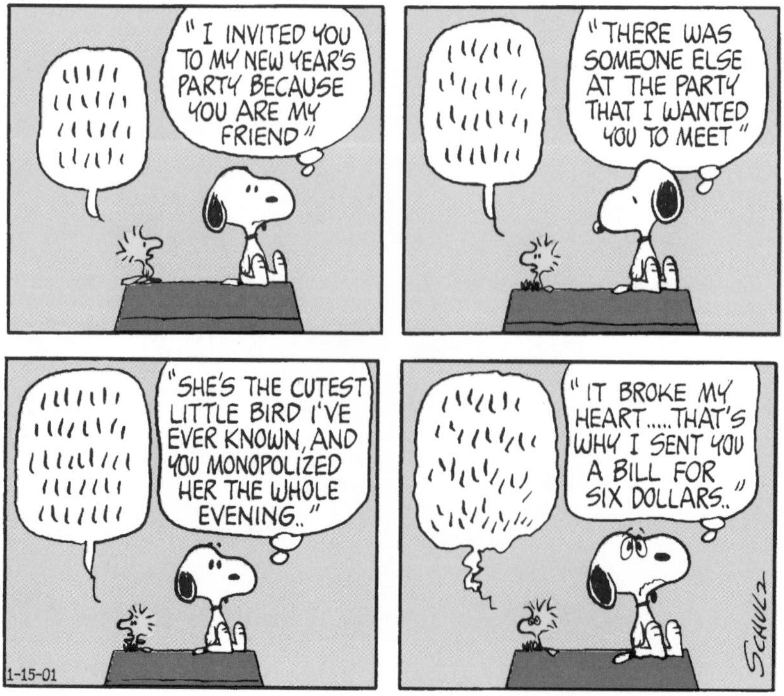
"I INVITED YOU TO MY NEW YEAR'S PARTY BECAUSE YOU ARE MY FRIEND"
"THERE WAS SOMEONE ELSE AT THE PARTY THAT I WANTED YOU TO MEET"
"SHE'S THE CUTEST LITTLE BIRD I'VE EVER KNOWN, AND YOU MONOPOLIZED HER THE WHOLE EVENING.."
1-15-01
"IT BROKE MY HEART.....THAT'S WHY I SENT YOU A BILL FOR SIX DOLLARS.."
SCHULZ

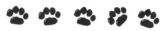

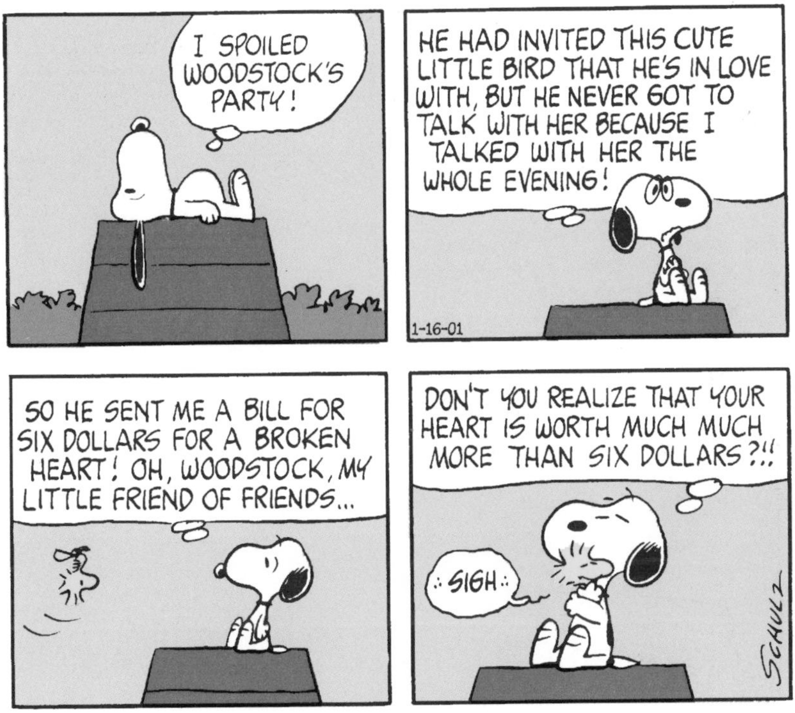
I SPOILED WOODSTOCK'S PARTY!
HE HAD INVITED THIS CUTE LITTLE BIRD THAT HE'S IN LOVE WITH, BUT HE NEVER GOT TO TALK WITH HER BECAUSE I TALKED WITH HER THE WHOLE EVENING!
1-16-01
SO HE SENT ME A BILL FOR SIX DOLLARS FOR A BROKEN HEART! OH, WOODSTOCK, MY LITTLE FRIEND OF FRIENDS...
DON'T YOU REALIZE THAT YOUR HEART IS WORTH MUCH MUCH MORE THAN SIX DOLLARS?!!
SIGH
SCHULZ

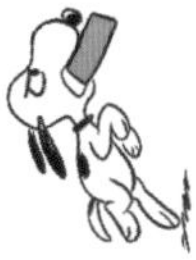

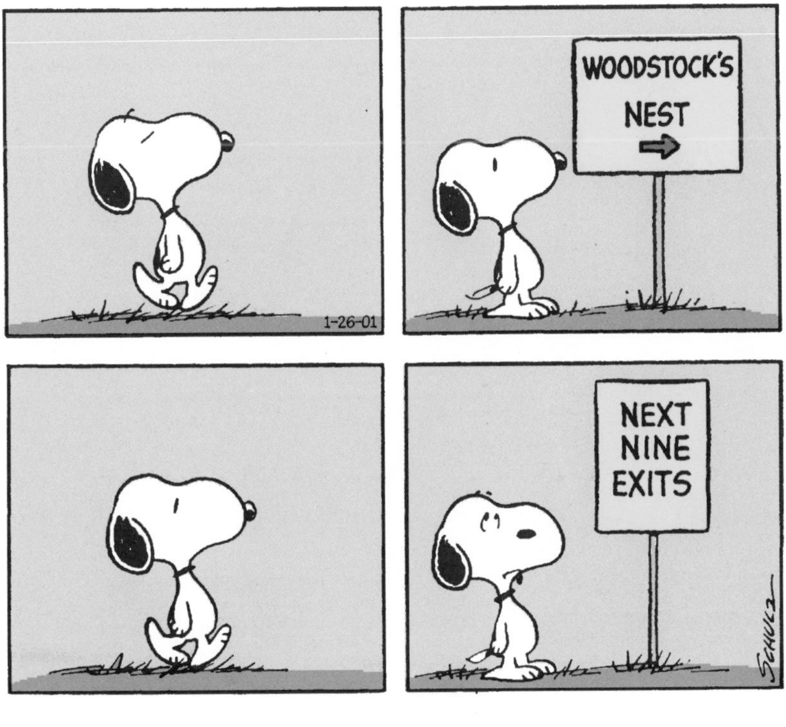
1-26-01
WOODSTOCK'S NEST
NEXT NINE EXITS
SCHULZ

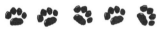

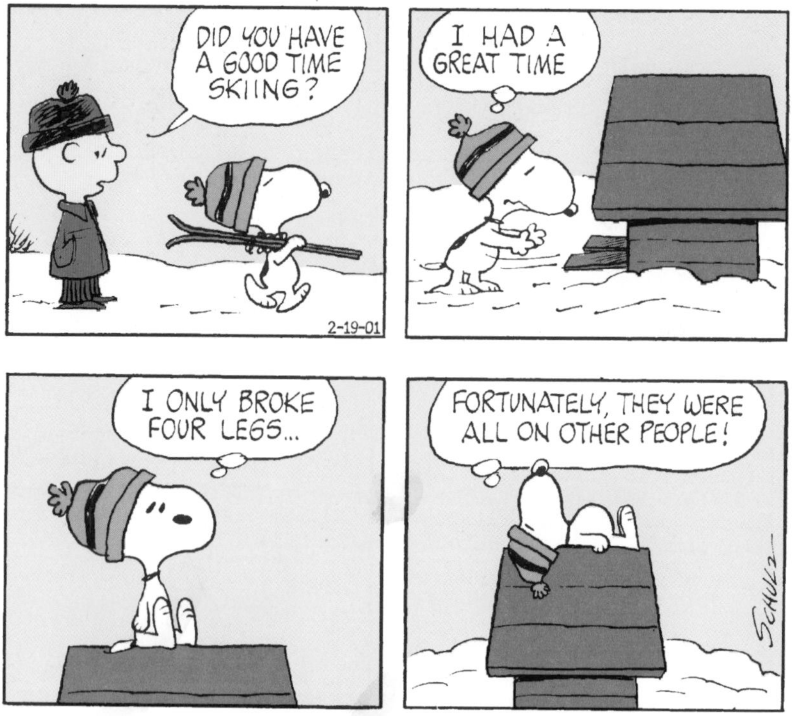
DID YOU HAVE A GOOD TIME SKIING?
2-19-01
I HAD A GREAT TIME
I ONLY BROKE FOUR LEGS...
FORTUNATELY, THEY WERE ALL ON OTHER PEOPLE!
SCHULZ

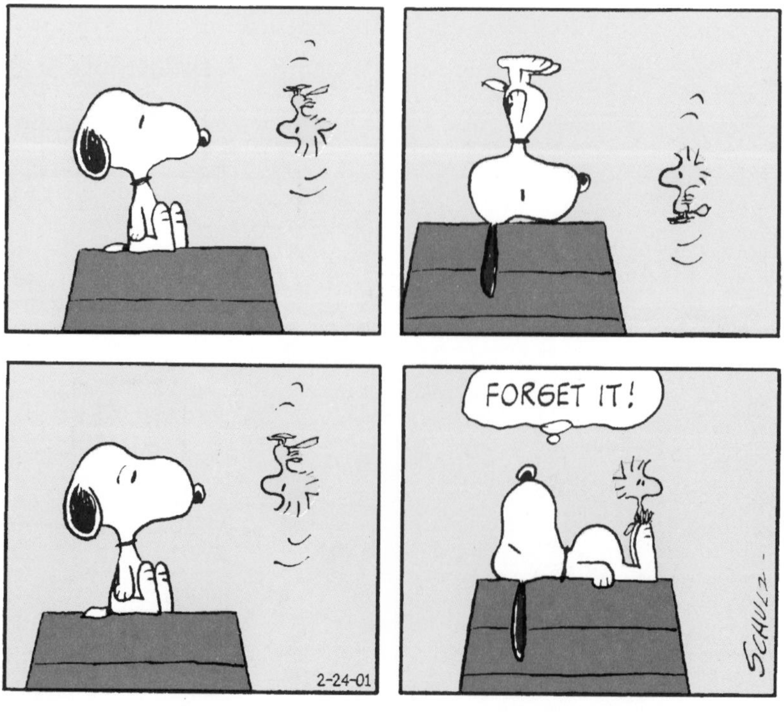
2-24-01
FORGET IT!
SCHULZ

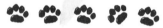

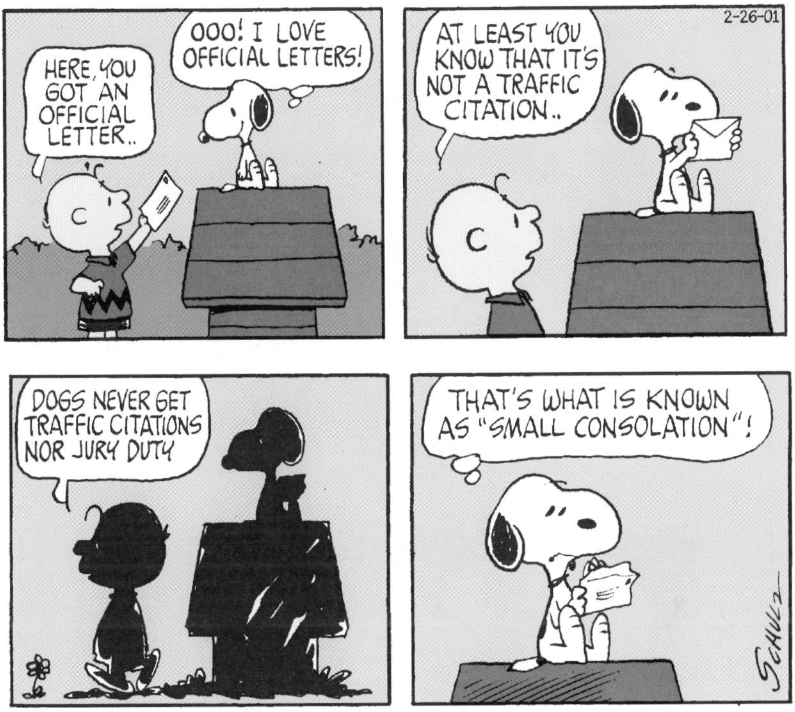
2-26-01
HERE, YOU GOT AN OFFICIAL LETTER..
OOO! I LOVE OFFICIAL LETTERS!
AT LEAST YOU KNOW THAT IT'S NOT A TRAFFIC CITATION..
DOGS NEVER GET TRAFFIC CITATIONS NOR JURY DUTY
THAT'S WHAT IS KNOWN AS "SMALL CONSOLATION"!
SCHULZ

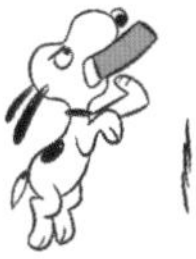

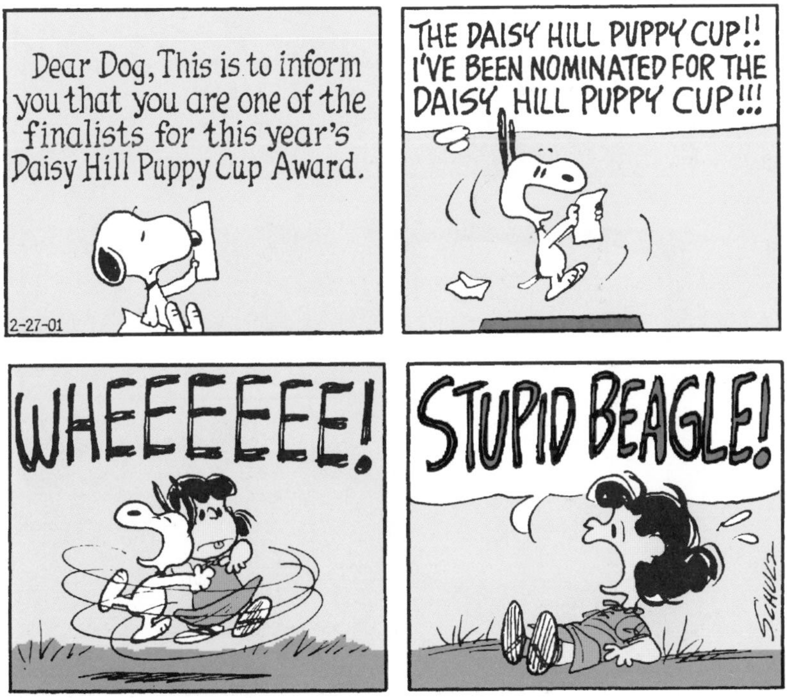
Dear Dog, This is to inform you that you are one of the finalists for this year's Daisy Hill Puppy Cup Award.
2-27-01
THE DAISY HILL PUPPY CUP!! I'VE BEEN NOMINATED FOR THE DAISY HILL PUPPY CUP!!!
WHEEEEEE!
STUPID BEAGLE!
SCHULZ

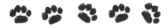

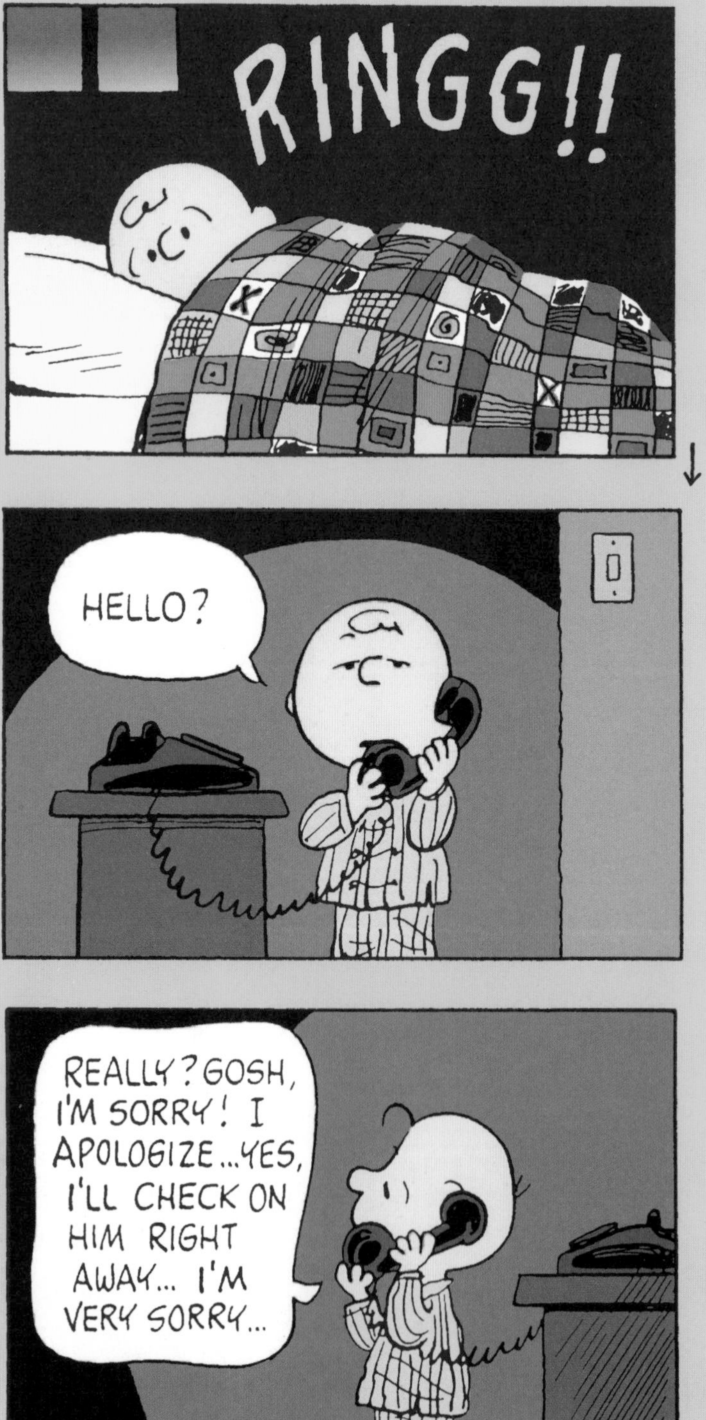
RINGG!!
HELLO?
REALLY? GOSH, I'M SORRY! I APOLOGIZE...YES, I'LL CHECK ON HIM RIGHT AWAY... I'M VERY SORRY...

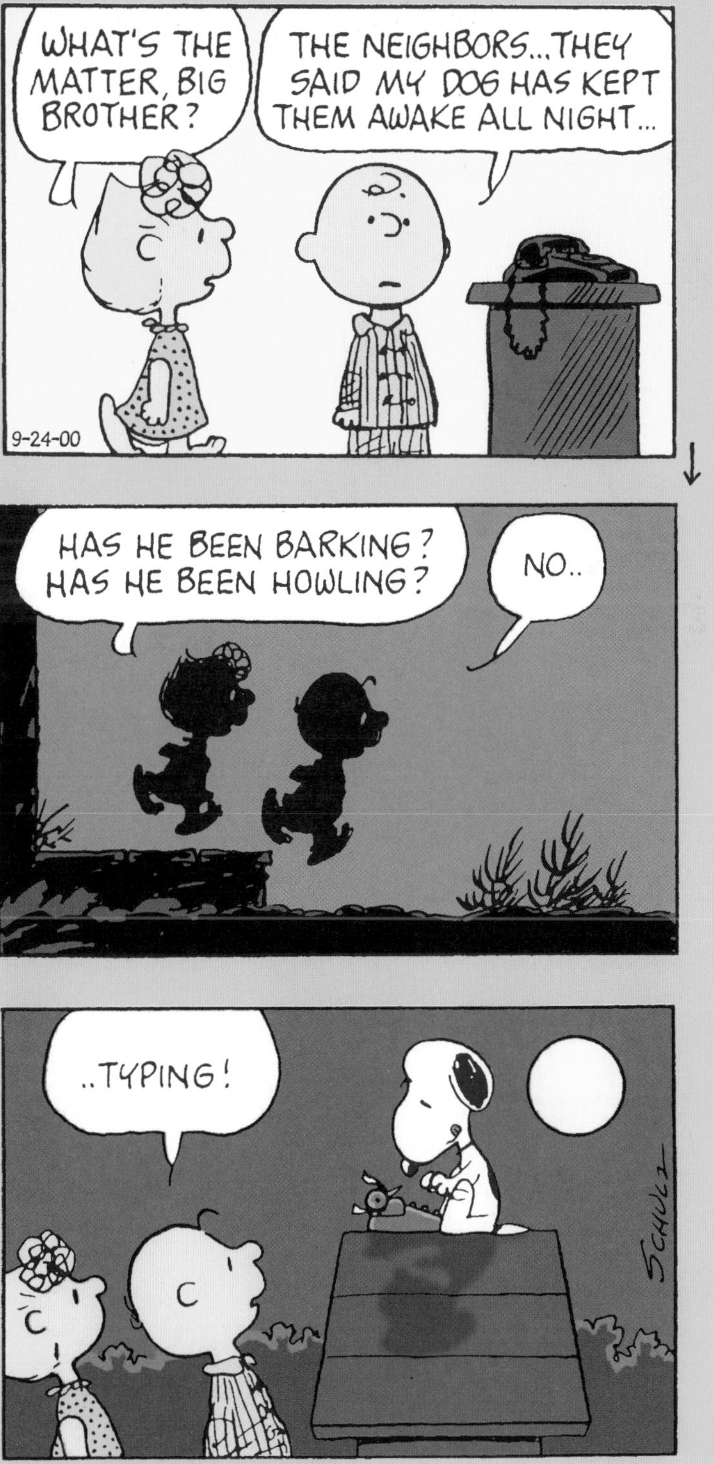
WHAT'S THE MATTER, BIG BROTHER?
THE NEIGHBORS...THEY SAID MY DOG HAS KEPT THEM AWAKE ALL NIGHT...
9-24-00
HAS HE BEEN BARKING? HAS HE BEEN HOWLING?
NO..
..TYPING!
SCHULZ

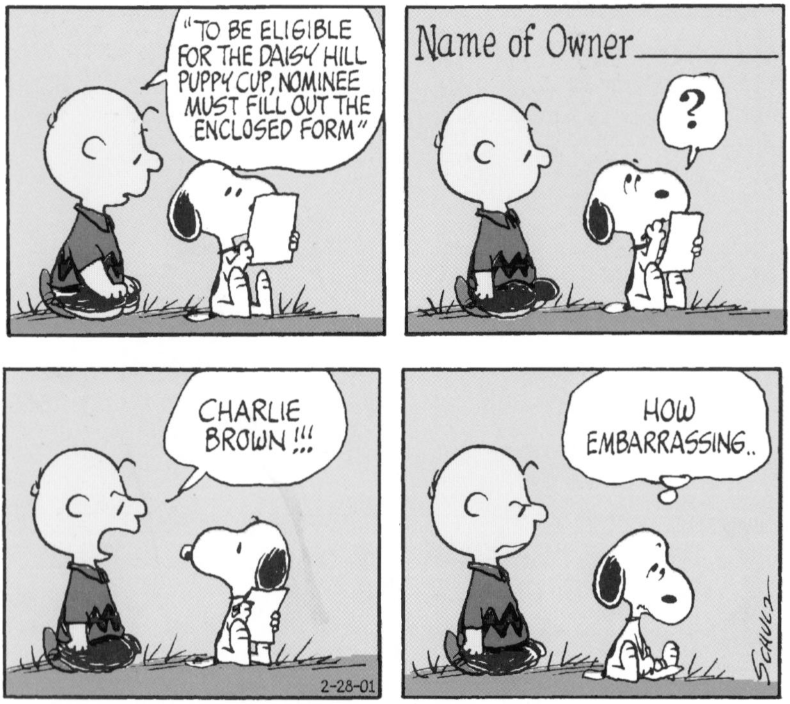
"TO BE ELIGIBLE FOR THE DAISY HILL PUPPY CUP, NOMINEE MUST FILL OUT THE ENCLOSED FORM"
Name of Owner
?
CHARLIE BROWN !!!
HOW EMBARRASSING..
2-28-01
SCHULZ

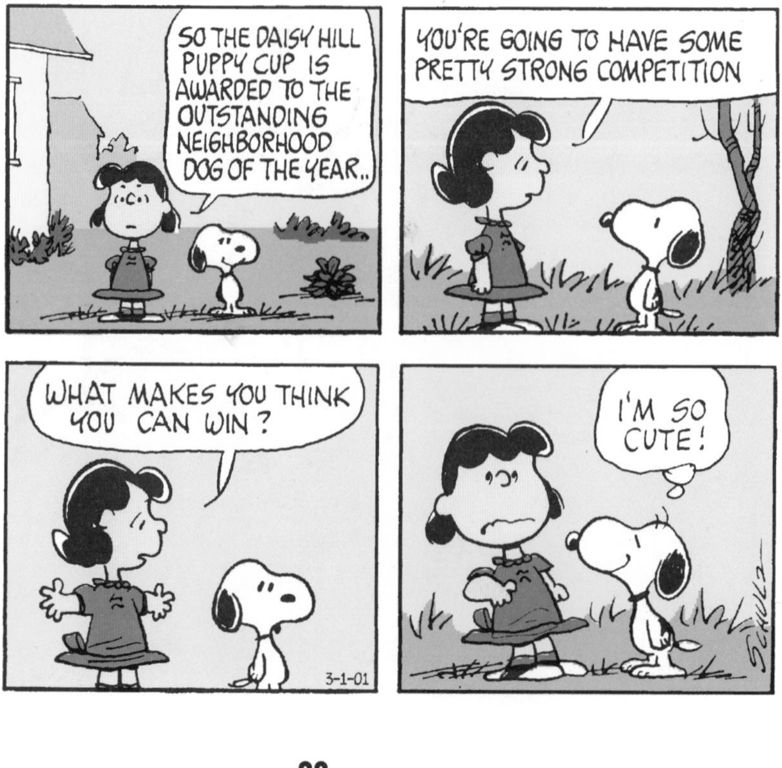
SO THE DAISY HILL PUPPY CUP IS AWARDED TO THE OUTSTANDING NEIGHBORHOOD DOG OF THE YEAR..
YOU'RE GOING TO HAVE SOME PRETTY STRONG COMPETITION
WHAT MAKES YOU THINK YOU CAN WIN?
I'M SO CUTE!
3-1-01
SCHULZ

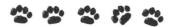

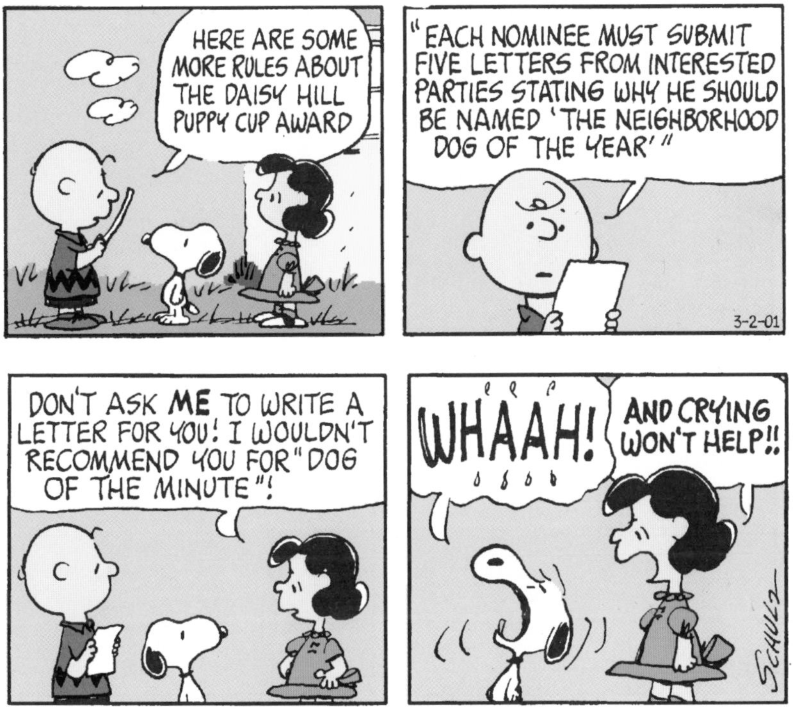
HERE ARE SOME MORE RULES ABOUT THE DAISY HILL PUPPY CUP AWARD
"EACH NOMINEE MUST SUBMIT FIVE LETTERS FROM INTERESTED PARTIES STATING WHY HE SHOULD BE NAMED 'THE NEIGHBORHOOD DOG OF THE YEAR'"
3-2-01
DON'T ASK ME TO WRITE A LETTER FOR YOU! I WOULDN'T RECOMMEND YOU FOR "DOG OF THE MINUTE"!
WHAAH!
AND CRYING WON'T HELP!!
SCHULZ

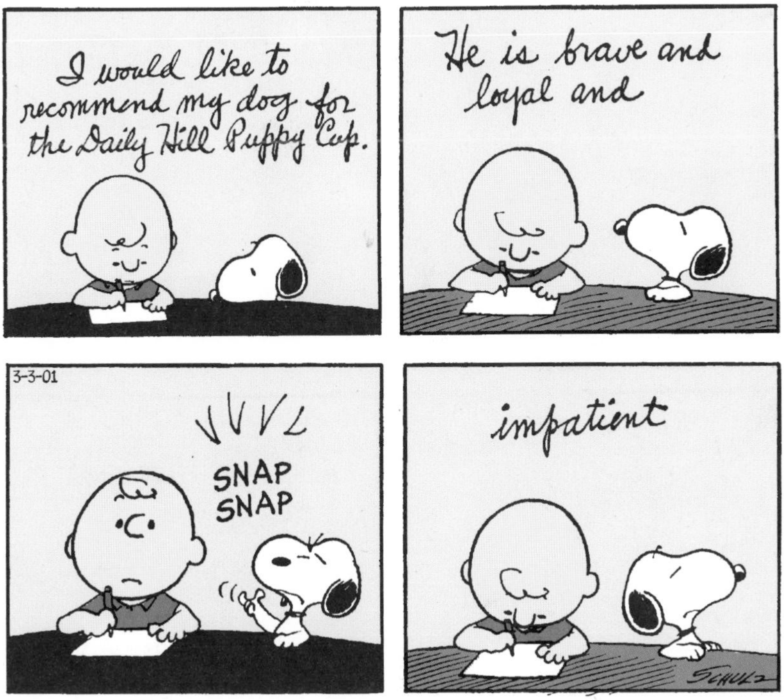
I would like to recommend my dog for the Daisy Hill Puppy Cup.
He is brave and loyal and
3-3-01
SNAP SNAP
impatient
SCHULZ

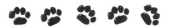

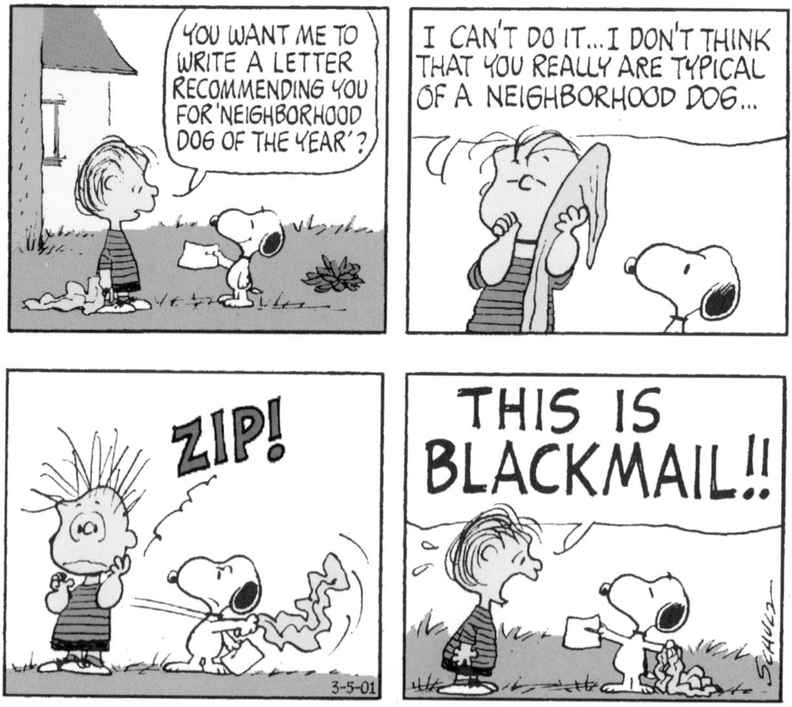
YOU WANT ME TO WRITE A LETTER RECOMMENDING YOU FOR 'NEIGHBORHOOD DOG OF THE YEAR'?
I CAN'T DO IT...I DON'T THINK THAT YOU REALLY ARE TYPICAL OF A NEIGHBORHOOD DOG...
ZIP!
3-5-01
THIS IS BLACKMAIL!!
SCHULZ

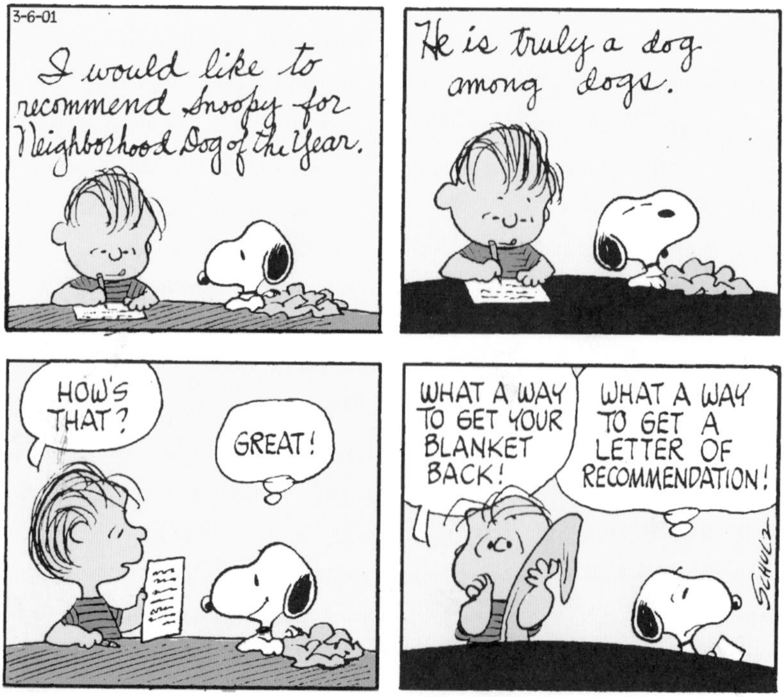
3-6-01
I would like to recommend Snoopy for Neighborhood Dog of the Year.
He is truly a dog among dogs.
HOW'S THAT?
GREAT!
WHAT A WAY TO GET YOUR BLANKET BACK!
WHAT A WAY TO GET A LETTER OF RECOMMENDATION!
SCHULZ

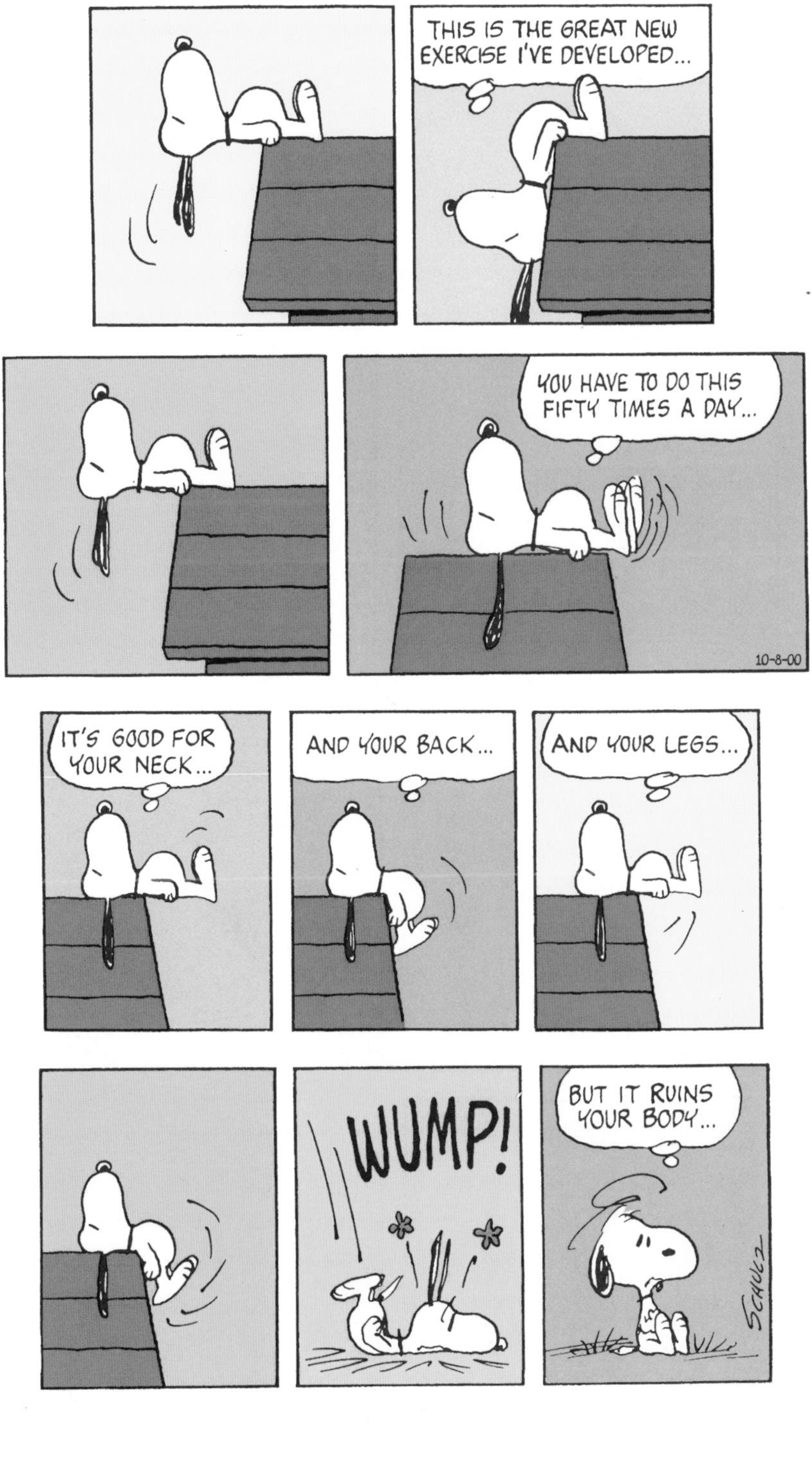
THIS IS THE GREAT NEW EXERCISE I'VE DEVELOPED...
YOU HAVE TO DO THIS FIFTY TIMES A DAY...
10-8-00
IT'S GOOD FOR YOUR NECK...
AND YOUR BACK...
AND YOUR LEGS...
WUMP!
BUT IT RUINS YOUR BODY...
SCHULZ

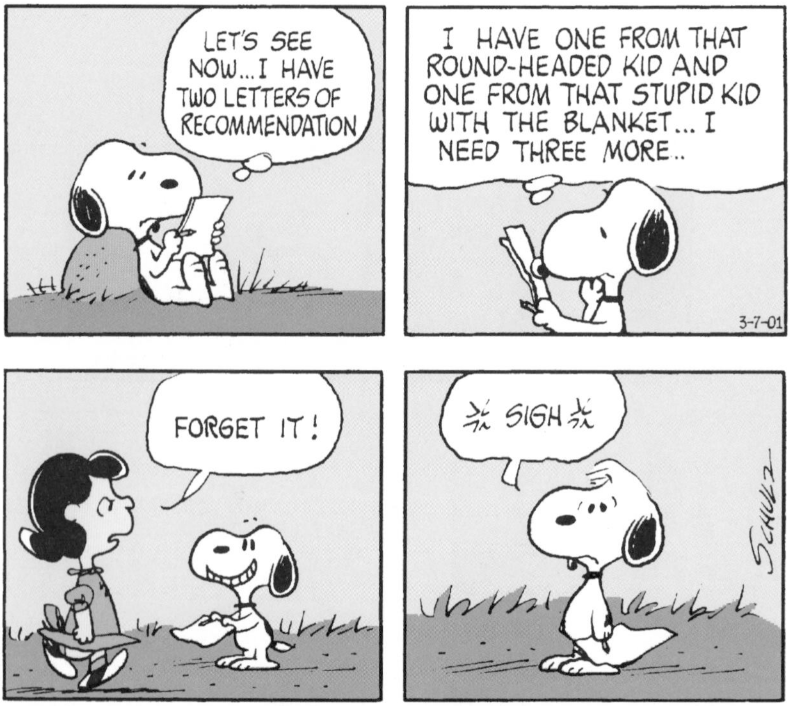
LET'S SEE NOW... I HAVE TWO LETTERS OF RECOMMENDATION
I HAVE ONE FROM THAT ROUND-HEADED KID AND ONE FROM THAT STUPID KID WITH THE BLANKET... I NEED THREE MORE..
3-7-01
FORGET IT!
SIGH
SCHULZ

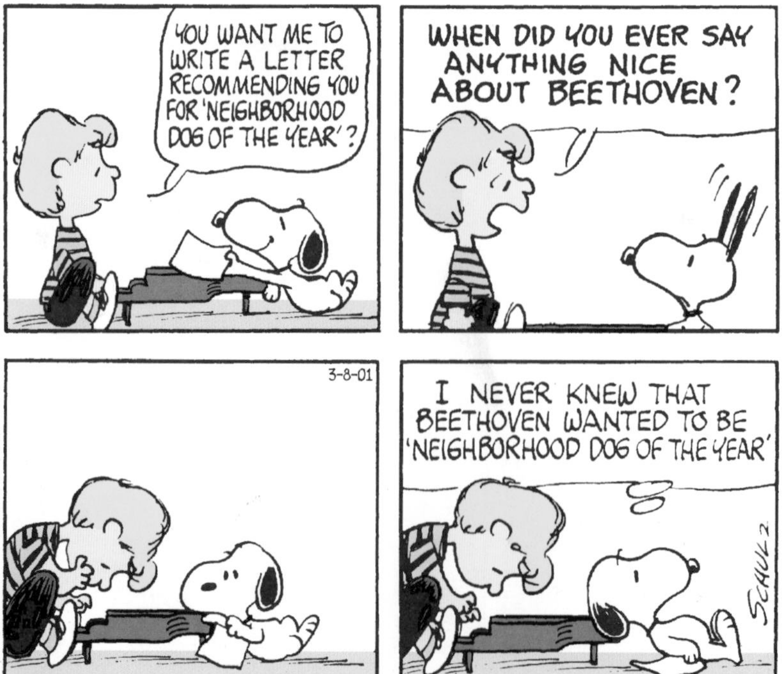
YOU WANT ME TO WRITE A LETTER RECOMMENDING YOU FOR 'NEIGHBORHOOD DOG OF THE YEAR'?
WHEN DID YOU EVER SAY ANYTHING NICE ABOUT BEETHOVEN?
3-8-01
I NEVER KNEW THAT BEETHOVEN WANTED TO BE 'NEIGHBORHOOD DOG OF THE YEAR'
SCHULZ

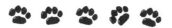

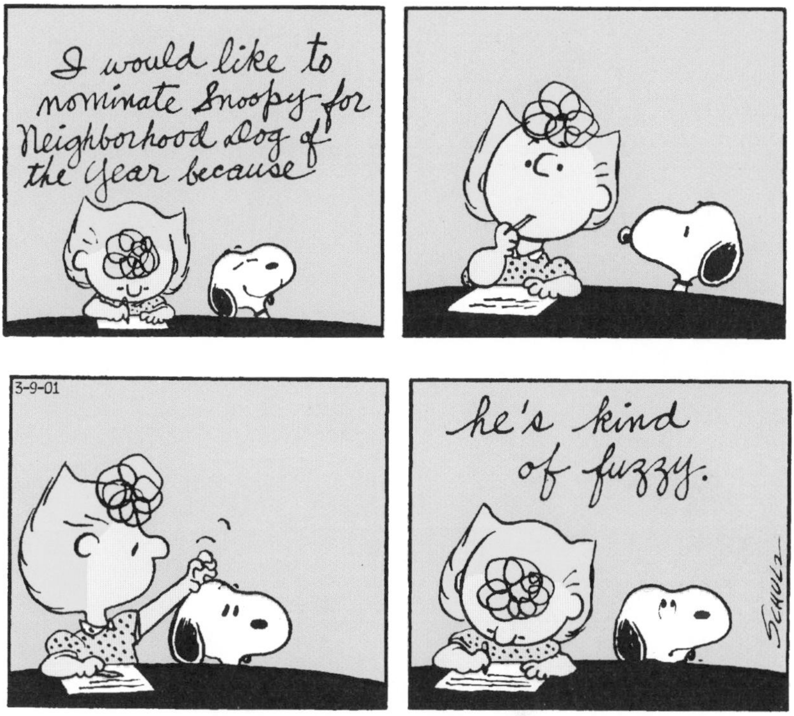

I would like to nominate Snoopy for Neighborhood Dog of the Year because
3-9-01
he's kind of fuzzy.
SCHULZ

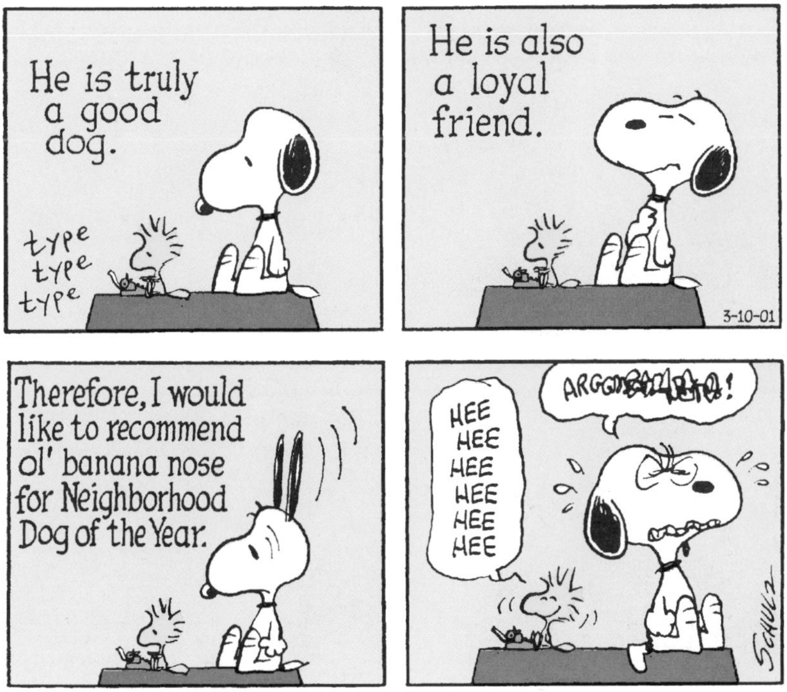

He is truly a good dog.
type type type
He is also a loyal friend.
3-10-01
Therefore, I would like to recommend ol' banana nose for Neighborhood Dog of the Year.
HEE HEE HEE HEE HEE HEE
SCHULZ

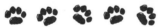

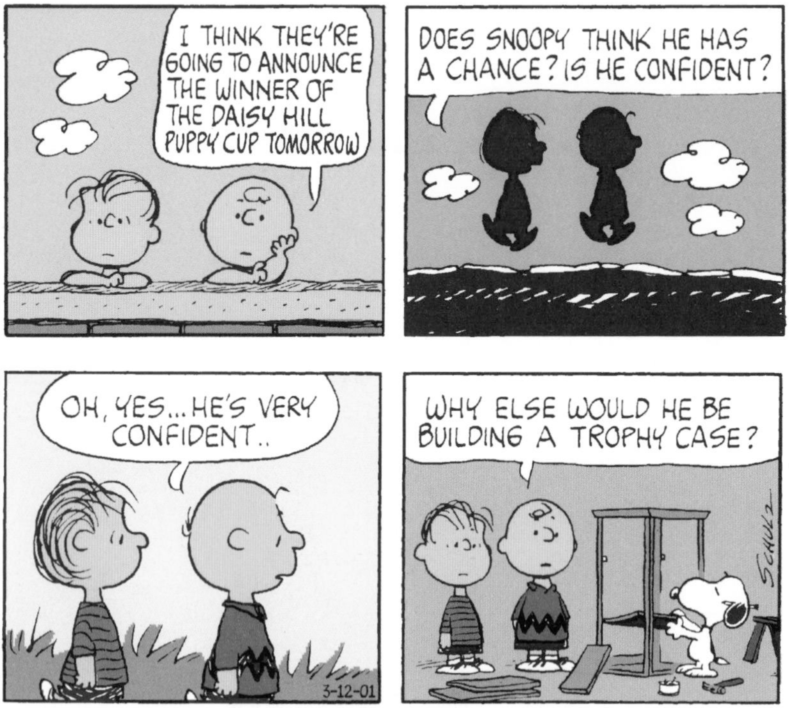
I THINK THEY'RE GOING TO ANNOUNCE THE WINNER OF THE DAISY HILL PUPPY CUP TOMORROW
DOES SNOOPY THINK HE HAS A CHANCE? IS HE CONFIDENT?
OH, YES... HE'S VERY CONFIDENT..
WHY ELSE WOULD HE BE BUILDING A TROPHY CASE?
SCHULZ
3-12-01

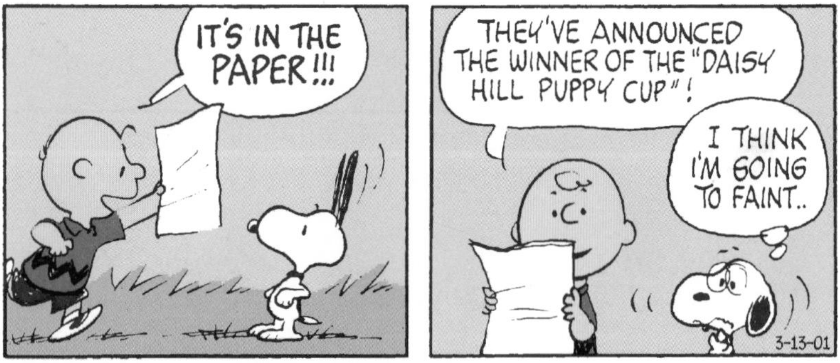
IT'S IN THE PAPER!!!
THEY'VE ANNOUNCED THE WINNER OF THE "DAISY HILL PUPPY CUP"!
I THINK I'M GOING TO FAINT..
3-13-01

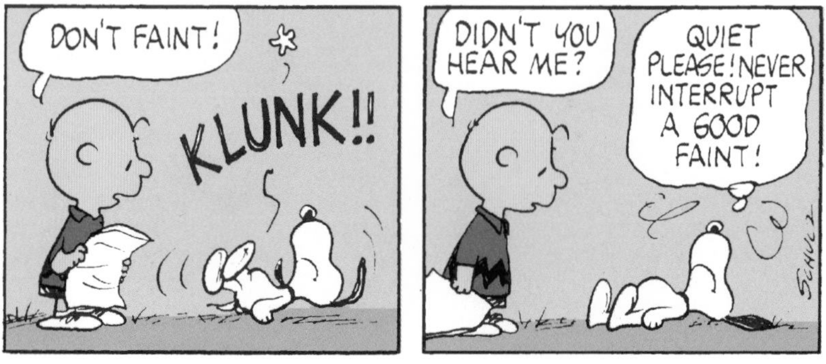
DON'T FAINT!
KLUNK!!
DIDN'T YOU HEAR ME?
QUIET PLEASE! NEVER INTERRUPT A GOOD FAINT!
SCHULZ

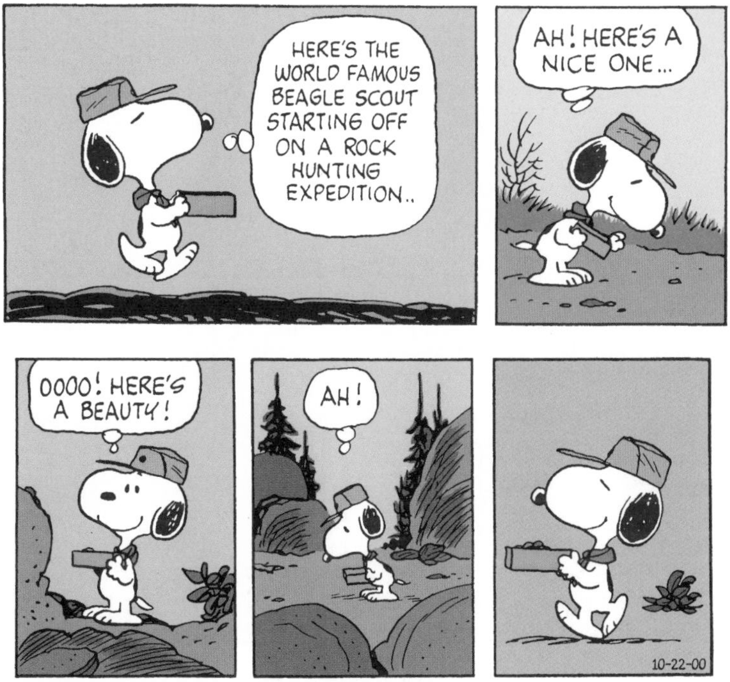
HERE'S THE WORLD FAMOUS BEAGLE SCOUT STARTING OFF ON A ROCK HUNTING EXPEDITION..
AH! HERE'S A NICE ONE...
OOOO! HERE'S A BEAUTY!
AH!
10-22-00

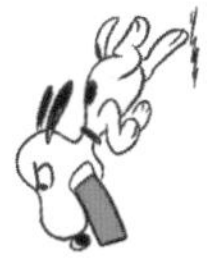

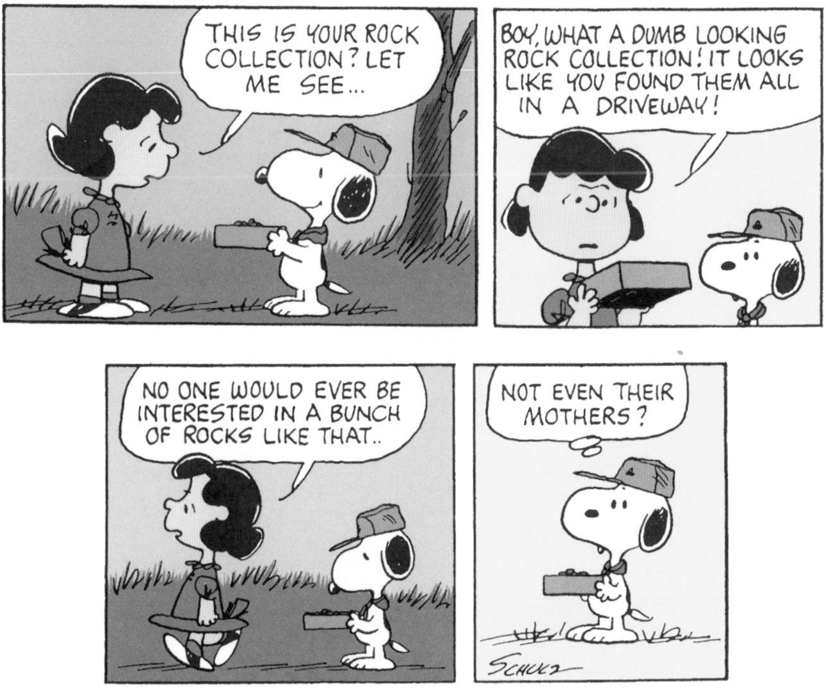
THIS IS YOUR ROCK COLLECTION? LET ME SEE...
BOY, WHAT A DUMB LOOKING ROCK COLLECTION! IT LOOKS LIKE YOU FOUND THEM ALL IN A DRIVEWAY!
NO ONE WOULD EVER BE INTERESTED IN A BUNCH OF ROCKS LIKE THAT..
NOT EVEN THEIR MOTHERS?
SCHULZ

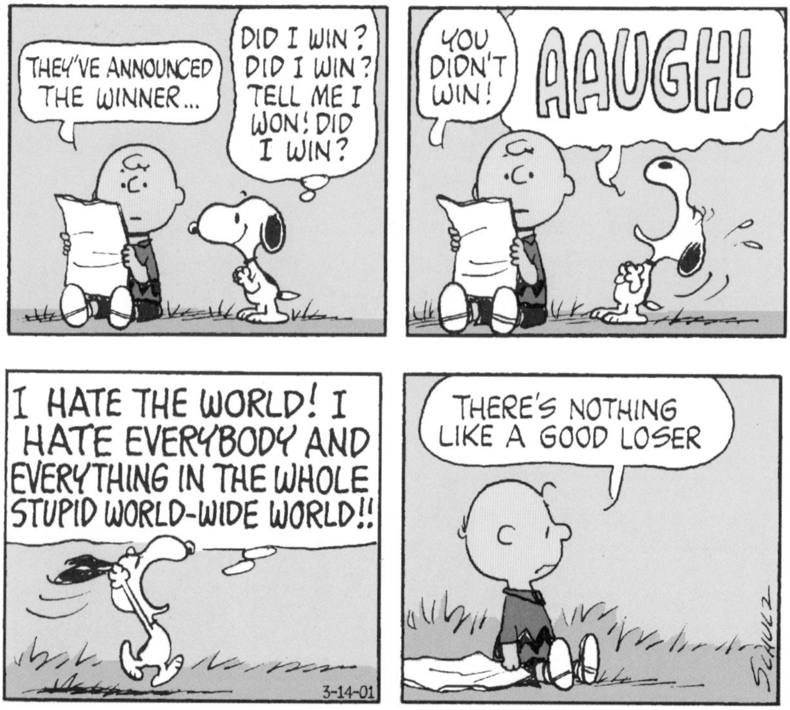
THEY'VE ANNOUNCED THE WINNER...
DID I WIN? DID I WIN? TELL ME I WON! DID I WIN?
YOU DIDN'T WIN!
AAUGH!
I HATE THE WORLD! I HATE EVERYBODY AND EVERYTHING IN THE WHOLE STUPID WORLD-WIDE WORLD!!
3-14-01
THERE'S NOTHING LIKE A GOOD LOSER
SCHULZ

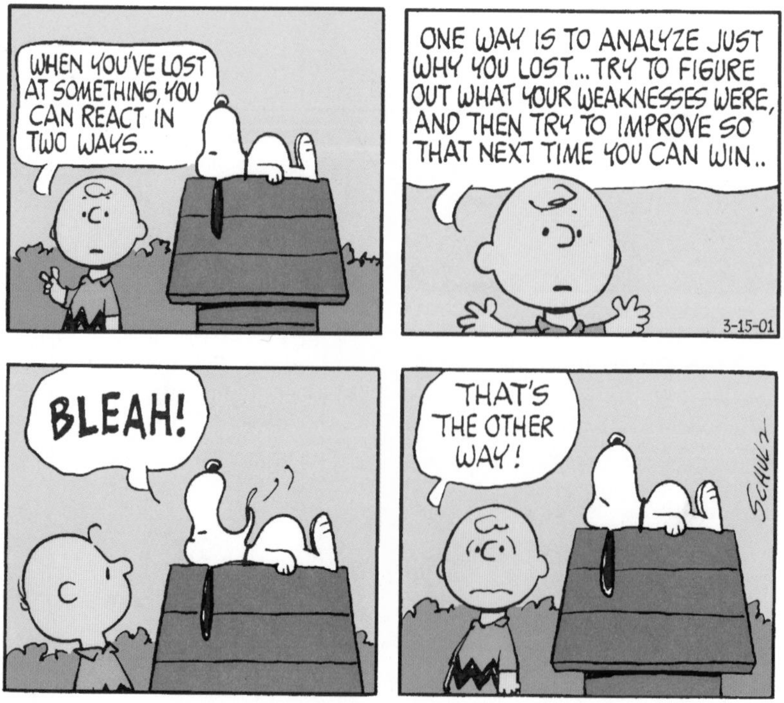
WHEN YOU'VE LOST AT SOMETHING, YOU CAN REACT IN TWO WAYS...
ONE WAY IS TO ANALYZE JUST WHY YOU LOST...TRY TO FIGURE OUT WHAT YOUR WEAKNESSES WERE, AND THEN TRY TO IMPROVE SO THAT NEXT TIME YOU CAN WIN..
3-15-01
BLEAH!
THAT'S THE OTHER WAY!
SCHULZ

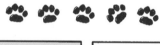

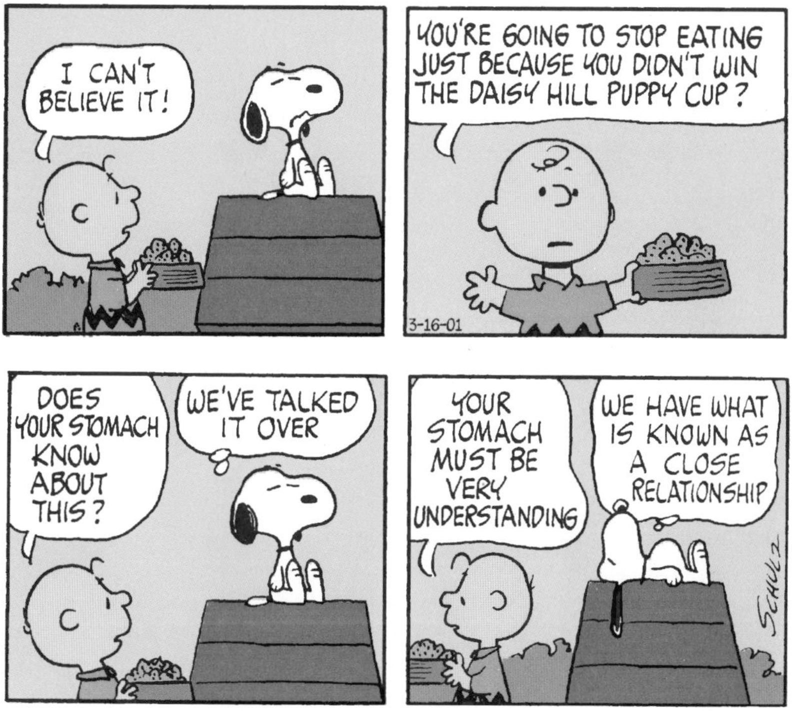
I CAN'T BELIEVE IT!
YOU'RE GOING TO STOP EATING JUST BECAUSE YOU DIDN'T WIN THE DAISY HILL PUPPY CUP?
3-16-01
DOES YOUR STOMACH KNOW ABOUT THIS?
WE'VE TALKED IT OVER
YOUR STOMACH MUST BE VERY UNDERSTANDING
WE HAVE WHAT IS KNOWN AS A CLOSE RELATIONSHIP
SCHULZ

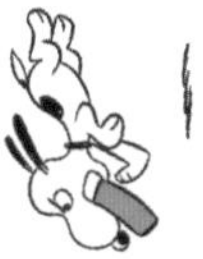

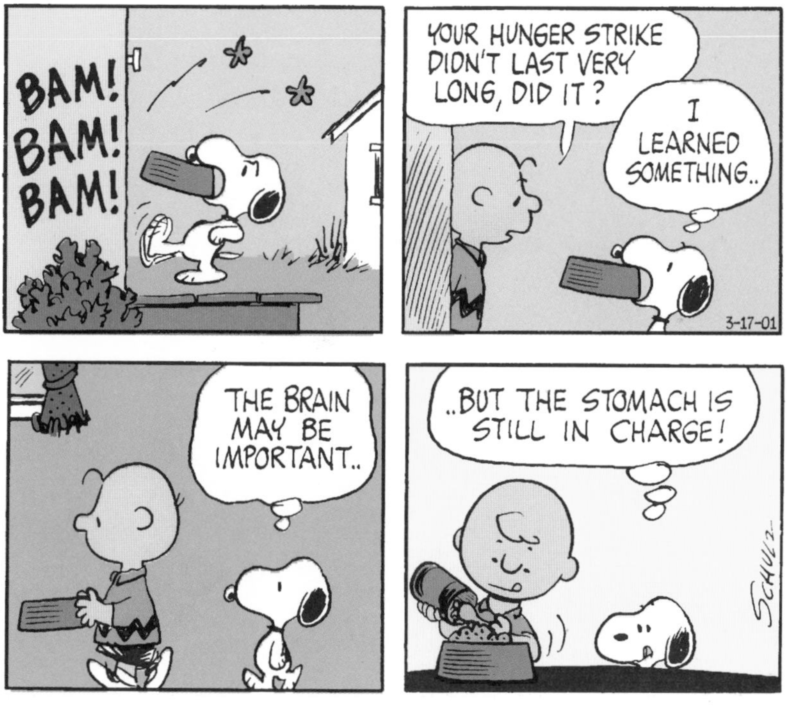
BAM! BAM! BAM!
YOUR HUNGER STRIKE DIDN'T LAST VERY LONG, DID IT?
I LEARNED SOMETHING..
3-17-01
THE BRAIN MAY BE IMPORTANT..
..BUT THE STOMACH IS STILL IN CHARGE!
SCHULZ

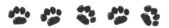

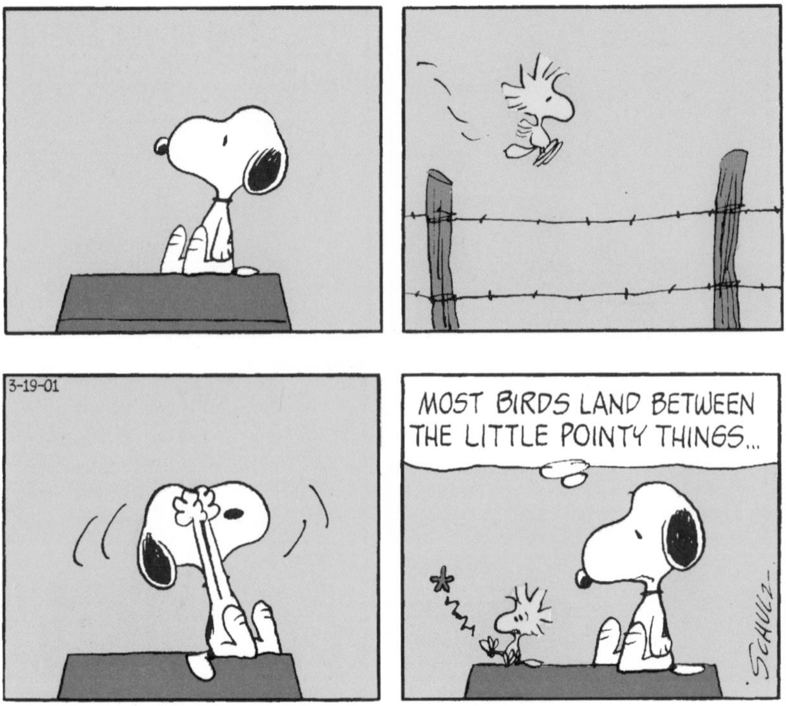
3-19-01
MOST BIRDS LAND BETWEEN THE LITTLE POINTY THINGS...
SCHULZ

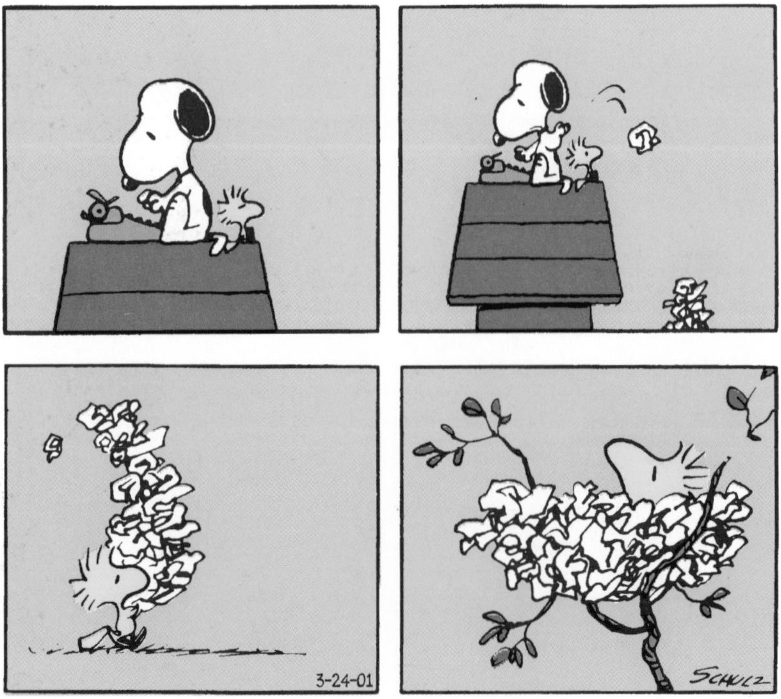
3-24-01
SCHULZ

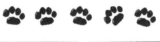

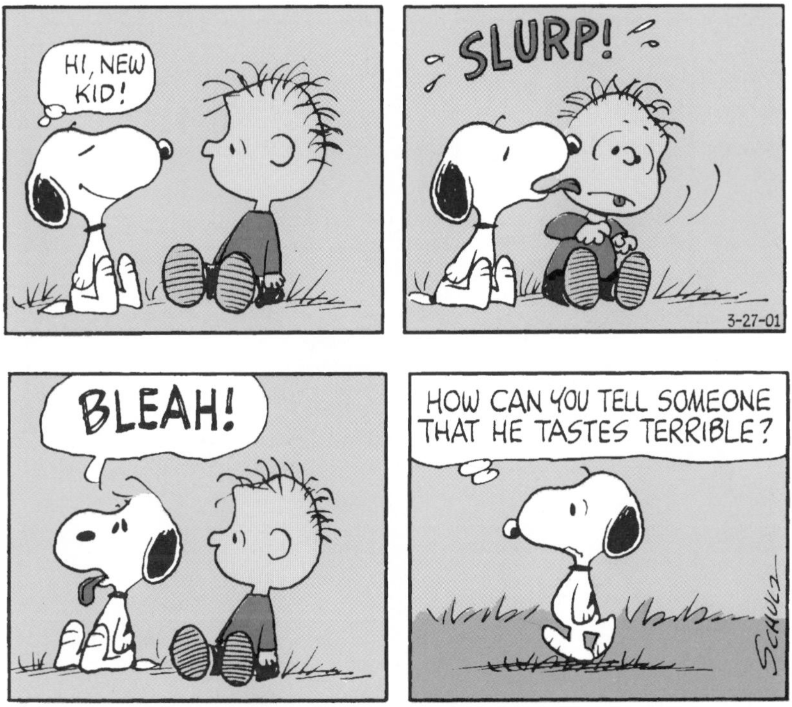
HI, NEW KID!
SLURP!
3-27-01
BLEAH!
HOW CAN YOU TELL SOMEONE THAT HE TASTES TERRIBLE?
SCHULZ

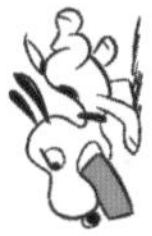

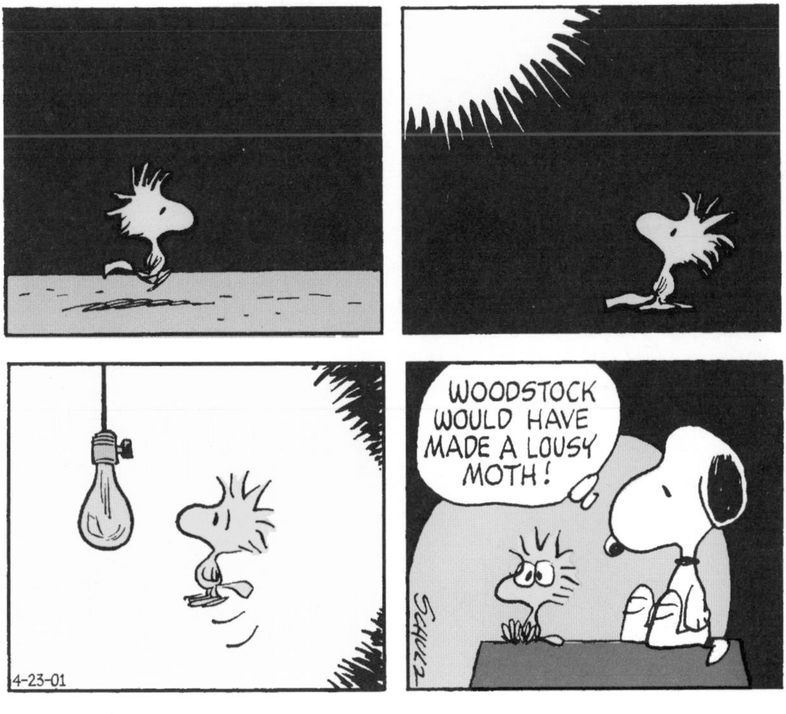
4-23-01
WOODSTOCK WOULD HAVE MADE A LOUSY MOTH!
SCHULZ

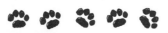

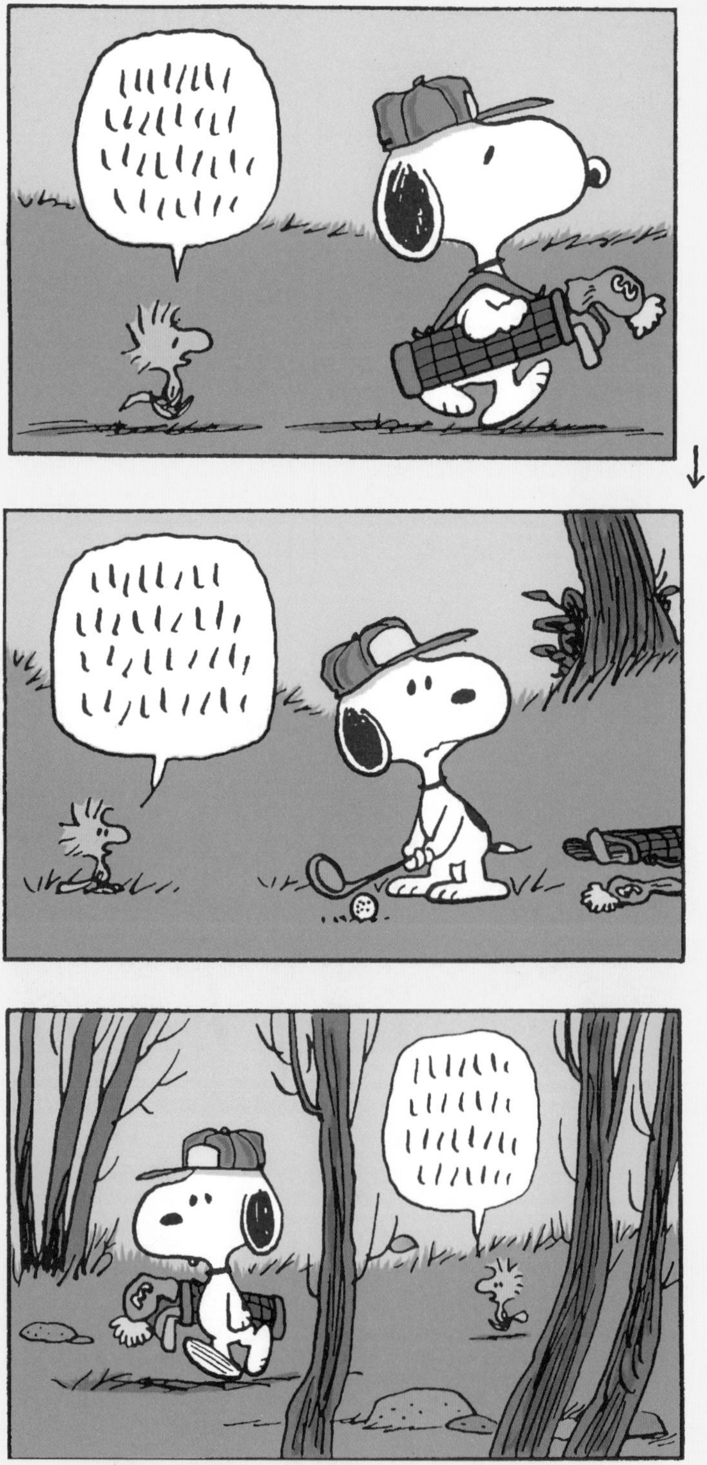

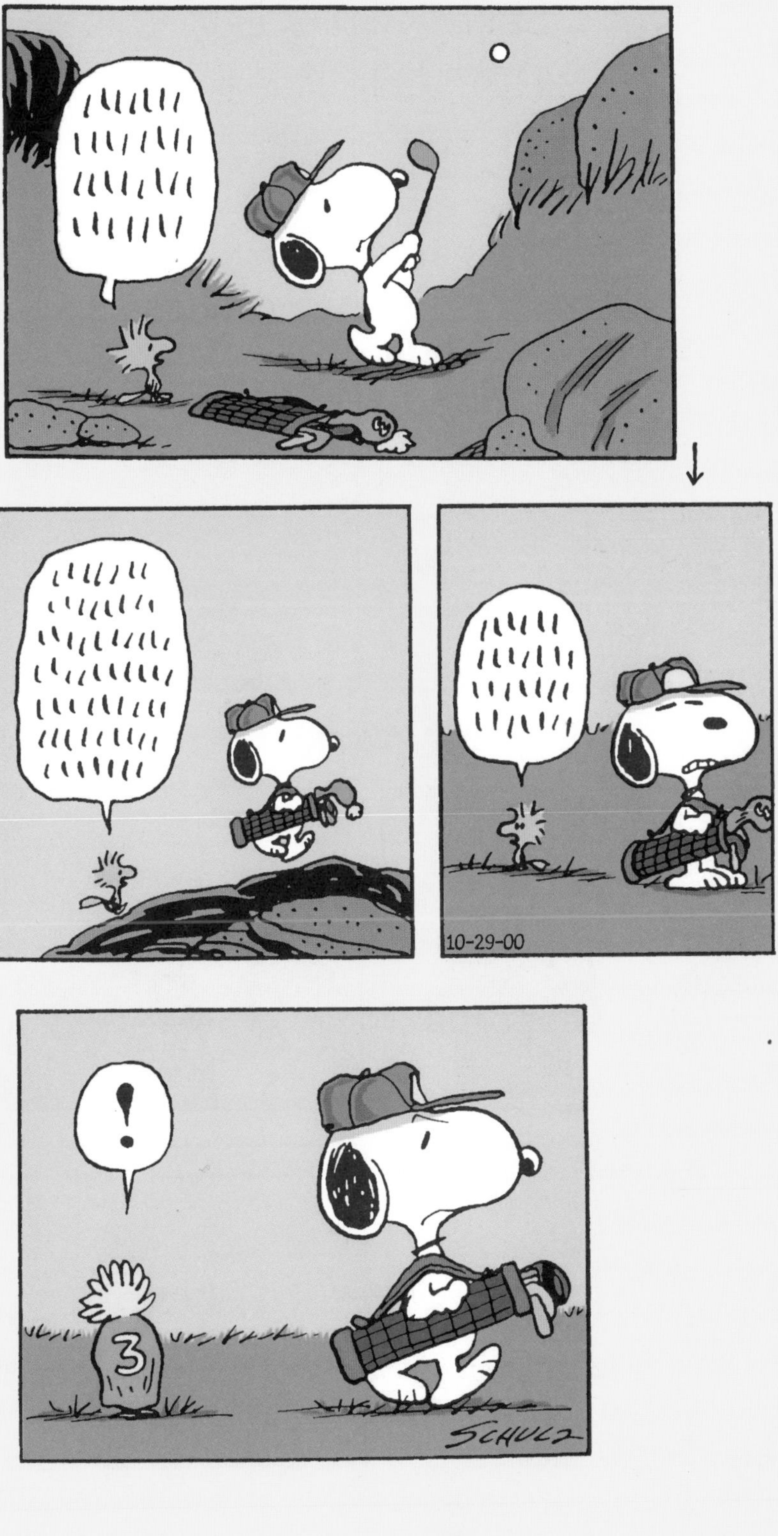
10-29-00
!
3
SCHULZ

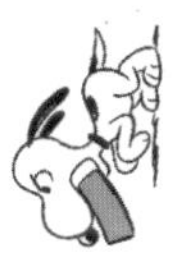

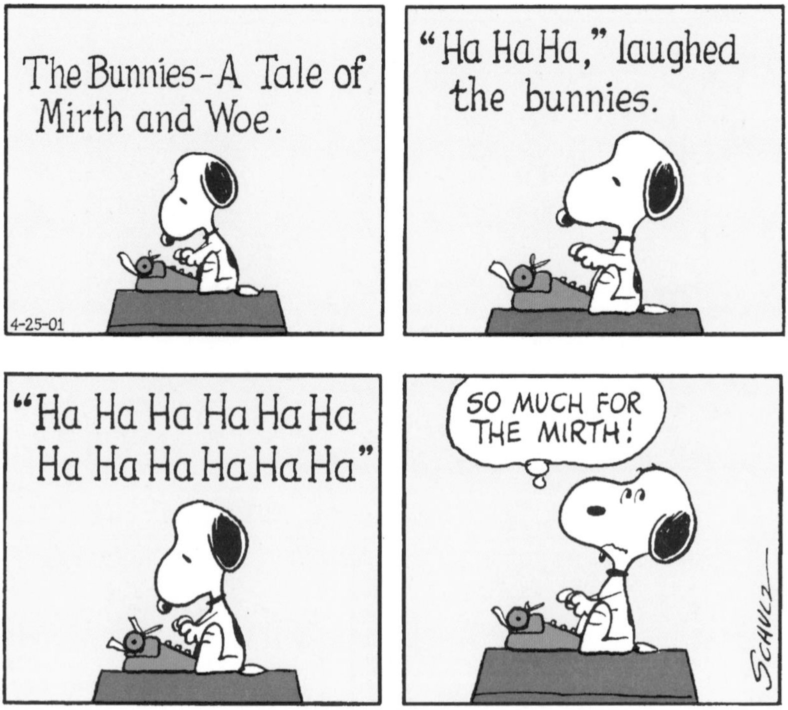
The Bunnies-A Tale of Mirth and Woe.
4-25-01
"Ha Ha Ha," laughed the bunnies.
"Ha Ha Ha Ha Ha Ha Ha Ha Ha Ha Ha Ha"
SO MUCH FOR THE MIRTH!
SCHULZ

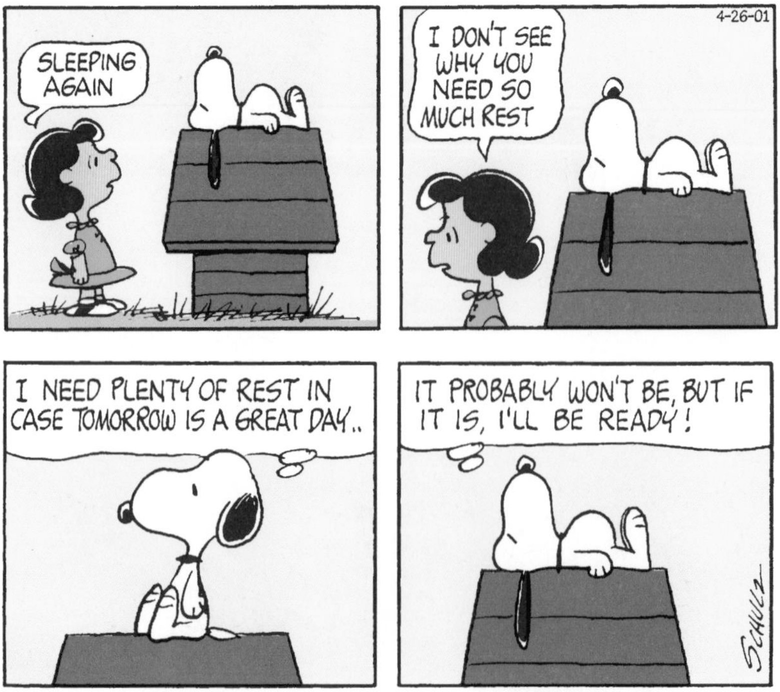
SLEEPING AGAIN
4-26-01
I DON'T SEE WHY YOU NEED SO MUCH REST
I NEED PLENTY OF REST IN CASE TOMORROW IS A GREAT DAY..
IT PROBABLY WON'T BE, BUT IF IT IS, I'LL BE READY!
SCHULZ

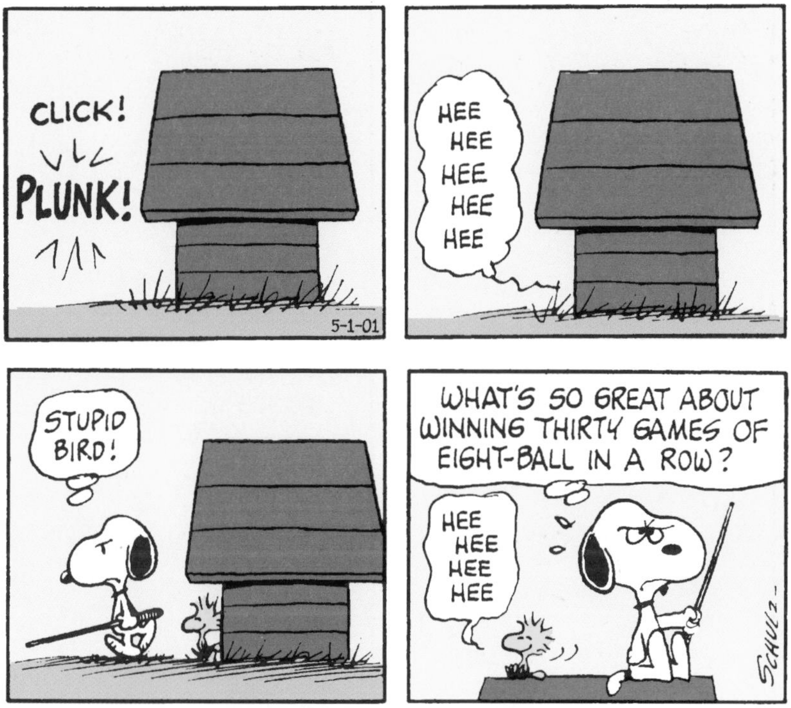
CLICK!
PLUNK!
5-1-01
HEE HEE HEE HEE HEE
STUPID BIRD!
WHAT'S SO GREAT ABOUT WINNING THIRTY GAMES OF EIGHT-BALL IN A ROW?
HEE HEE HEE HEE
SCHULZ

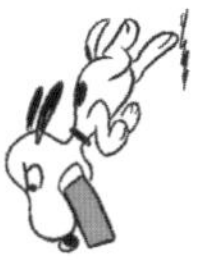

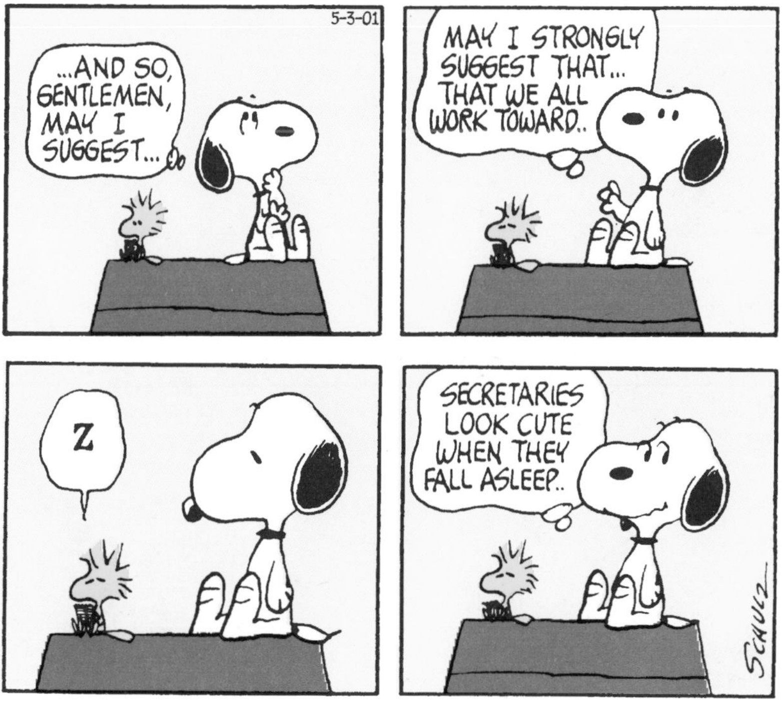
5-3-01
...AND SO, GENTLEMEN, MAY I SUGGEST...
MAY I STRONGLY SUGGEST THAT... THAT WE ALL WORK TOWARD..
Z
SECRETARIES LOOK CUTE WHEN THEY FALL ASLEEP..
SCHULZ

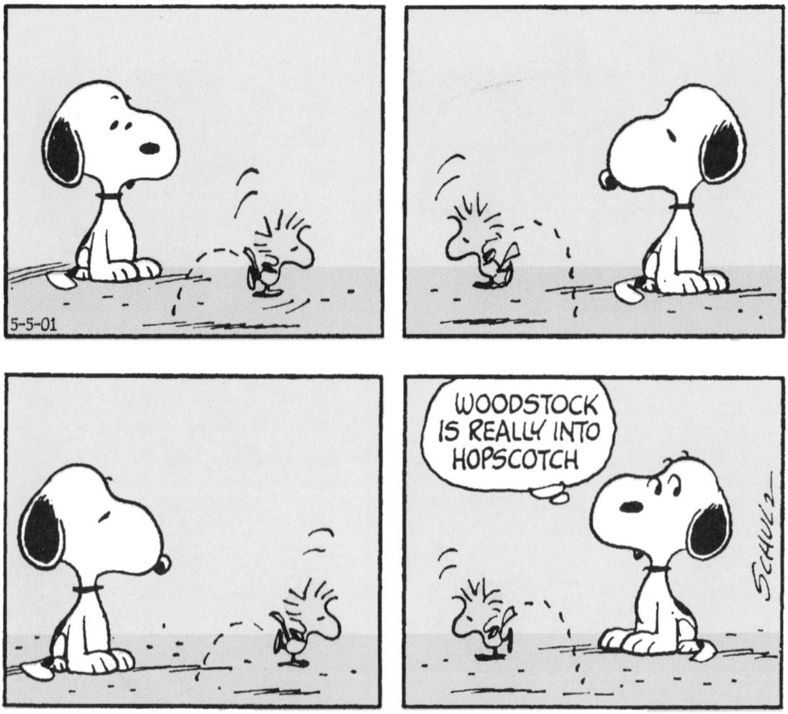
5-5-01
WOODSTOCK IS REALLY INTO HOPSCOTCH
SCHULZ

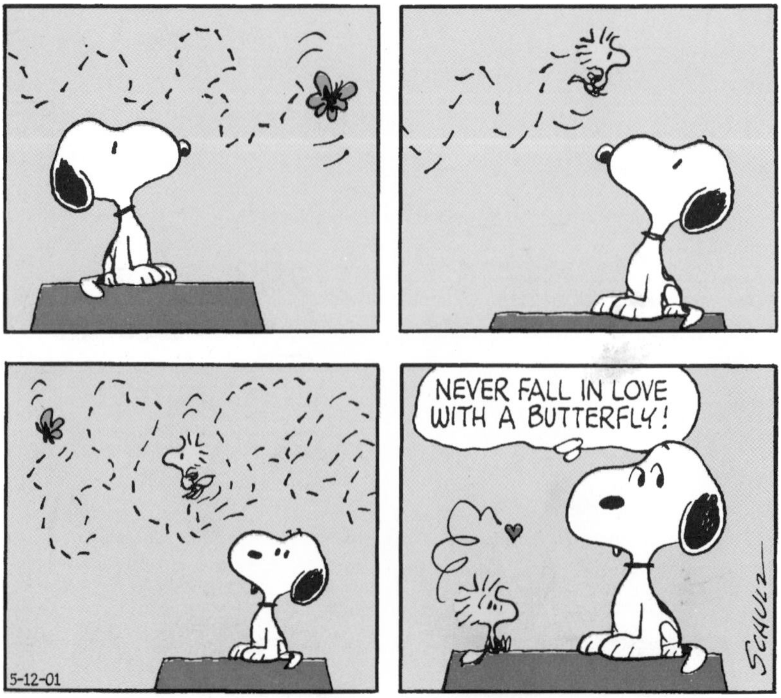
5-12-01
NEVER FALL IN LOVE WITH A BUTTERFLY!
SCHULZ

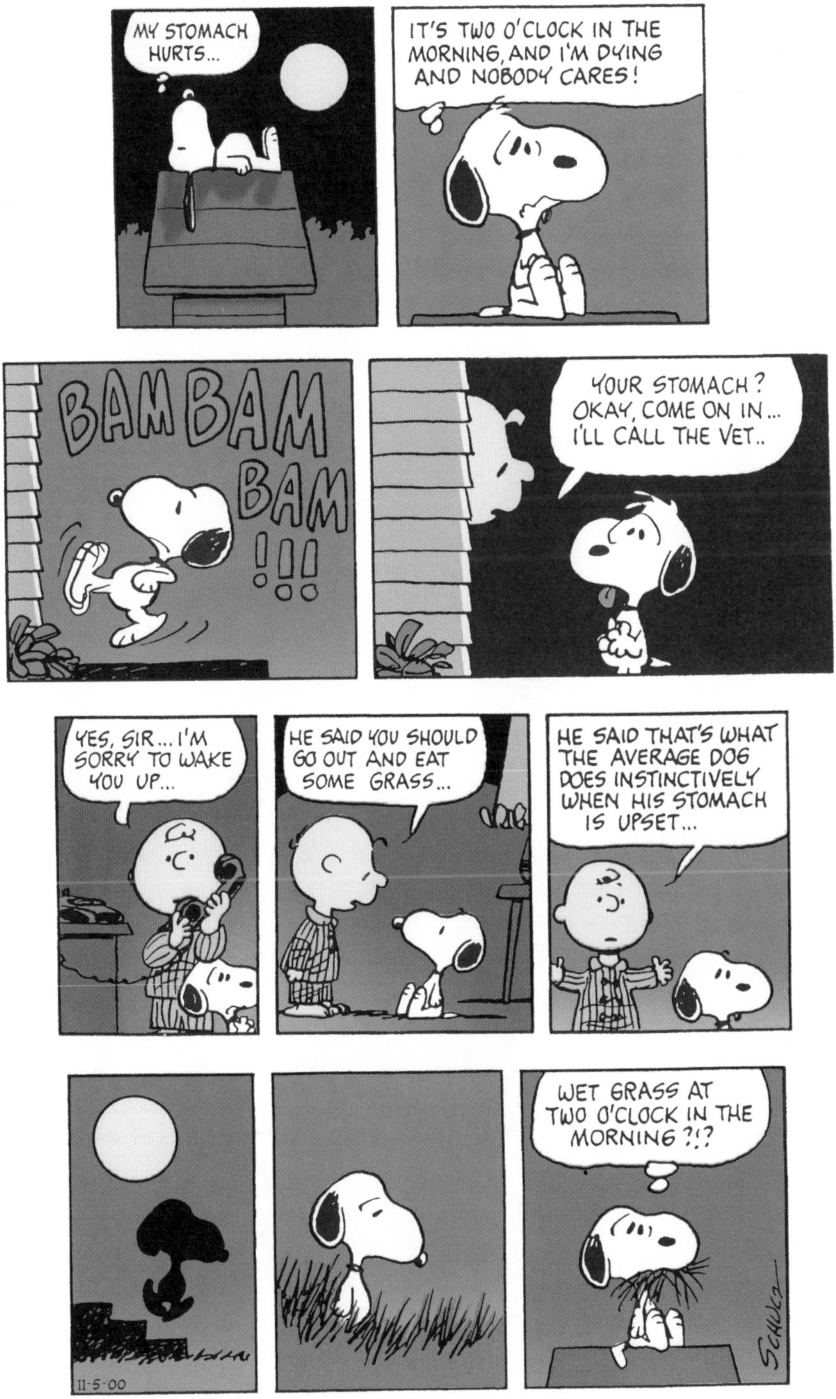
MY STOMACH HURTS...
IT'S TWO O'CLOCK IN THE MORNING, AND I'M DYING AND NOBODY CARES!
BAM BAM BAM !!!
YOUR STOMACH? OKAY, COME ON IN... I'LL CALL THE VET..
YES, SIR... I'M SORRY TO WAKE YOU UP...
HE SAID YOU SHOULD GO OUT AND EAT SOME GRASS...
HE SAID THAT'S WHAT THE AVERAGE DOG DOES INSTINCTIVELY WHEN HIS STOMACH IS UPSET...
11-5-00
WET GRASS AT TWO O'CLOCK IN THE MORNING ?!?
SCHULZ

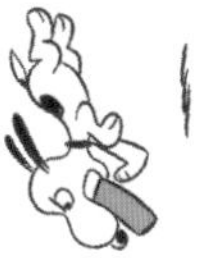

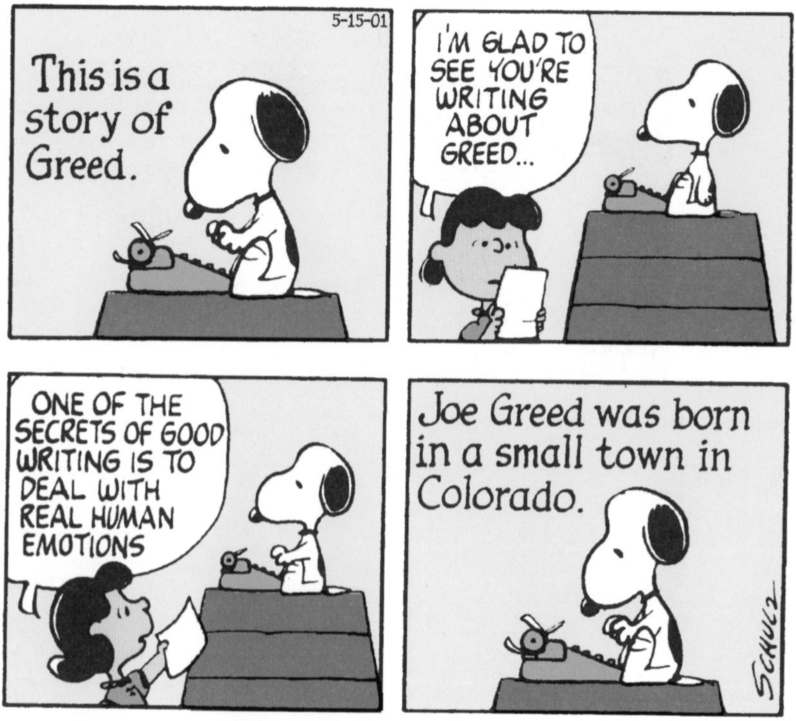
5-15-01
This is a story of Greed.
I'M GLAD TO SEE YOU'RE WRITING ABOUT GREED...
ONE OF THE SECRETS OF GOOD WRITING IS TO DEAL WITH REAL HUMAN EMOTIONS
Joe Greed was born in a small town in Colorado.
SCHULZ

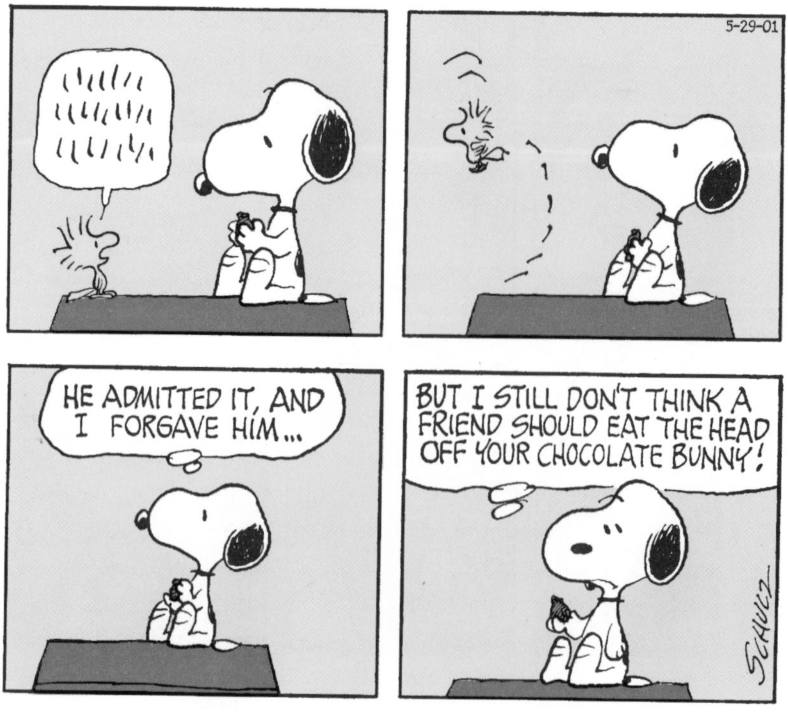
5-29-01
HE ADMITTED IT, AND I FORGAVE HIM...
BUT I STILL DON'T THINK A FRIEND SHOULD EAT THE HEAD OFF YOUR CHOCOLATE BUNNY!
SCHULZ

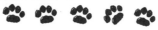

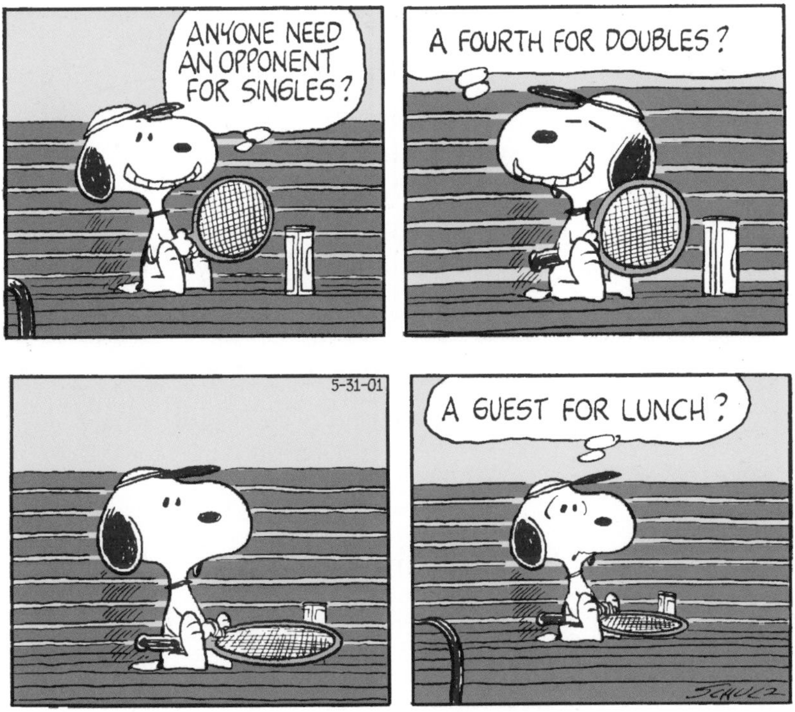
ANYONE NEED AN OPPONENT FOR SINGLES?
A FOURTH FOR DOUBLES?
5-31-01
A GUEST FOR LUNCH?

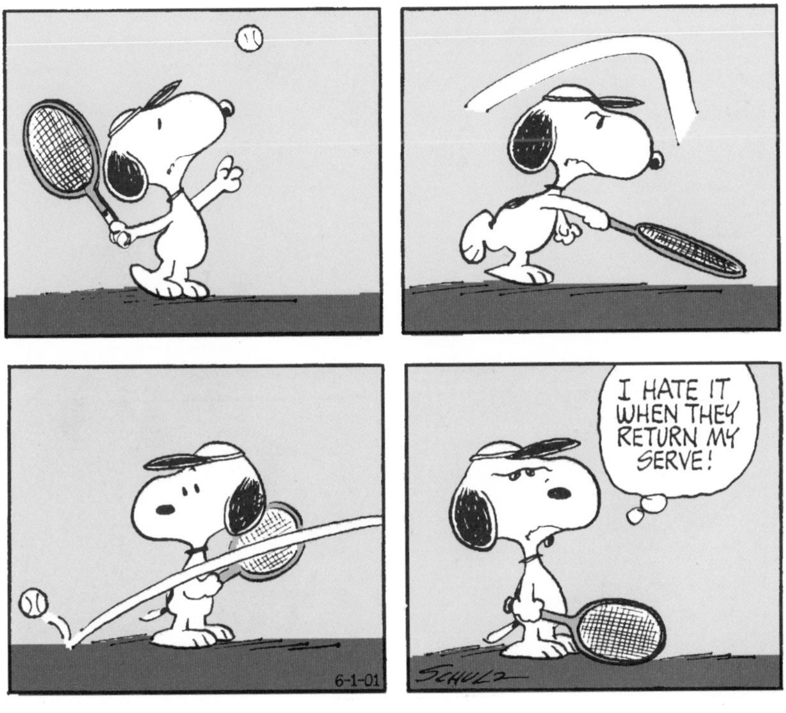
6-1-01
I HATE IT WHEN THEY RETURN MY SERVE!

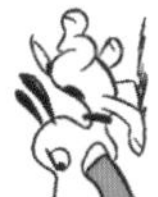

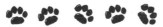

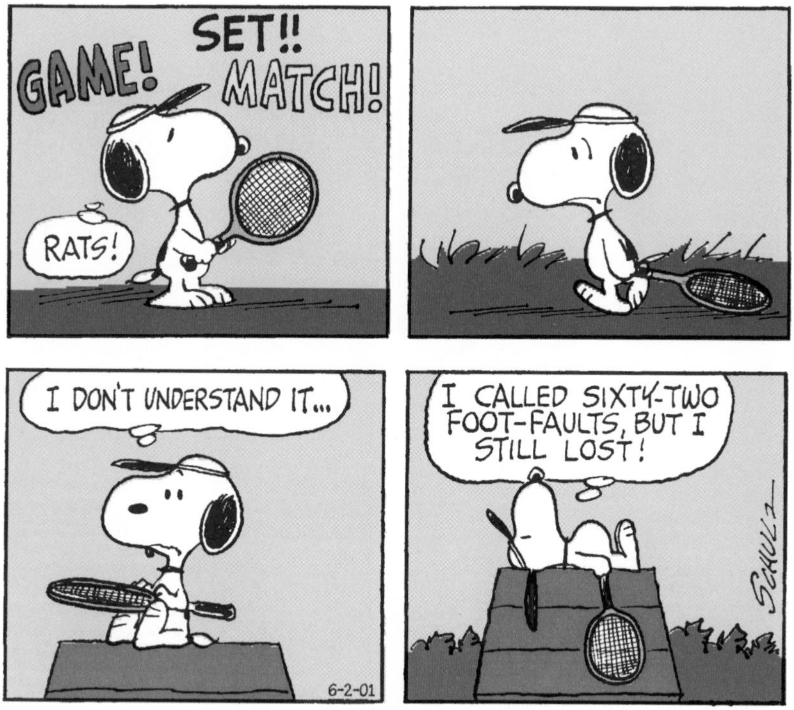
GAME! SET!! MATCH!
RATS!
I DON'T UNDERSTAND IT...
6-2-01
I CALLED SIXTY-TWO FOOT-FAULTS, BUT I STILL LOST!
SCHULZ

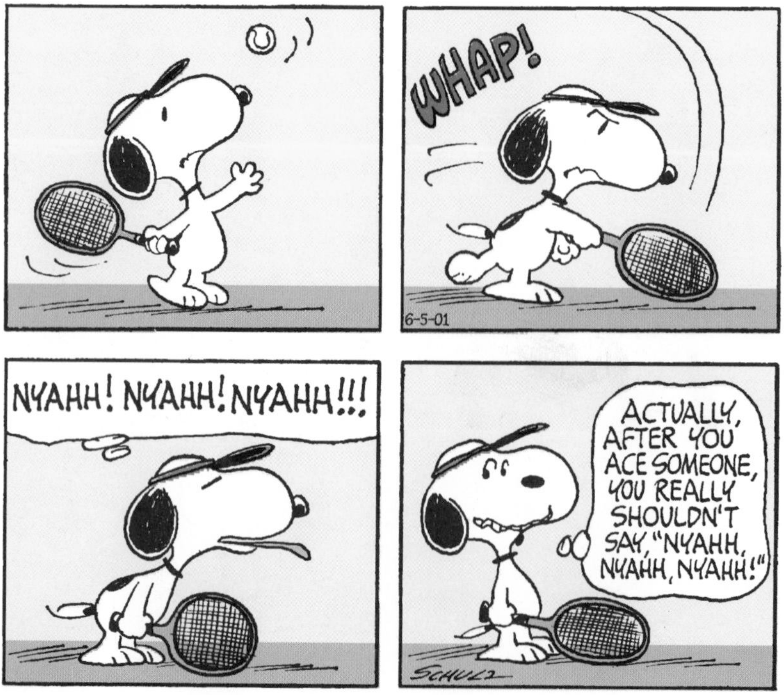
WHAP!
6-5-01
NYAHH! NYAHH! NYAHH!!!
ACTUALLY, AFTER YOU ACE SOMEONE, YOU REALLY SHOULDN'T SAY, "NYAHH, NYAHH, NYAHH!"
SCHULZ

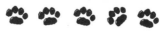

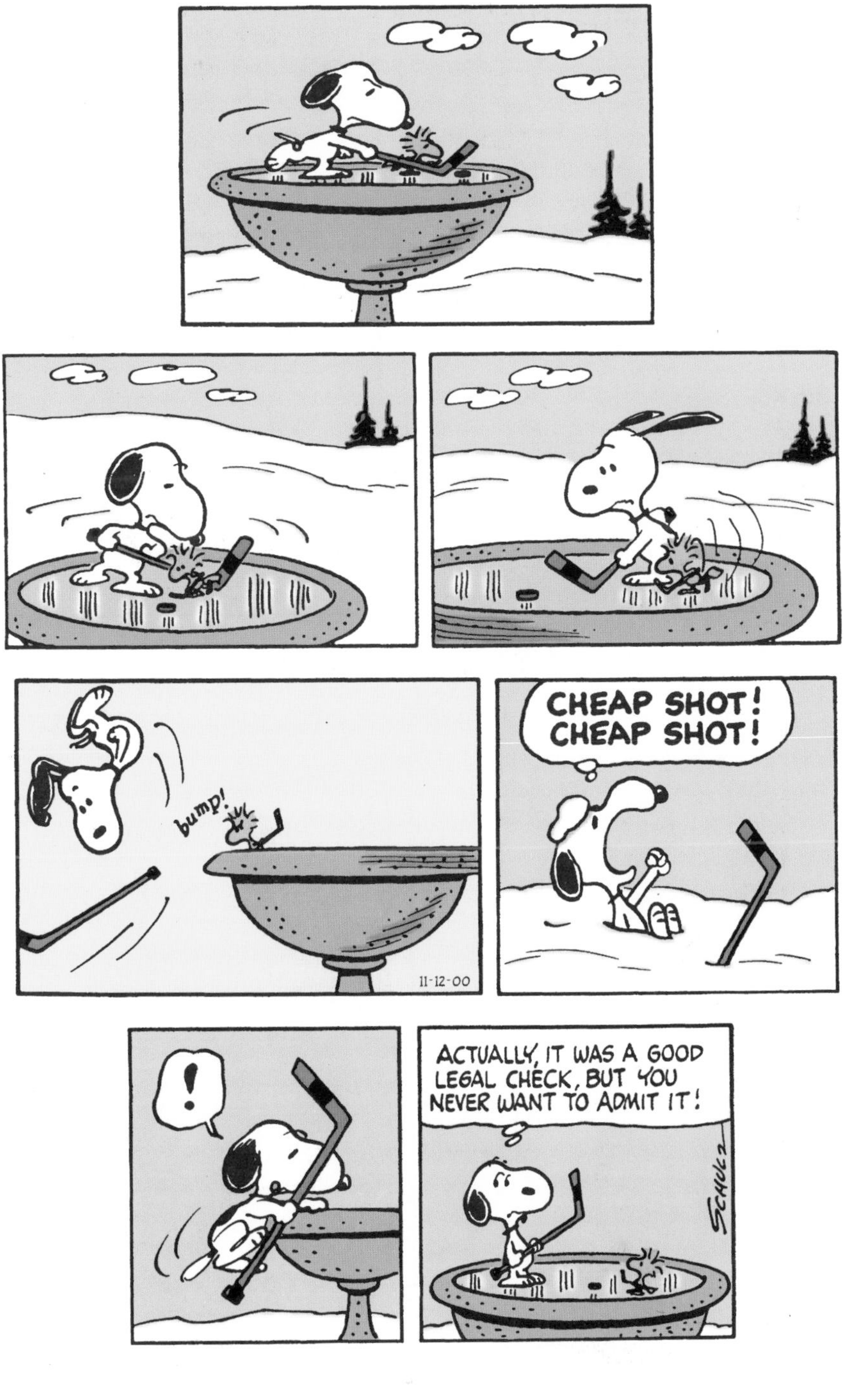
bump!
11-12-00
CHEAP SHOT! CHEAP SHOT!
!
ACTUALLY, IT WAS A GOOD LEGAL CHECK, BUT YOU NEVER WANT TO ADMIT IT!
SCHULZ

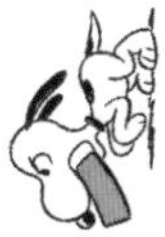

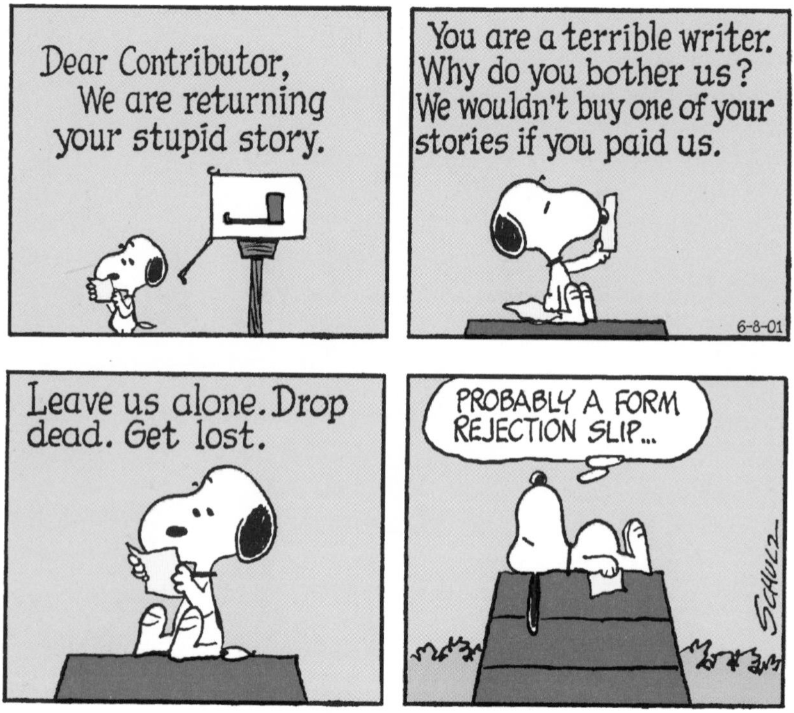
Dear Contributor,
We are returning your stupid story.
You are a terrible writer. Why do you bother us? We wouldn't buy one of your stories if you paid us.
6-8-01
Leave us alone. Drop dead. Get lost.
PROBABLY A FORM REJECTION SLIP...
SCHULZ

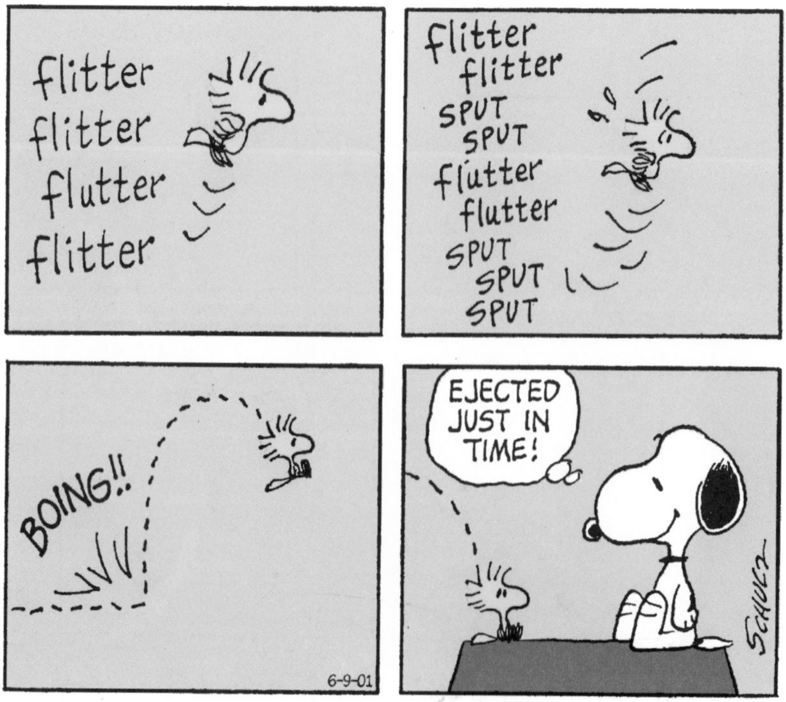
flitter
flitter
flutter
flitter
flitter
flitter
SPUT
SPUT
flutter
flutter
SPUT
SPUT
SPUT
BOING!!
6-9-01
EJECTED JUST IN TIME!
SCHULZ

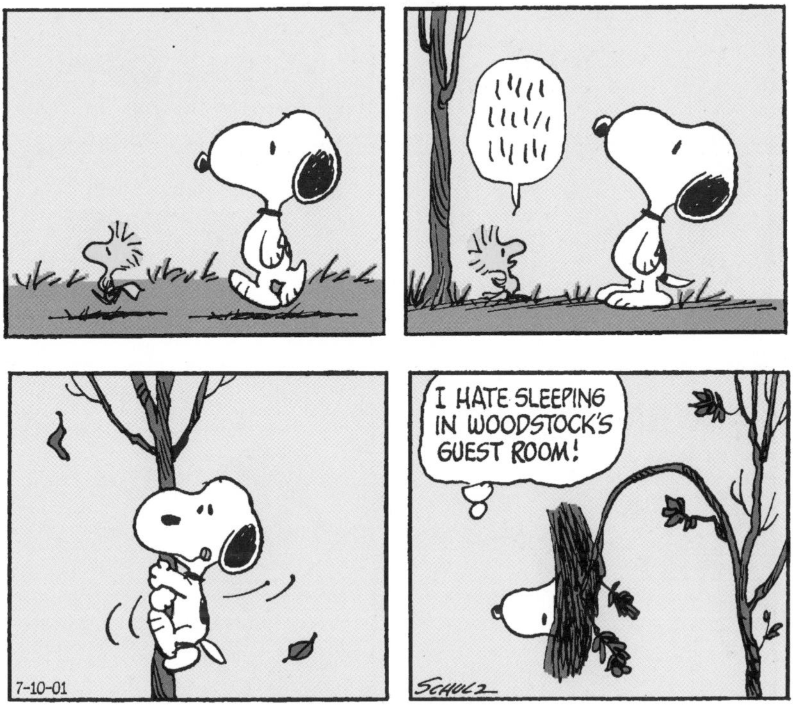
I HATE SLEEPING IN WOODSTOCK'S GUEST ROOM!
7-10-01
SCHULZ

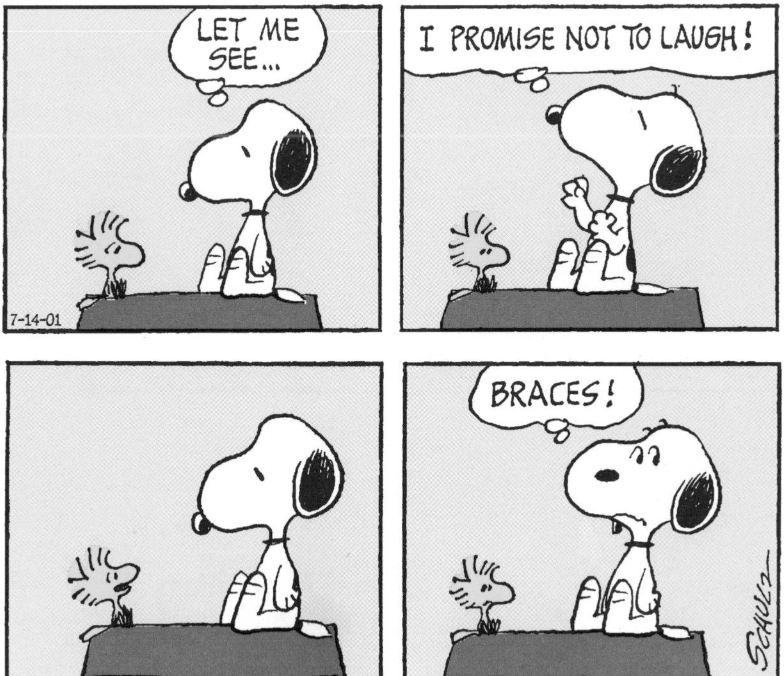
LET ME SEE...
7-14-01
I PROMISE NOT TO LAUGH!
BRACES!
SCHULZ

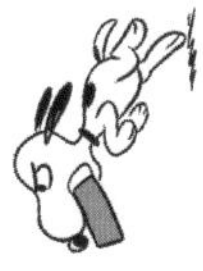

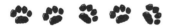

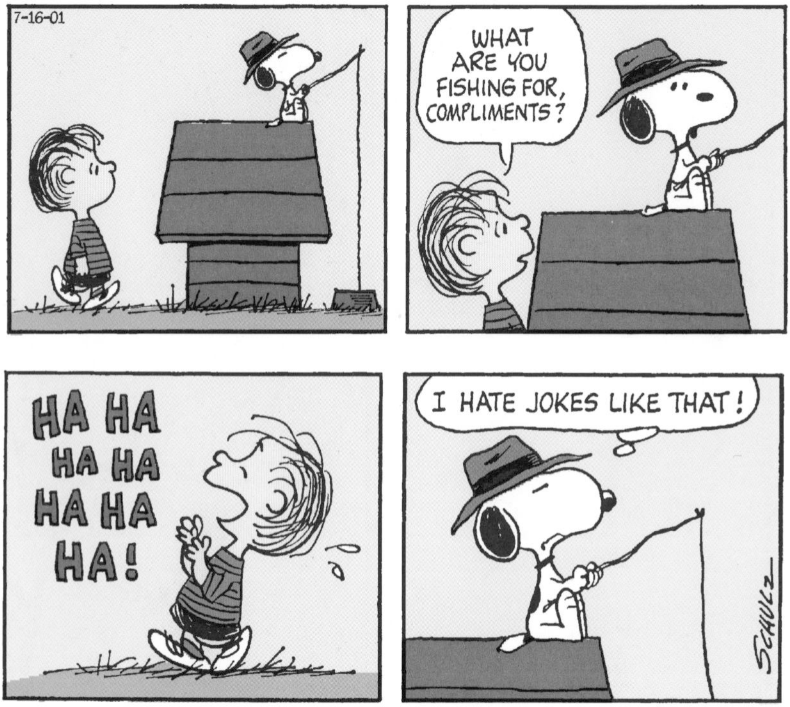
7-16-01
WHAT ARE YOU FISHING FOR, COMPLIMENTS?
HA HA HA HA HA HA HA!
I HATE JOKES LIKE THAT!
SCHULZ

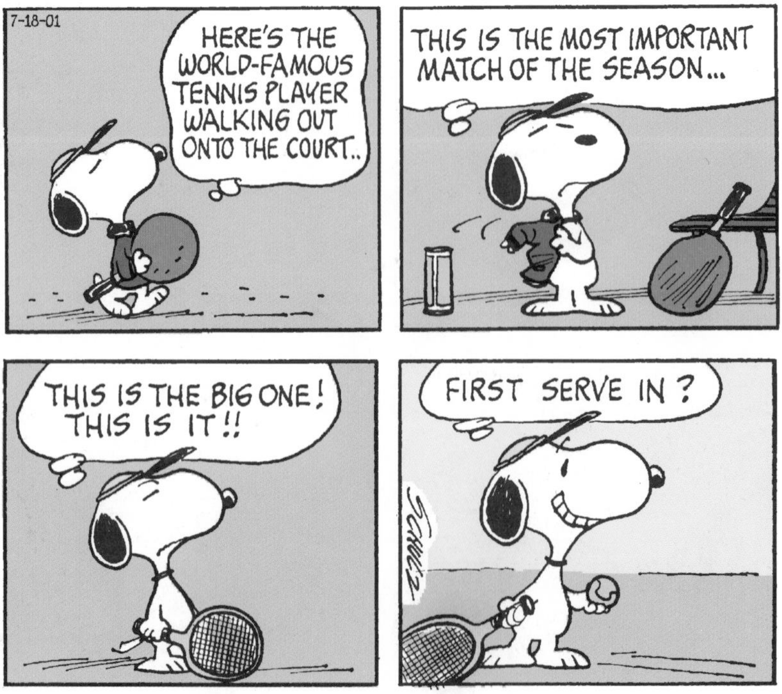
7-18-01
HERE'S THE WORLD-FAMOUS TENNIS PLAYER WALKING OUT ONTO THE COURT..
THIS IS THE MOST IMPORTANT MATCH OF THE SEASON...
THIS IS THE BIG ONE! THIS IS IT!!
FIRST SERVE IN?
SCHULZ

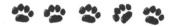

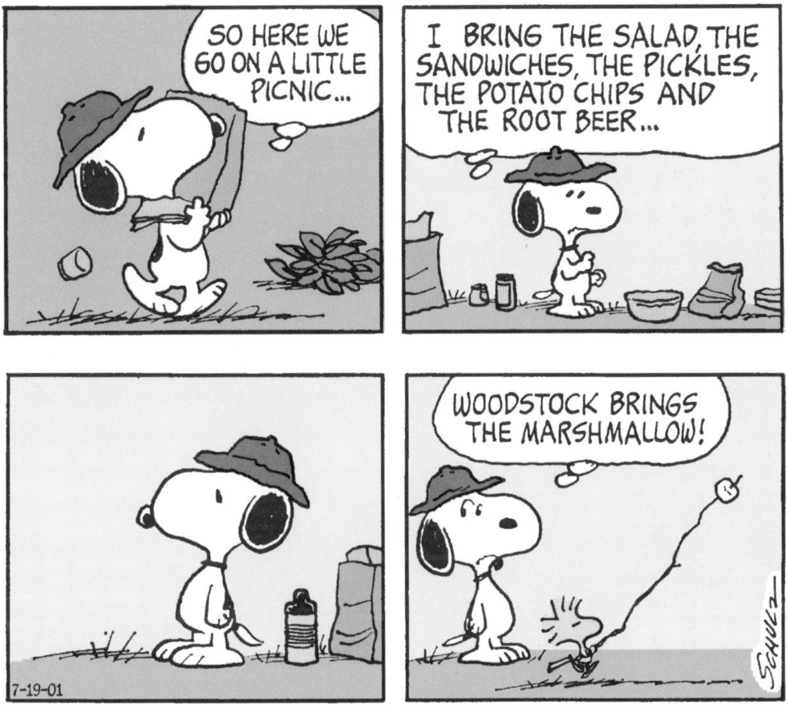
SO HERE WE GO ON A LITTLE PICNIC...
I BRING THE SALAD, THE SANDWICHES, THE PICKLES, THE POTATO CHIPS AND THE ROOT BEER...
7-19-01
WOODSTOCK BRINGS THE MARSHMALLOW!
SCHULZ

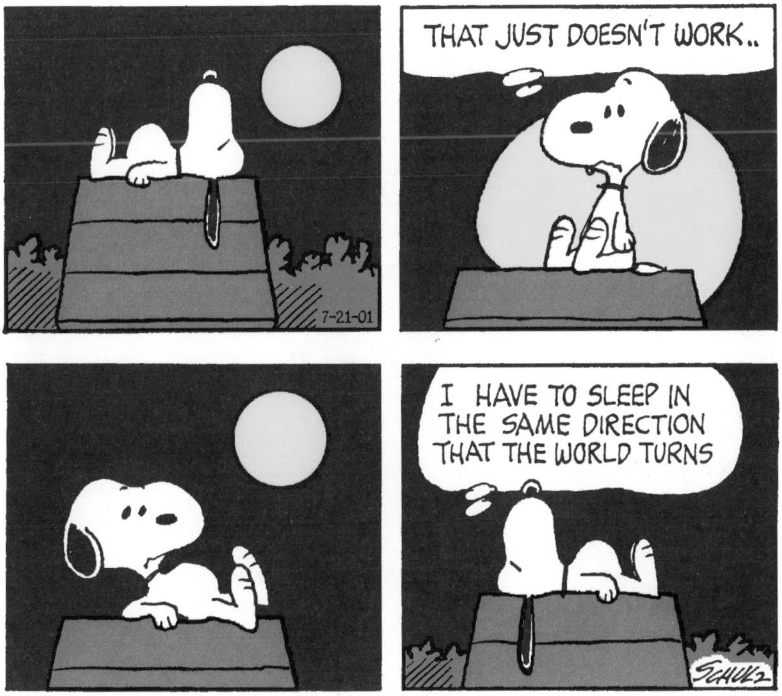
7-21-01
THAT JUST DOESN'T WORK..
I HAVE TO SLEEP IN THE SAME DIRECTION THAT THE WORLD TURNS
SCHULZ

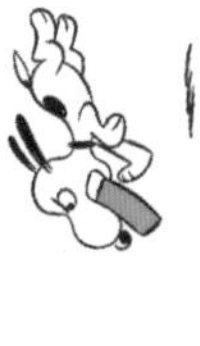

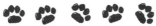

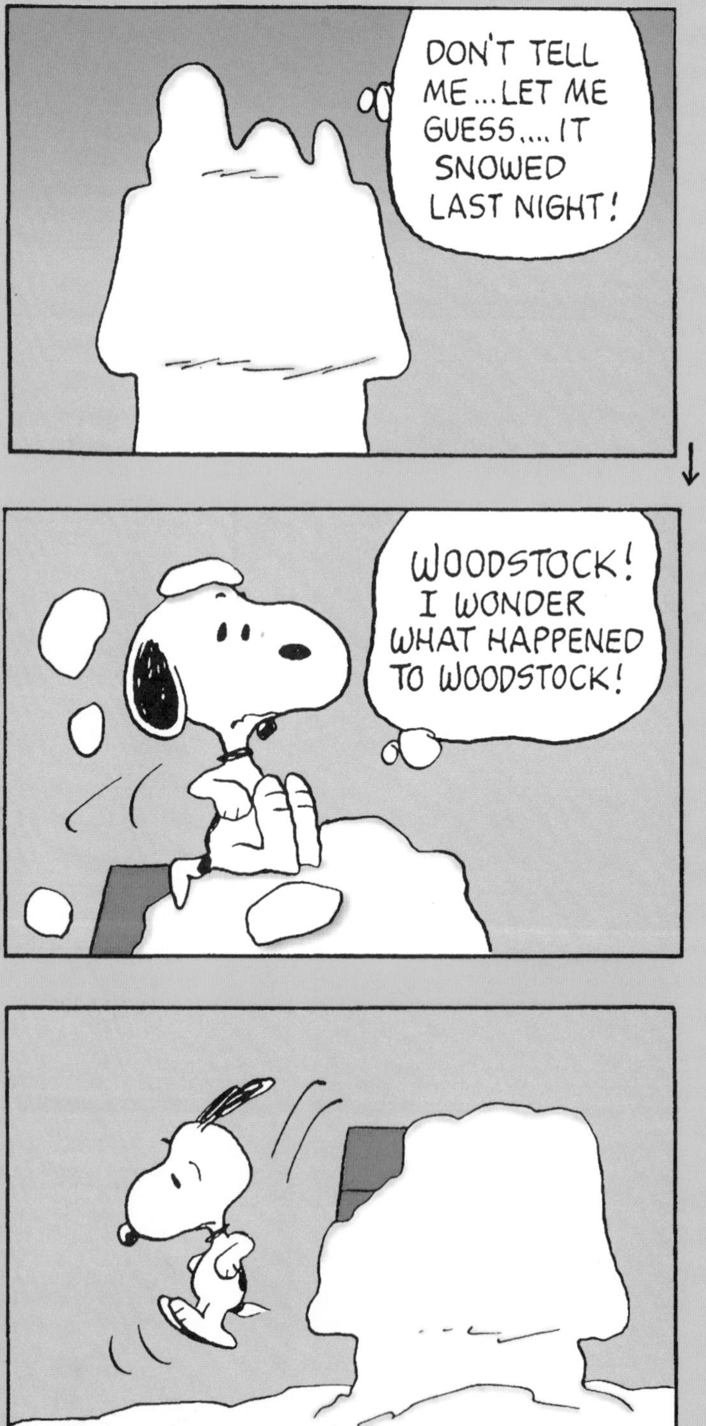
DON'T TELL ME...LET ME GUESS.... IT SNOWED LAST NIGHT!
WOODSTOCK! I WONDER WHAT HAPPENED TO WOODSTOCK!

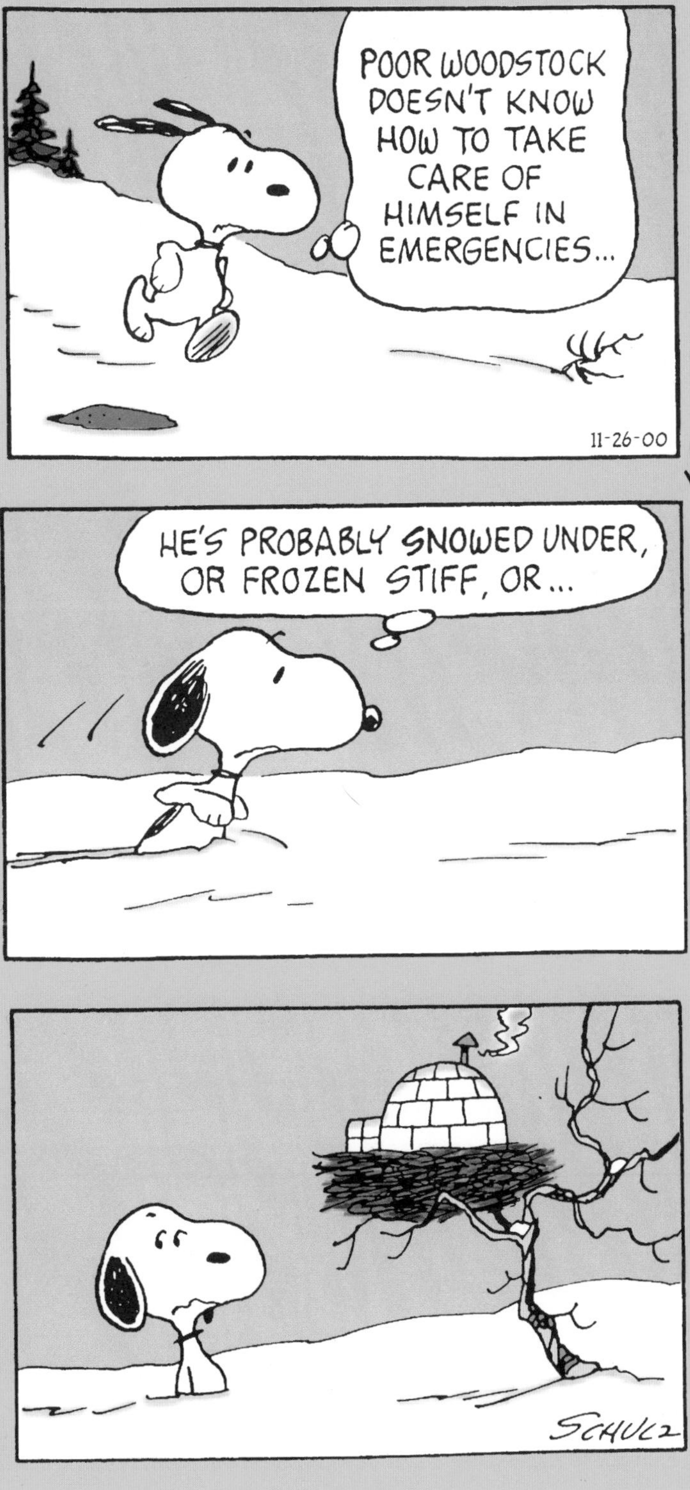
POOR WOODSTOCK DOESN'T KNOW HOW TO TAKE CARE OF HIMSELF IN EMERGENCIES...
11-26-00
HE'S PROBABLY SNOWED UNDER, OR FROZEN STIFF, OR...
SCHULZ

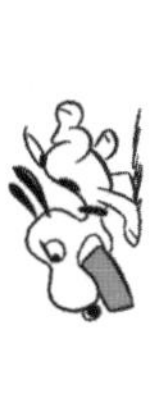

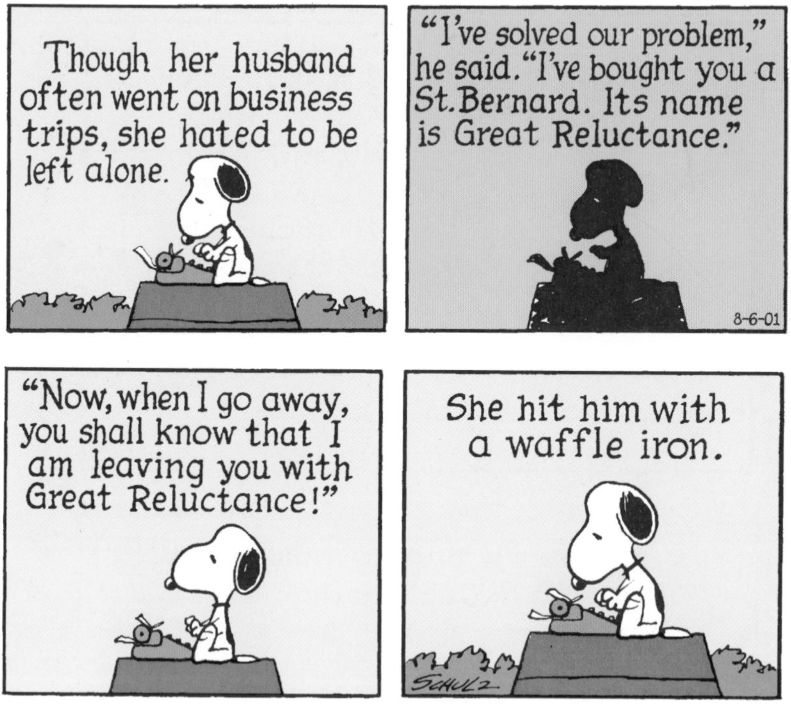
Though her husband often went on business trips, she hated to be left alone.
"I've solved our problem," he said. "I've bought you a St. Bernard. Its name is Great Reluctance."
8-6-01
"Now, when I go away, you shall know that I am leaving you with Great Reluctance!"
She hit him with a waffle iron.
SCHULZ

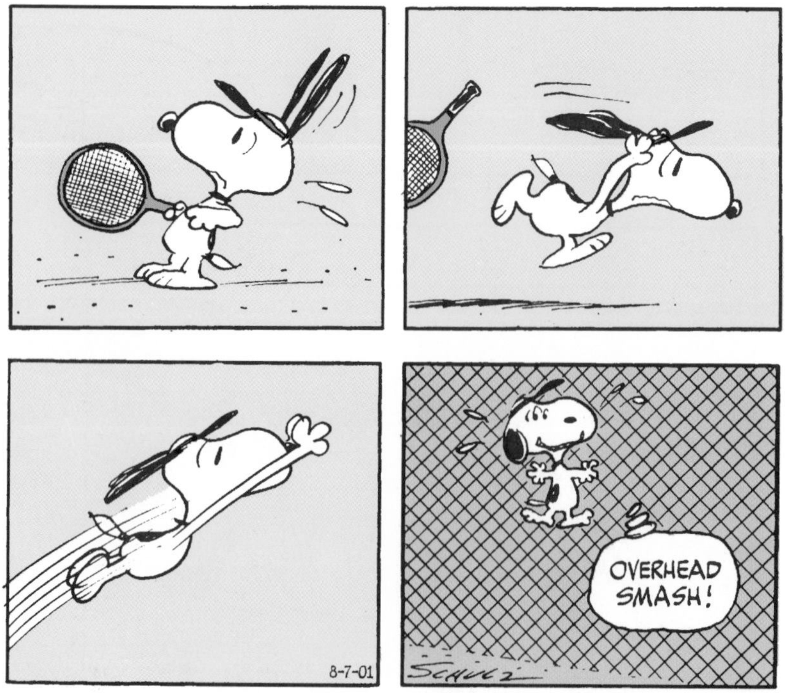
8-7-01
OVERHEAD SMASH!
SCHULZ

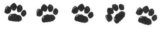

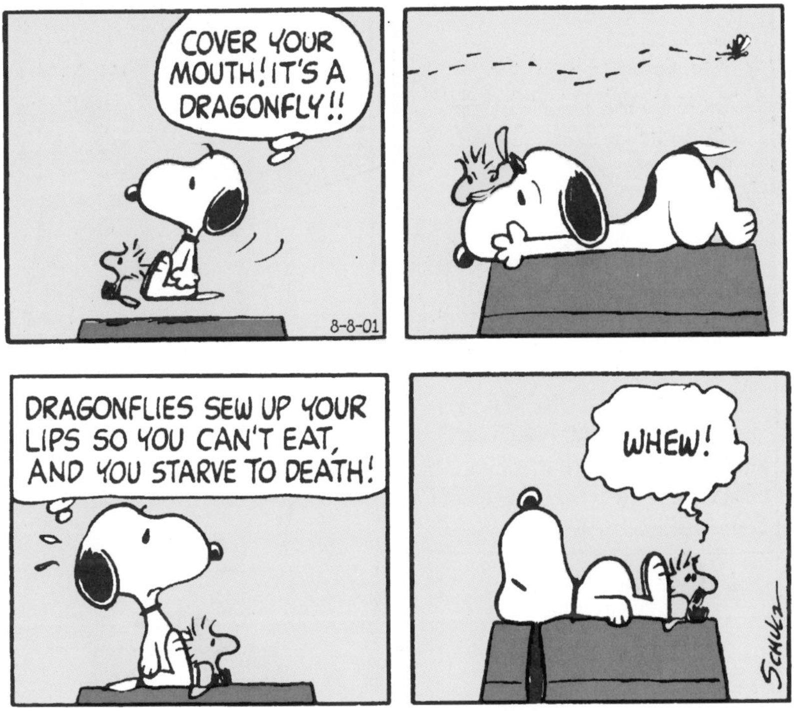
COVER YOUR MOUTH! IT'S A DRAGONFLY!!
8-8-01
DRAGONFLIES SEW UP YOUR LIPS SO YOU CAN'T EAT, AND YOU STARVE TO DEATH!
WHEW!
SCHULZ

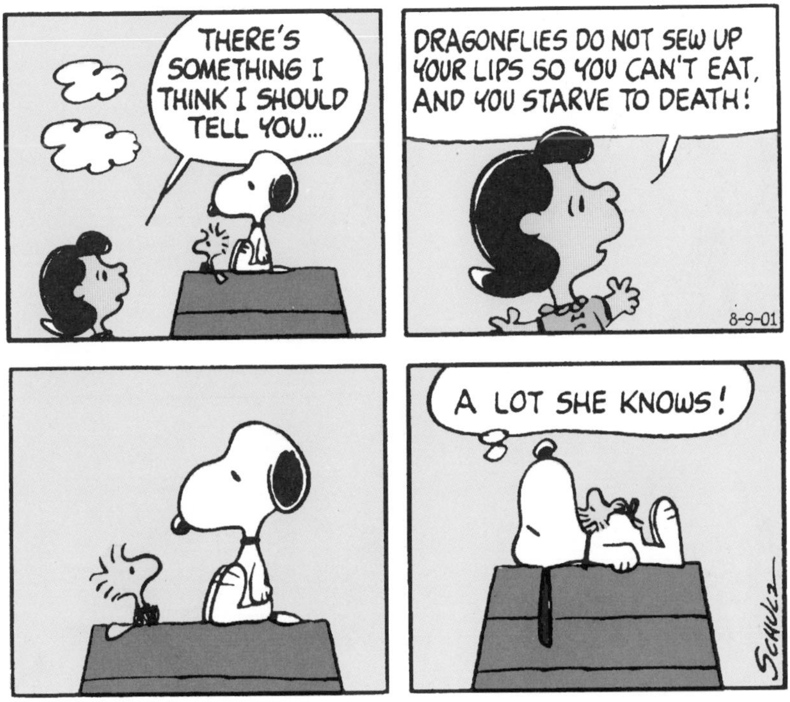
THERE'S SOMETHING I THINK I SHOULD TELL YOU...
DRAGONFLIES DO NOT SEW UP YOUR LIPS SO YOU CAN'T EAT, AND YOU STARVE TO DEATH!
8-9-01
A LOT SHE KNOWS!
SCHULZ

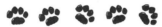

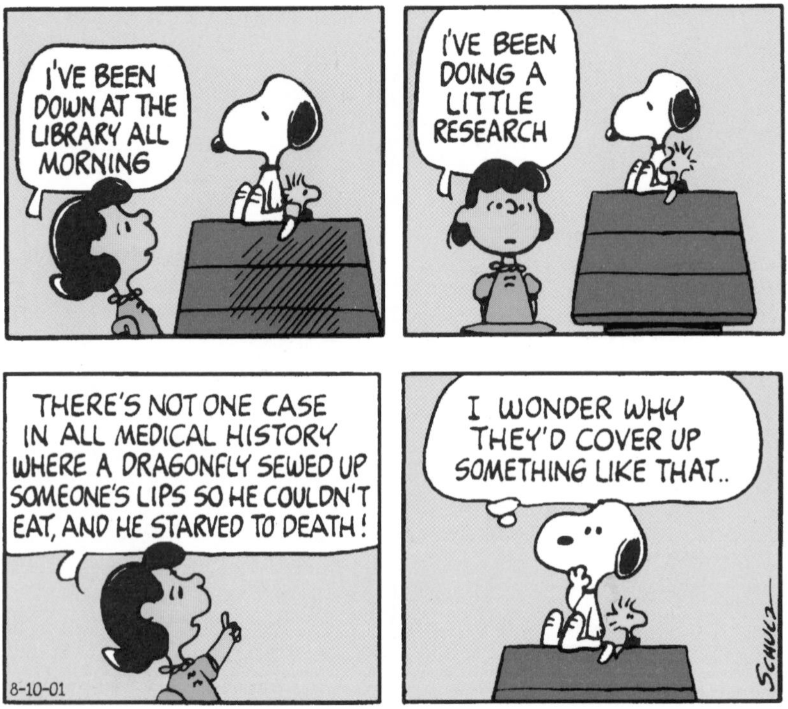
I'VE BEEN DOWN AT THE LIBRARY ALL MORNING
I'VE BEEN DOING A LITTLE RESEARCH
THERE'S NOT ONE CASE IN ALL MEDICAL HISTORY WHERE A DRAGONFLY SEWED UP SOMEONE'S LIPS SO HE COULDN'T EAT, AND HE STARVED TO DEATH!
8-10-01
I WONDER WHY THEY'D COVER UP SOMETHING LIKE THAT..
SCHULZ

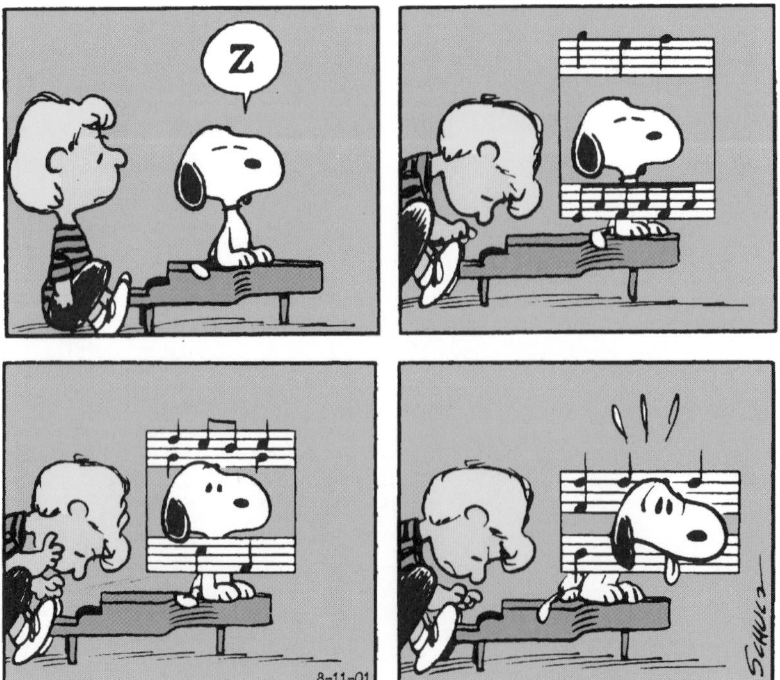
Z
8-11-01
SCHULZ

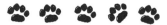

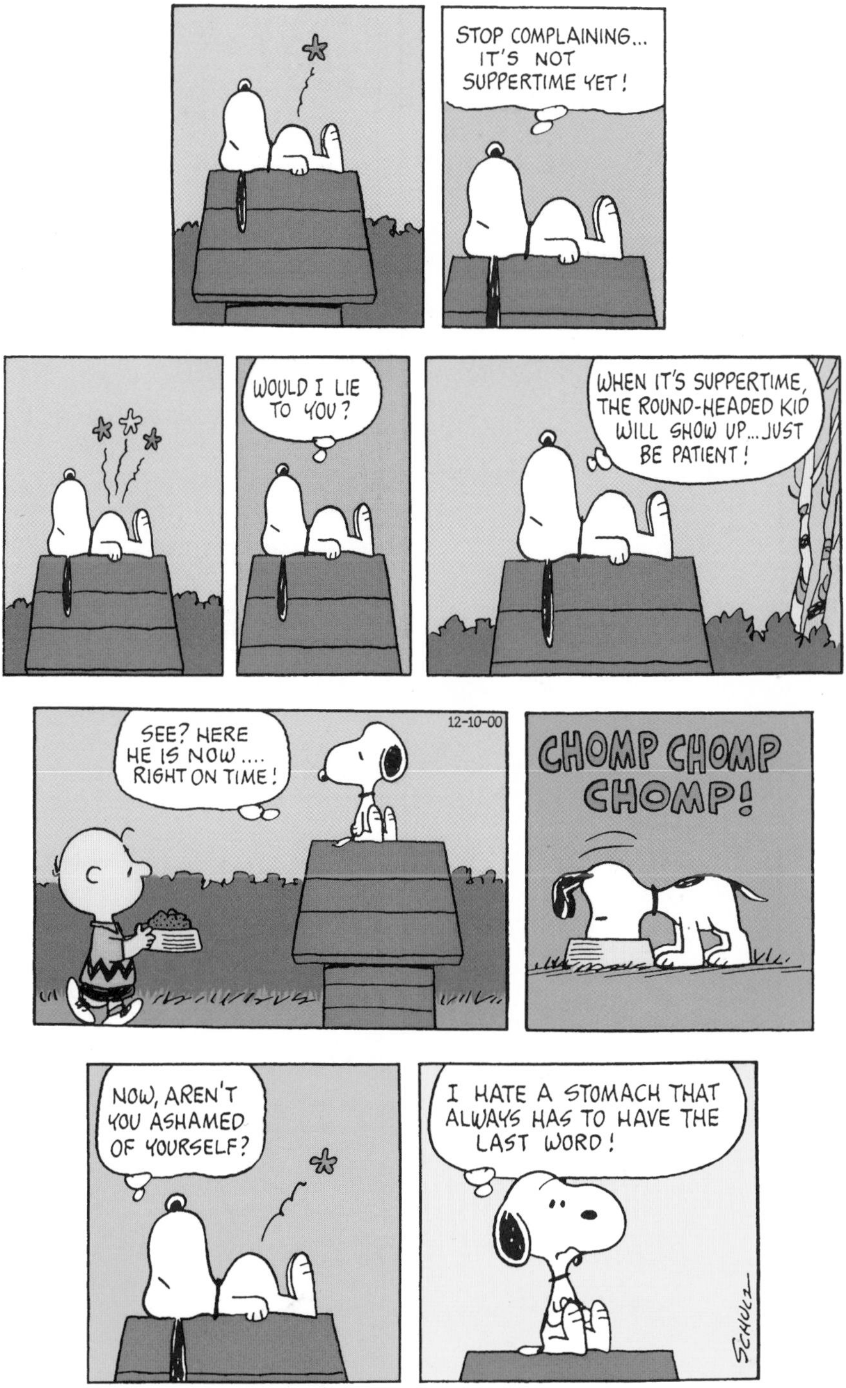
STOP COMPLAINING... IT'S NOT SUPPERTIME YET!
WOULD I LIE TO YOU?
WHEN IT'S SUPPERTIME, THE ROUND-HEADED KID WILL SHOW UP... JUST BE PATIENT!
SEE? HERE HE IS NOW.... RIGHT ON TIME!
12-10-00
CHOMP CHOMP CHOMP!
NOW, AREN'T YOU ASHAMED OF YOURSELF?
I HATE A STOMACH THAT ALWAYS HAS TO HAVE THE LAST WORD!
SCHULZ

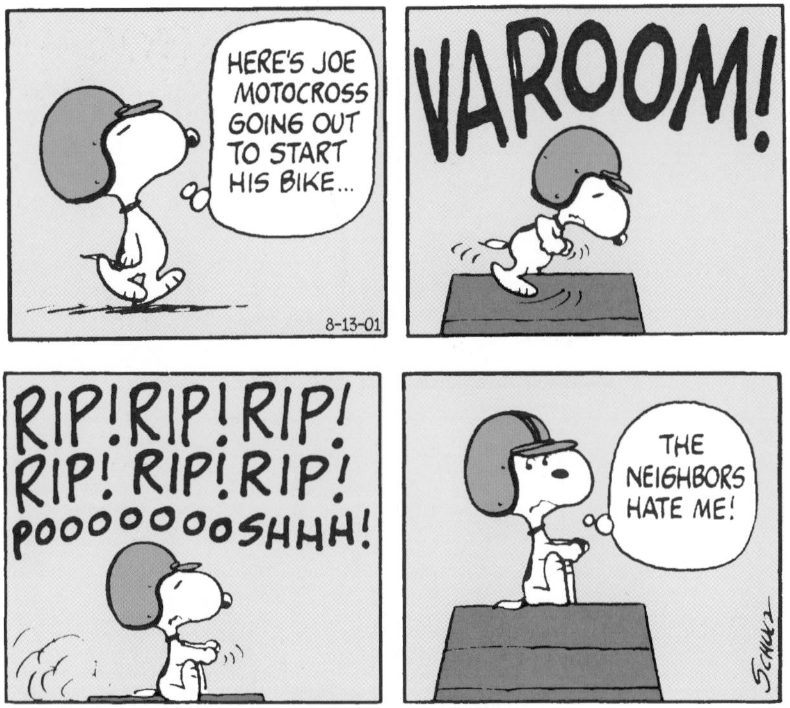
HERE'S JOE MOTOCROSS GOING OUT TO START HIS BIKE...
8-13-01
VAROOM!
RIP! RIP! RIP! RIP! RIP! RIP!
POOOOOOOOSHHH!
THE NEIGHBORS HATE ME!
SCHULZ

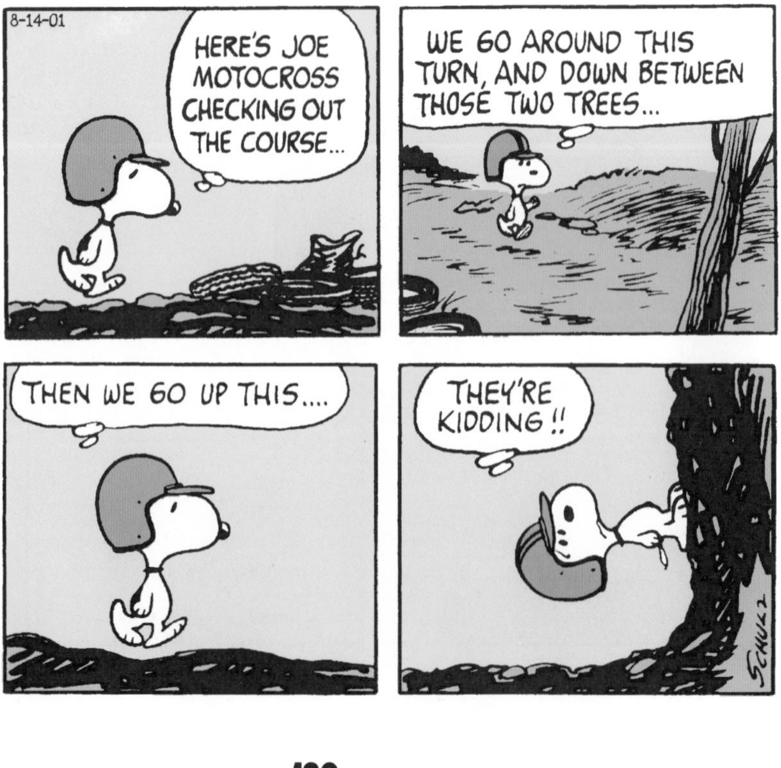
8-14-01
HERE'S JOE MOTOCROSS CHECKING OUT THE COURSE...
WE GO AROUND THIS TURN, AND DOWN BETWEEN THOSE TWO TREES...
THEN WE GO UP THIS....
THEY'RE KIDDING!!
SCHULZ

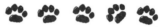

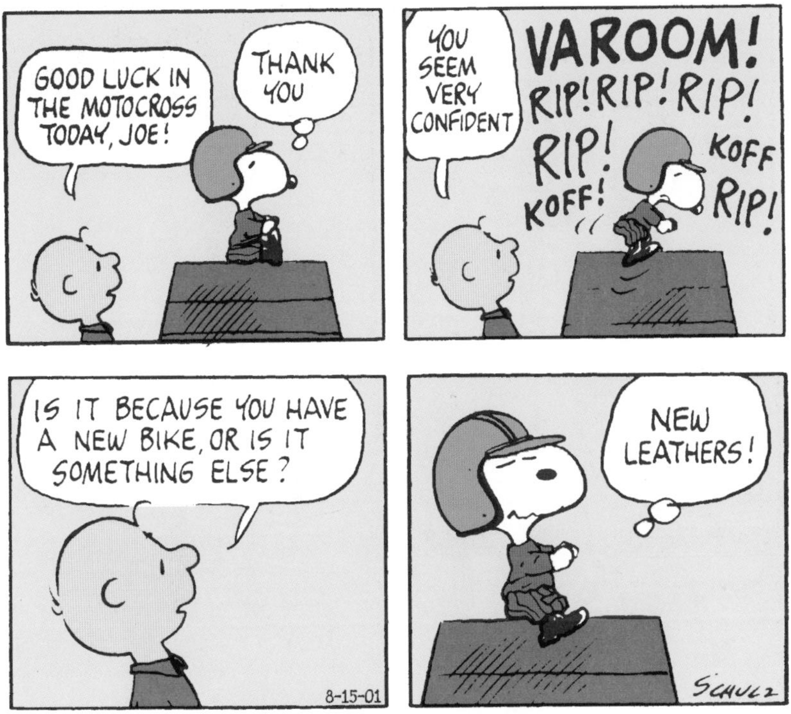

GOOD LUCK IN THE MOTOCROSS TODAY, JOE!
THANK YOU
YOU SEEM VERY CONFIDENT
VAROOM!
RIP! RIP! RIP!
RIP!
KOFF
KOFF!
RIP!
IS IT BECAUSE YOU HAVE A NEW BIKE, OR IS IT SOMETHING ELSE?
8-15-01
NEW LEATHERS!
SCHULZ

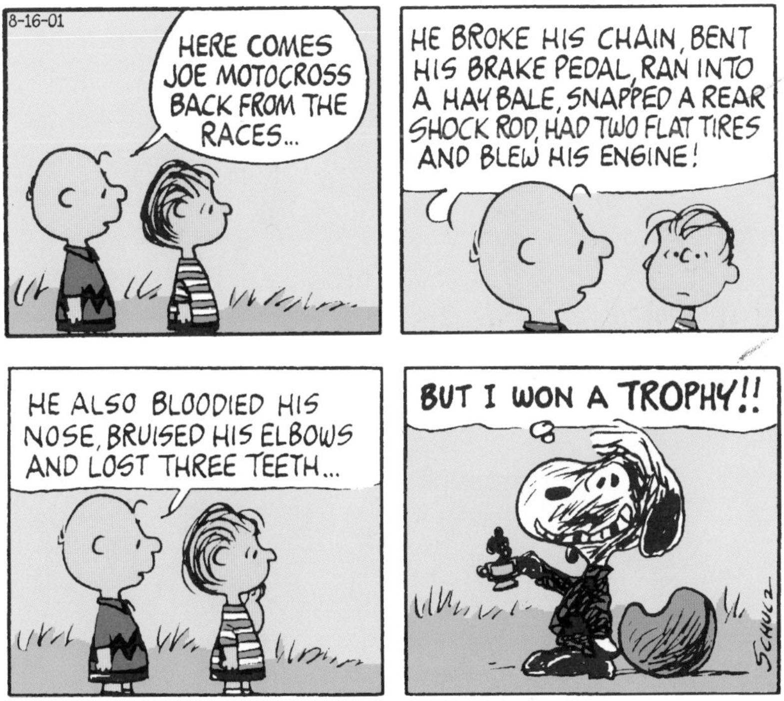

8-16-01
HERE COMES JOE MOTOCROSS BACK FROM THE RACES...
HE BROKE HIS CHAIN, BENT HIS BRAKE PEDAL, RAN INTO A HAY BALE, SNAPPED A REAR SHOCK ROD, HAD TWO FLAT TIRES AND BLEW HIS ENGINE!
HE ALSO BLOODIED HIS NOSE, BRUISED HIS ELBOWS AND LOST THREE TEETH...
BUT I WON A TROPHY!!
SCHULZ

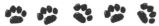

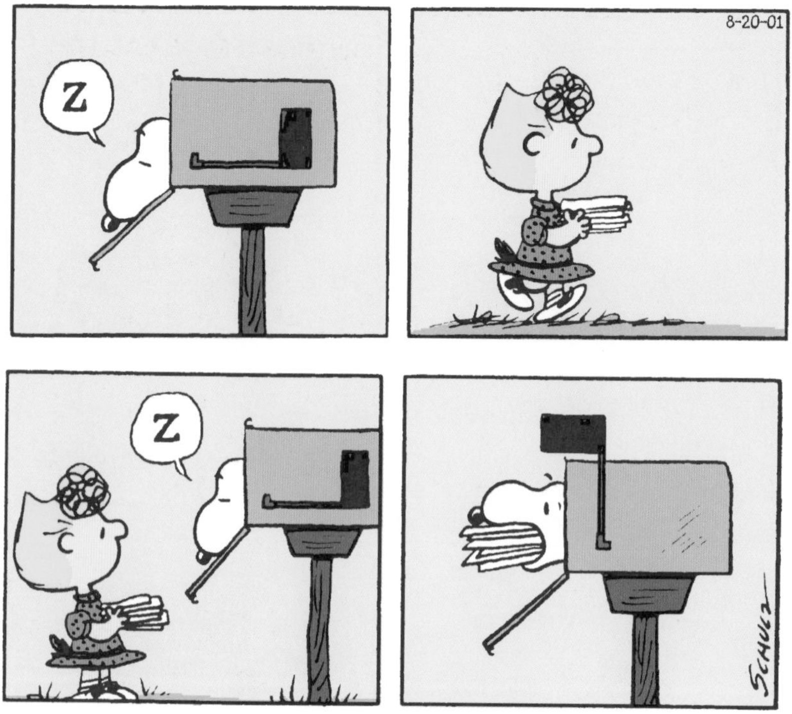

Z
8-20-01
Z

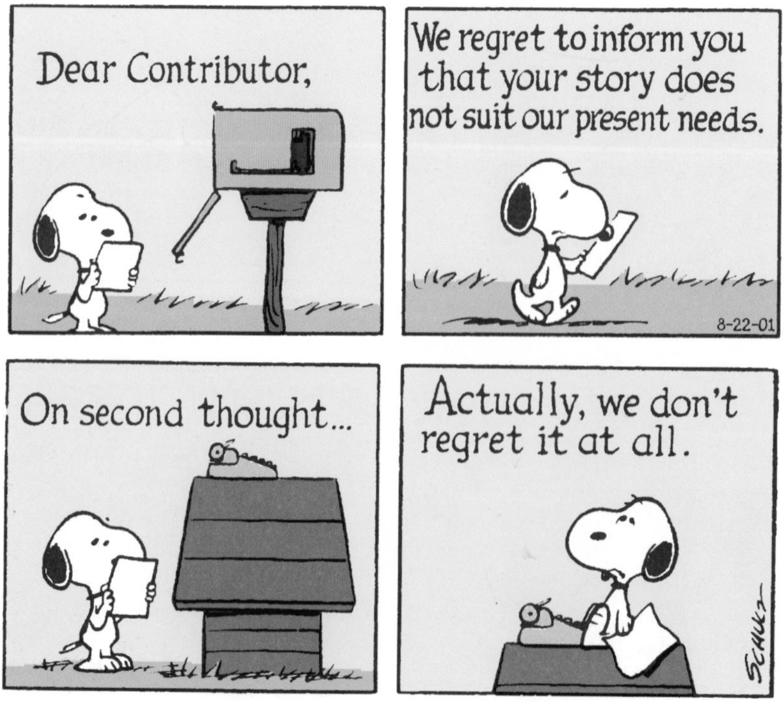

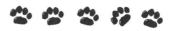

Dear Contributor,
We regret to inform you that your story does not suit our present needs.
8-22-01
On second thought...
Actually, we don't regret it at all.

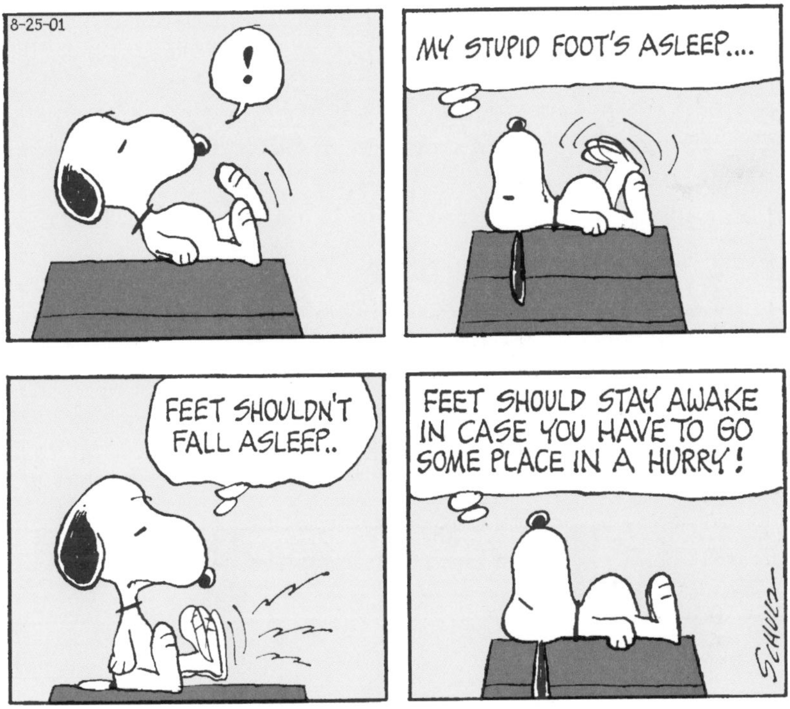
8-25-01
!
MY STUPID FOOT'S ASLEEP....
FEET SHOULDN'T FALL ASLEEP..
FEET SHOULD STAY AWAKE IN CASE YOU HAVE TO GO SOME PLACE IN A HURRY!
SCHULZ

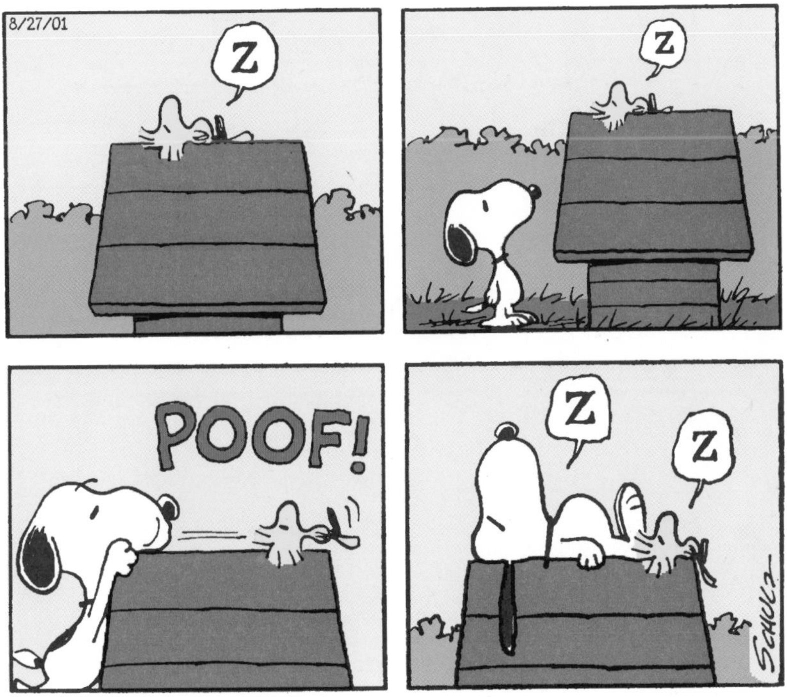
8/27/01
Z
Z
POOF!
Z
Z
SCHULZ

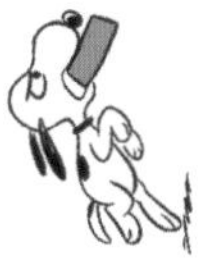

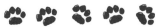

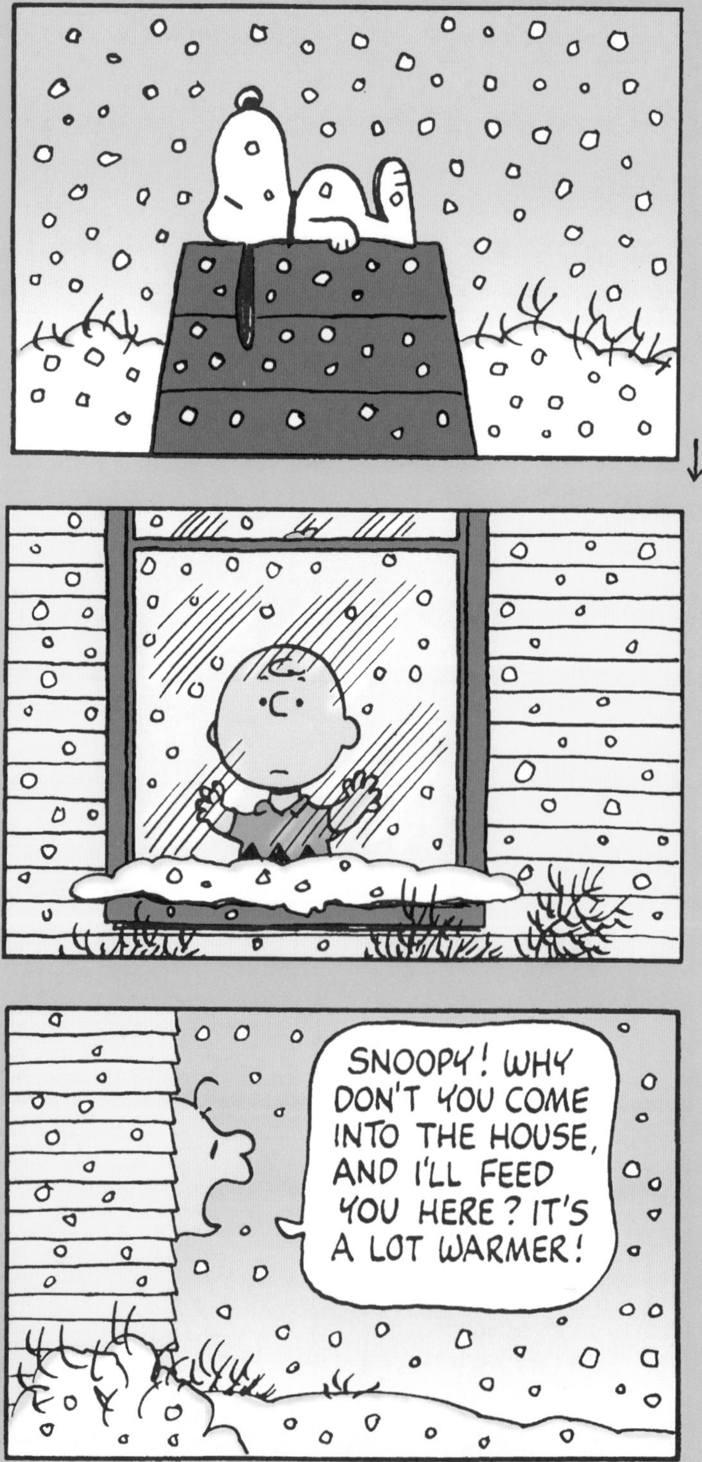
SNOOPY! WHY DON'T YOU COME INTO THE HOUSE, AND I'LL FEED YOU HERE? IT'S A LOT WARMER!

HOW NICE... AN INVITATION TO DINNER..
TAP TAP TAP
12/31/00
WHY DOES HE HAVE TO MAKE A BIG DEAL OUT OF EVERYTHING ?

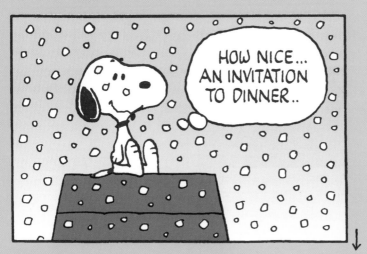

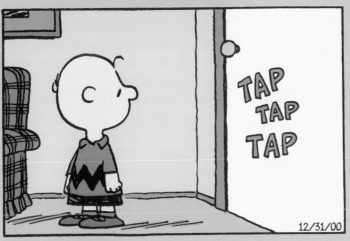

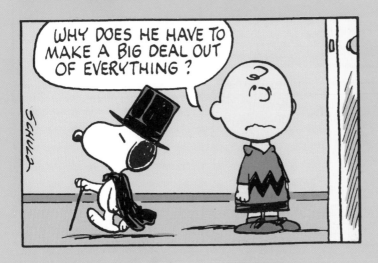

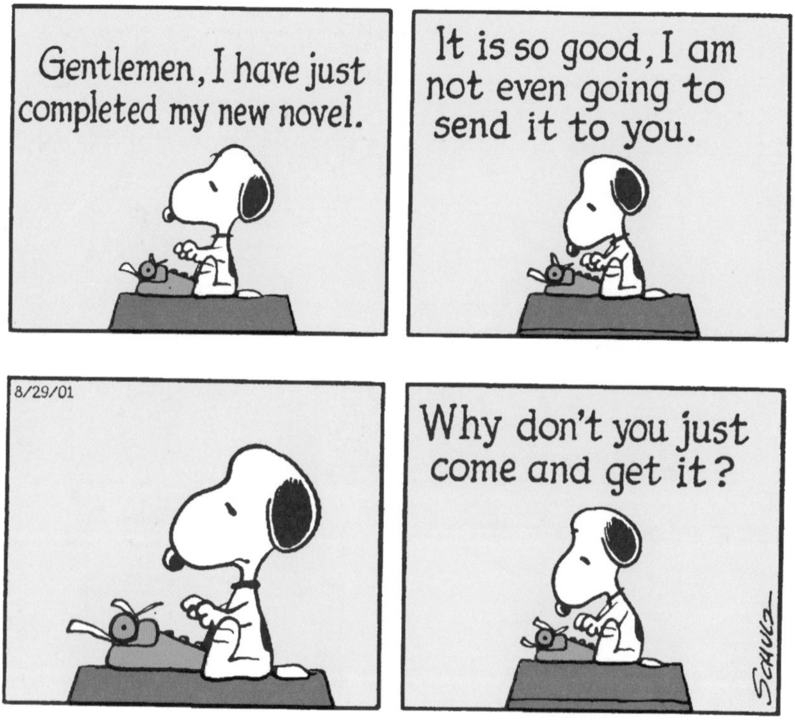
Gentlemen, I have just completed my new novel.
It is so good, I am not even going to send it to you.
8/29/01
Why don't you just come and get it?

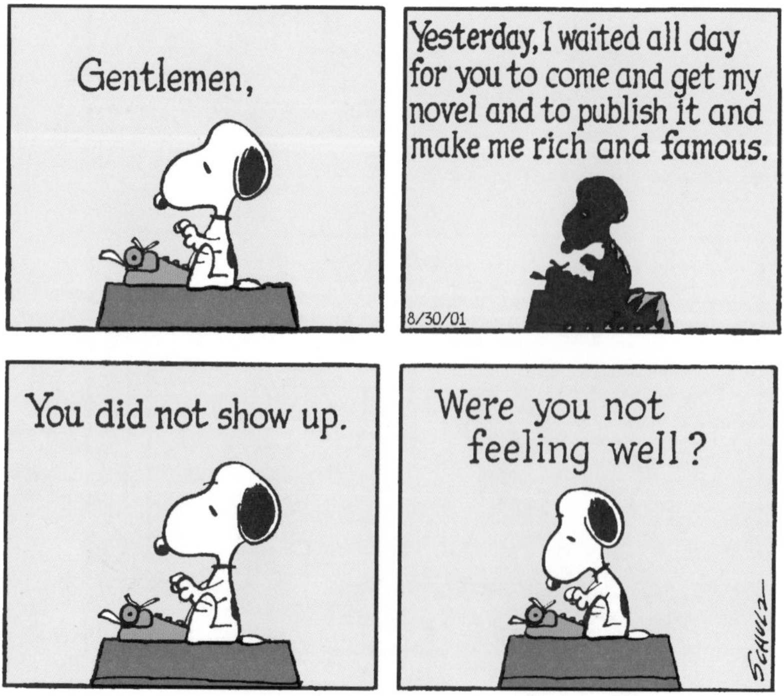
Gentlemen,
Yesterday, I waited all day for you to come and get my novel and to publish it and make me rich and famous.
8/30/01
You did not show up.
Were you not feeling well?

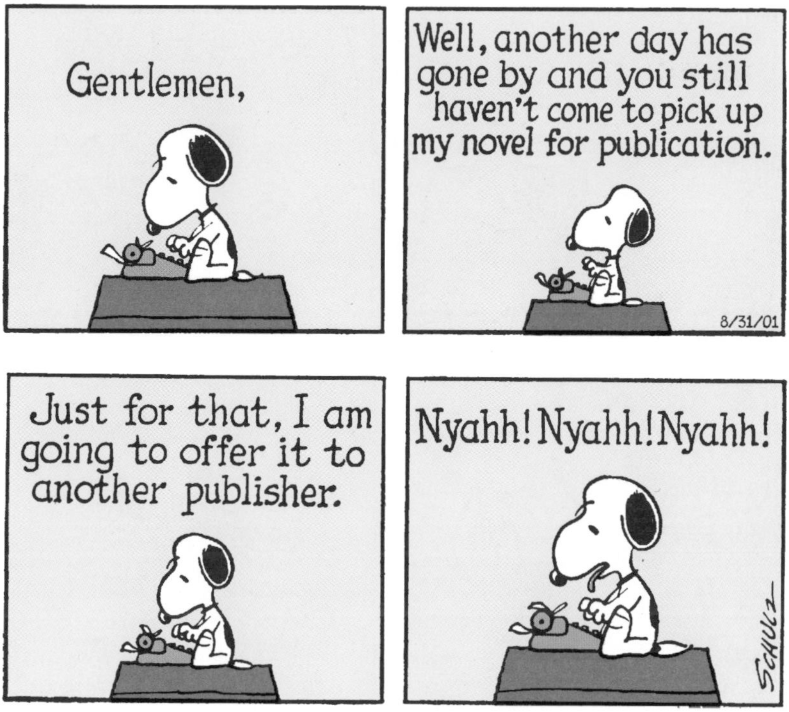
Gentlemen,
Well, another day has gone by and you still haven't come to pick up my novel for publication.
8/31/01
Just for that, I am going to offer it to another publisher.
Nyahh! Nyahh! Nyahh!
SCHULZ

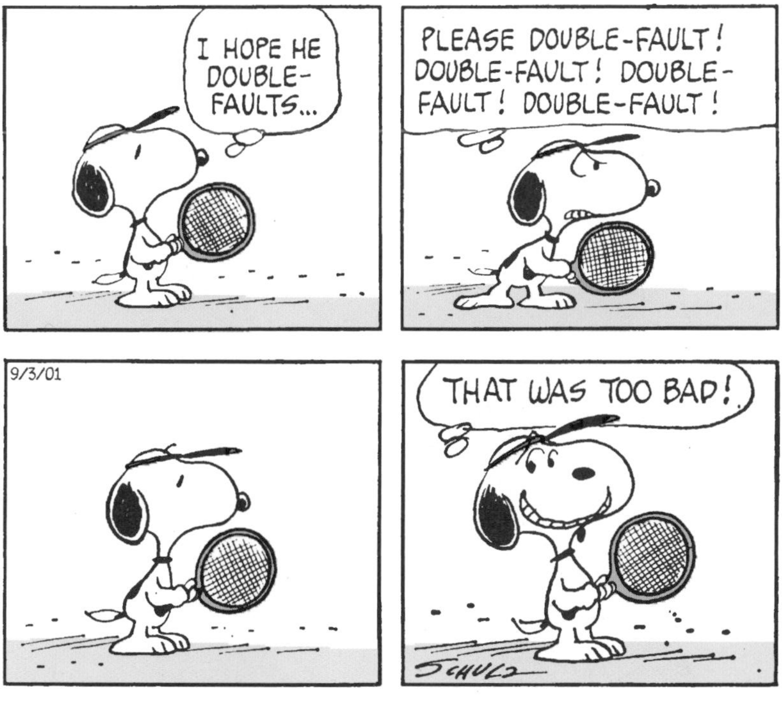
I HOPE HE DOUBLE-FAULTS...
PLEASE DOUBLE-FAULT! DOUBLE-FAULT! DOUBLE-FAULT! DOUBLE-FAULT!
9/3/01
THAT WAS TOO BAD!
SCHULZ

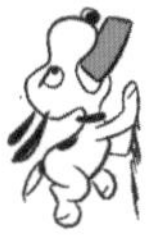

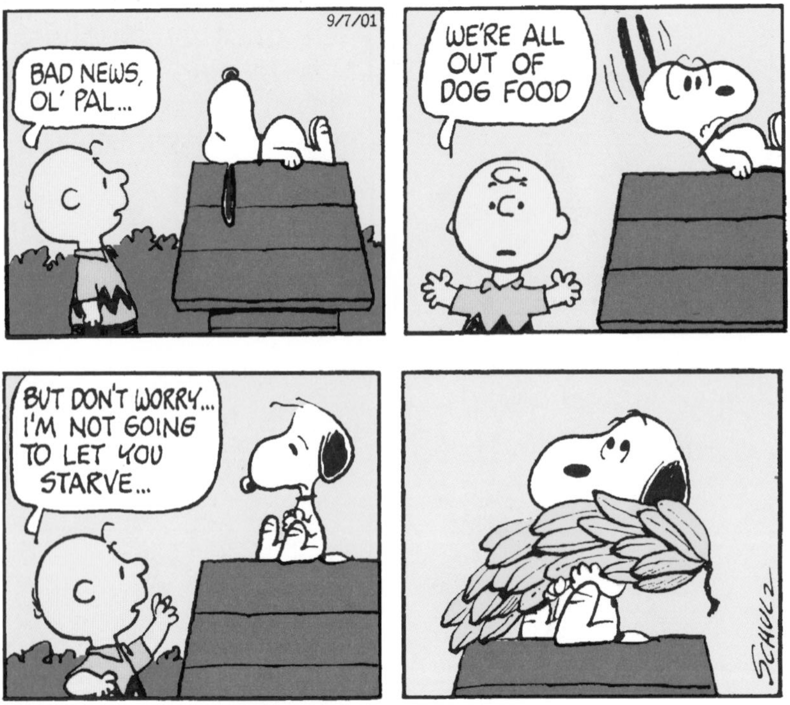
9/7/01
BAD NEWS, OL' PAL...
WE'RE ALL OUT OF DOG FOOD
BUT DON'T WORRY... I'M NOT GOING TO LET YOU STARVE...
SCHULZ

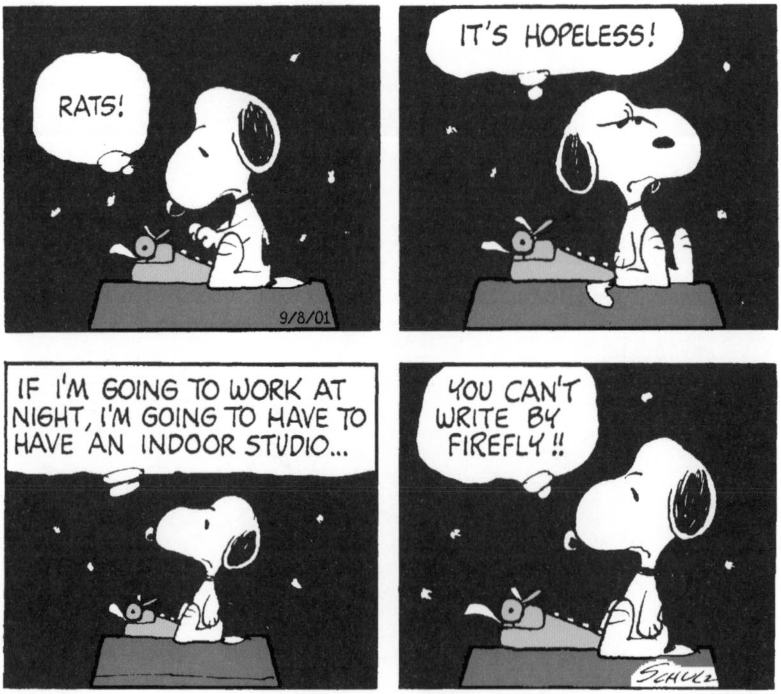
RATS!
9/8/01
IT'S HOPELESS!
IF I'M GOING TO WORK AT NIGHT, I'M GOING TO HAVE TO HAVE AN INDOOR STUDIO...
YOU CAN'T WRITE BY FIREFLY !!
SCHULZ

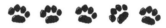

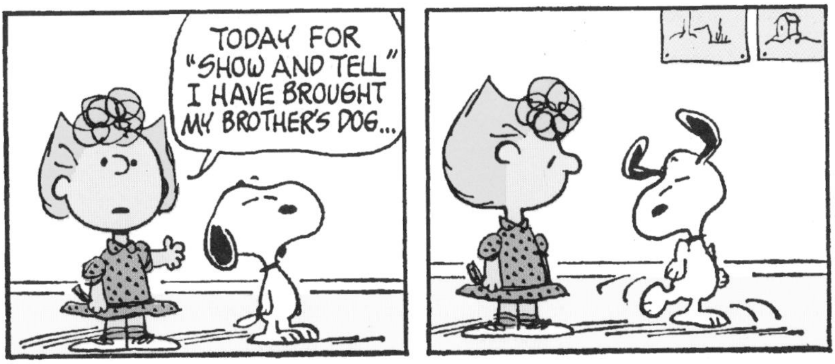
TODAY FOR "SHOW AND TELL" I HAVE BROUGHT MY BROTHER'S DOG...

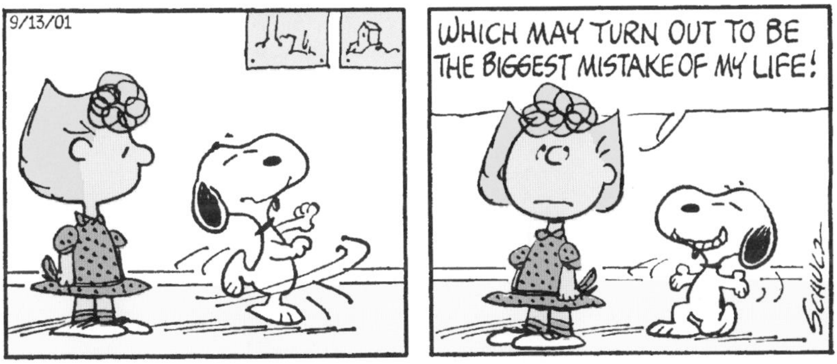
9/13/01
WHICH MAY TURN OUT TO BE THE BIGGEST MISTAKE OF MY LIFE!
SCHULZ

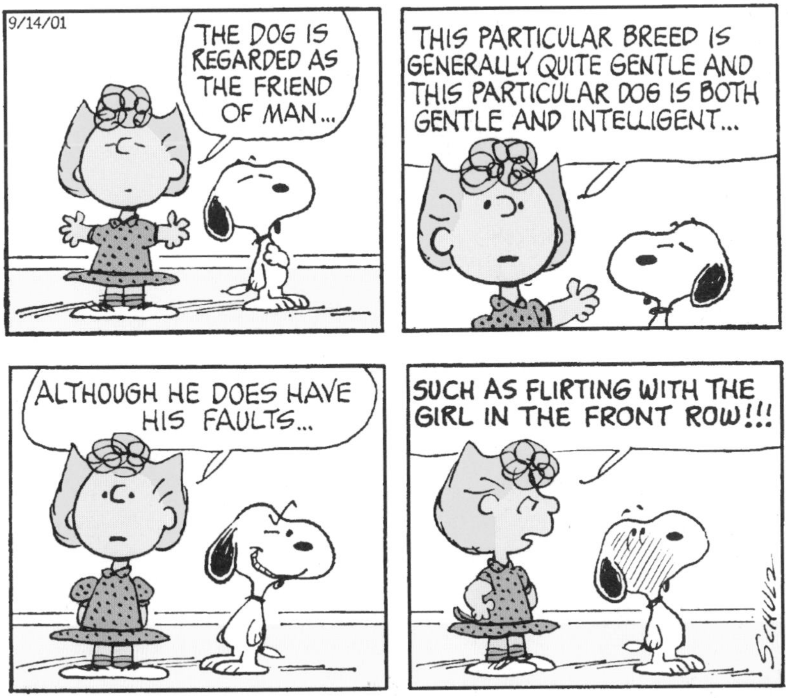
9/14/01
THE DOG IS REGARDED AS THE FRIEND OF MAN...
THIS PARTICULAR BREED IS GENERALLY QUITE GENTLE AND THIS PARTICULAR DOG IS BOTH GENTLE AND INTELLIGENT...
ALTHOUGH HE DOES HAVE HIS FAULTS...
SUCH AS FLIRTING WITH THE GIRL IN THE FRONT ROW!!!
SCHULZ

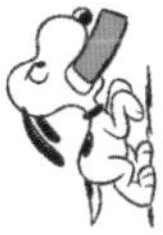

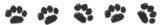

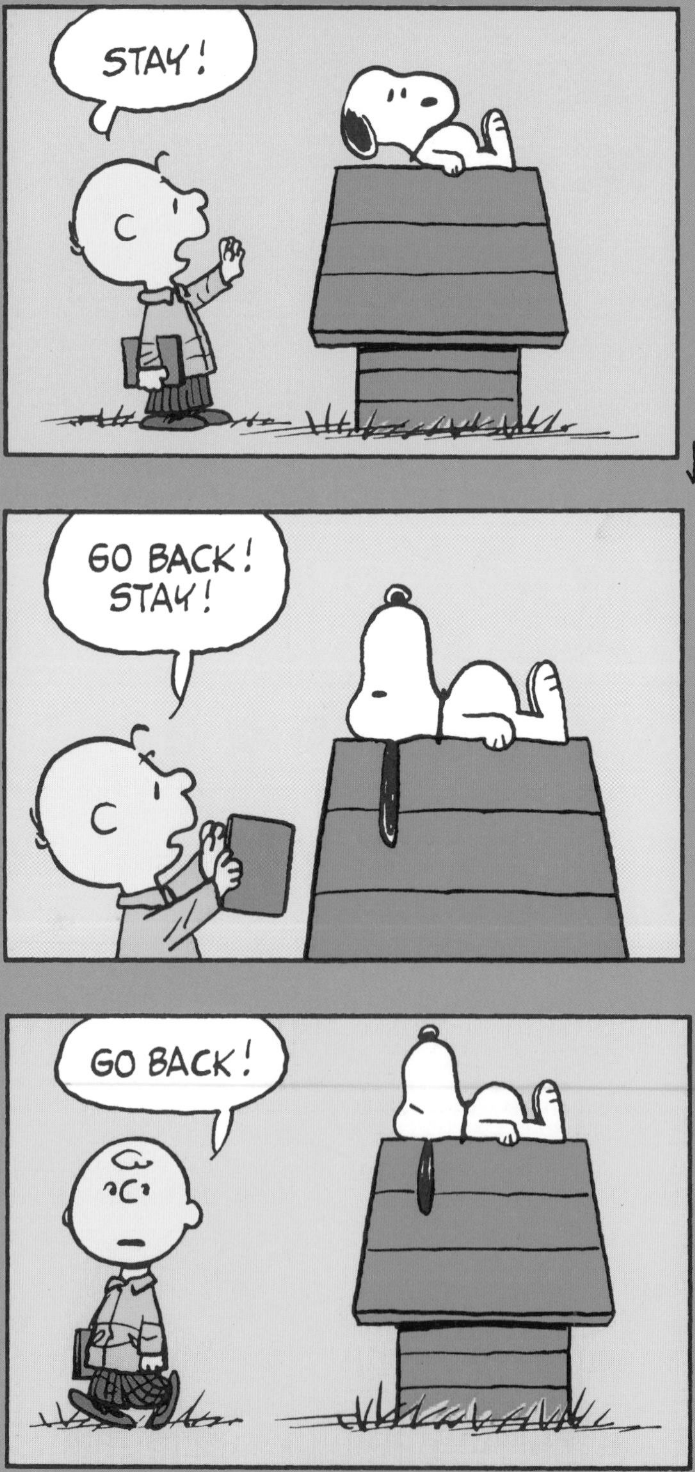
STAY!
GO BACK! STAY!
GO BACK!

BACK, I SAY! BACK!
SIGH SOME KIDS HAVE DOGS WHO TRY TO FOLLOW THEM TO SCHOOL...
1-14-01
SCHULZ

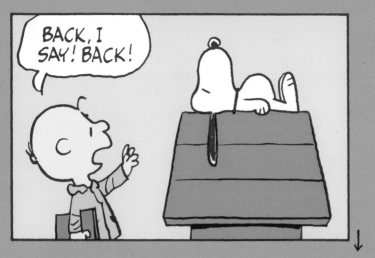

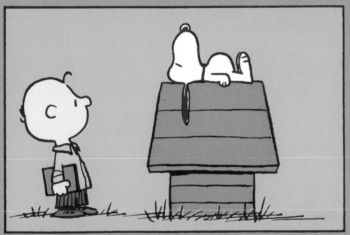

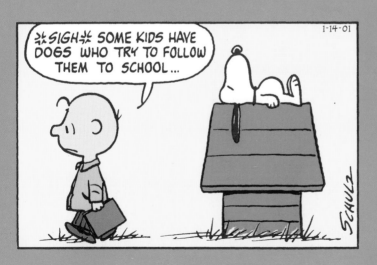

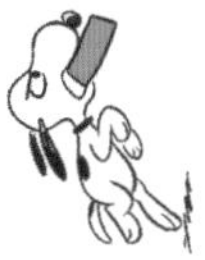

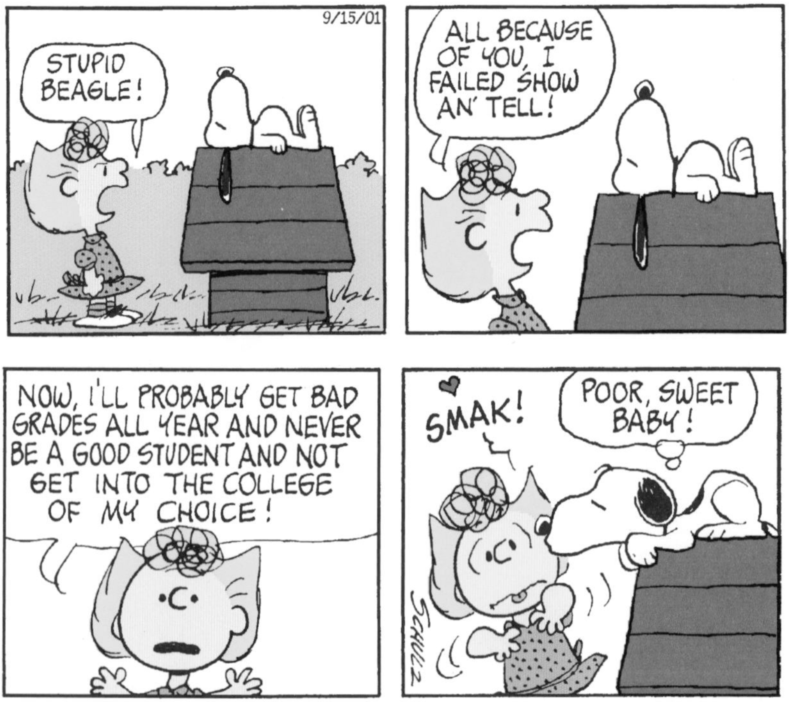
9/15/01
STUPID BEAGLE!
ALL BECAUSE OF YOU, I FAILED SHOW AN' TELL!
NOW, I'LL PROBABLY GET BAD GRADES ALL YEAR AND NEVER BE A GOOD STUDENT AND NOT GET INTO THE COLLEGE OF MY CHOICE!
SMAK!
POOR, SWEET BABY!
SCHULZ

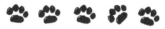

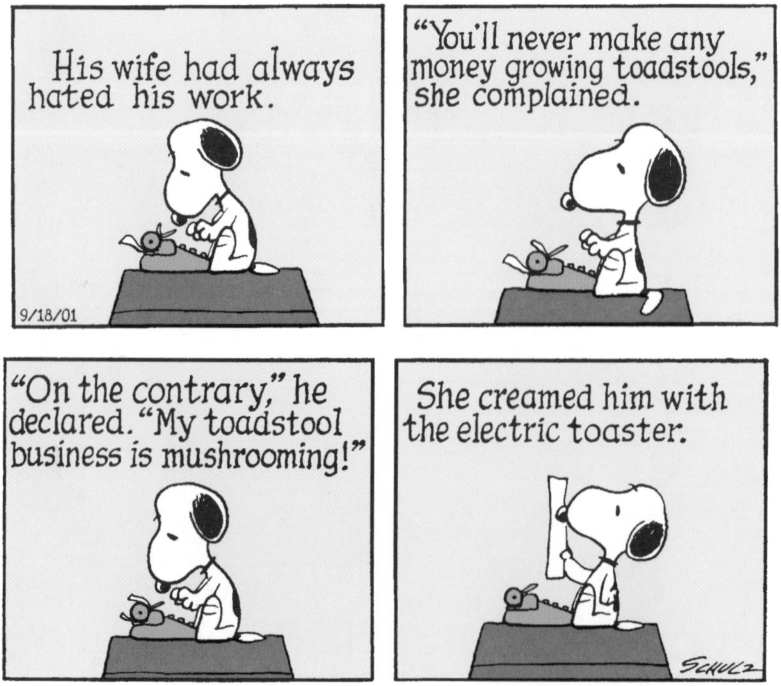
His wife had always hated his work.
9/18/01
"You'll never make any money growing toadstools," she complained.
"On the contrary," he declared. "My toadstool business is mushrooming!"
She creamed him with the electric toaster.
SCHULZ

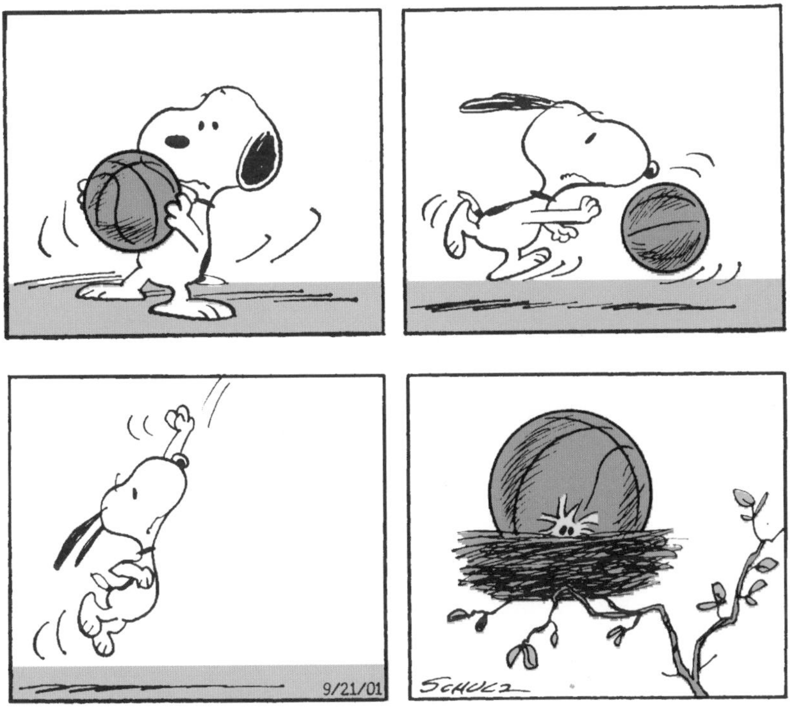
9/21/01
SCHULZ

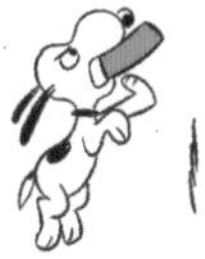

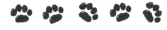

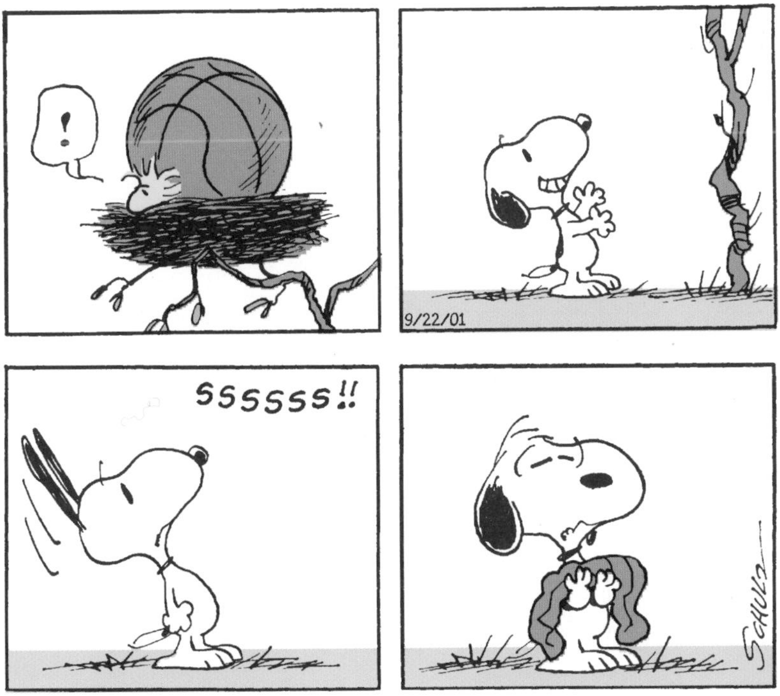
!
9/22/01
SSSSSS!!
SCHULZ

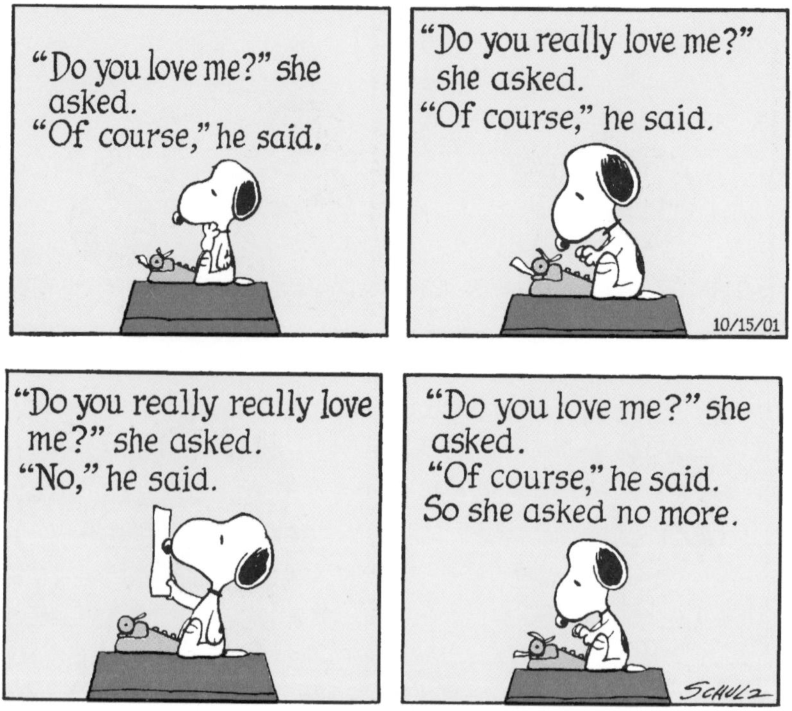
"Do you love me?" she asked.
"Of course," he said.
"Do you really love me?" she asked.
"Of course," he said.
10/15/01
"Do you really really love me?" she asked.
"No," he said.
"Do you love me?" she asked.
"Of course," he said.
So she asked no more.
SCHULZ

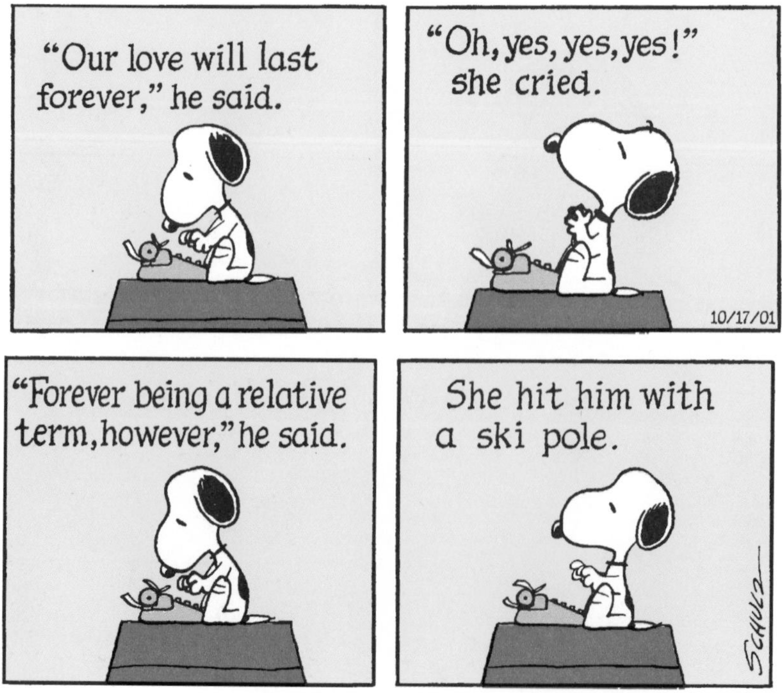
"Our love will last forever," he said.
"Oh, yes, yes, yes!" she cried.
10/17/01
"Forever being a relative term, however," he said.
She hit him with a ski pole.
SCHULZ

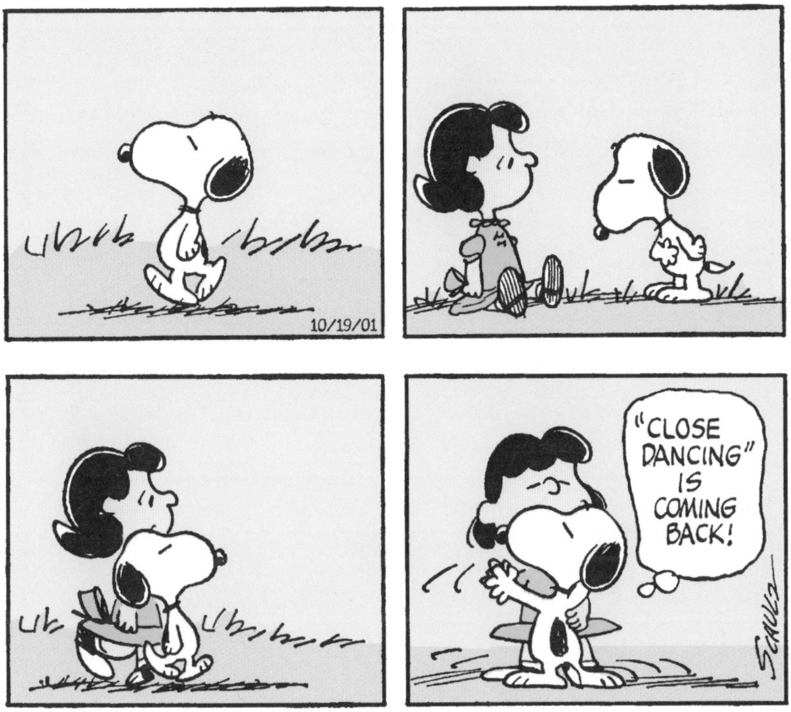
10/19/01
"CLOSE DANCING" IS COMING BACK!
SCHULZ

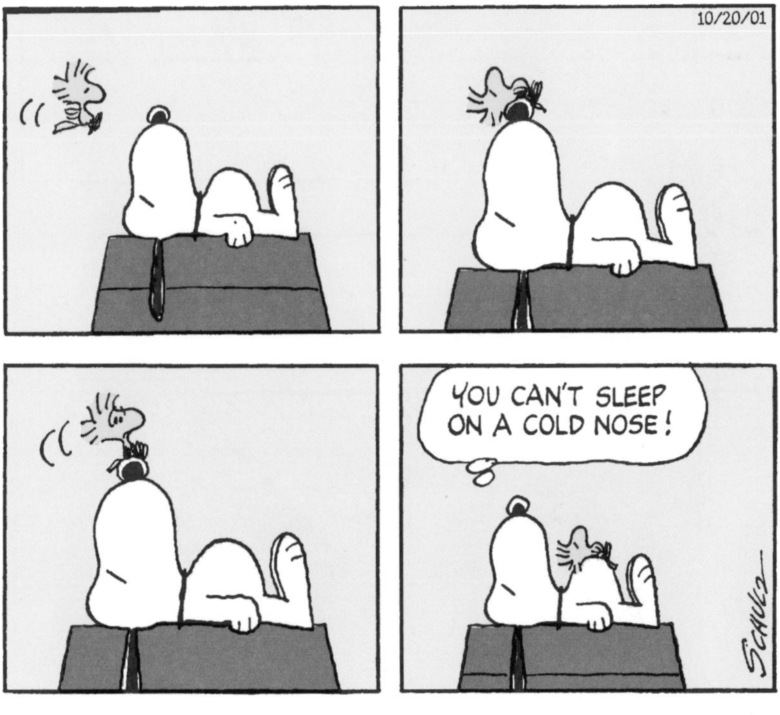
10/20/01
YOU CAN'T SLEEP ON A COLD NOSE!
SCHULZ

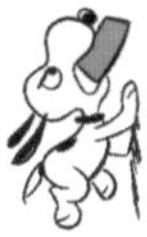

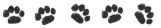

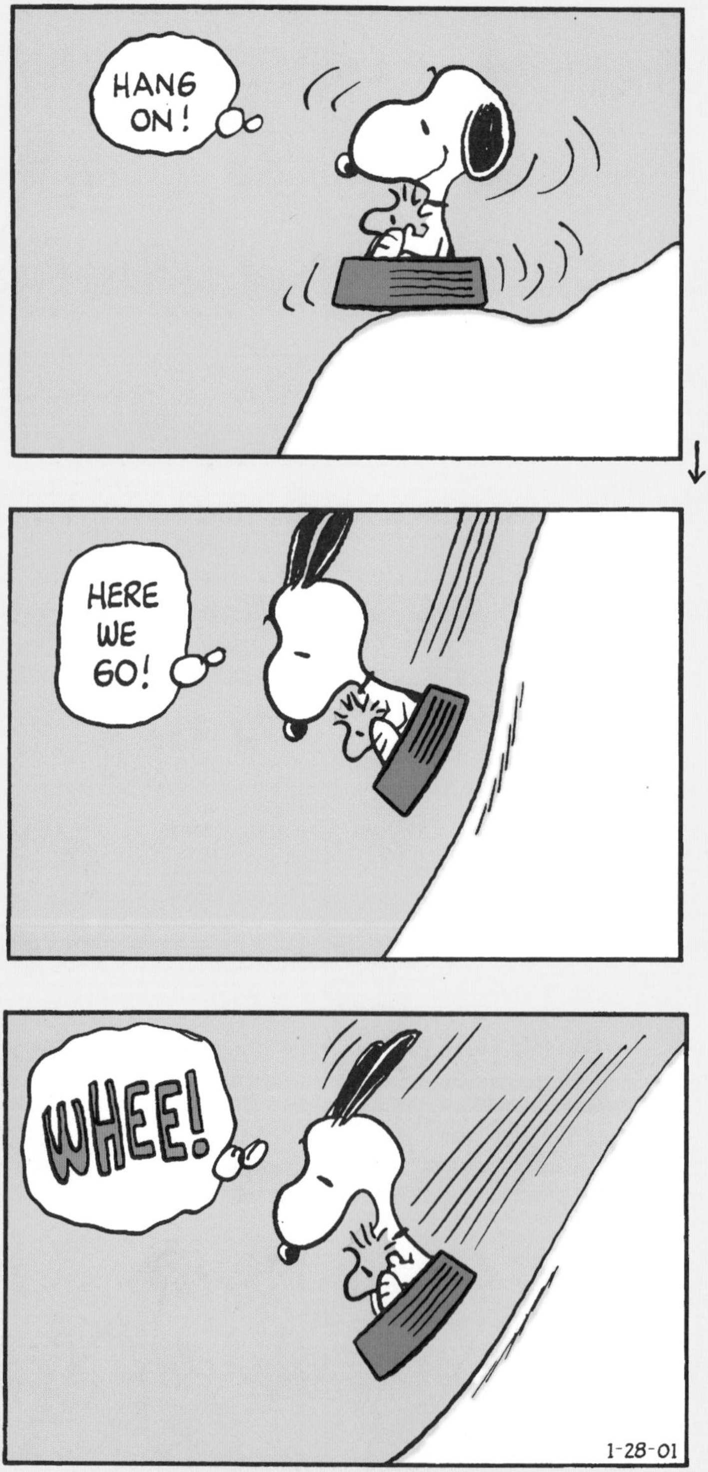
HANG ON!
HERE WE GO!
WHEE!
1-28-01

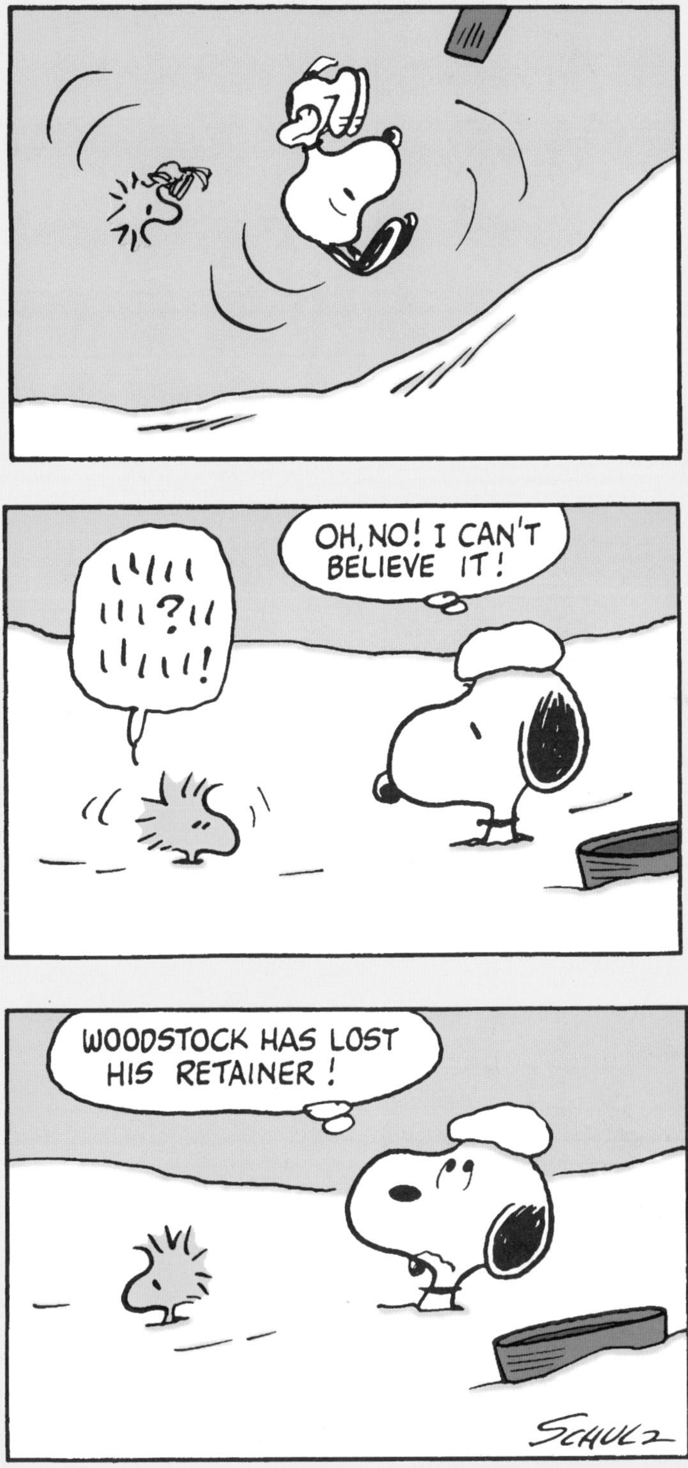
OH, NO! I CAN'T BELIEVE IT!
WOODSTOCK HAS LOST HIS RETAINER!
SCHULZ

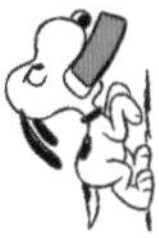

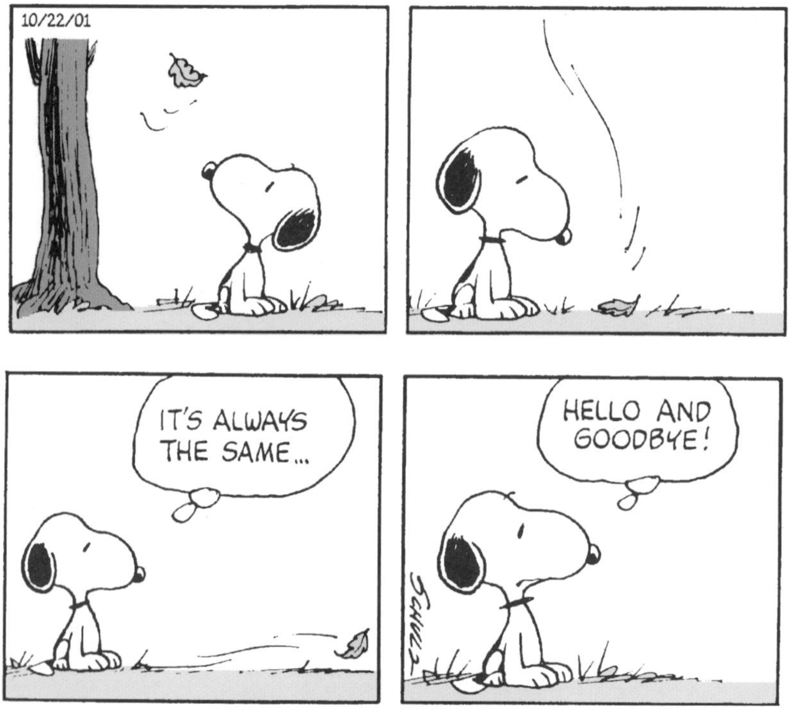
10/22/01
IT'S ALWAYS THE SAME...
HELLO AND GOODBYE!
SCHULZ

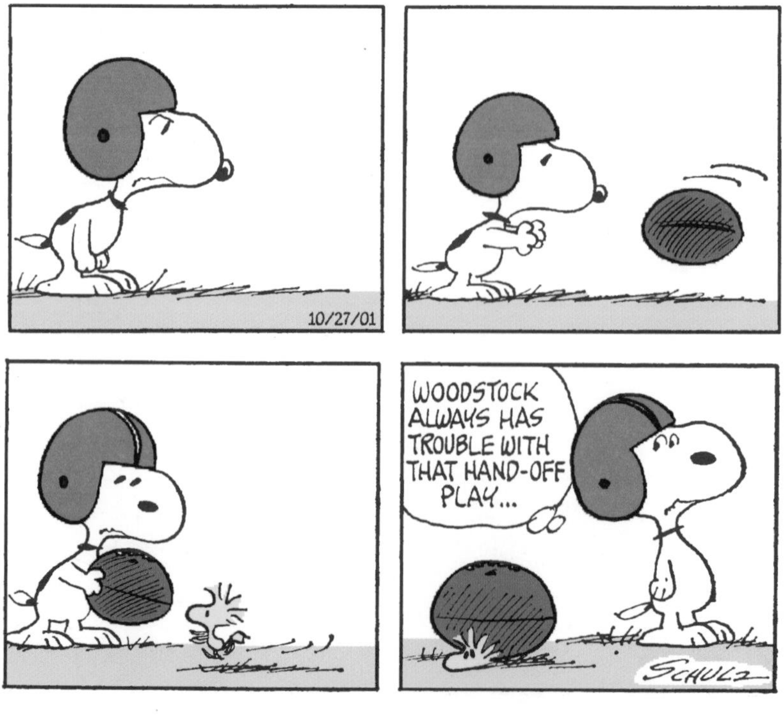
10/27/01
WOODSTOCK ALWAYS HAS TROUBLE WITH THAT HAND-OFF PLAY...
SCHULZ

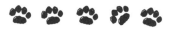

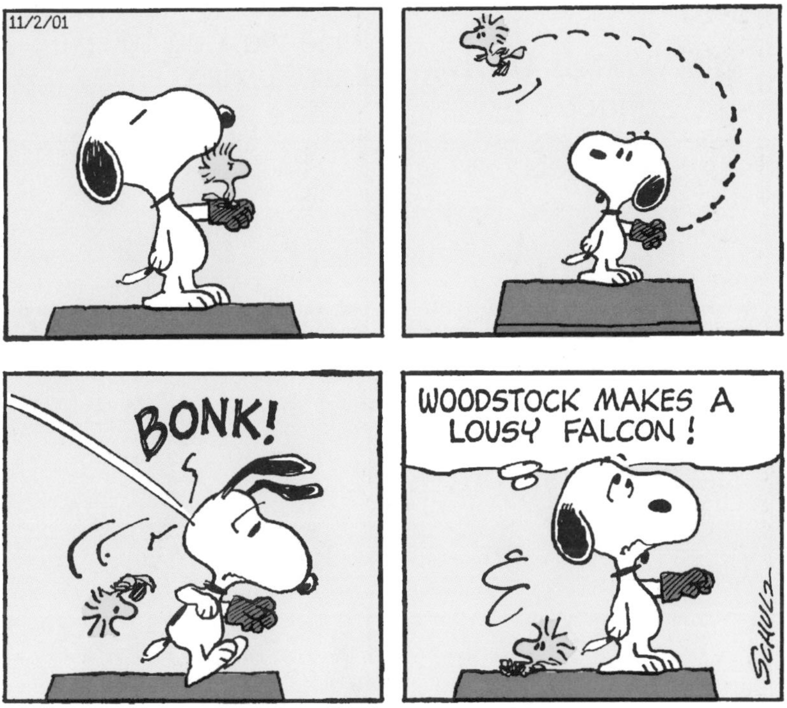
11/2/01
BONK!
WOODSTOCK MAKES A LOUSY FALCON!
SCHULZ

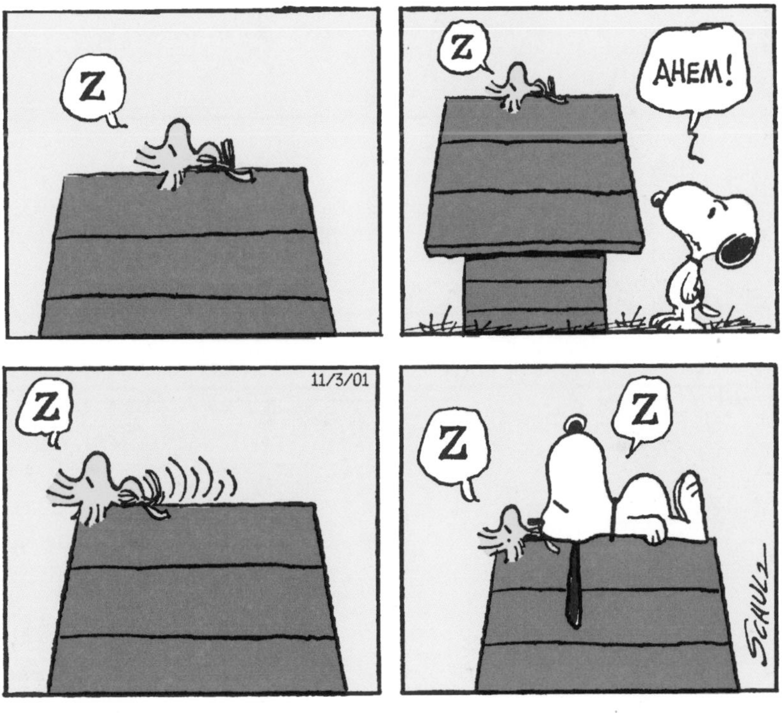
Z
Z
AHEM!
Z
11/3/01
Z
Z
SCHULZ

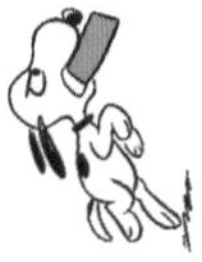

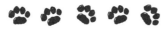

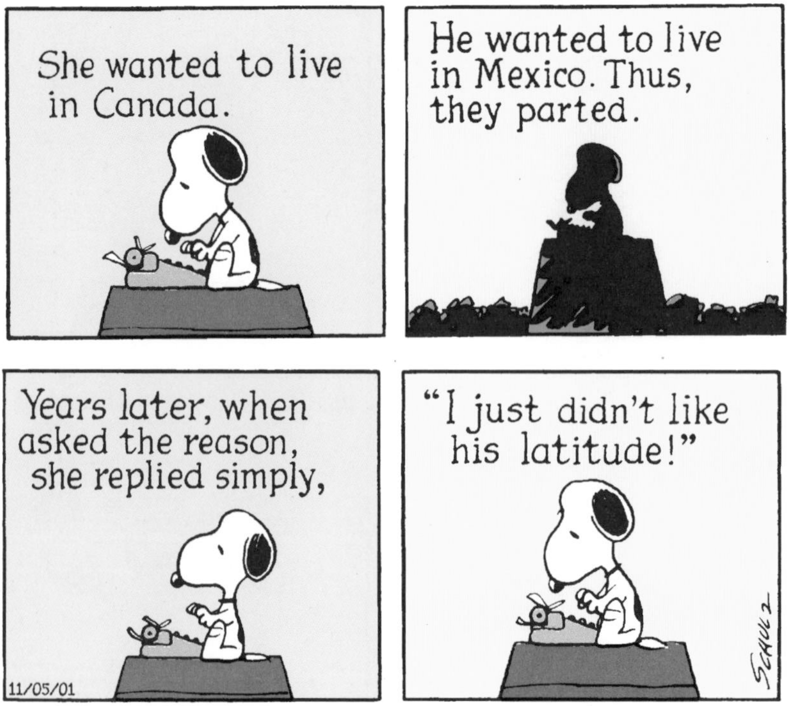
She wanted to live in Canada.
He wanted to live in Mexico. Thus, they parted.
Years later, when asked the reason, she replied simply,
"I just didn't like his latitude!"
11/05/01

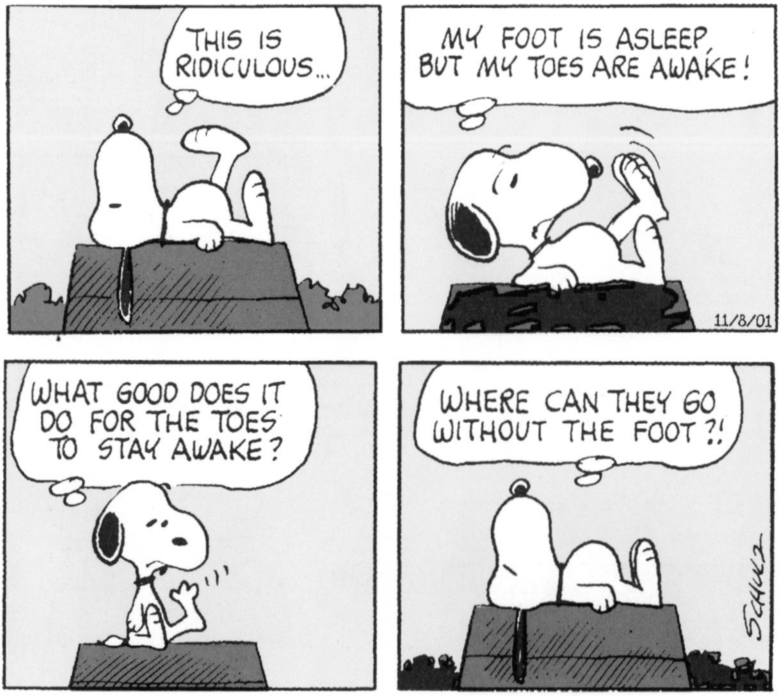
THIS IS RIDICULOUS...
MY FOOT IS ASLEEP, BUT MY TOES ARE AWAKE!
11/8/01
WHAT GOOD DOES IT DO FOR THE TOES TO STAY AWAKE?
WHERE CAN THEY GO WITHOUT THE FOOT?!

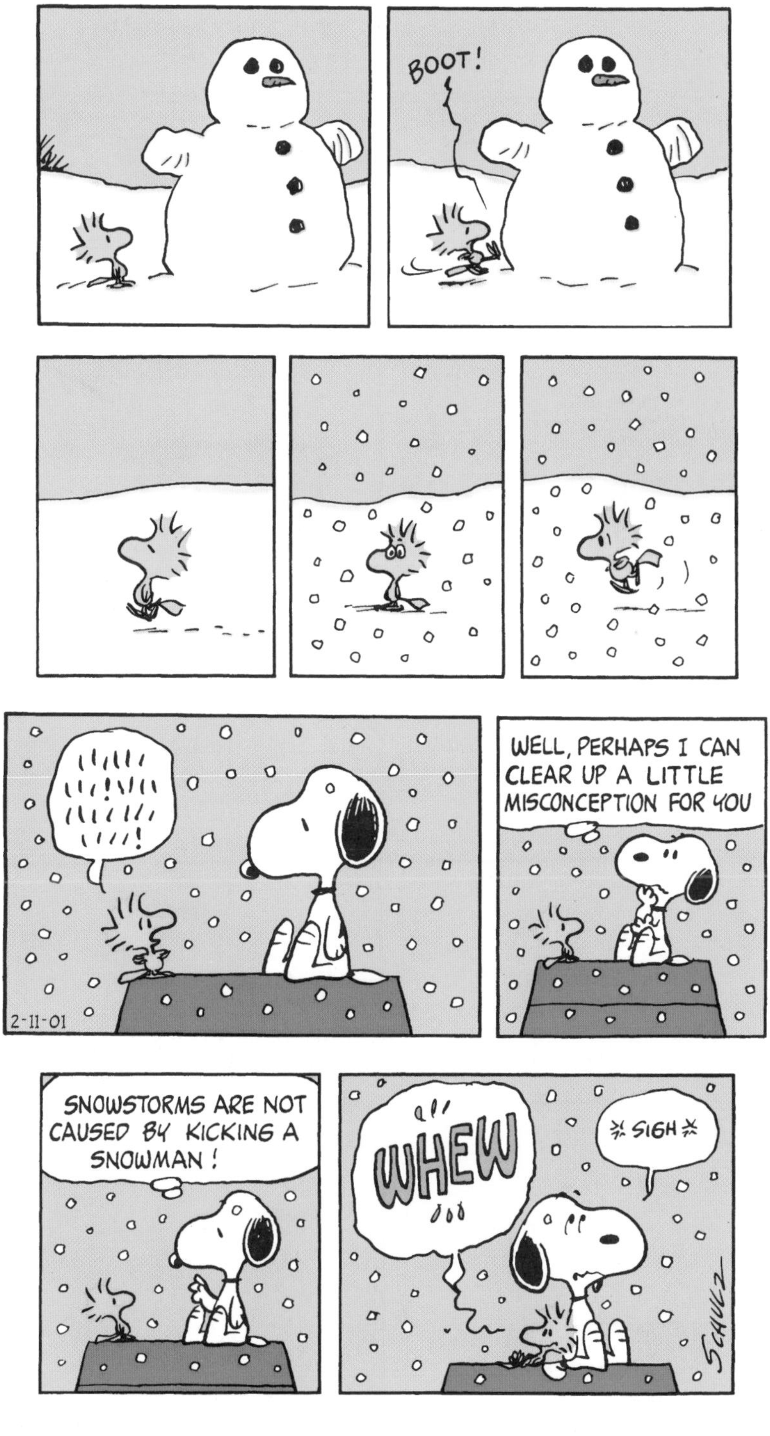
BOOT!
WELL, PERHAPS I CAN CLEAR UP A LITTLE MISCONCEPTION FOR YOU
SNOWSTORMS ARE NOT CAUSED BY KICKING A SNOWMAN!
WHEW
SIGH
2-11-01
SCHULZ

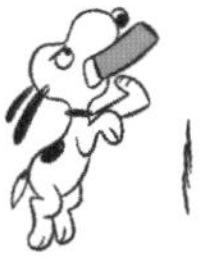

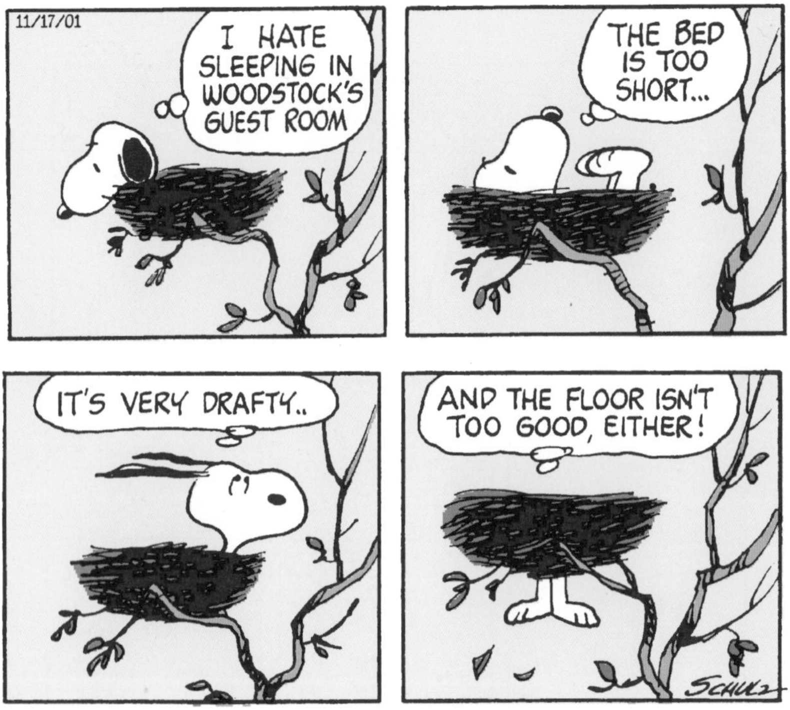
11/17/01
I HATE SLEEPING IN WOODSTOCK'S GUEST ROOM
THE BED IS TOO SHORT...
IT'S VERY DRAFTY..
AND THE FLOOR ISN'T TOO GOOD, EITHER!

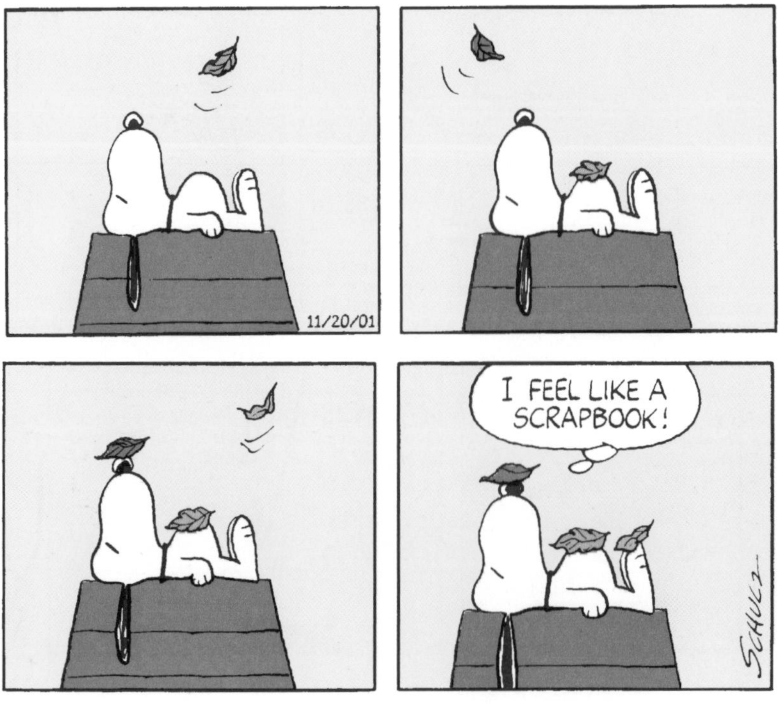
11/20/01
I FEEL LIKE A SCRAPBOOK!

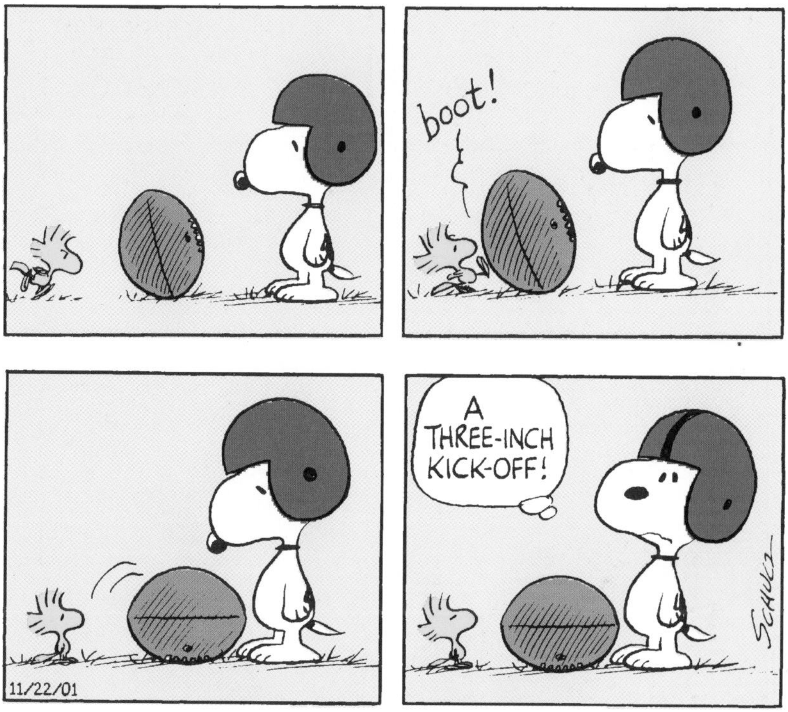
boot!
A THREE-INCH KICK-OFF!
SCHULZ
11/22/01

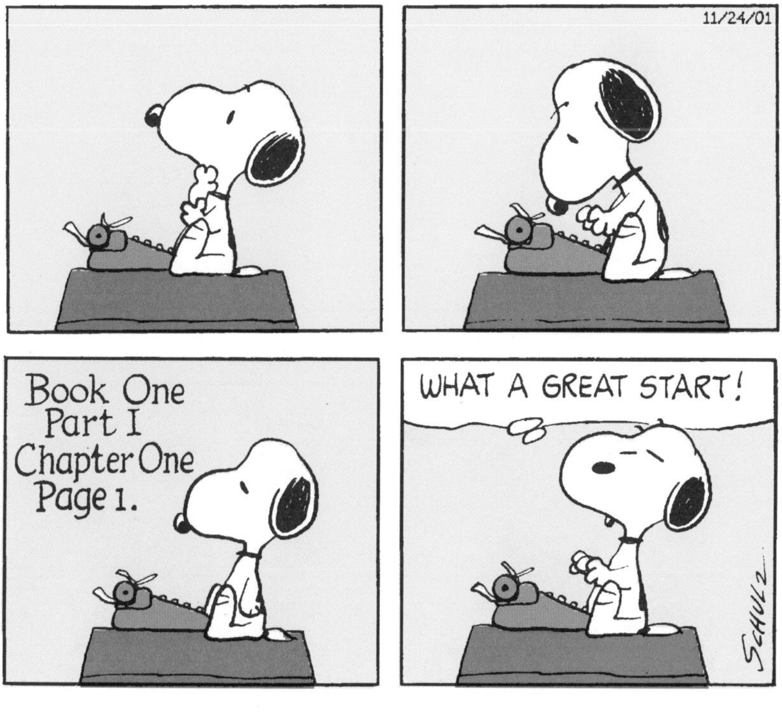
11/24/01
Book One Part I Chapter One Page 1.
WHAT A GREAT START!
SCHULZ

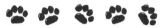

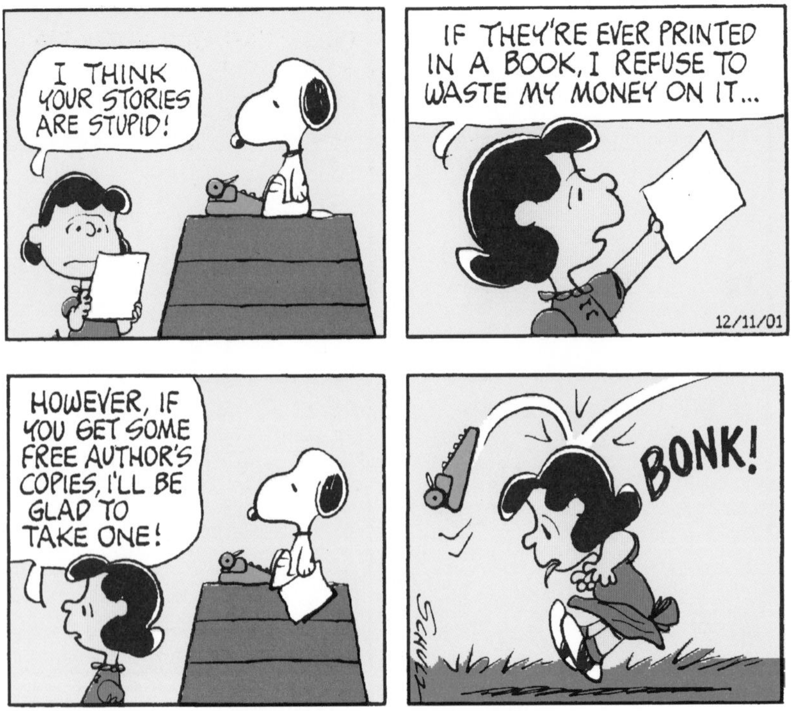
I THINK YOUR STORIES ARE STUPID!
IF THEY'RE EVER PRINTED IN A BOOK, I REFUSE TO WASTE MY MONEY ON IT...
12/11/01
HOWEVER, IF YOU GET SOME FREE AUTHOR'S COPIES, I'LL BE GLAD TO TAKE ONE!
BONK!
SCHULZ

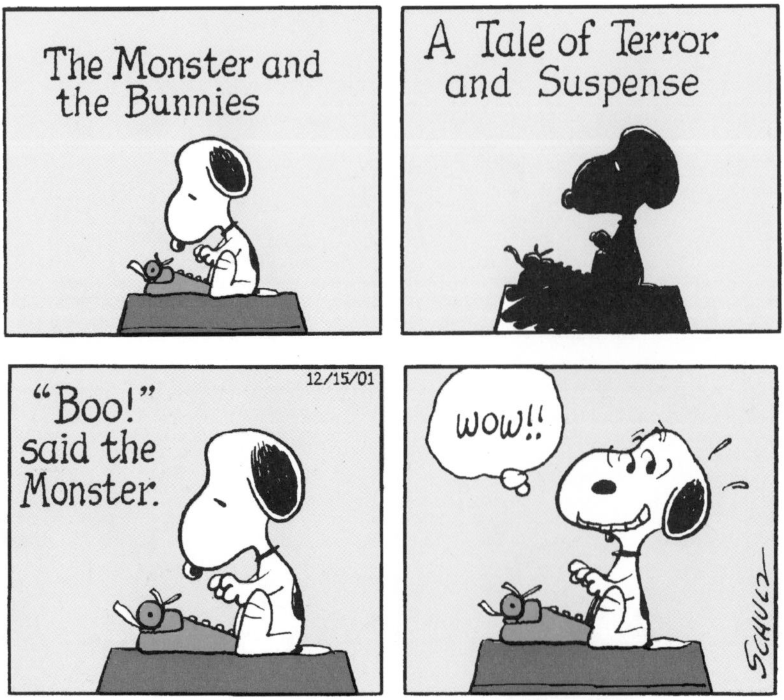
The Monster and the Bunnies
A Tale of Terror and Suspense
12/15/01
"Boo!" said the Monster.
WOW!!
SCHULZ

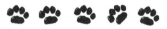

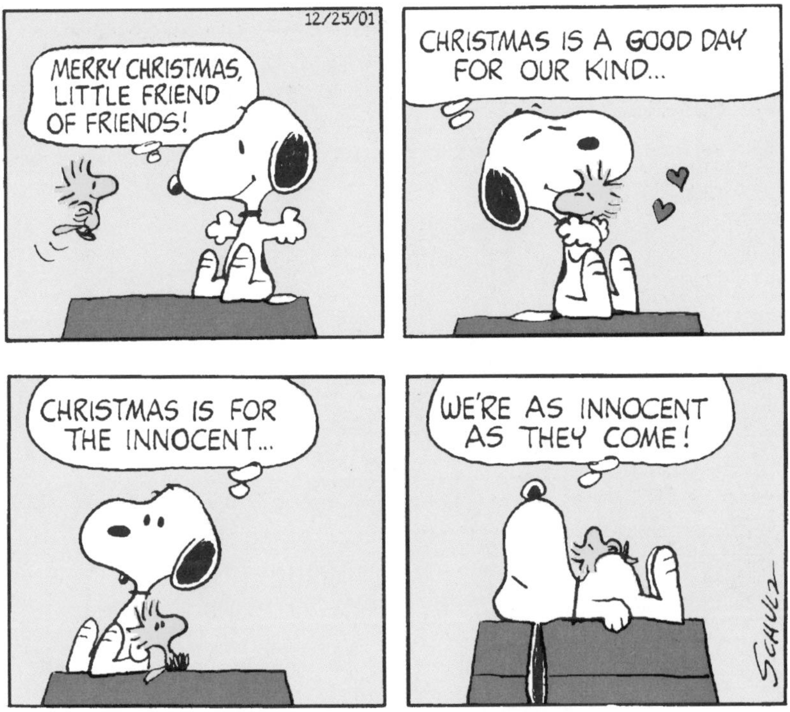
12/25/01
MERRY CHRISTMAS, LITTLE FRIEND OF FRIENDS!
CHRISTMAS IS A GOOD DAY FOR OUR KIND...
CHRISTMAS IS FOR THE INNOCENT...
WE'RE AS INNOCENT AS THEY COME!
SCHULZ

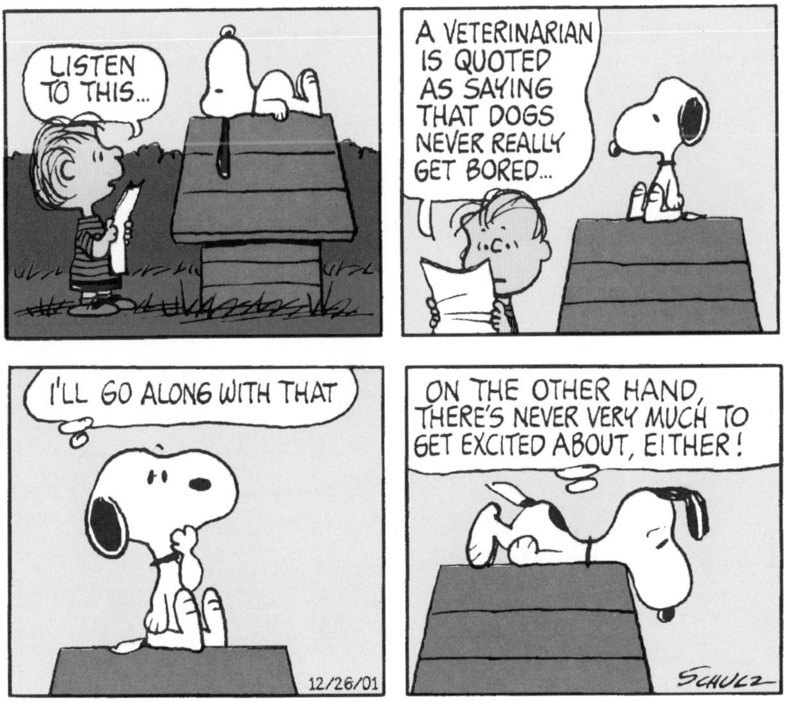
LISTEN TO THIS...
A VETERINARIAN IS QUOTED AS SAYING THAT DOGS NEVER REALLY GET BORED...
I'LL GO ALONG WITH THAT
12/26/01
ON THE OTHER HAND, THERE'S NEVER VERY MUCH TO GET EXCITED ABOUT, EITHER!
SCHULZ

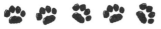

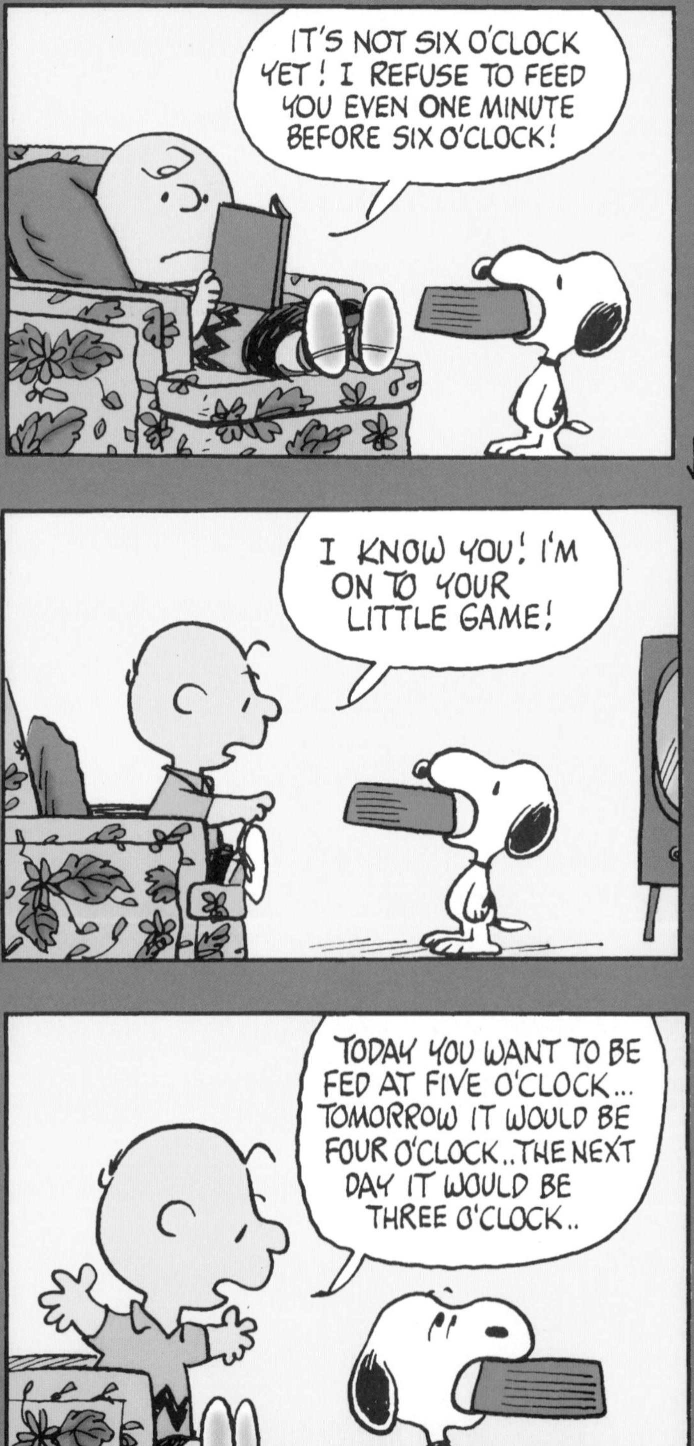
IT'S NOT SIX O'CLOCK YET! I REFUSE TO FEED YOU EVEN ONE MINUTE BEFORE SIX O'CLOCK!
I KNOW YOU! I'M ON TO YOUR LITTLE GAME!
TODAY YOU WANT TO BE FED AT FIVE O'CLOCK... TOMORROW IT WOULD BE FOUR O'CLOCK..THE NEXT DAY IT WOULD BE THREE O'CLOCK..

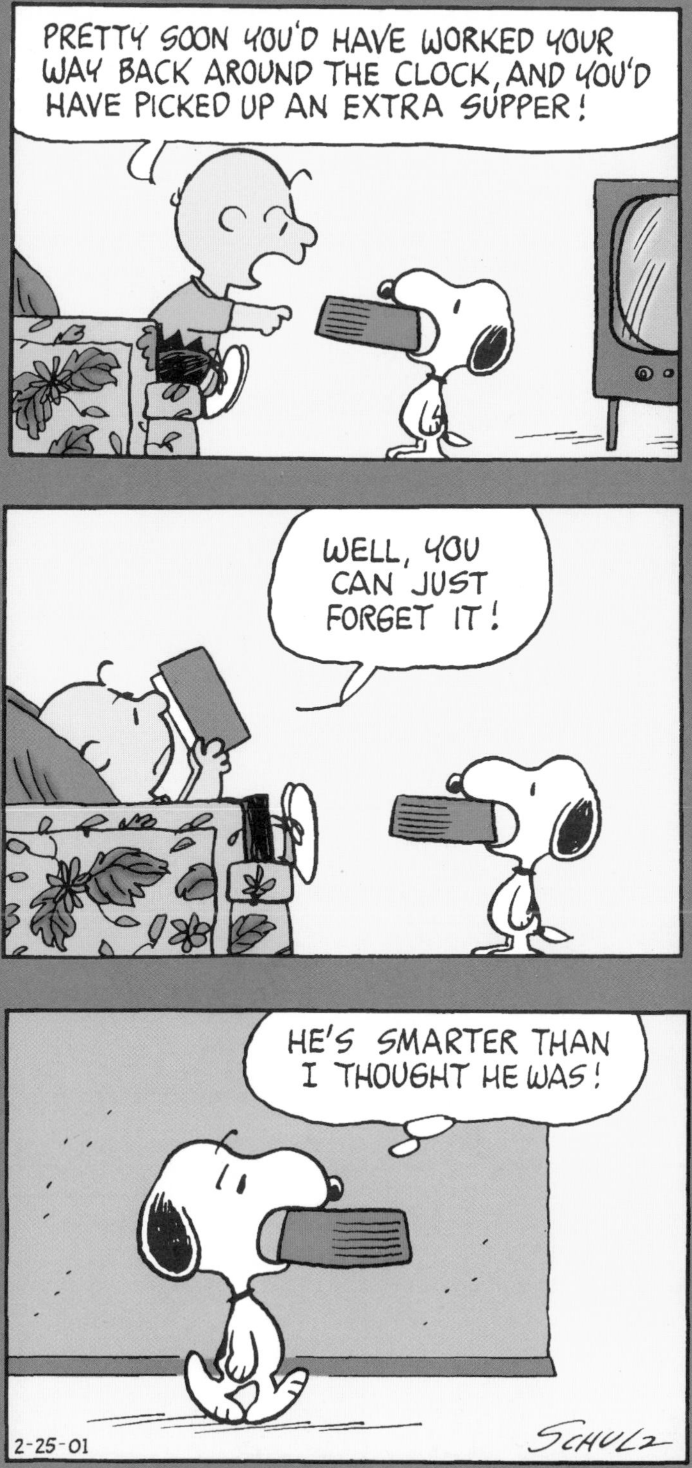
PRETTY SOON YOU'D HAVE WORKED YOUR WAY BACK AROUND THE CLOCK, AND YOU'D HAVE PICKED UP AN EXTRA SUPPER!
WELL, YOU CAN JUST FORGET IT!
HE'S SMARTER THAN I THOUGHT HE WAS!
2-25-01
SCHULZ

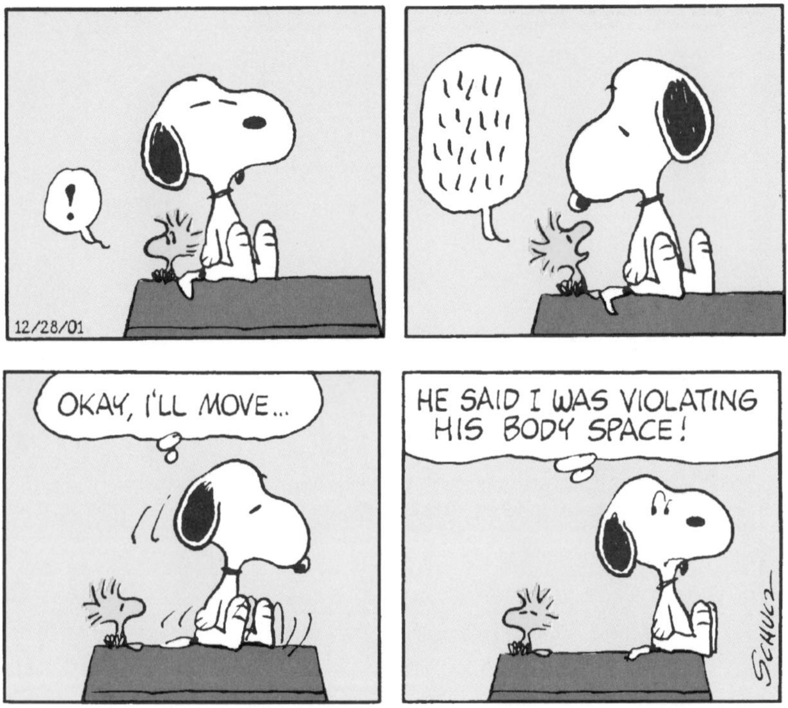
!
12/28/01
OKAY, I'LL MOVE...
HE SAID I WAS VIOLATING HIS BODY SPACE!
SCHULZ

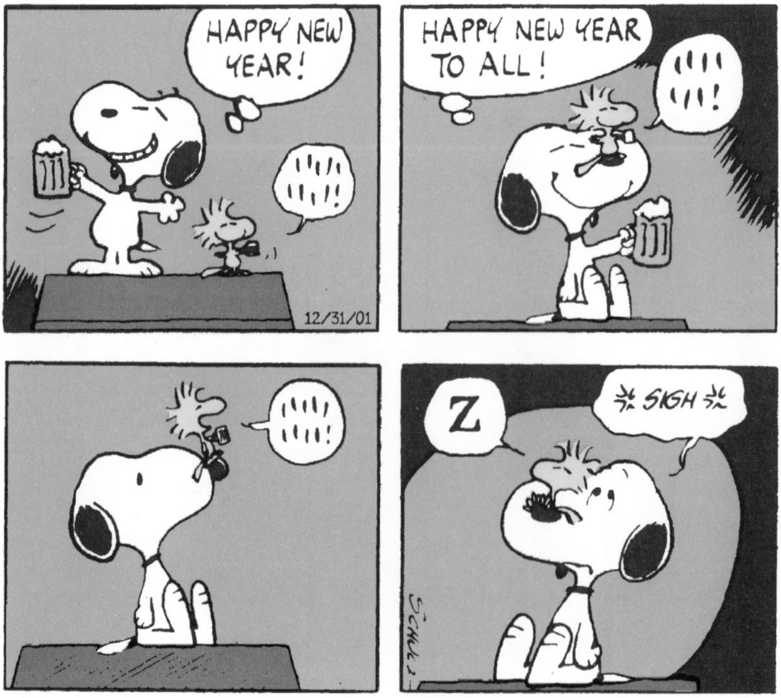
HAPPY NEW YEAR!
12/31/01
HAPPY NEW YEAR TO ALL!
Z
SIGH
SCHULZ

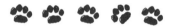

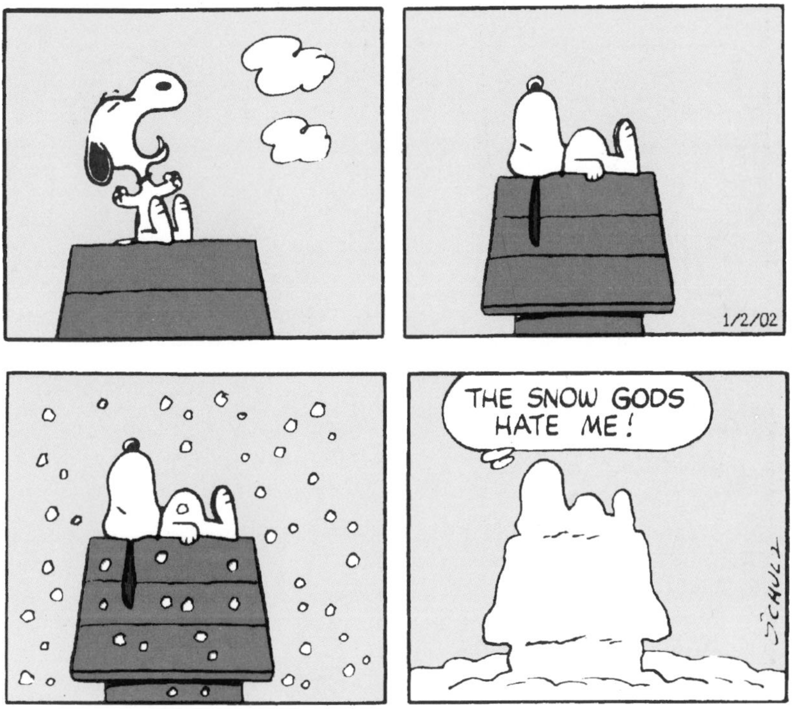
1/2/02
THE SNOW GODS HATE ME!
SCHULZ

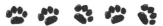

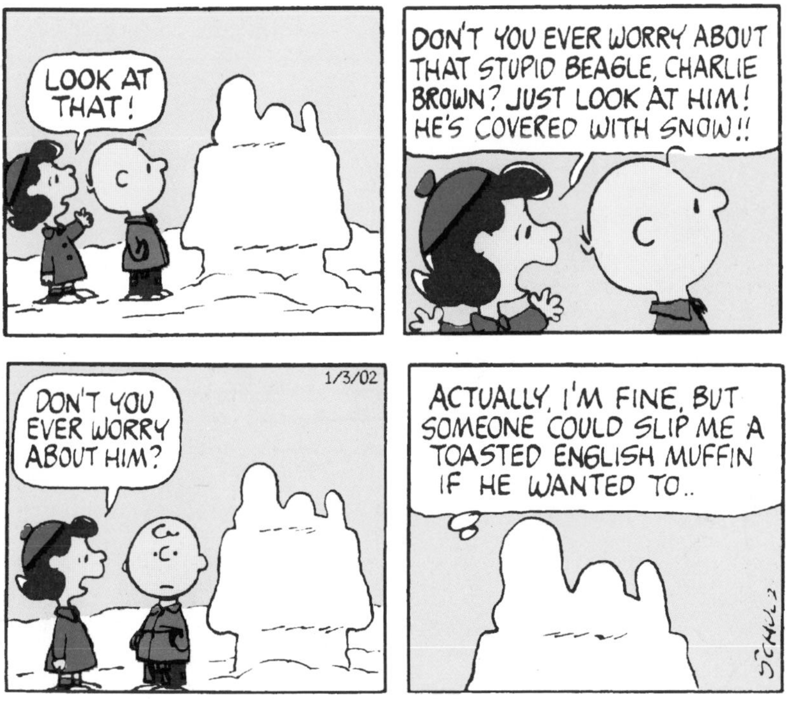
LOOK AT THAT!
DON'T YOU EVER WORRY ABOUT THAT STUPID BEAGLE, CHARLIE BROWN? JUST LOOK AT HIM! HE'S COVERED WITH SNOW!!
1/3/02
DON'T YOU EVER WORRY ABOUT HIM?
ACTUALLY, I'M FINE, BUT SOMEONE COULD SLIP ME A TOASTED ENGLISH MUFFIN IF HE WANTED TO..
SCHULZ

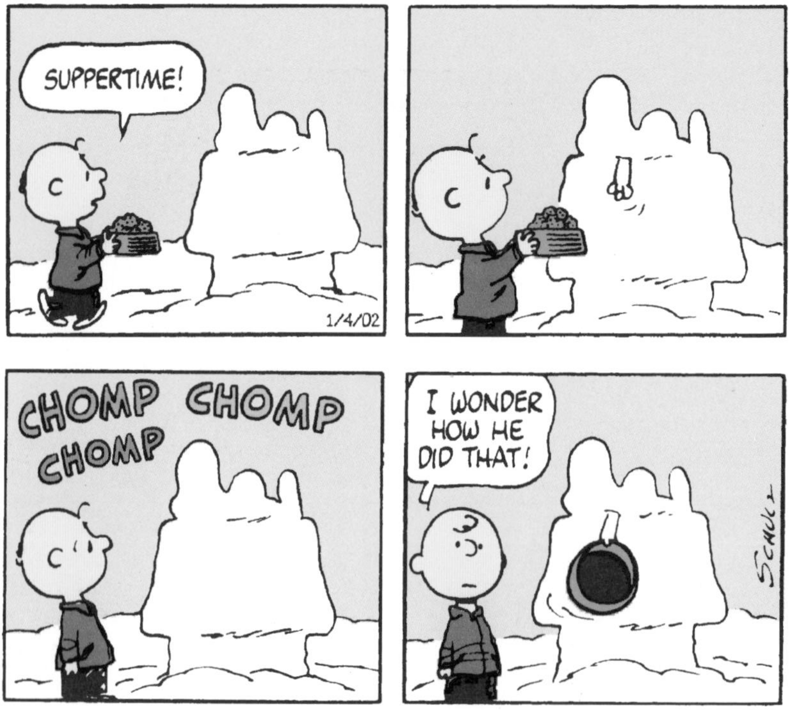
SUPPERTIME!
1/4/02
CHOMP CHOMP
CHOMP
I WONDER HOW HE DID THAT!
SCHULZ

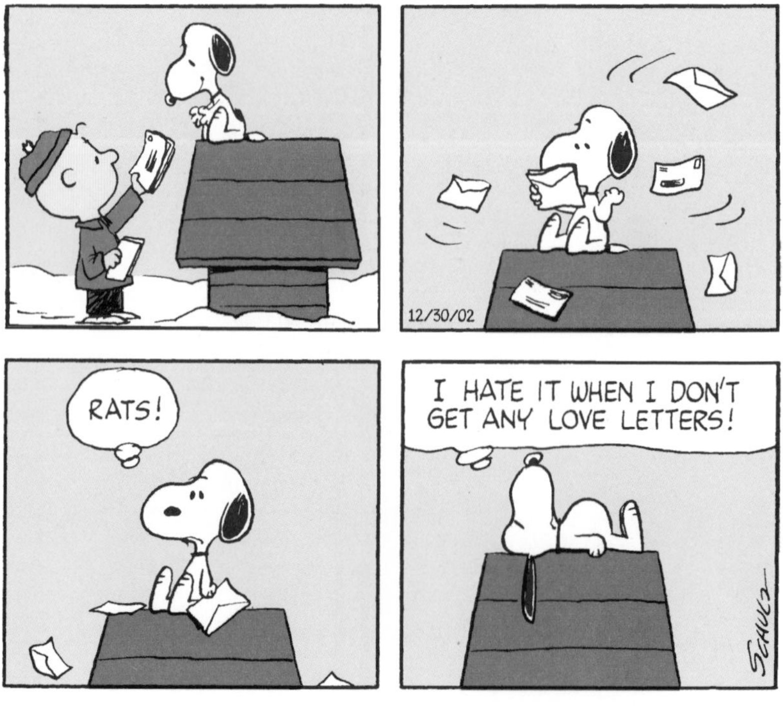
12/30/02
RATS!
I HATE IT WHEN I DON'T GET ANY LOVE LETTERS!
SCHULZ

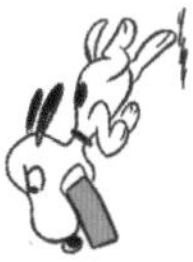

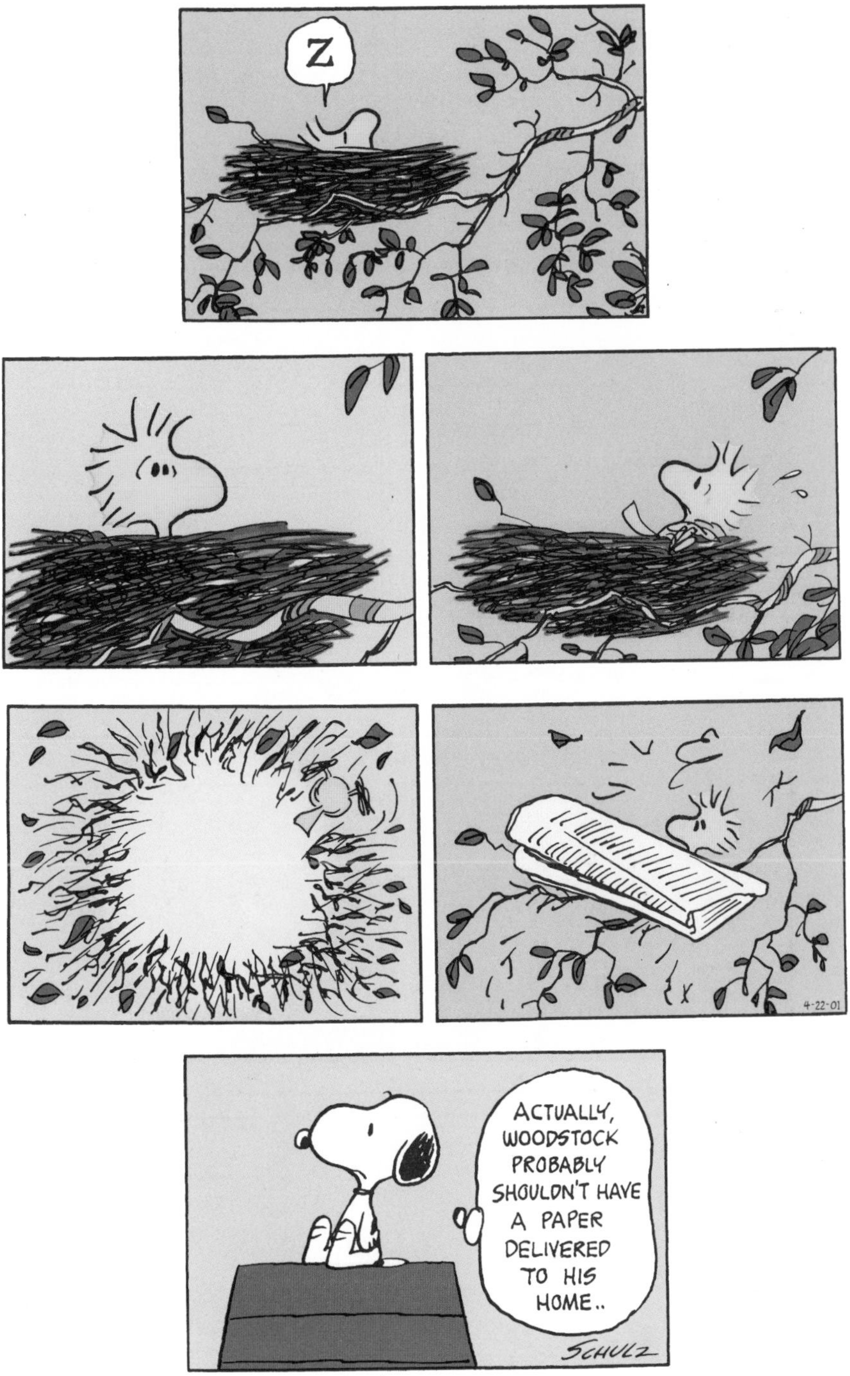
Z
4-22-01
ACTUALLY, WOODSTOCK PROBABLY SHOULDN'T HAVE A PAPER DELIVERED TO HIS HOME..
SCHULZ

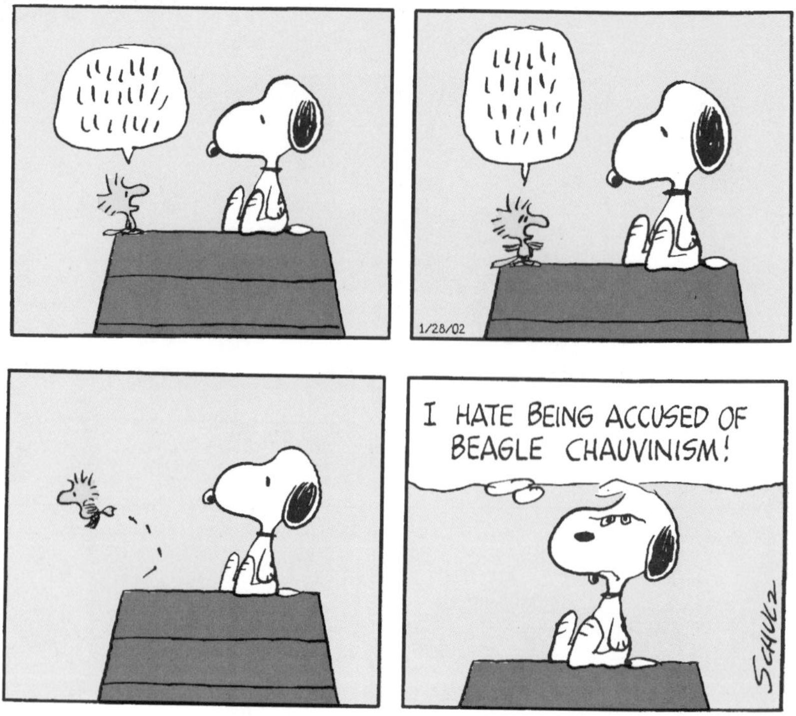
1/28/02
I HATE BEING ACCUSED OF BEAGLE CHAUVINISM!
SCHULZ

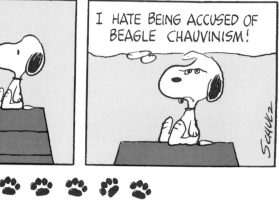

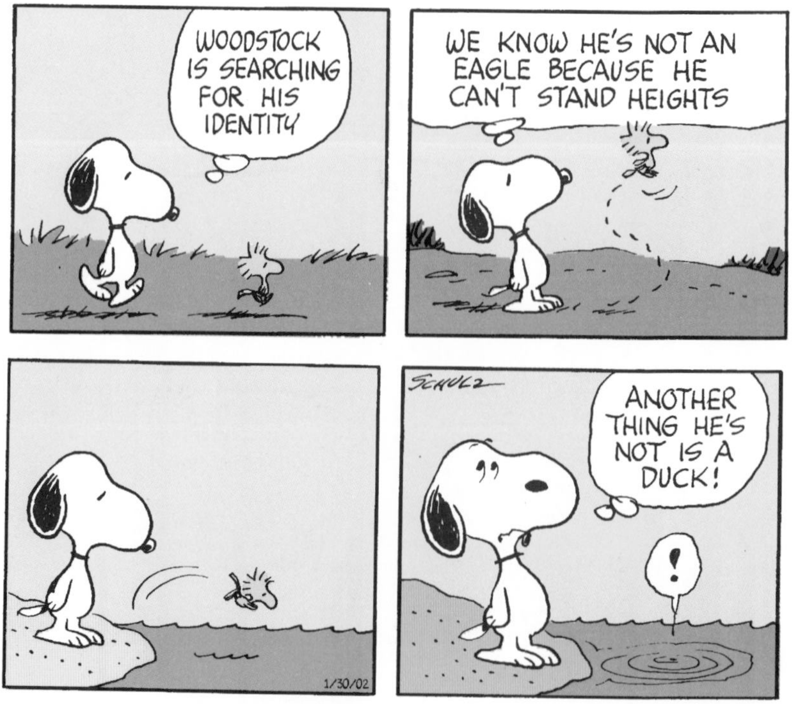
WOODSTOCK IS SEARCHING FOR HIS IDENTITY
WE KNOW HE'S NOT AN EAGLE BECAUSE HE CAN'T STAND HEIGHTS
1/30/02
SCHULZ
ANOTHER THING HE'S NOT IS A DUCK!
!

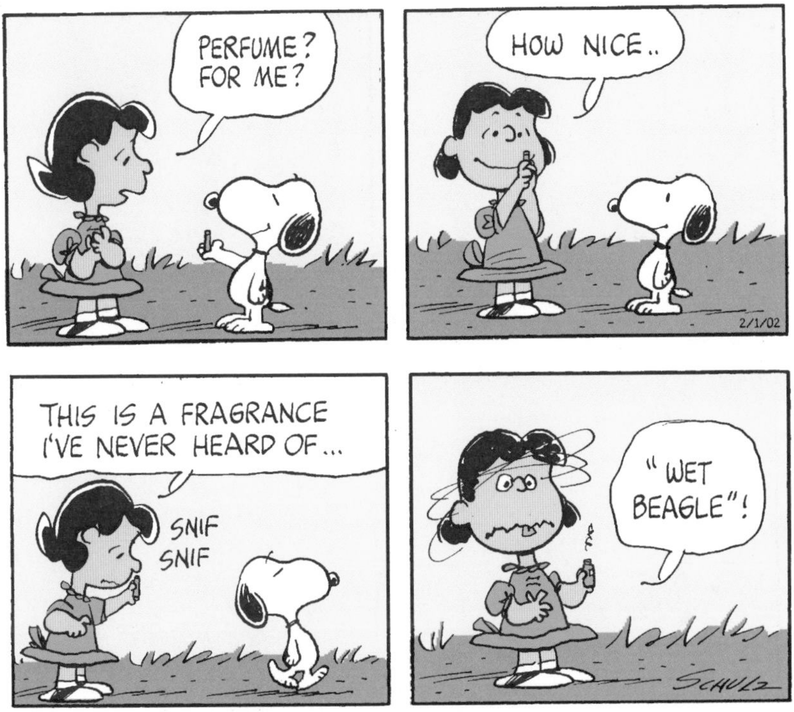
PERFUME? FOR ME?
HOW NICE..
2/1/02
THIS IS A FRAGRANCE I'VE NEVER HEARD OF...
SNIF SNIF
"WET BEAGLE"!
SCHULZ

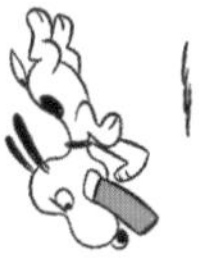

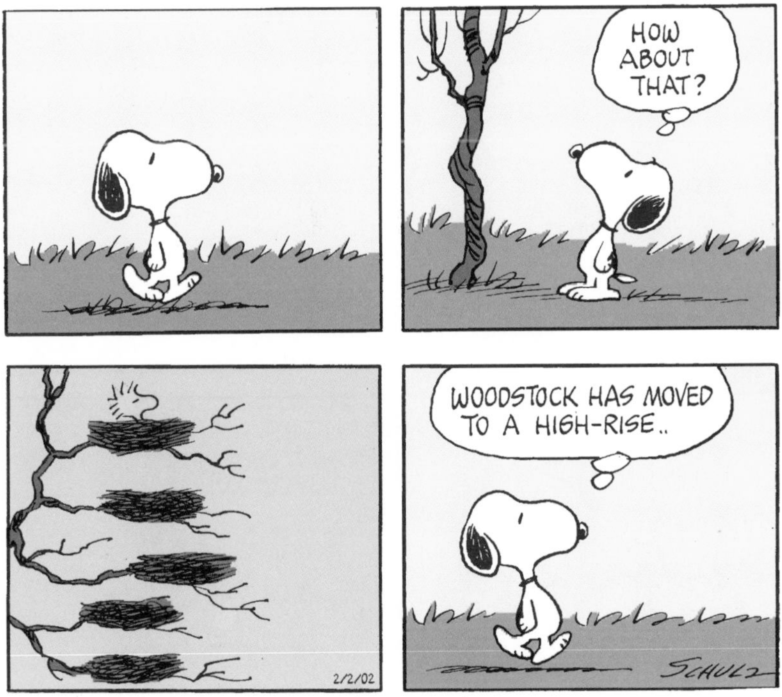
HOW ABOUT THAT?
2/2/02
WOODSTOCK HAS MOVED TO A HIGH-RISE..
SCHULZ

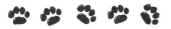

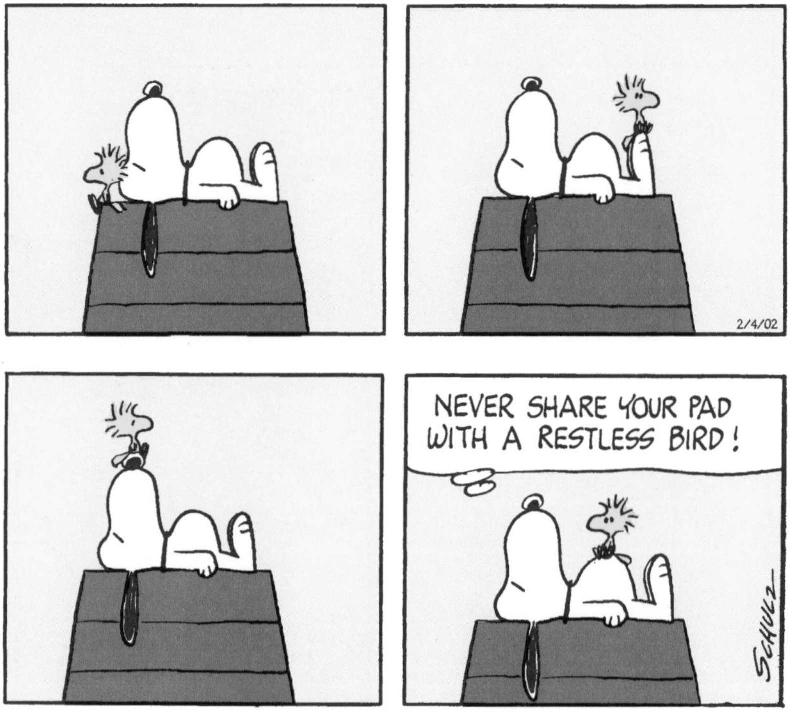
2/4/02
NEVER SHARE YOUR PAD WITH A RESTLESS BIRD!
SCHULZ

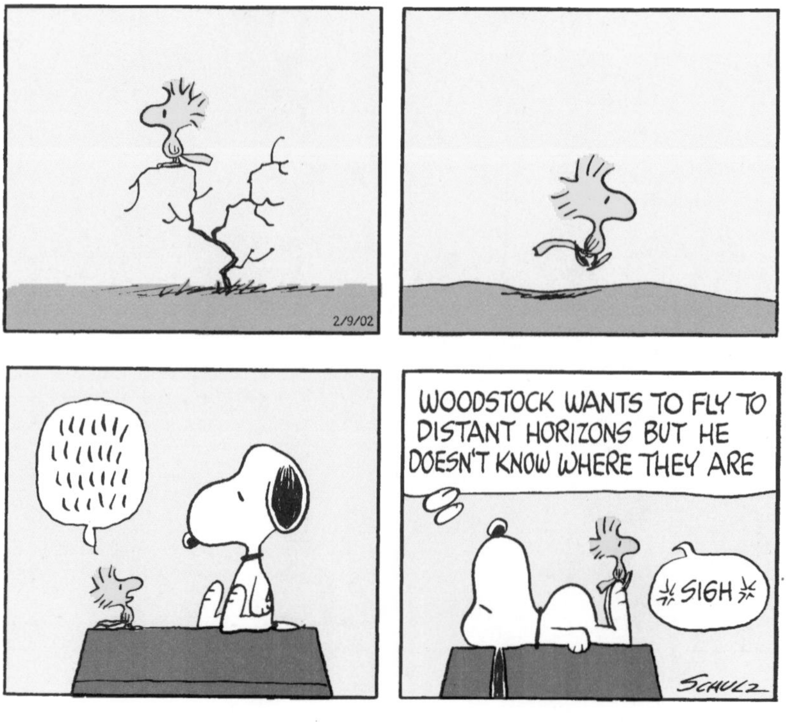
2/9/02
WOODSTOCK WANTS TO FLY TO DISTANT HORIZONS BUT HE DOESN'T KNOW WHERE THEY ARE
SIGH
SCHULZ

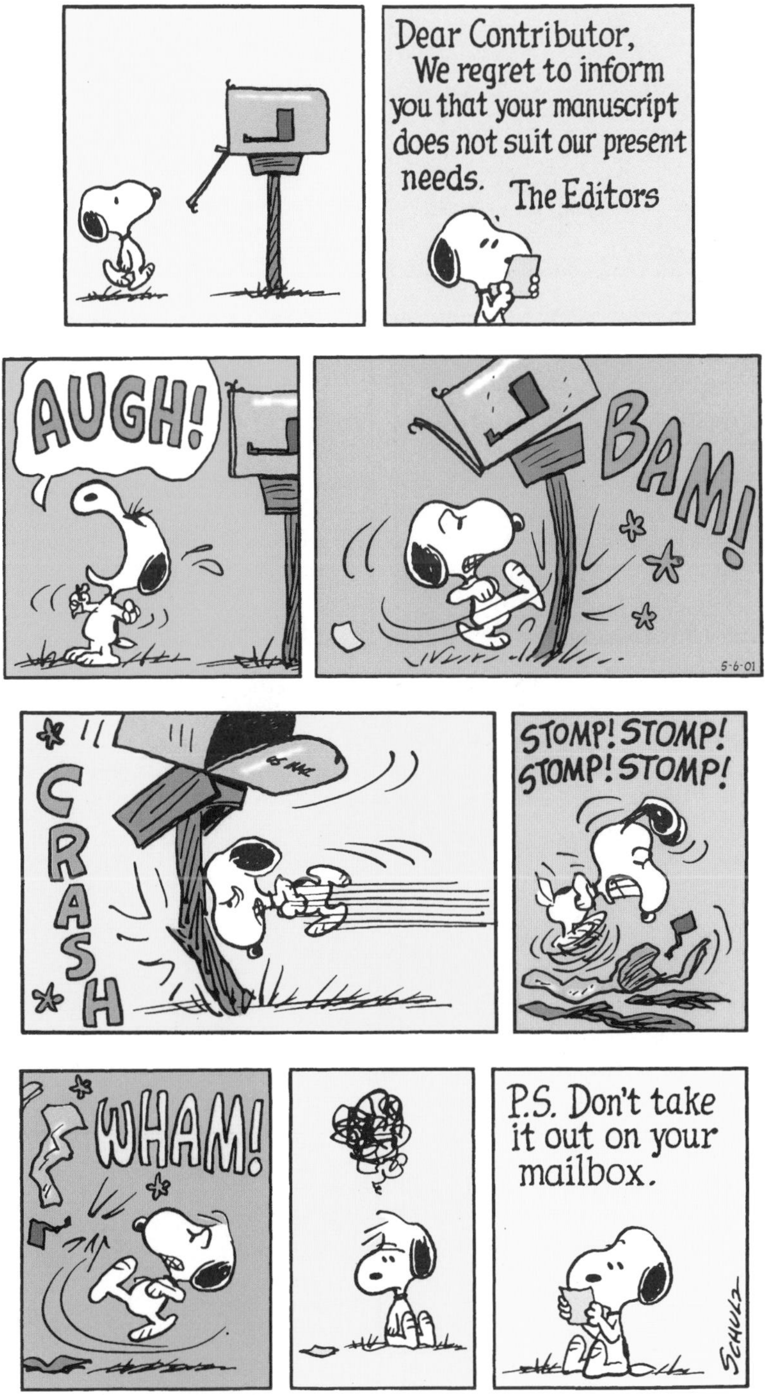
Dear Contributor,
We regret to inform you that your manuscript does not suit our present needs.
The Editors
AUGH!
BAM!
5-6-01
CRASH
STOMP! STOMP!
STOMP! STOMP!
WHAM!
P.S. Don't take it out on your mailbox.
SCHULZ

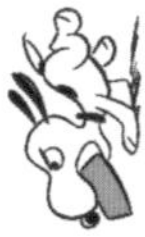

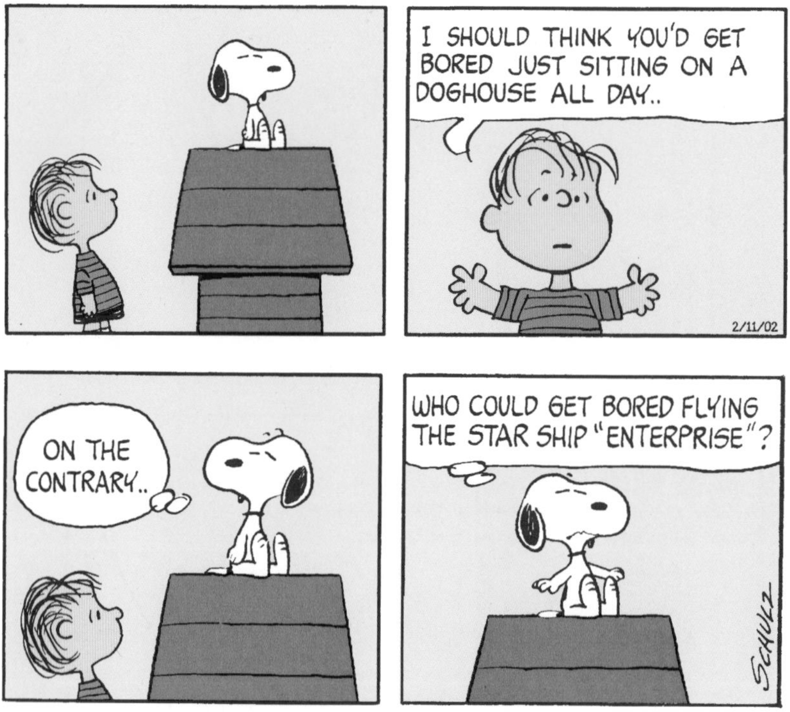
I SHOULD THINK YOU'D GET BORED JUST SITTING ON A DOGHOUSE ALL DAY..
2/11/02
ON THE CONTRARY..
WHO COULD GET BORED FLYING THE STAR SHIP "ENTERPRISE"?
SCHULZ

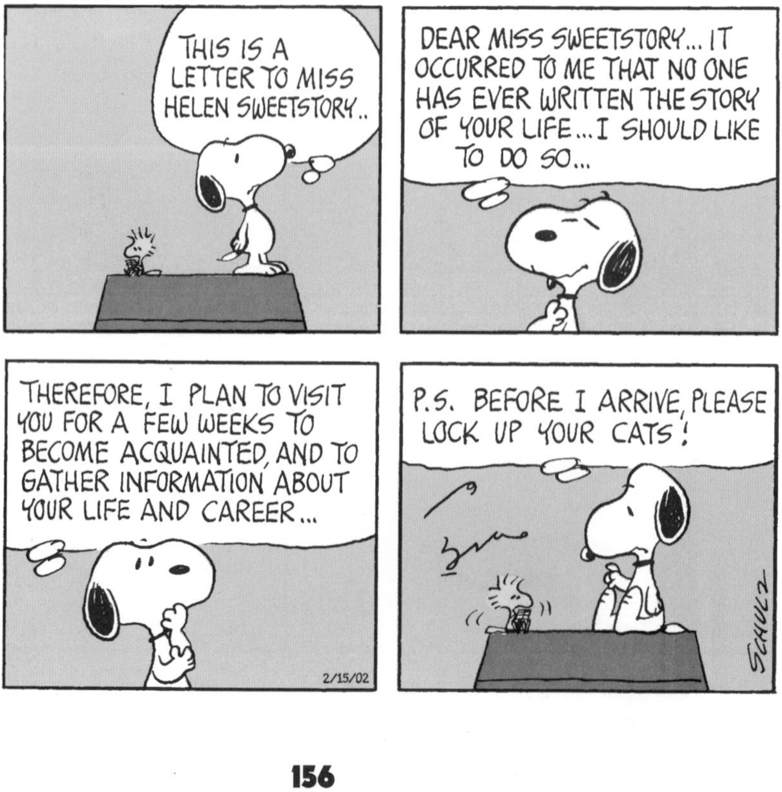
THIS IS A LETTER TO MISS HELEN SWEETSTORY..
DEAR MISS SWEETSTORY... IT OCCURRED TO ME THAT NO ONE HAS EVER WRITTEN THE STORY OF YOUR LIFE...I SHOULD LIKE TO DO SO...
THEREFORE, I PLAN TO VISIT YOU FOR A FEW WEEKS TO BECOME ACQUAINTED, AND TO GATHER INFORMATION ABOUT YOUR LIFE AND CAREER...
2/15/02
P.S. BEFORE I ARRIVE, PLEASE LOCK UP YOUR CATS!
SCHULZ

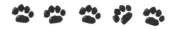

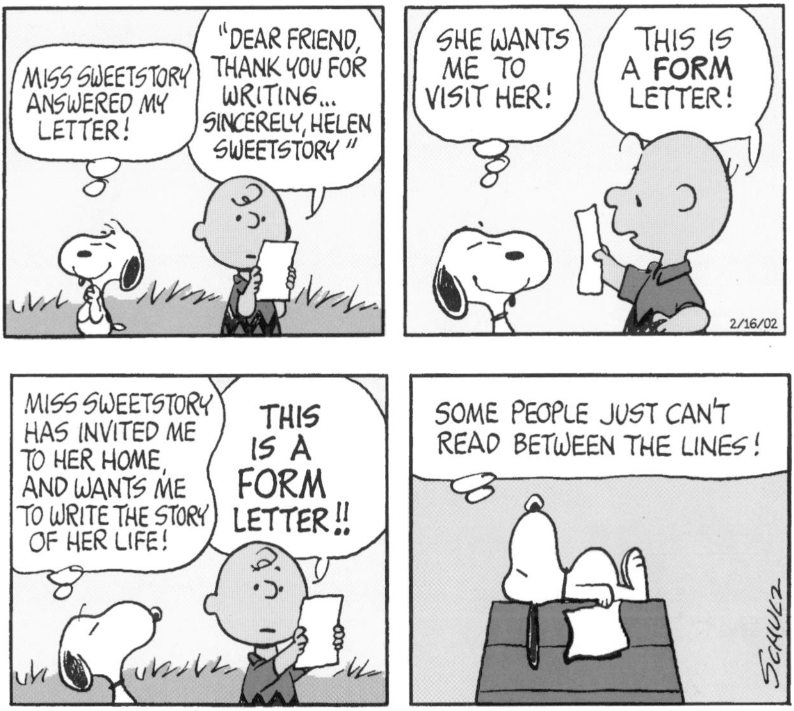
MISS SWEETSTORY ANSWERED MY LETTER!
"DEAR FRIEND, THANK YOU FOR WRITING... SINCERELY, HELEN SWEETSTORY"
SHE WANTS ME TO VISIT HER!
THIS IS A FORM LETTER!
2/16/02
MISS SWEETSTORY HAS INVITED ME TO HER HOME, AND WANTS ME TO WRITE THE STORY OF HER LIFE!
THIS IS A FORM LETTER!!
SOME PEOPLE JUST CAN'T READ BETWEEN THE LINES!
SCHULZ

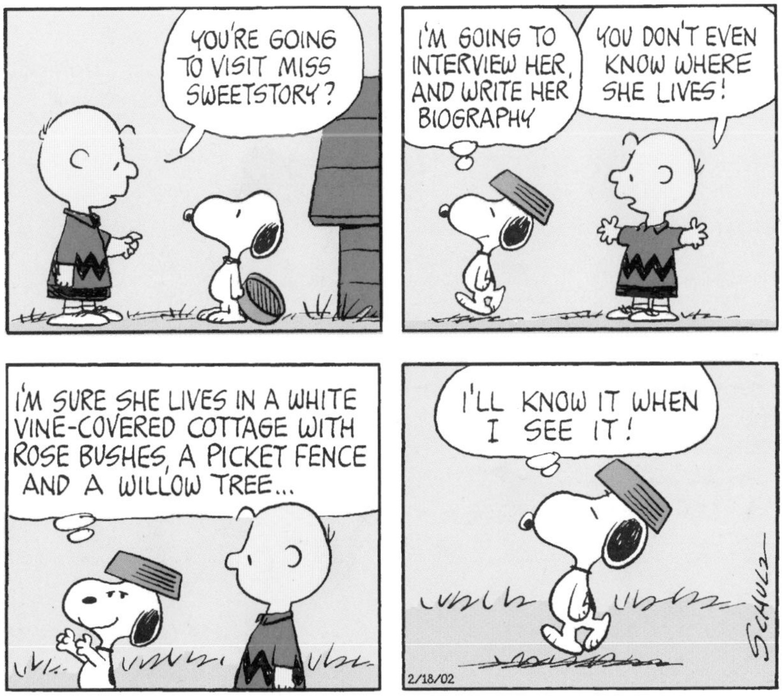
YOU'RE GOING TO VISIT MISS SWEETSTORY?
I'M GOING TO INTERVIEW HER, AND WRITE HER BIOGRAPHY
YOU DON'T EVEN KNOW WHERE SHE LIVES!
I'M SURE SHE LIVES IN A WHITE VINE-COVERED COTTAGE WITH ROSE BUSHES, A PICKET FENCE AND A WILLOW TREE...
I'LL KNOW IT WHEN I SEE IT!
SCHULZ
2/18/02

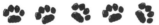

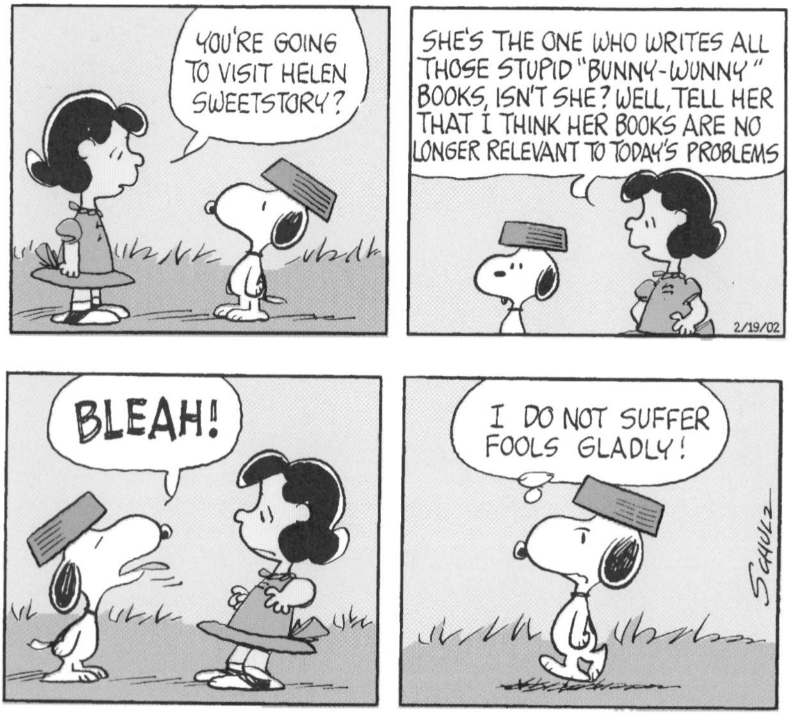
YOU'RE GOING TO VISIT HELEN SWEETSTORY?
SHE'S THE ONE WHO WRITES ALL THOSE STUPID "BUNNY-WUNNY" BOOKS, ISN'T SHE? WELL, TELL HER THAT I THINK HER BOOKS ARE NO LONGER RELEVANT TO TODAY'S PROBLEMS
2/19/02
BLEAH!
I DO NOT SUFFER FOOLS GLADLY!
SCHULZ

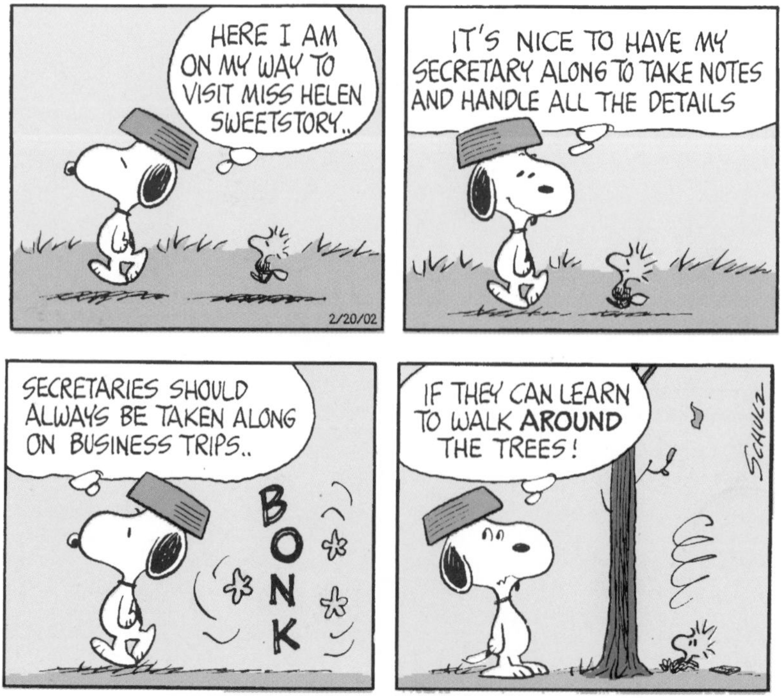
HERE I AM ON MY WAY TO VISIT MISS HELEN SWEETSTORY..
2/20/02
IT'S NICE TO HAVE MY SECRETARY ALONG TO TAKE NOTES AND HANDLE ALL THE DETAILS
SECRETARIES SHOULD ALWAYS BE TAKEN ALONG ON BUSINESS TRIPS..
BONK
IF THEY CAN LEARN TO WALK **AROUND** THE TREES!
SCHULZ

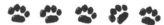

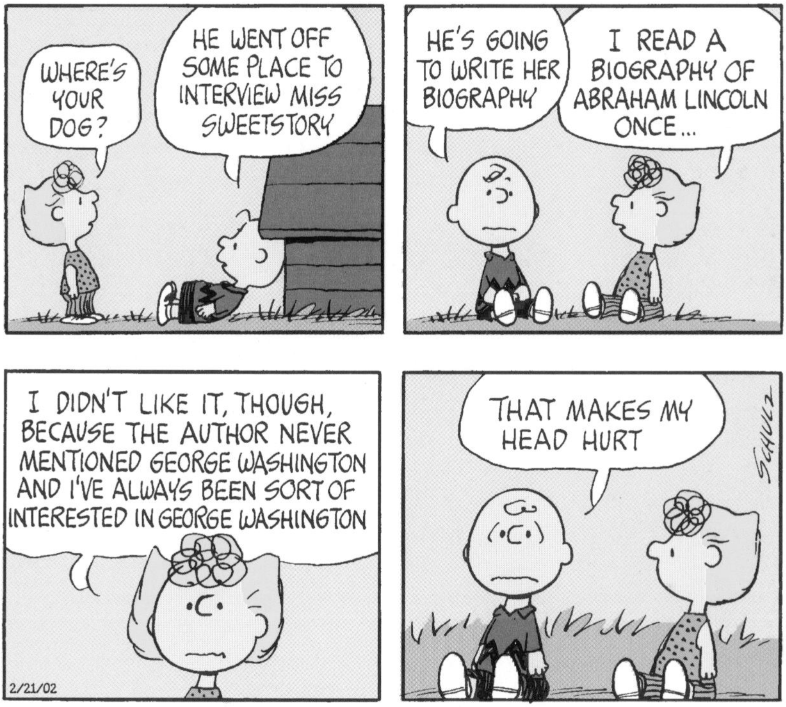
WHERE'S YOUR DOG?
HE WENT OFF SOME PLACE TO INTERVIEW MISS SWEETSTORY
HE'S GOING TO WRITE HER BIOGRAPHY
I READ A BIOGRAPHY OF ABRAHAM LINCOLN ONCE...
I DIDN'T LIKE IT, THOUGH, BECAUSE THE AUTHOR NEVER MENTIONED GEORGE WASHINGTON AND I'VE ALWAYS BEEN SORT OF INTERESTED IN GEORGE WASHINGTON
2/21/02
THAT MAKES MY HEAD HURT
SCHULZ

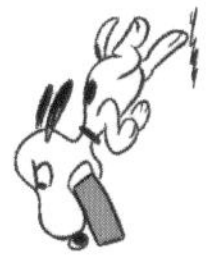

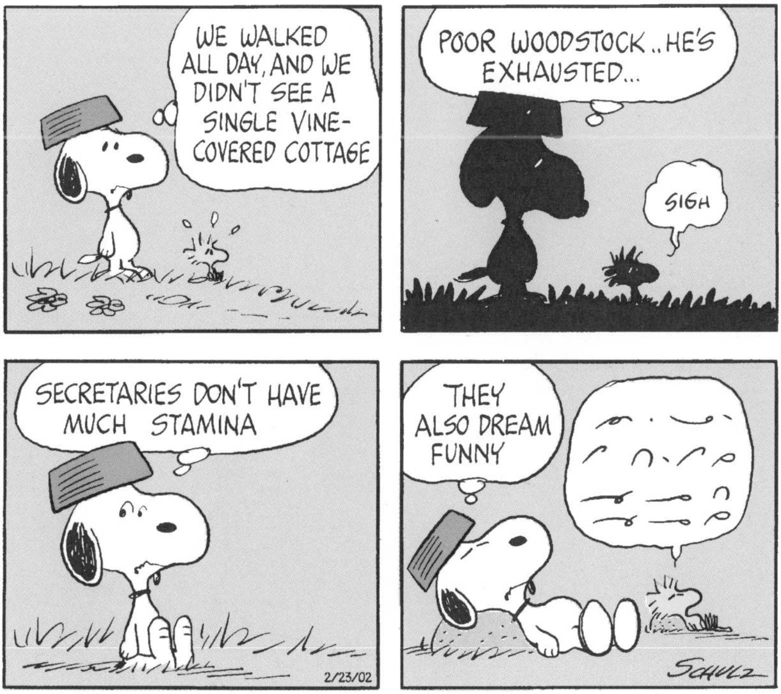
WE WALKED ALL DAY, AND WE DIDN'T SEE A SINGLE VINE-COVERED COTTAGE
POOR WOODSTOCK..HE'S EXHAUSTED...
SIGH
SECRETARIES DON'T HAVE MUCH STAMINA
2/23/02
THEY ALSO DREAM FUNNY
SCHULZ

SUPPERTIME!
5-20-01

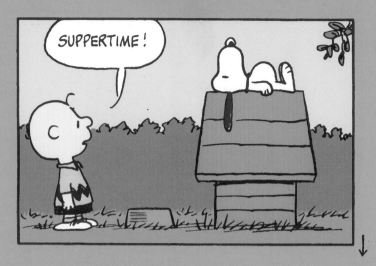

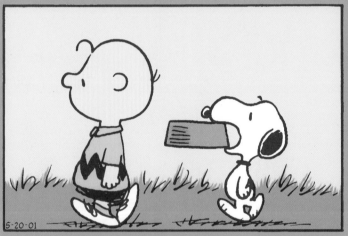

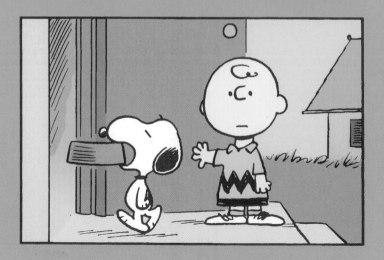

THANK YOU
YOU DON'T GET A TIP FOR CARRYING IN YOUR OWN DISH!
SCHULZ

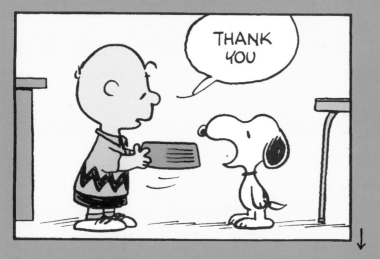

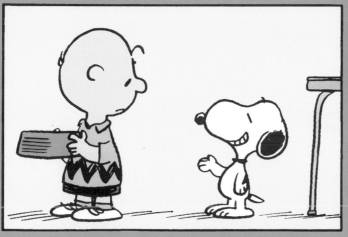

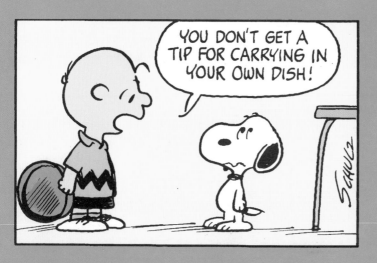

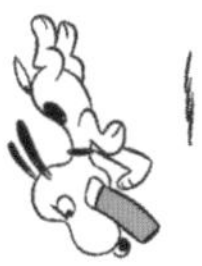

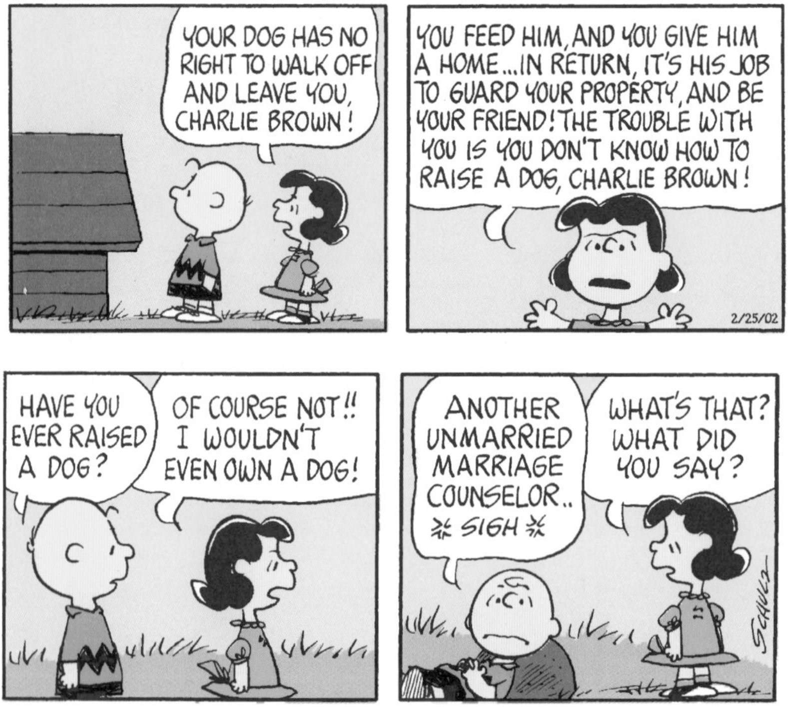
YOUR DOG HAS NO RIGHT TO WALK OFF AND LEAVE YOU, CHARLIE BROWN!
YOU FEED HIM, AND YOU GIVE HIM A HOME...IN RETURN, IT'S HIS JOB TO GUARD YOUR PROPERTY, AND BE YOUR FRIEND! THE TROUBLE WITH YOU IS YOU DON'T KNOW HOW TO RAISE A DOG, CHARLIE BROWN!
2/25/02
HAVE YOU EVER RAISED A DOG?
OF COURSE NOT!! I WOULDN'T EVEN OWN A DOG!
ANOTHER UNMARRIED MARRIAGE COUNSELOR.. SIGH
WHAT'S THAT? WHAT DID YOU SAY?
SCHULZ

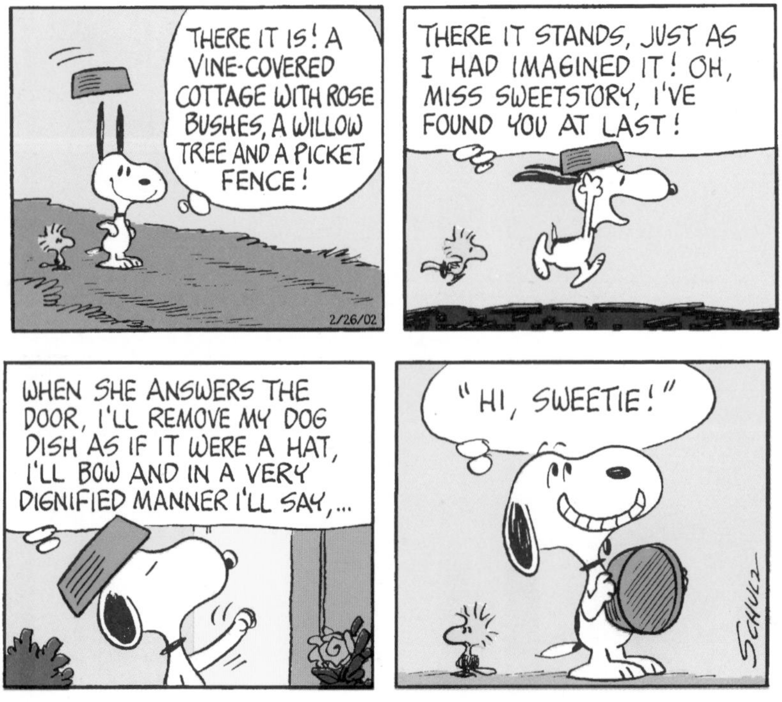
THERE IT IS! A VINE-COVERED COTTAGE WITH ROSE BUSHES, A WILLOW TREE AND A PICKET FENCE!
2/26/02
THERE IT STANDS, JUST AS I HAD IMAGINED IT! OH, MISS SWEETSTORY, I'VE FOUND YOU AT LAST!
WHEN SHE ANSWERS THE DOOR, I'LL REMOVE MY DOG DISH AS IF IT WERE A HAT, I'LL BOW AND IN A VERY DIGNIFIED MANNER I'LL SAY,...
"HI, SWEETIE!"
SCHULZ

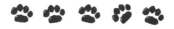

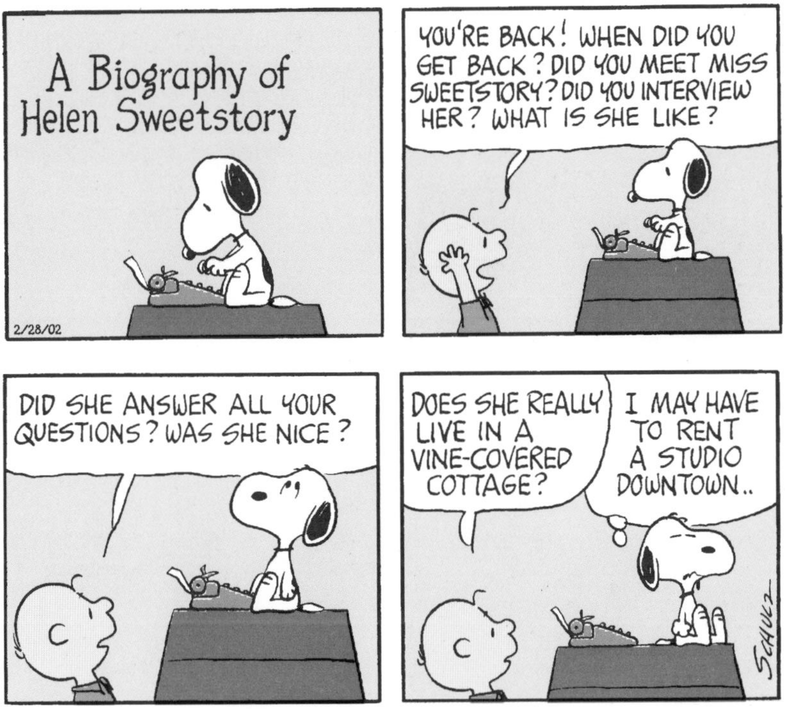
A Biography of Helen Sweetstory
2/28/02
YOU'RE BACK! WHEN DID YOU GET BACK? DID YOU MEET MISS SWEETSTORY? DID YOU INTERVIEW HER? WHAT IS SHE LIKE?
DID SHE ANSWER ALL YOUR QUESTIONS? WAS SHE NICE?
DOES SHE REALLY LIVE IN A VINE-COVERED COTTAGE?
I MAY HAVE TO RENT A STUDIO DOWNTOWN..
SCHULZ

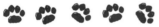

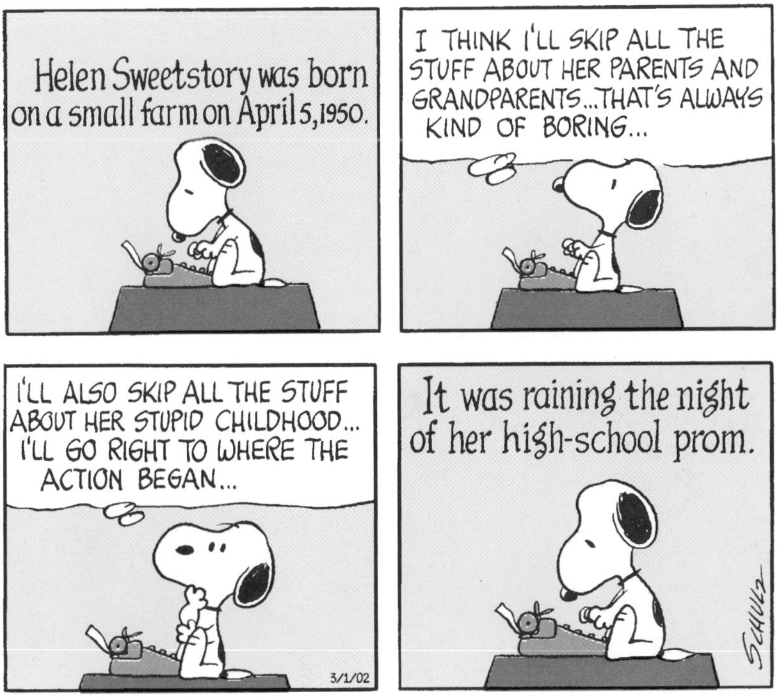
Helen Sweetstory was born on a small farm on April 5, 1950.
I THINK I'LL SKIP ALL THE STUFF ABOUT HER PARENTS AND GRANDPARENTS...THAT'S ALWAYS KIND OF BORING...
I'LL ALSO SKIP ALL THE STUFF ABOUT HER STUPID CHILDHOOD... I'LL GO RIGHT TO WHERE THE ACTION BEGAN...
3/1/02
It was raining the night of her high-school prom.
SCHULZ

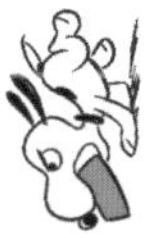

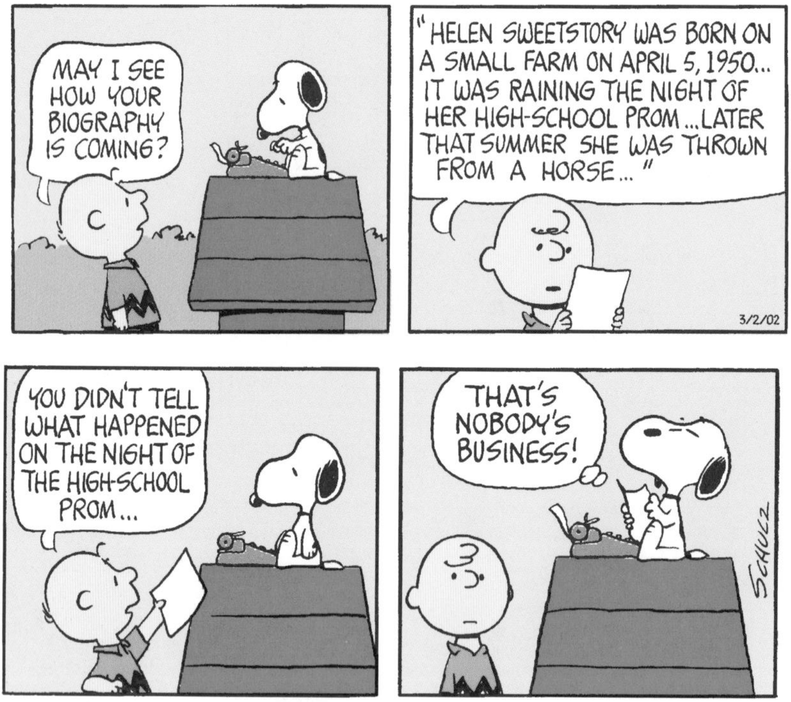
MAY I SEE HOW YOUR BIOGRAPHY IS COMING?
"HELEN SWEETSTORY WAS BORN ON A SMALL FARM ON APRIL 5, 1950... IT WAS RAINING THE NIGHT OF HER HIGH-SCHOOL PROM ...LATER THAT SUMMER SHE WAS THROWN FROM A HORSE..."
3/2/02
YOU DIDN'T TELL WHAT HAPPENED ON THE NIGHT OF THE HIGH-SCHOOL PROM...
THAT'S NOBODY'S BUSINESS!
SCHULZ

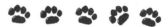

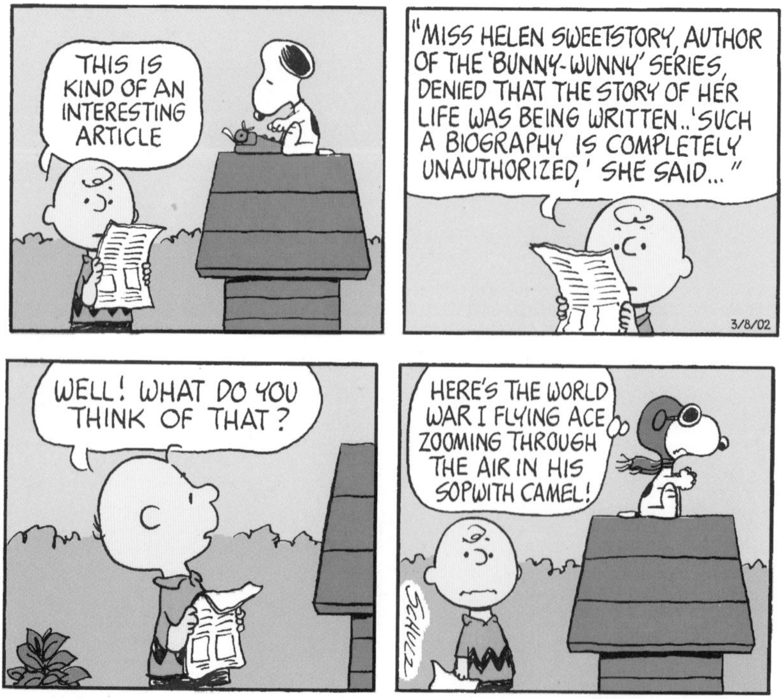
THIS IS KIND OF AN INTERESTING ARTICLE
"MISS HELEN SWEETSTORY, AUTHOR OF THE 'BUNNY-WUNNY' SERIES, DENIED THAT THE STORY OF HER LIFE WAS BEING WRITTEN..'SUCH A BIOGRAPHY IS COMPLETELY UNAUTHORIZED,' SHE SAID..."
3/8/02
WELL! WHAT DO YOU THINK OF THAT?
HERE'S THE WORLD WAR I FLYING ACE ZOOMING THROUGH THE AIR IN HIS SOPWITH CAMEL!
SCHULZ

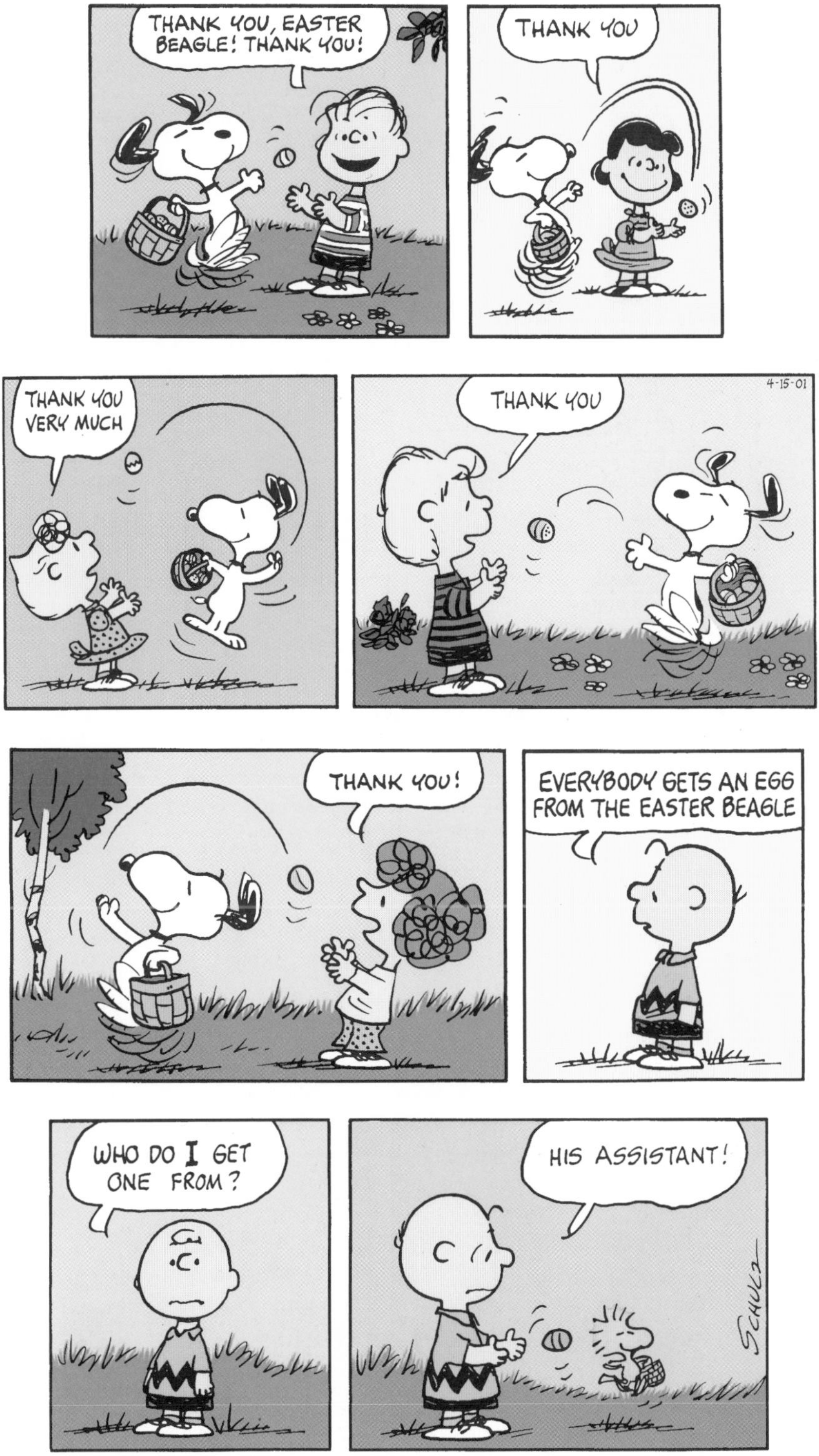
THANK YOU, EASTER BEAGLE! THANK YOU!
THANK YOU
THANK YOU VERY MUCH
4-15-01
THANK YOU
THANK YOU!
EVERYBODY GETS AN EGG FROM THE EASTER BEAGLE
WHO DO I GET ONE FROM?
HIS ASSISTANT!
SCHULZ

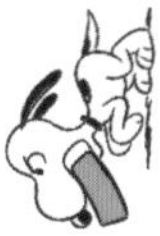

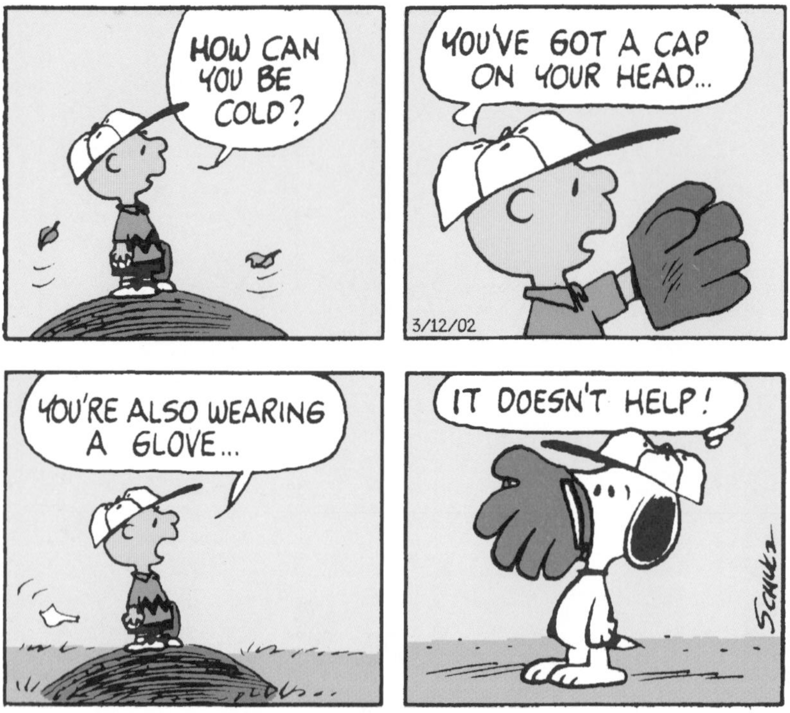
HOW CAN YOU BE COLD?
YOU'VE GOT A CAP ON YOUR HEAD...
3/12/02
YOU'RE ALSO WEARING A GLOVE...
IT DOESN'T HELP!

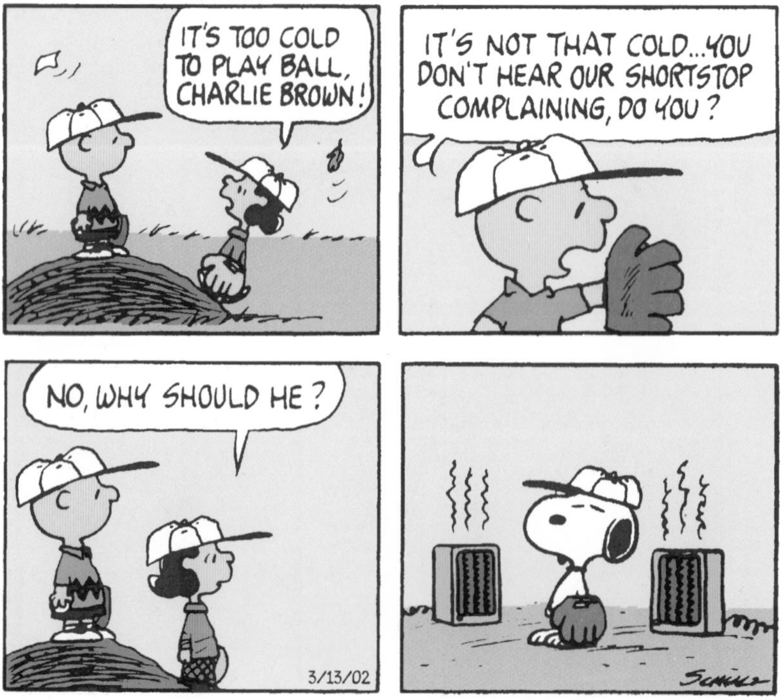
IT'S TOO COLD TO PLAY BALL, CHARLIE BROWN!
IT'S NOT THAT COLD...YOU DON'T HEAR OUR SHORTSTOP COMPLAINING, DO YOU?
NO, WHY SHOULD HE?
3/13/02

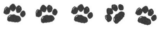

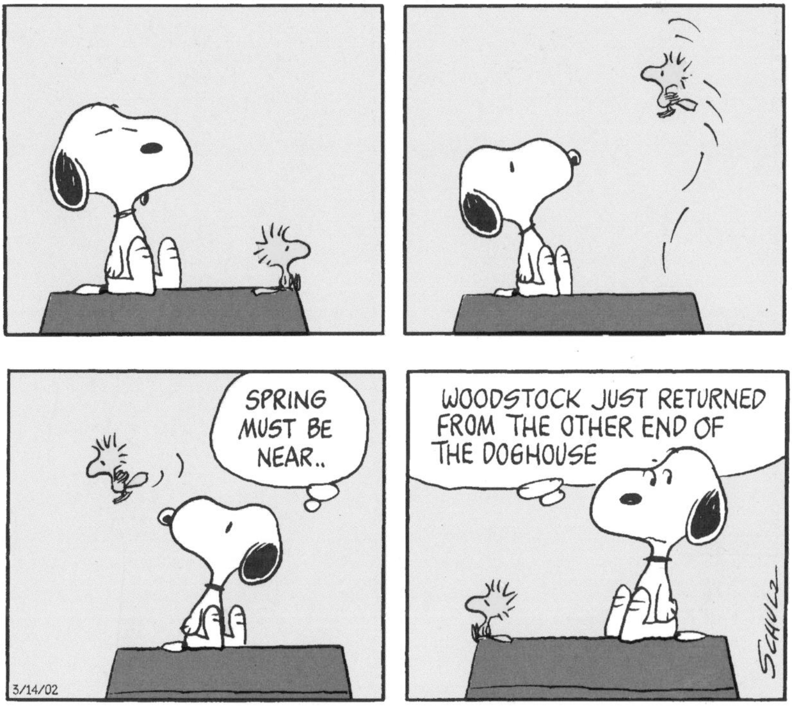
SPRING MUST BE NEAR..
WOODSTOCK JUST RETURNED FROM THE OTHER END OF THE DOGHOUSE
3/14/02

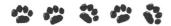

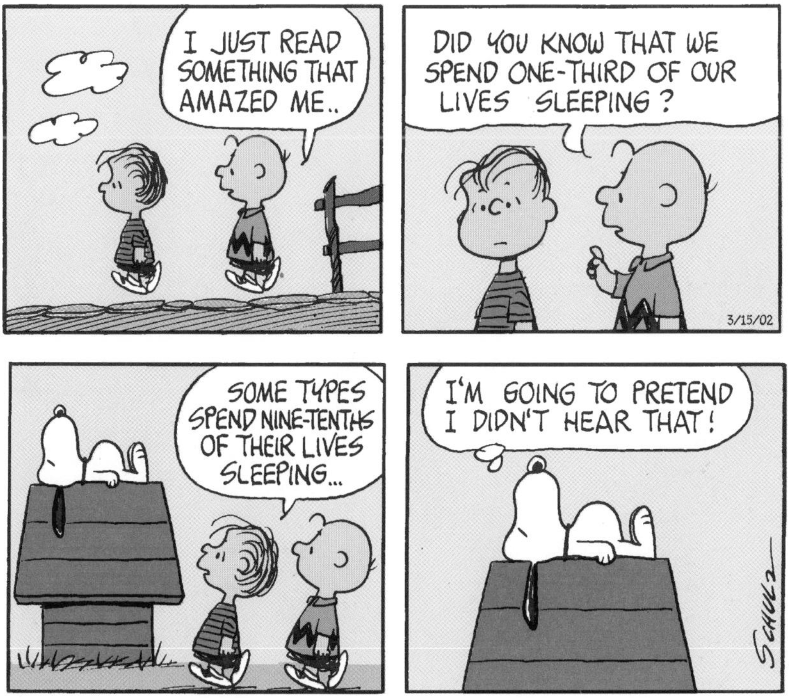
I JUST READ SOMETHING THAT AMAZED ME..
DID YOU KNOW THAT WE SPEND ONE-THIRD OF OUR LIVES SLEEPING?
3/15/02
SOME TYPES SPEND NINE-TENTHS OF THEIR LIVES SLEEPING...
I'M GOING TO PRETEND I DIDN'T HEAR THAT!

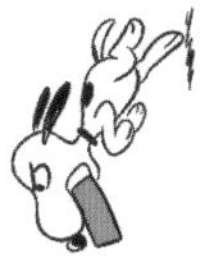

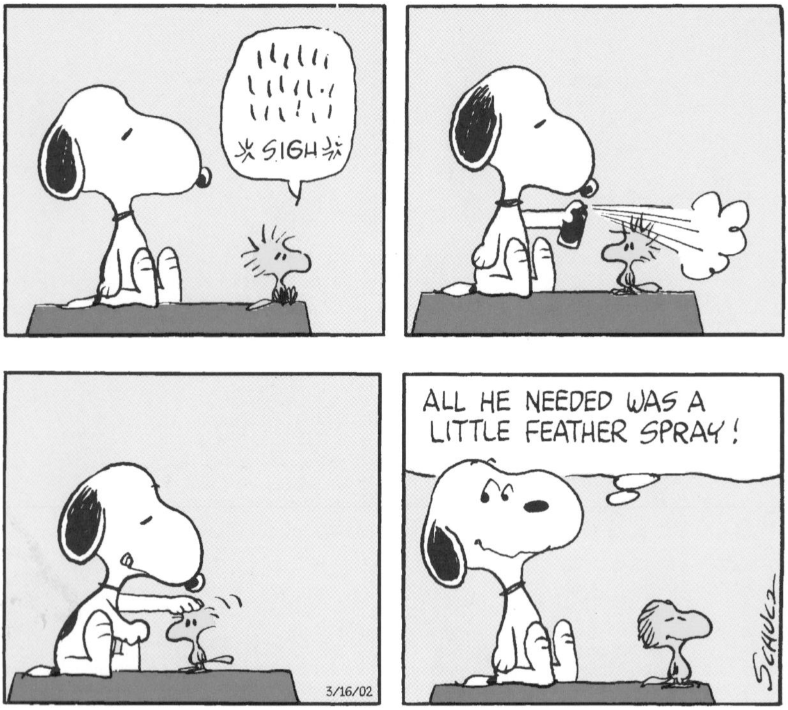
SIGH
ALL HE NEEDED WAS A LITTLE FEATHER SPRAY!
3/16/02
SCHULZ

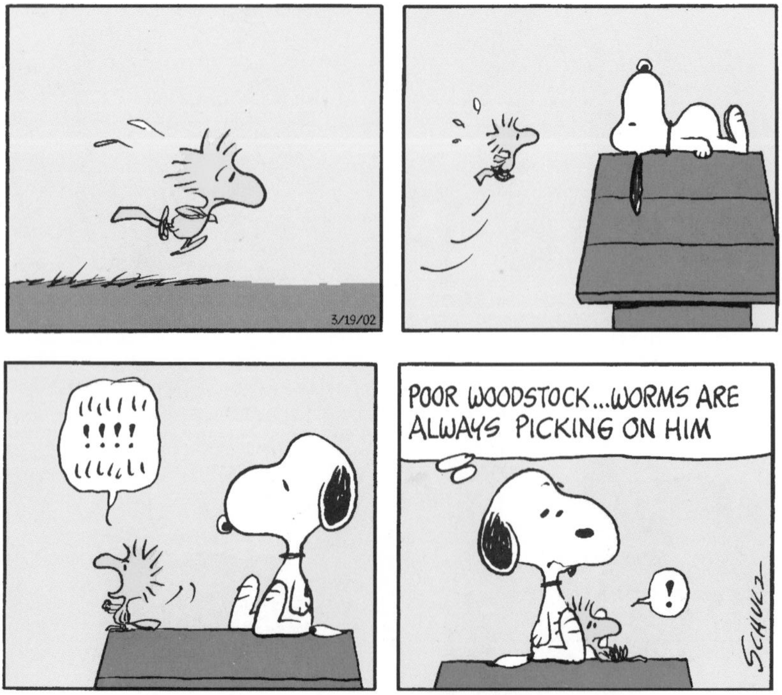
3/19/02
!!!!
POOR WOODSTOCK...WORMS ARE ALWAYS PICKING ON HIM
!
SCHULZ

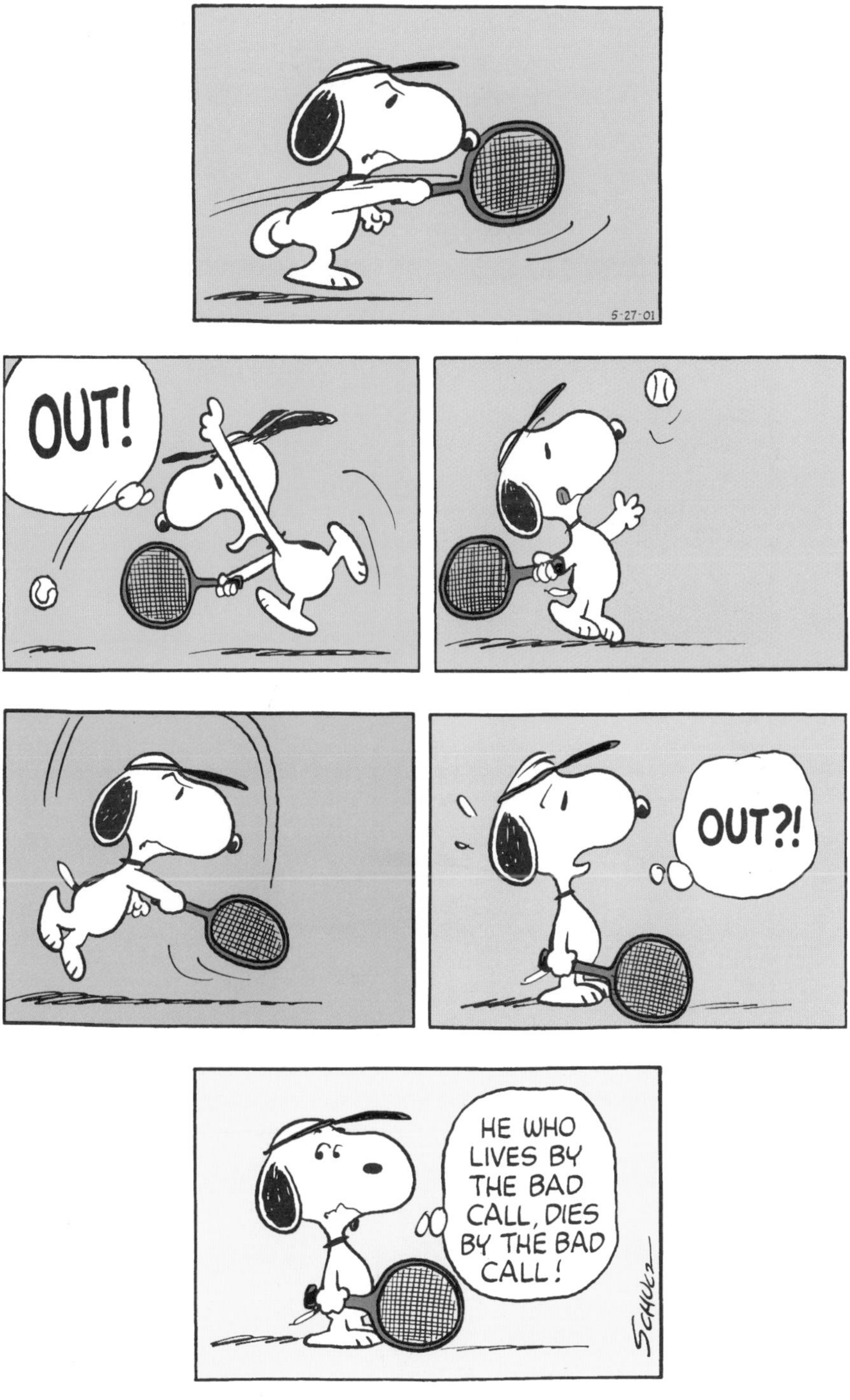
5-27-01
OUT!
OUT?!
HE WHO LIVES BY THE BAD CALL, DIES BY THE BAD CALL!
SCHULZ

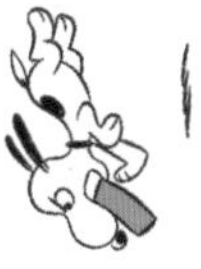

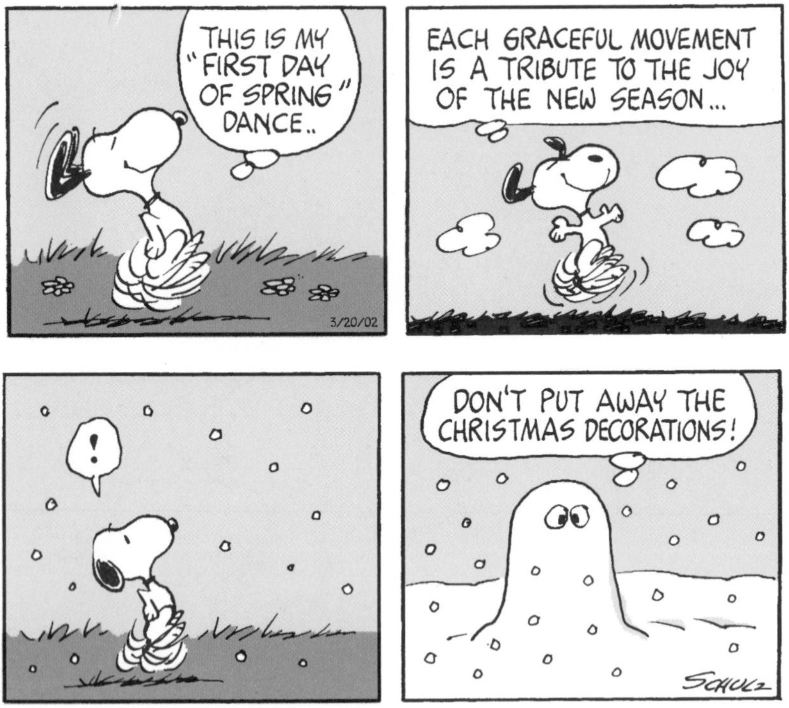
THIS IS MY "FIRST DAY OF SPRING" DANCE..
3/20/02
EACH GRACEFUL MOVEMENT IS A TRIBUTE TO THE JOY OF THE NEW SEASON...
!
DON'T PUT AWAY THE CHRISTMAS DECORATIONS!
SCHULZ

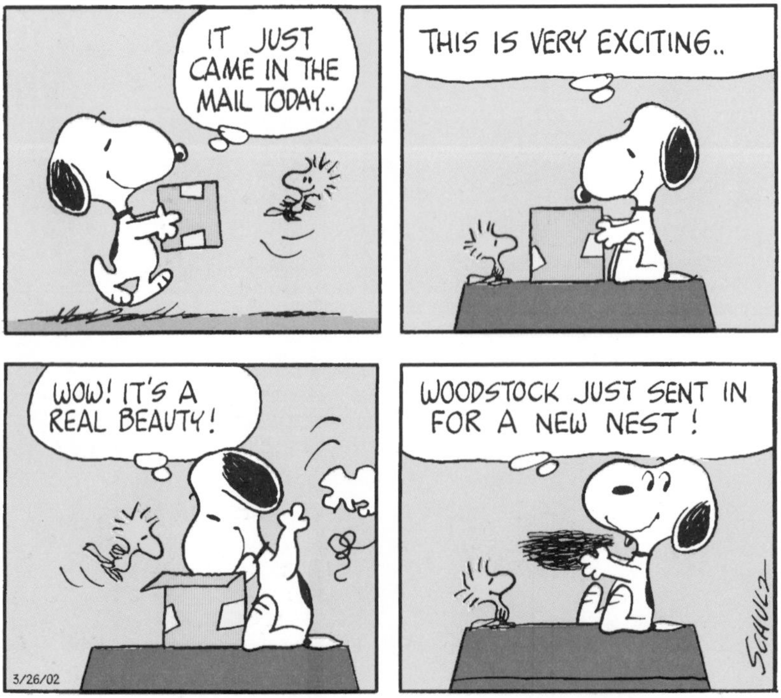
IT JUST CAME IN THE MAIL TODAY..
THIS IS VERY EXCITING..
WOW! IT'S A REAL BEAUTY!
3/26/02
WOODSTOCK JUST SENT IN FOR A NEW NEST!
SCHULZ

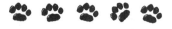

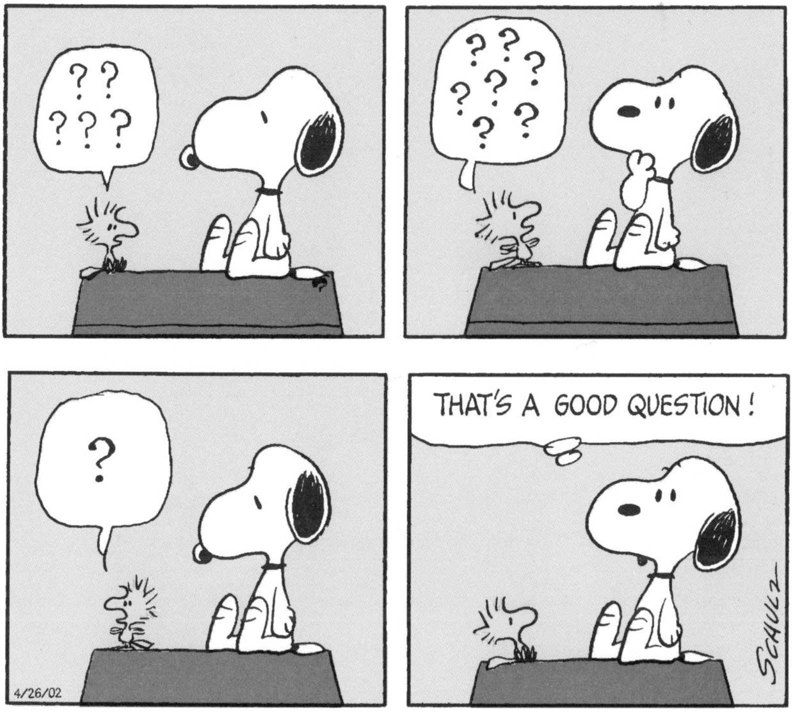
??
???
???
???
?
THAT'S A GOOD QUESTION!
4/26/02
SCHULZ

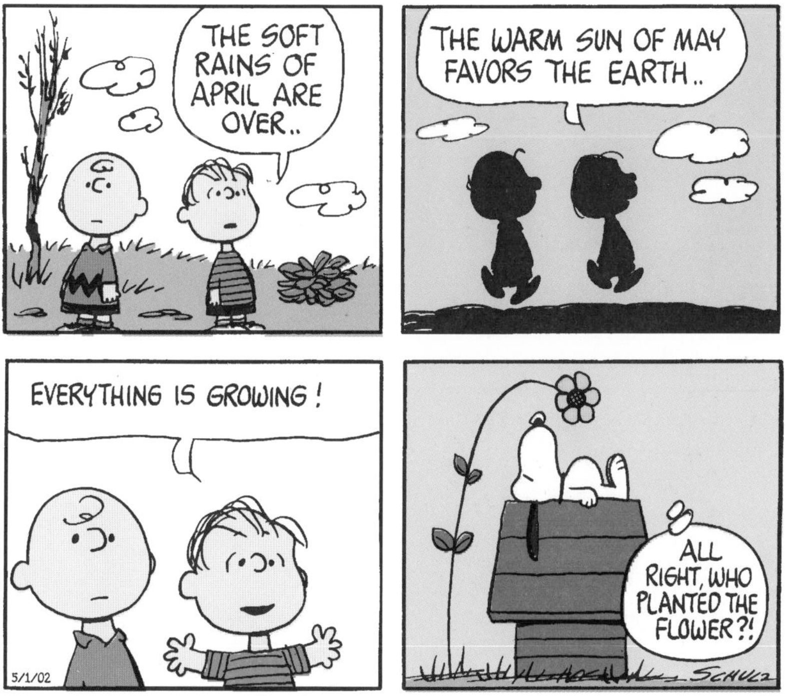
THE SOFT RAINS OF APRIL ARE OVER..
THE WARM SUN OF MAY FAVORS THE EARTH..
EVERYTHING IS GROWING!
ALL RIGHT, WHO PLANTED THE FLOWER?!
5/1/02
SCHULZ

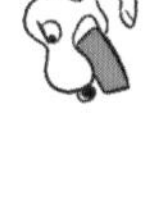

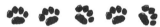

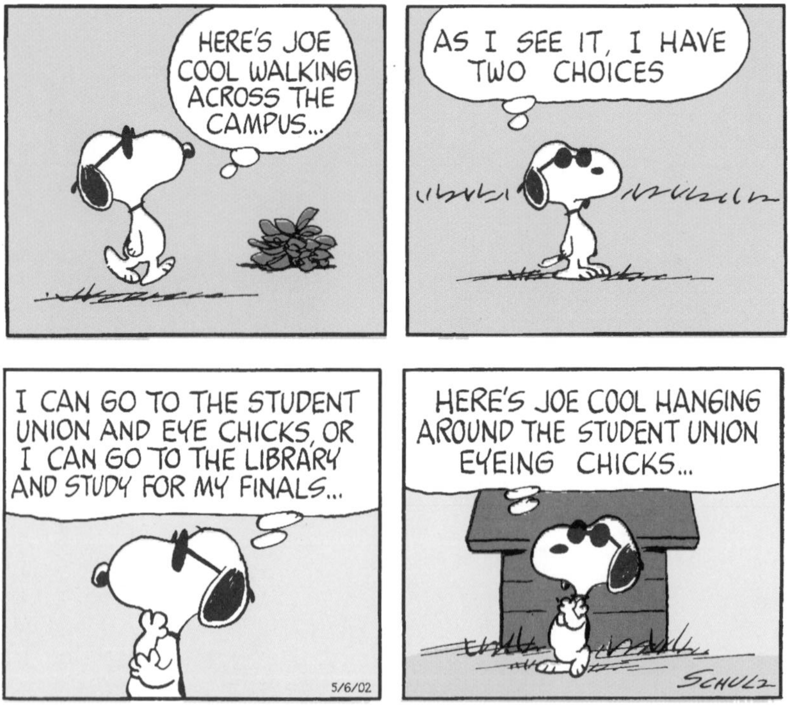
HERE'S JOE COOL WALKING ACROSS THE CAMPUS...
AS I SEE IT, I HAVE TWO CHOICES
I CAN GO TO THE STUDENT UNION AND EYE CHICKS, OR I CAN GO TO THE LIBRARY AND STUDY FOR MY FINALS...
5/6/02
HERE'S JOE COOL HANGING AROUND THE STUDENT UNION EYEING CHICKS...
SCHULZ

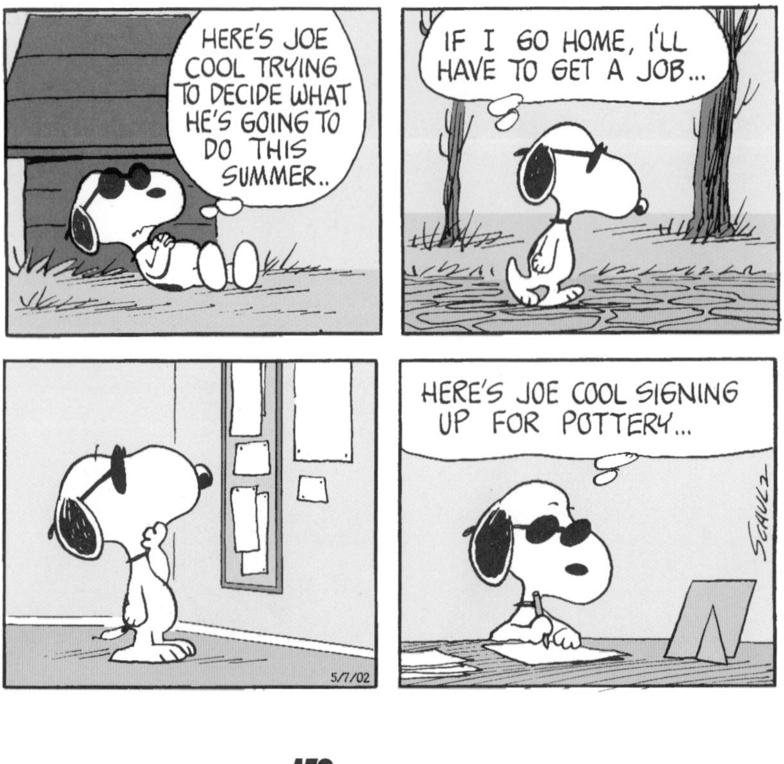
HERE'S JOE COOL TRYING TO DECIDE WHAT HE'S GOING TO DO THIS SUMMER..
IF I GO HOME, I'LL HAVE TO GET A JOB...
5/7/02
HERE'S JOE COOL SIGNING UP FOR POTTERY...
SCHULZ

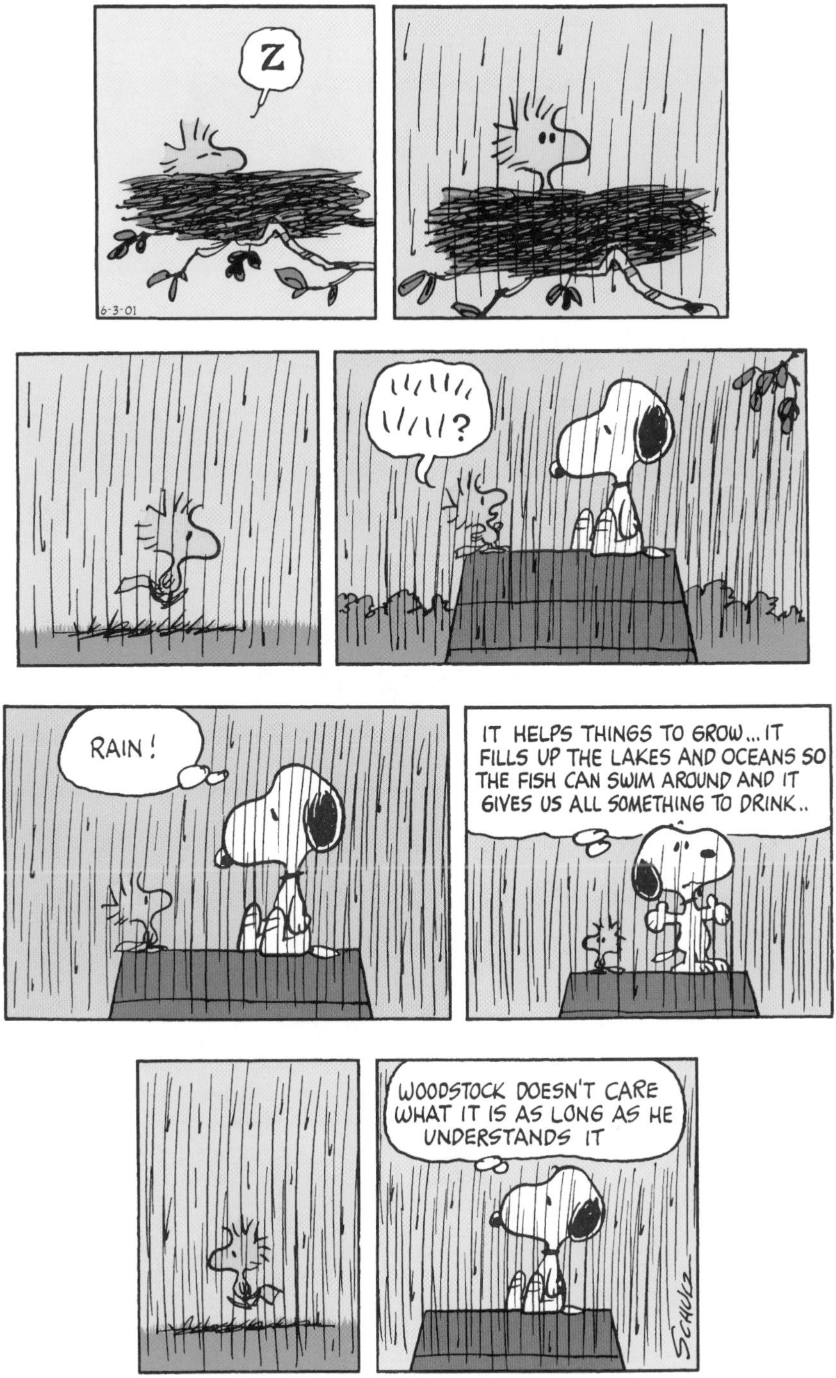
Z
6-3-01
\/\/\/\/ \/\/\/?
RAIN!
IT HELPS THINGS TO GROW... IT FILLS UP THE LAKES AND OCEANS SO THE FISH CAN SWIM AROUND AND IT GIVES US ALL SOMETHING TO DRINK..
WOODSTOCK DOESN'T CARE WHAT IT IS AS LONG AS HE UNDERSTANDS IT
SCHULZ

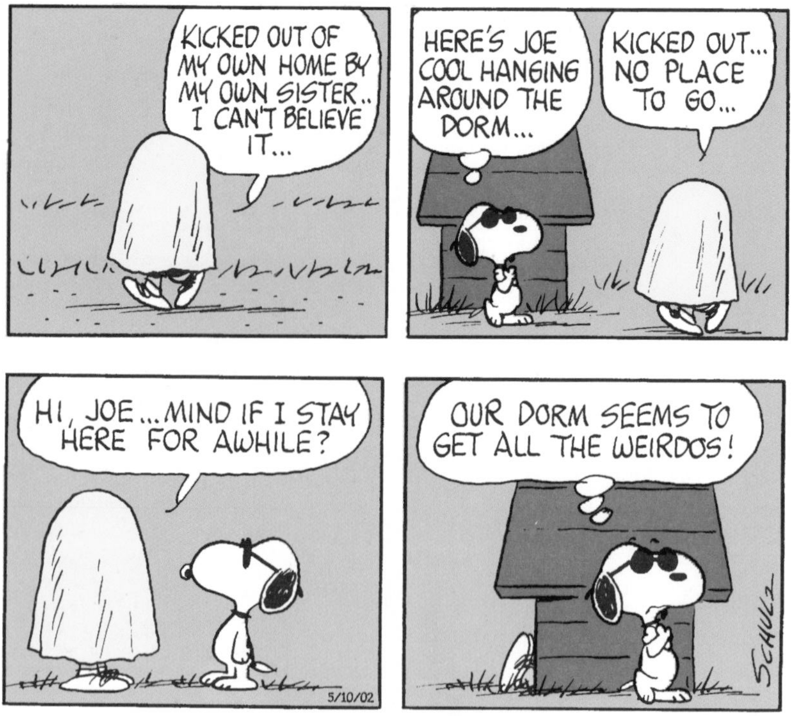
KICKED OUT OF MY OWN HOME BY MY OWN SISTER.. I CAN'T BELIEVE IT...
HERE'S JOE COOL HANGING AROUND THE DORM...
KICKED OUT... NO PLACE TO GO...
HI, JOE...MIND IF I STAY HERE FOR AWHILE?
OUR DORM SEEMS TO GET ALL THE WEIRDOS!
5/10/02
SCHULZ

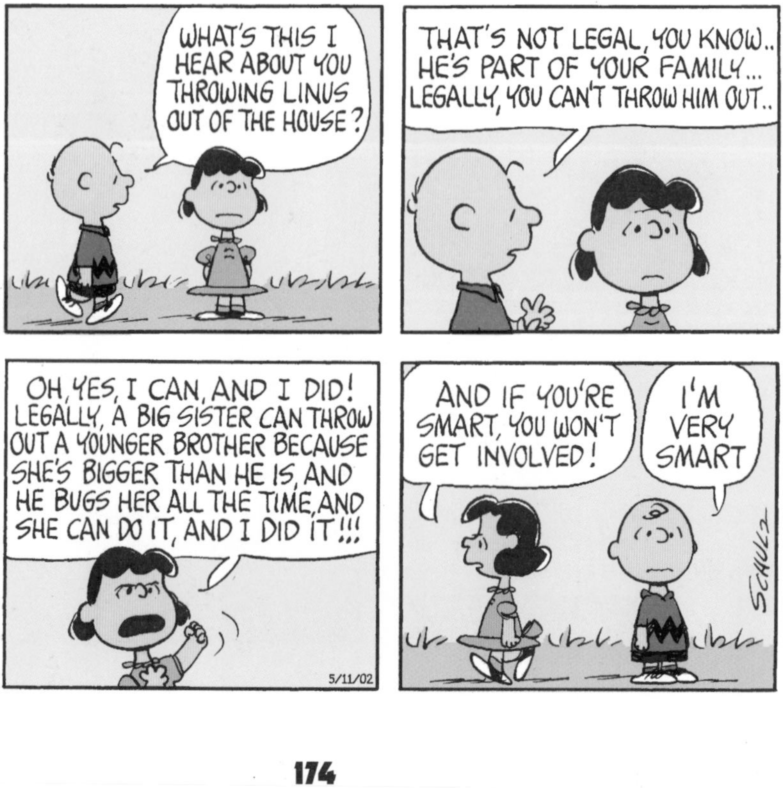
WHAT'S THIS I HEAR ABOUT YOU THROWING LINUS OUT OF THE HOUSE?
THAT'S NOT LEGAL, YOU KNOW.. HE'S PART OF YOUR FAMILY... LEGALLY, YOU CAN'T THROW HIM OUT..
OH, YES, I CAN, AND I DID! LEGALLY, A BIG SISTER CAN THROW OUT A YOUNGER BROTHER BECAUSE SHE'S BIGGER THAN HE IS, AND HE BUGS HER ALL THE TIME, AND SHE CAN DO IT, AND I DID IT!!!
5/11/02
AND IF YOU'RE SMART, YOU WON'T GET INVOLVED!
I'M VERY SMART
SCHULZ

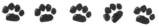

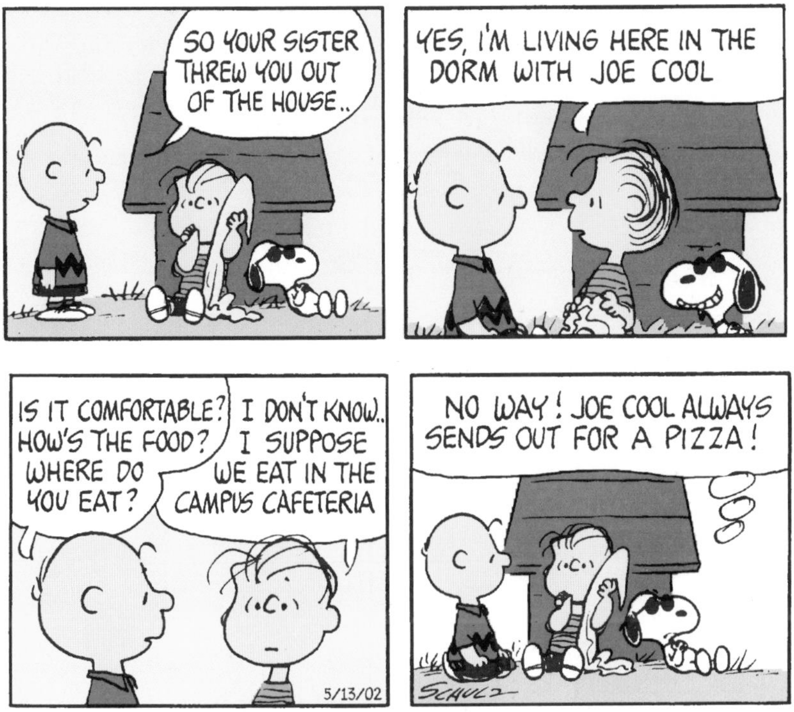
SO YOUR SISTER THREW YOU OUT OF THE HOUSE..
YES, I'M LIVING HERE IN THE DORM WITH JOE COOL
IS IT COMFORTABLE? HOW'S THE FOOD? WHERE DO YOU EAT?
I DON'T KNOW.. I SUPPOSE WE EAT IN THE CAMPUS CAFETERIA
5/13/02
NO WAY! JOE COOL ALWAYS SENDS OUT FOR A PIZZA!
SCHULZ

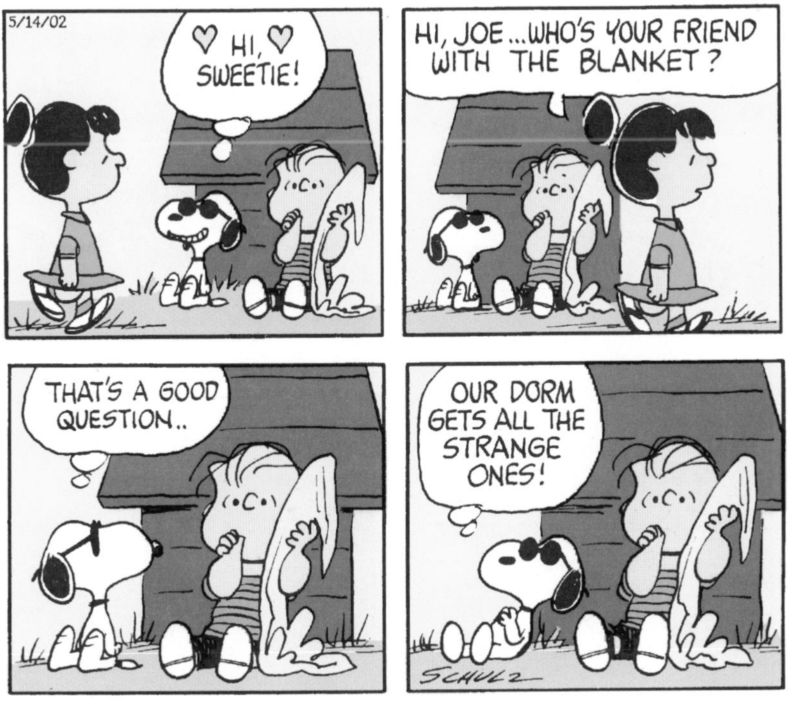
5/14/02
♡ HI, ♡ SWEETIE!
HI, JOE...WHO'S YOUR FRIEND WITH THE BLANKET?
THAT'S A GOOD QUESTION..
OUR DORM GETS ALL THE STRANGE ONES!
SCHULZ

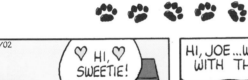

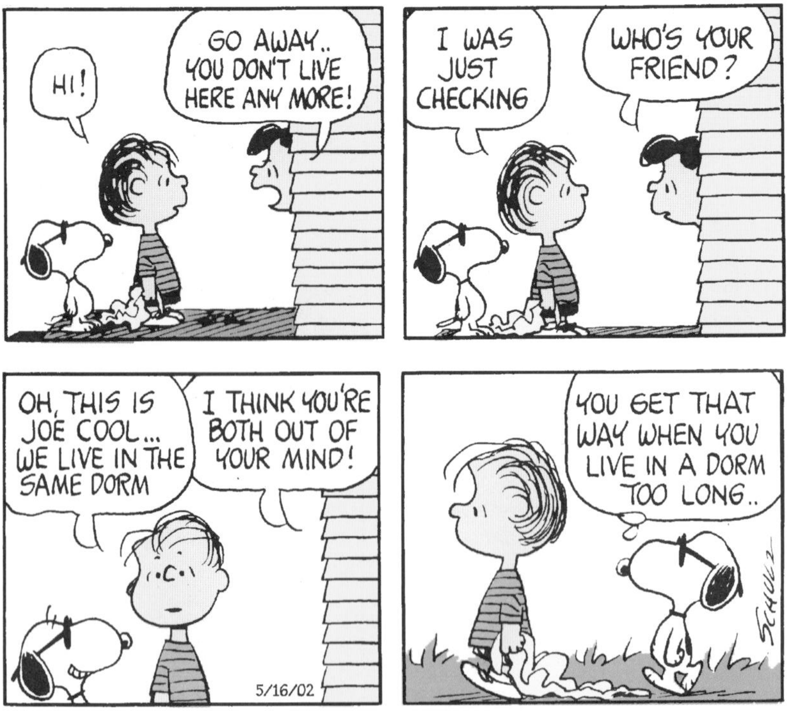
HI!
GO AWAY..
YOU DON'T LIVE
HERE ANY MORE!
I WAS
JUST
CHECKING
WHO'S YOUR
FRIEND?
OH, THIS IS
JOE COOL...
WE LIVE IN THE
SAME DORM
I THINK YOU'RE
BOTH OUT OF
YOUR MIND!
5/16/02
YOU GET THAT
WAY WHEN YOU
LIVE IN A DORM
TOO LONG..
SCHULZ

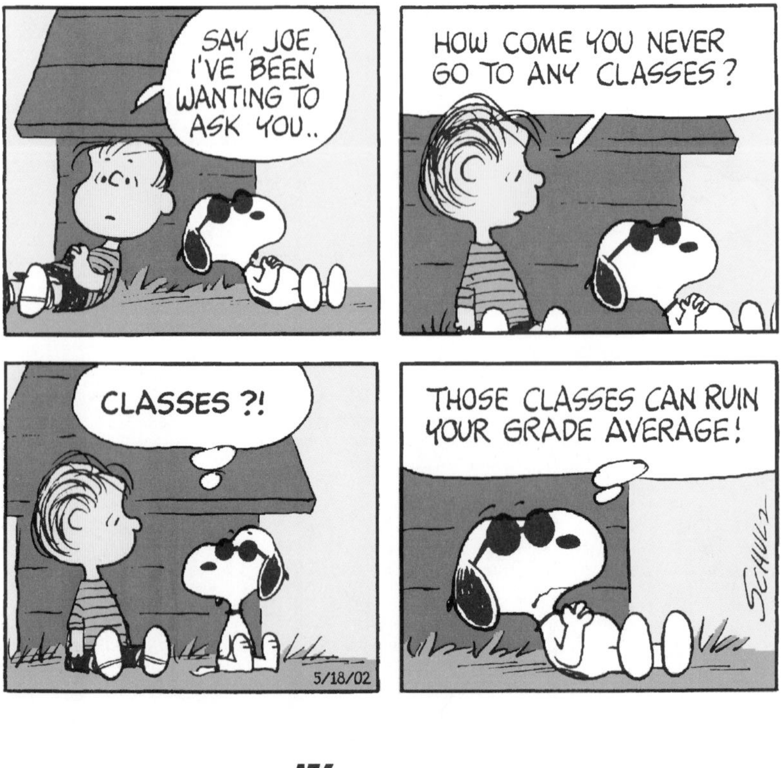
SAY, JOE,
I'VE BEEN
WANTING TO
ASK YOU..
HOW COME YOU NEVER
GO TO ANY CLASSES?
CLASSES ?!
5/18/02
THOSE CLASSES CAN RUIN
YOUR GRADE AVERAGE!
SCHULZ

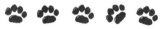

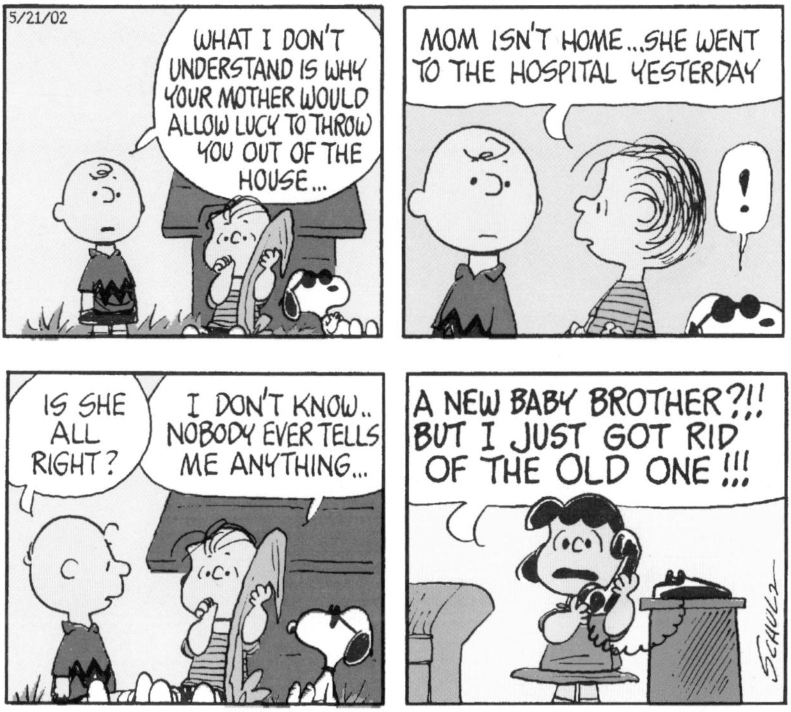
5/21/02
WHAT I DON'T UNDERSTAND IS WHY YOUR MOTHER WOULD ALLOW LUCY TO THROW YOU OUT OF THE HOUSE...
MOM ISN'T HOME...SHE WENT TO THE HOSPITAL YESTERDAY
!
IS SHE ALL RIGHT?
I DON'T KNOW.. NOBODY EVER TELLS ME ANYTHING...
A NEW BABY BROTHER?!! BUT I JUST GOT RID OF THE OLD ONE!!!

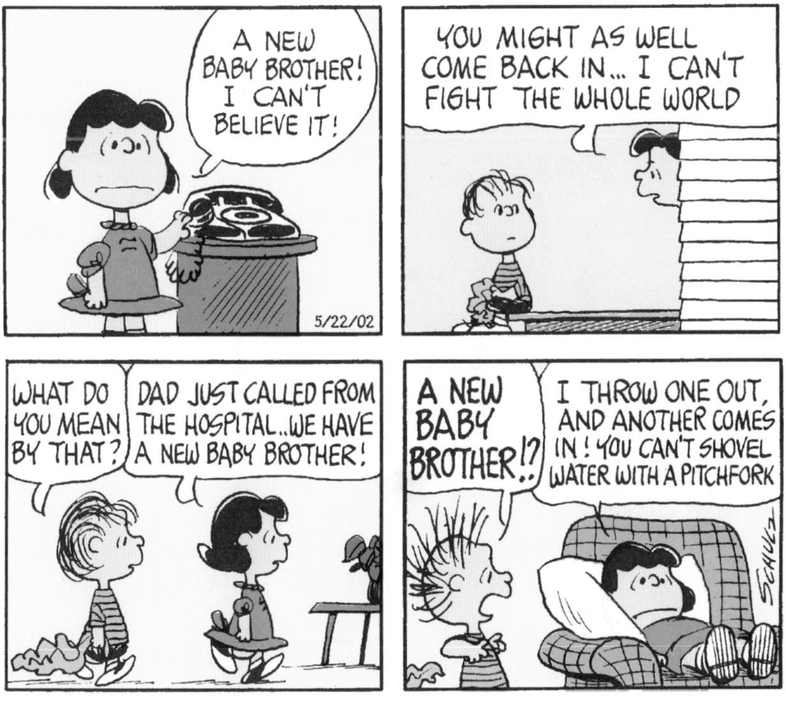
A NEW BABY BROTHER! I CAN'T BELIEVE IT!
5/22/02
YOU MIGHT AS WELL COME BACK IN... I CAN'T FIGHT THE WHOLE WORLD
WHAT DO YOU MEAN BY THAT?
DAD JUST CALLED FROM THE HOSPITAL..WE HAVE A NEW BABY BROTHER!
A NEW BABY BROTHER!?
I THROW ONE OUT, AND ANOTHER COMES IN! YOU CAN'T SHOVEL WATER WITH A PITCHFORK

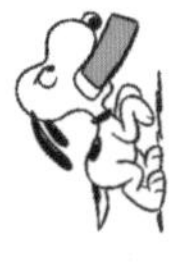

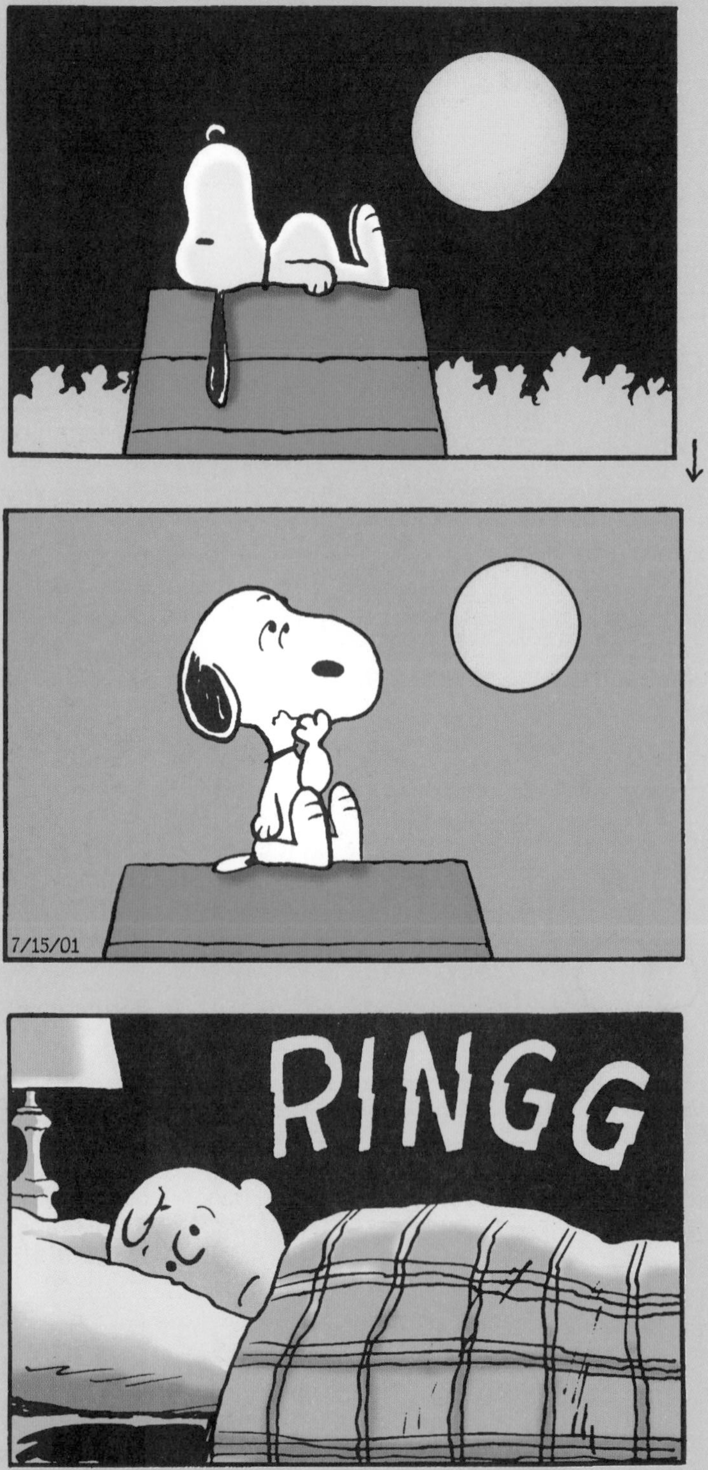
7/15/01
RINGG

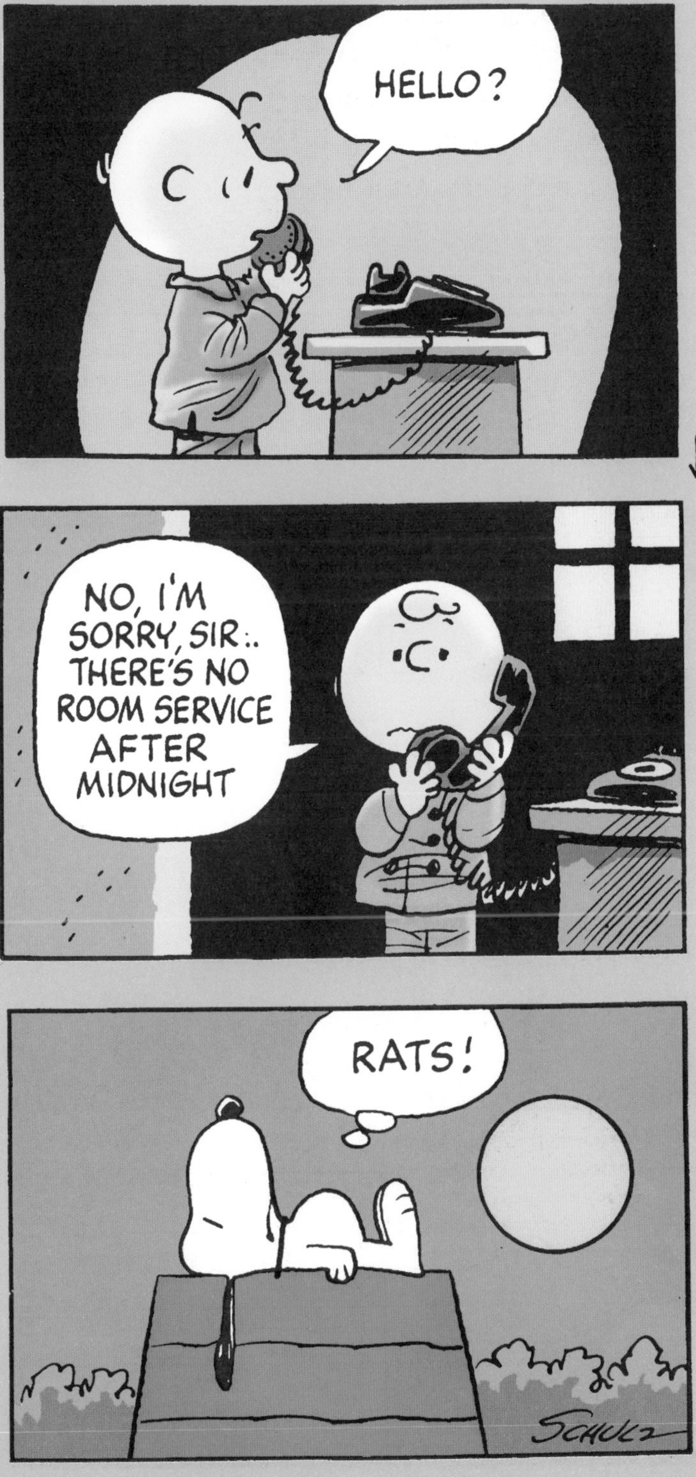
HELLO?
NO, I'M SORRY, SIR.. THERE'S NO ROOM SERVICE AFTER MIDNIGHT
RATS!
SCHULZ

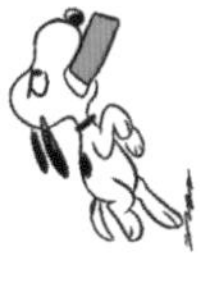

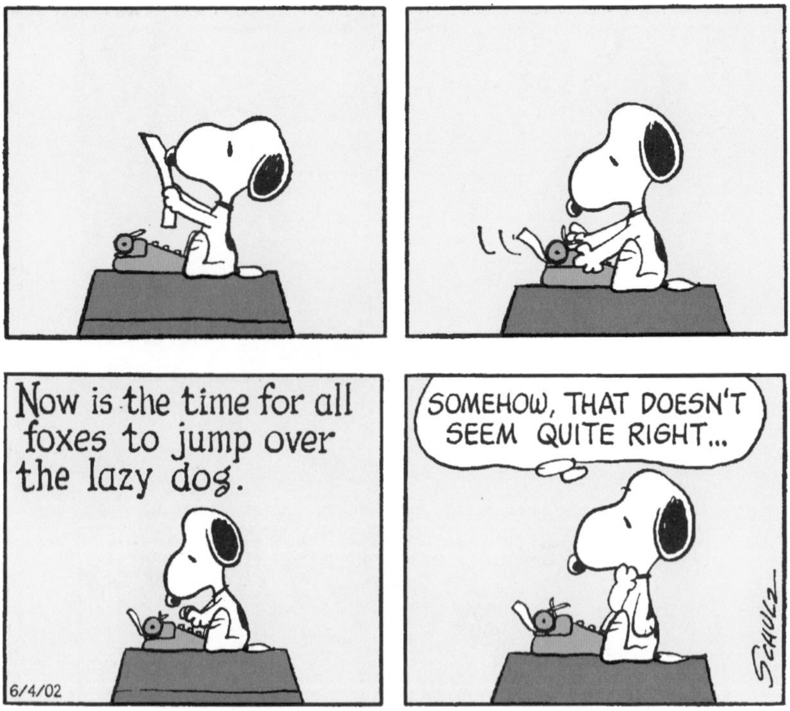
Now is the time for all foxes to jump over the lazy dog.
6/4/02
SOMEHOW, THAT DOESN'T SEEM QUITE RIGHT...
SCHULZ

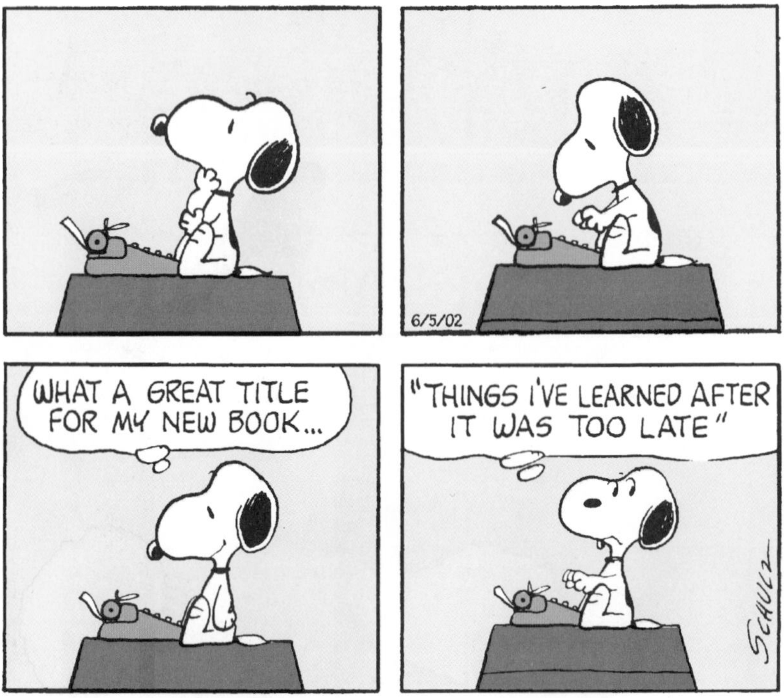
6/5/02
WHAT A GREAT TITLE FOR MY NEW BOOK...
"THINGS I'VE LEARNED AFTER IT WAS TOO LATE"
SCHULZ

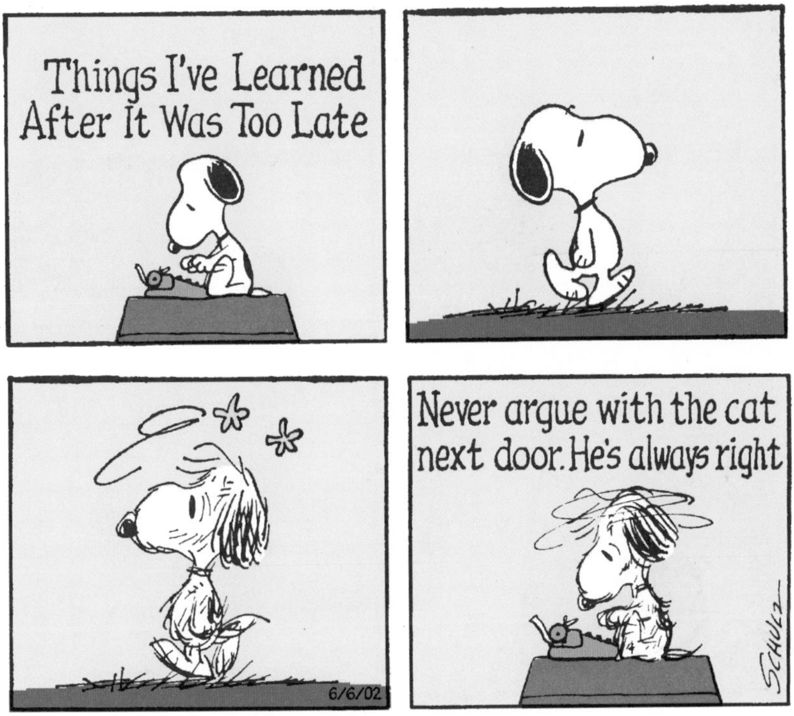
Things I've Learned After It Was Too Late
Never argue with the cat next door. He's always right
6/6/02
SCHULZ

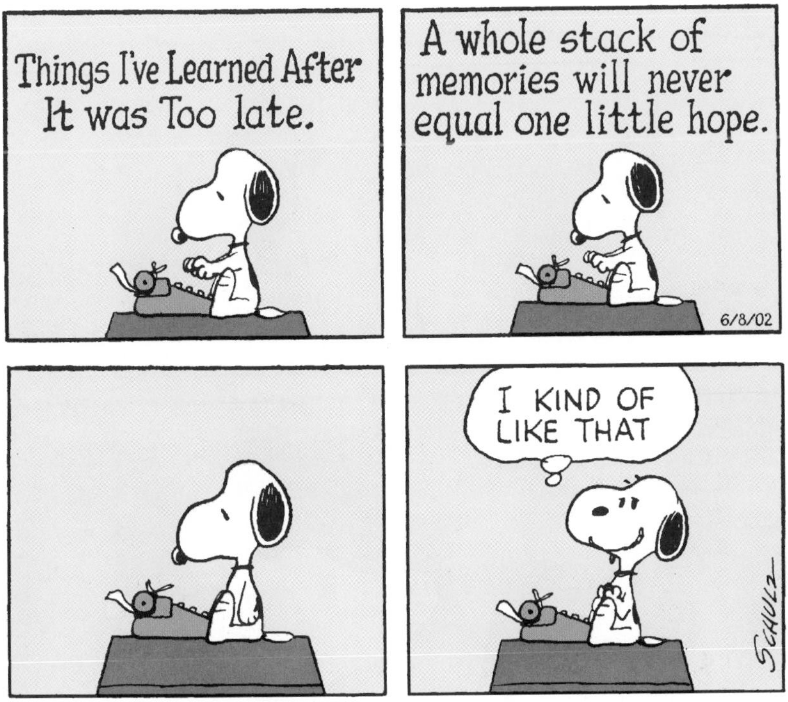
Things I've Learned After It was Too late.
A whole stack of memories will never equal one little hope.
6/8/02
I KIND OF LIKE THAT
SCHULZ

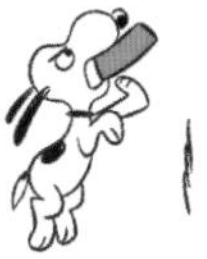

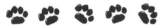

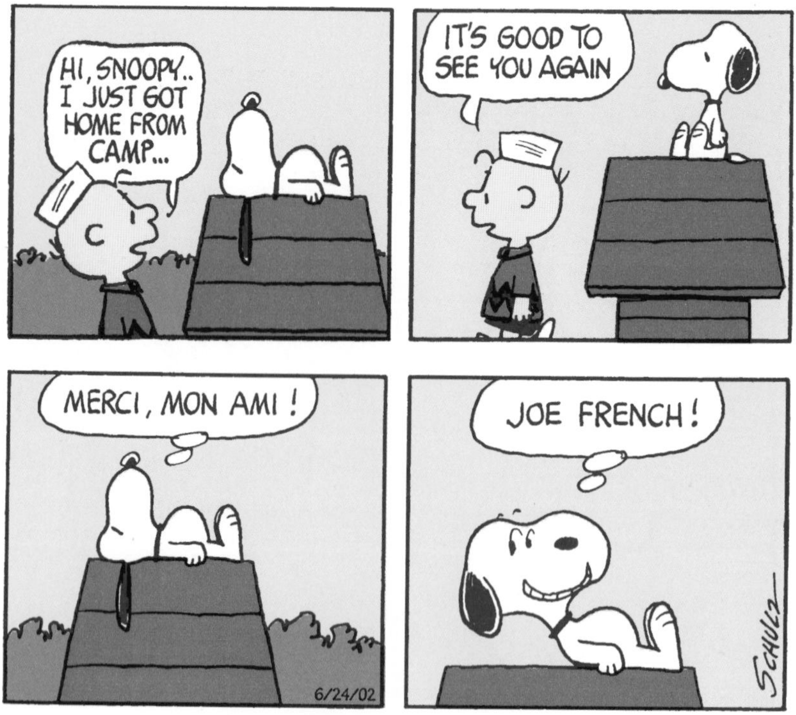
HI, SNOOPY.. I JUST GOT HOME FROM CAMP...
IT'S GOOD TO SEE YOU AGAIN
MERCI, MON AMI !
JOE FRENCH !
6/24/02
SCHULZ

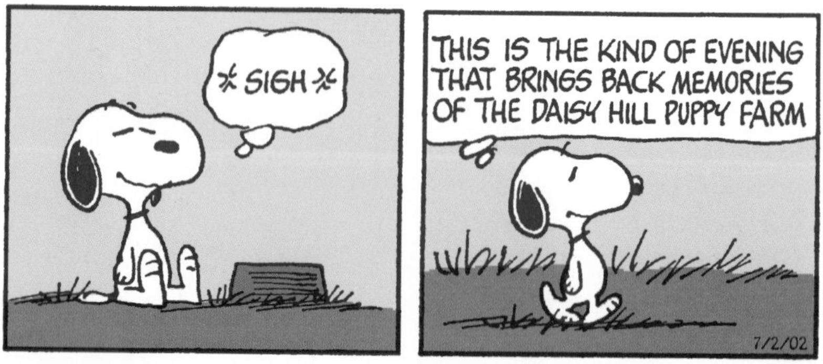
SIGH
THIS IS THE KIND OF EVENING THAT BRINGS BACK MEMORIES OF THE DAISY HILL PUPPY FARM
7/2/02

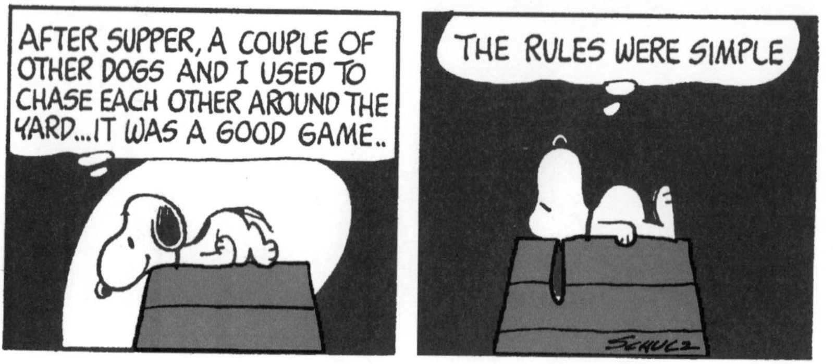
AFTER SUPPER, A COUPLE OF OTHER DOGS AND I USED TO CHASE EACH OTHER AROUND THE YARD...IT WAS A GOOD GAME..
THE RULES WERE SIMPLE
SCHULZ

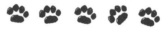

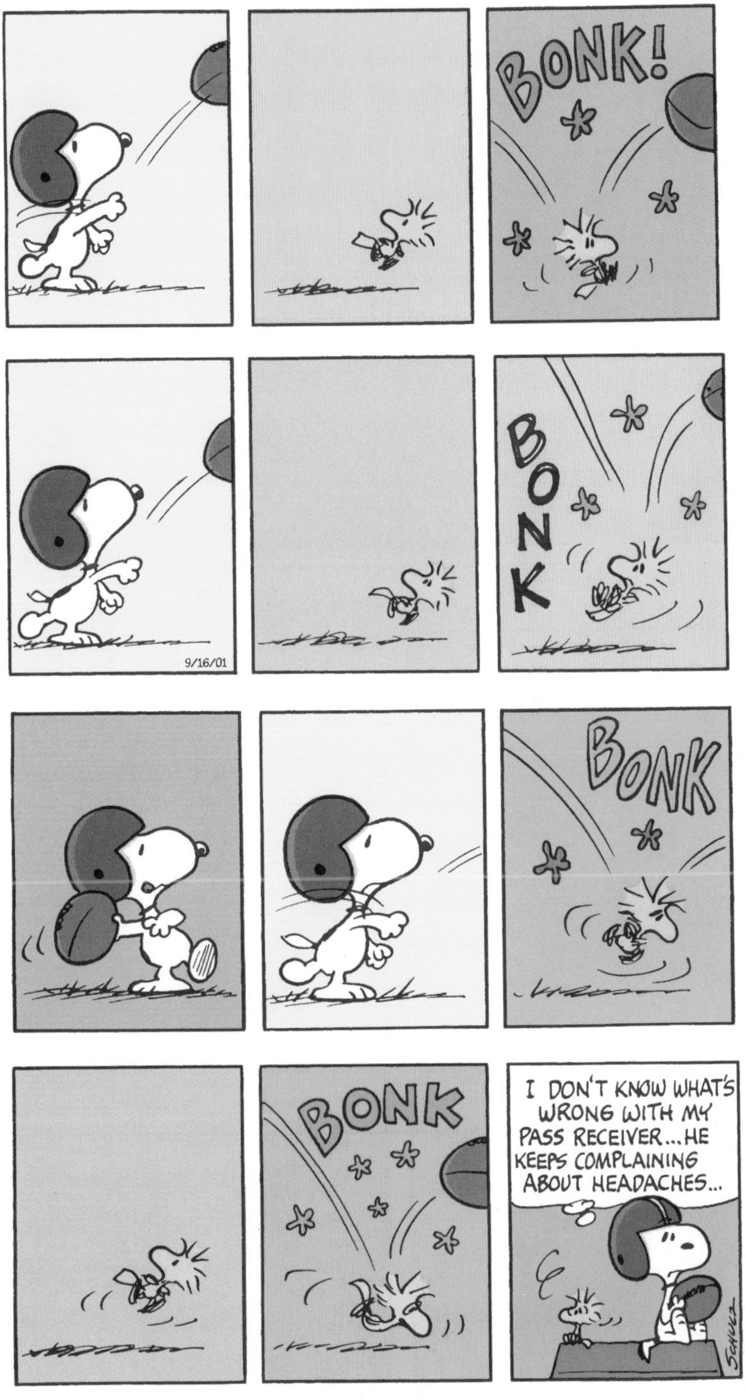
BONK!
9/16/01
BONK
BONK
BONK
I DON'T KNOW WHAT'S WRONG WITH MY PASS RECEIVER... HE KEEPS COMPLAINING ABOUT HEADACHES...
SCHULZ

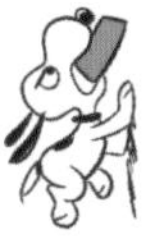

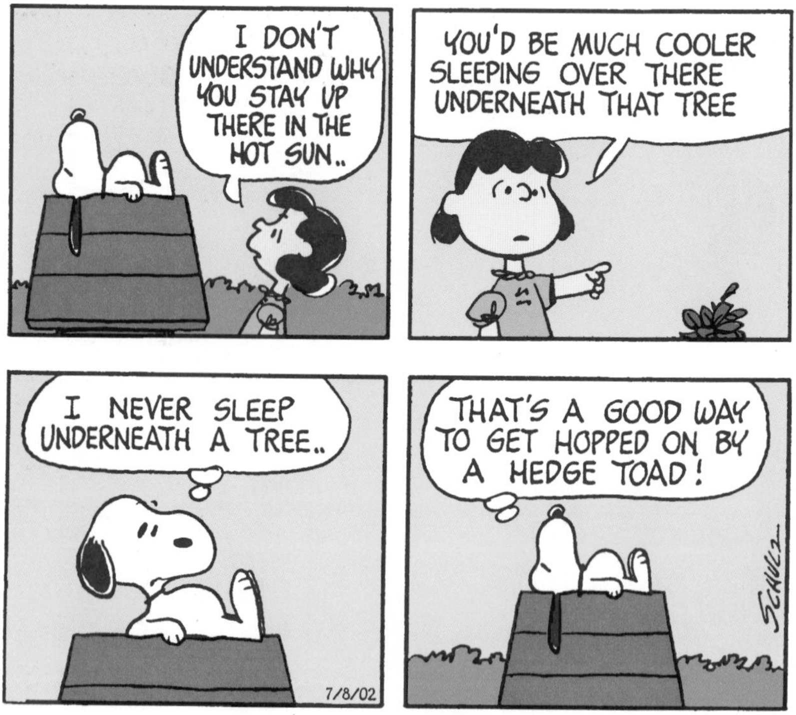
I DON'T UNDERSTAND WHY YOU STAY UP THERE IN THE HOT SUN..
YOU'D BE MUCH COOLER SLEEPING OVER THERE UNDERNEATH THAT TREE
I NEVER SLEEP UNDERNEATH A TREE..
7/8/02
THAT'S A GOOD WAY TO GET HOPPED ON BY A HEDGE TOAD!

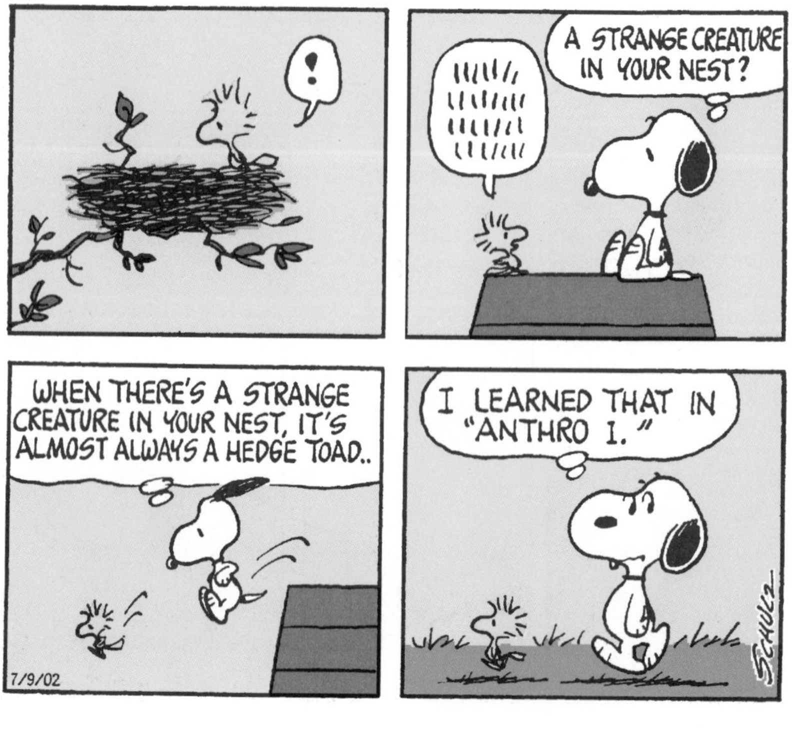
!
A STRANGE CREATURE IN YOUR NEST?
WHEN THERE'S A STRANGE CREATURE IN YOUR NEST, IT'S ALMOST ALWAYS A HEDGE TOAD..
7/9/02
I LEARNED THAT IN "ANTHRO I."

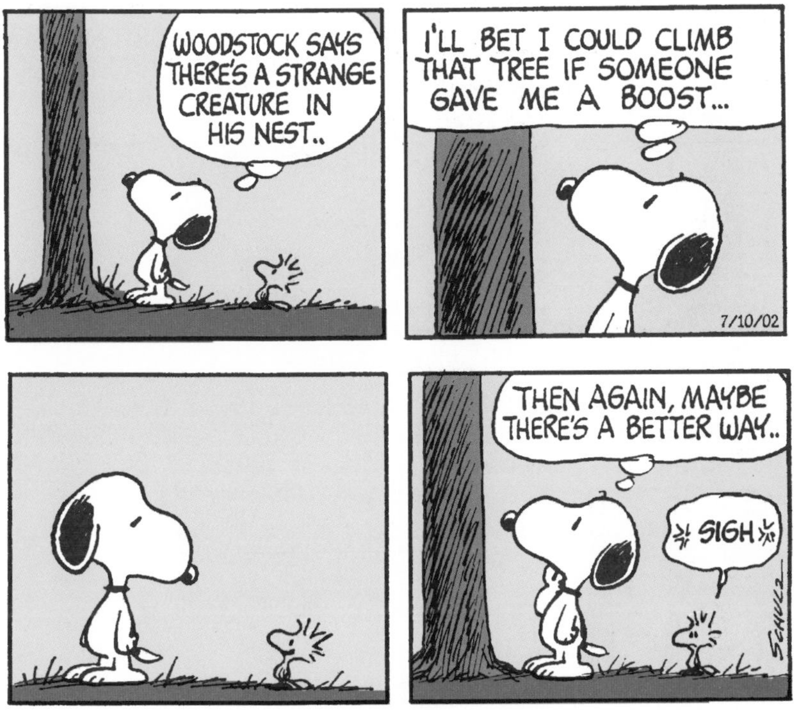
WOODSTOCK SAYS THERE'S A STRANGE CREATURE IN HIS NEST..
I'LL BET I COULD CLIMB THAT TREE IF SOMEONE GAVE ME A BOOST...
7/10/02
THEN AGAIN, MAYBE THERE'S A BETTER WAY..
SIGH
SCHULZ

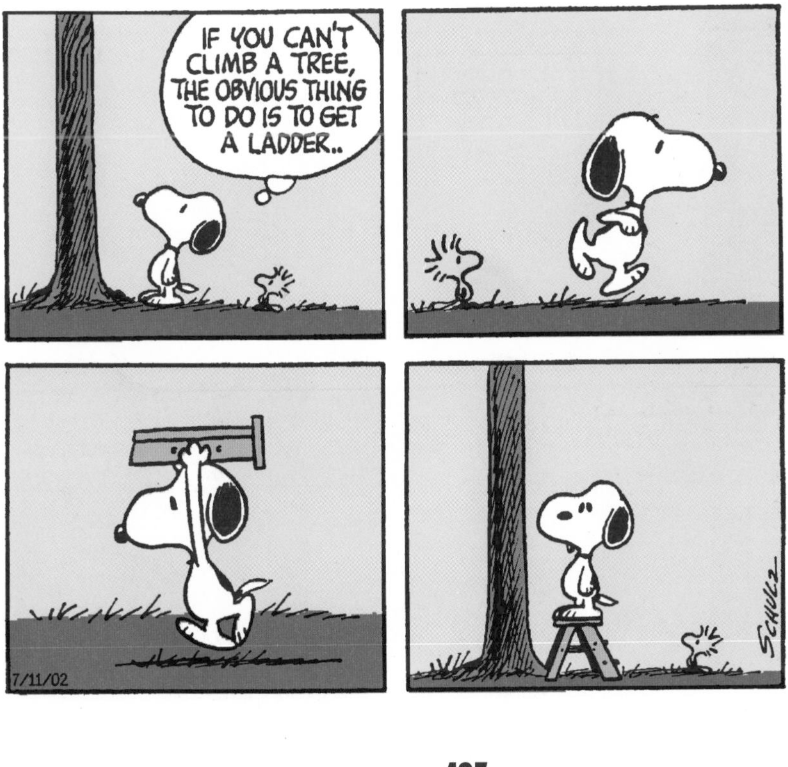
IF YOU CAN'T CLIMB A TREE, THE OBVIOUS THING TO DO IS TO GET A LADDER..
7/11/02
SCHULZ

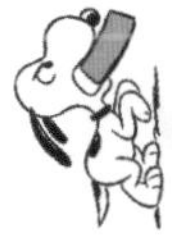

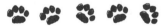

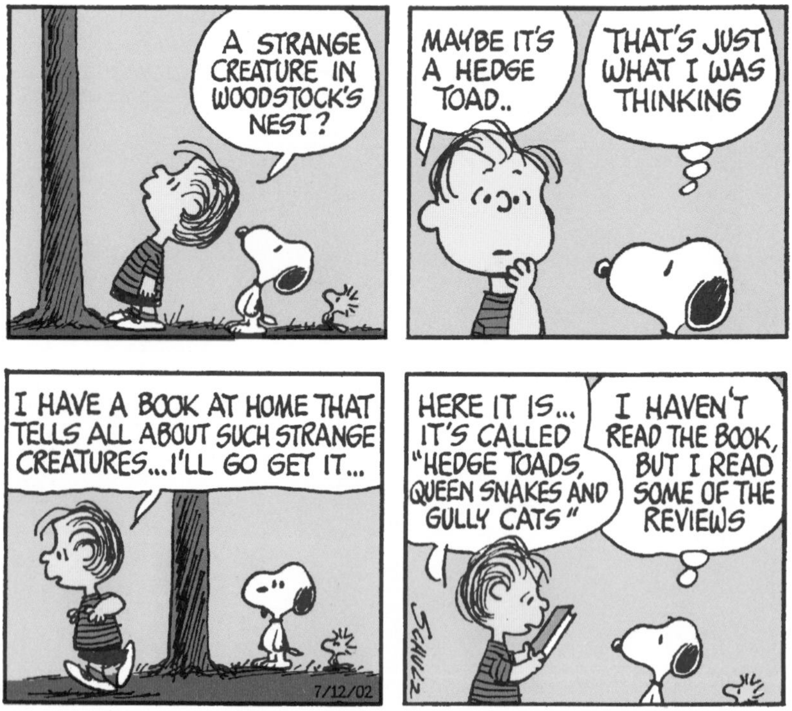
A STRANGE CREATURE IN WOODSTOCK'S NEST?
MAYBE IT'S A HEDGE TOAD..
THAT'S JUST WHAT I WAS THINKING
I HAVE A BOOK AT HOME THAT TELLS ALL ABOUT SUCH STRANGE CREATURES...I'LL GO GET IT...
7/12/02
HERE IT IS... IT'S CALLED "HEDGE TOADS, QUEEN SNAKES AND GULLY CATS"
I HAVEN'T READ THE BOOK, BUT I READ SOME OF THE REVIEWS
SCHULZ

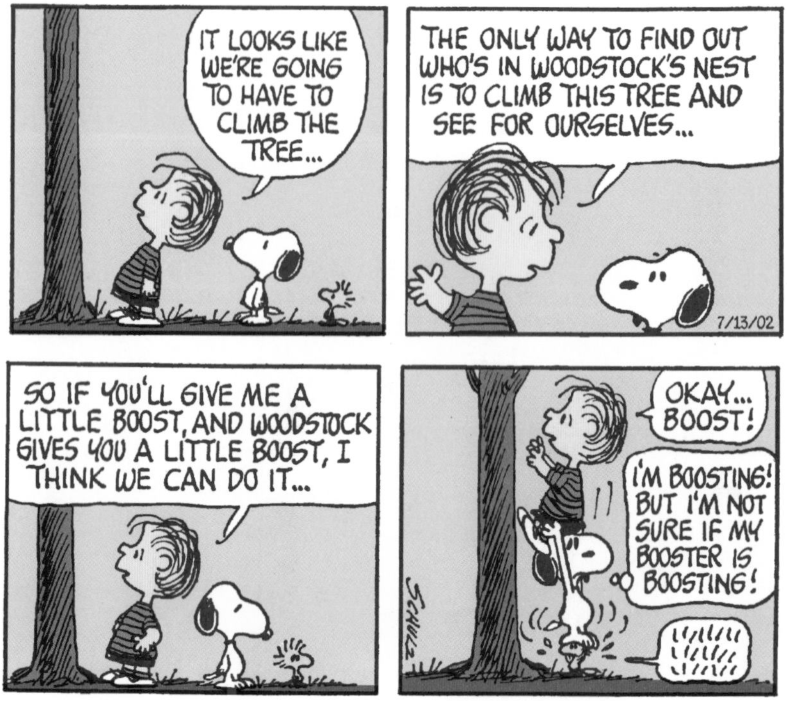
IT LOOKS LIKE WE'RE GOING TO HAVE TO CLIMB THE TREE...
THE ONLY WAY TO FIND OUT WHO'S IN WOODSTOCK'S NEST IS TO CLIMB THIS TREE AND SEE FOR OURSELVES...
7/13/02
SO IF YOU'LL GIVE ME A LITTLE BOOST, AND WOODSTOCK GIVES YOU A LITTLE BOOST, I THINK WE CAN DO IT...
OKAY... BOOST!
I'M BOOSTING! BUT I'M NOT SURE IF MY BOOSTER IS BOOSTING!
SCHULZ

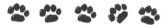

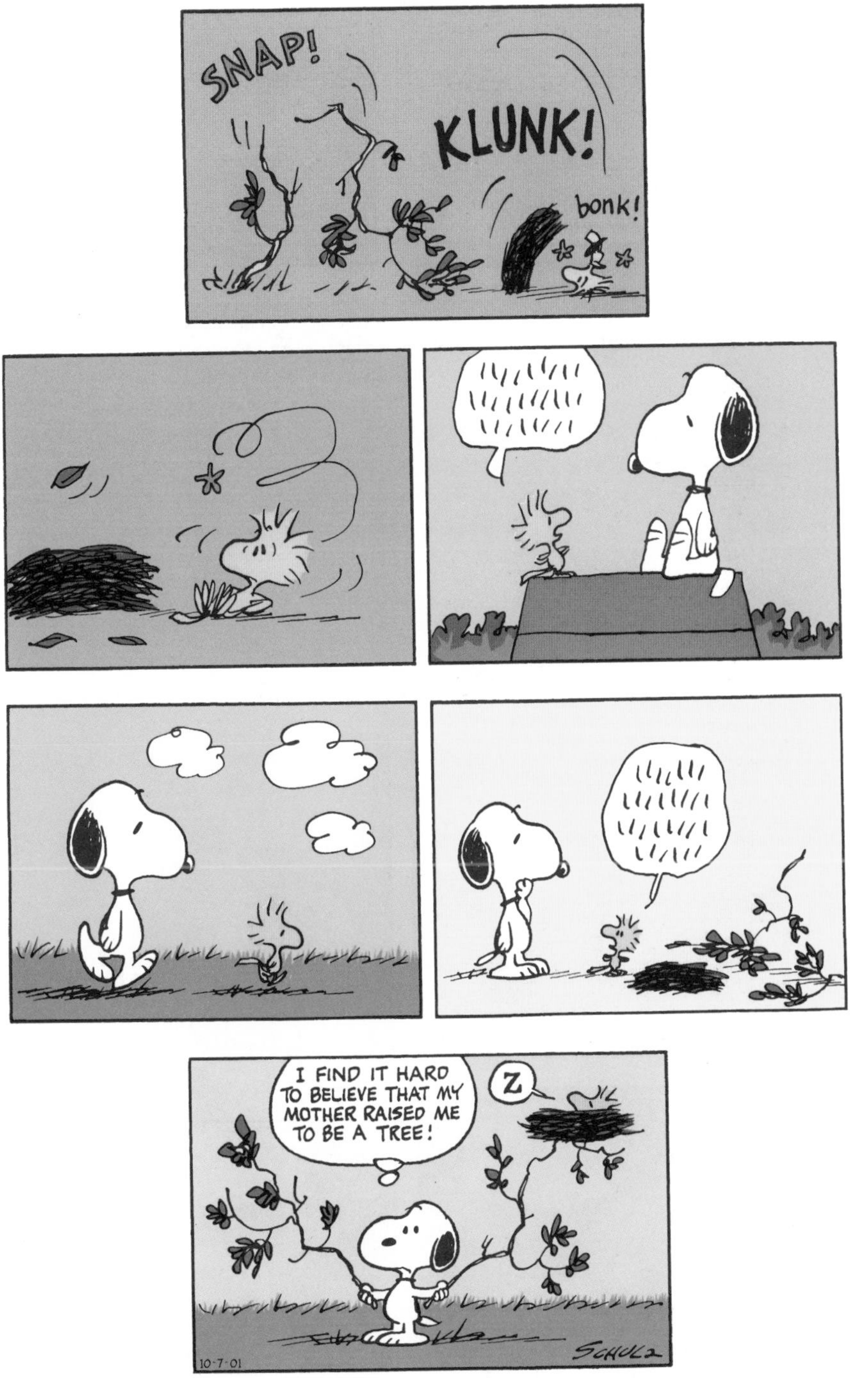
SNAP!
KLUNK!
bonk!
I FIND IT HARD TO BELIEVE THAT MY MOTHER RAISED ME TO BE A TREE!
Z
SCHULZ
10-7-01

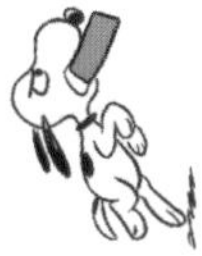

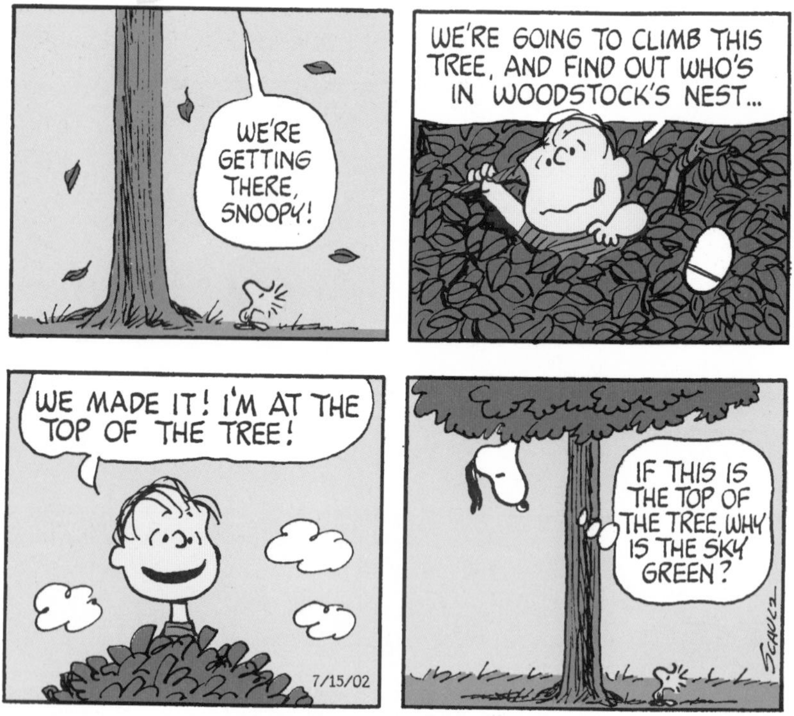
WE'RE GETTING THERE, SNOOPY!
WE'RE GOING TO CLIMB THIS TREE, AND FIND OUT WHO'S IN WOODSTOCK'S NEST...
WE MADE IT! I'M AT THE TOP OF THE TREE!
7/15/02
IF THIS IS THE TOP OF THE TREE, WHY IS THE SKY GREEN?
SCHULZ

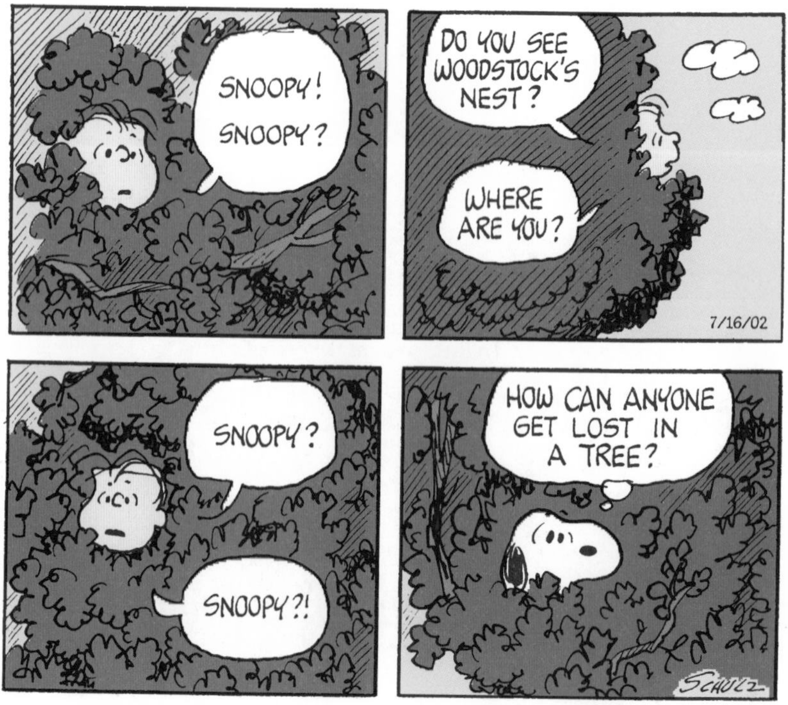
SNOOPY!
SNOOPY?
DO YOU SEE WOODSTOCK'S NEST?
WHERE ARE YOU?
7/16/02
SNOOPY?
SNOOPY?!
HOW CAN ANYONE GET LOST IN A TREE?
SCHULZ

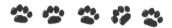

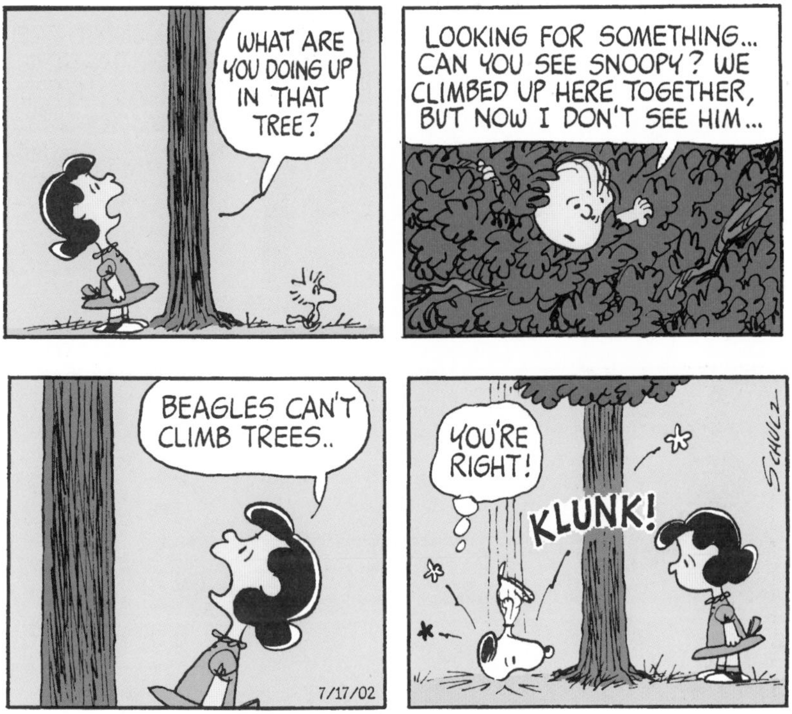
WHAT ARE YOU DOING UP IN THAT TREE?
LOOKING FOR SOMETHING... CAN YOU SEE SNOOPY? WE CLIMBED UP HERE TOGETHER, BUT NOW I DON'T SEE HIM...
BEAGLES CAN'T CLIMB TREES..
7/17/02
YOU'RE RIGHT!
KLUNK!
SCHULZ

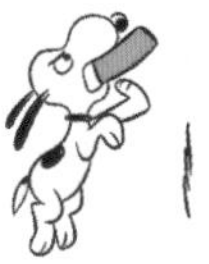

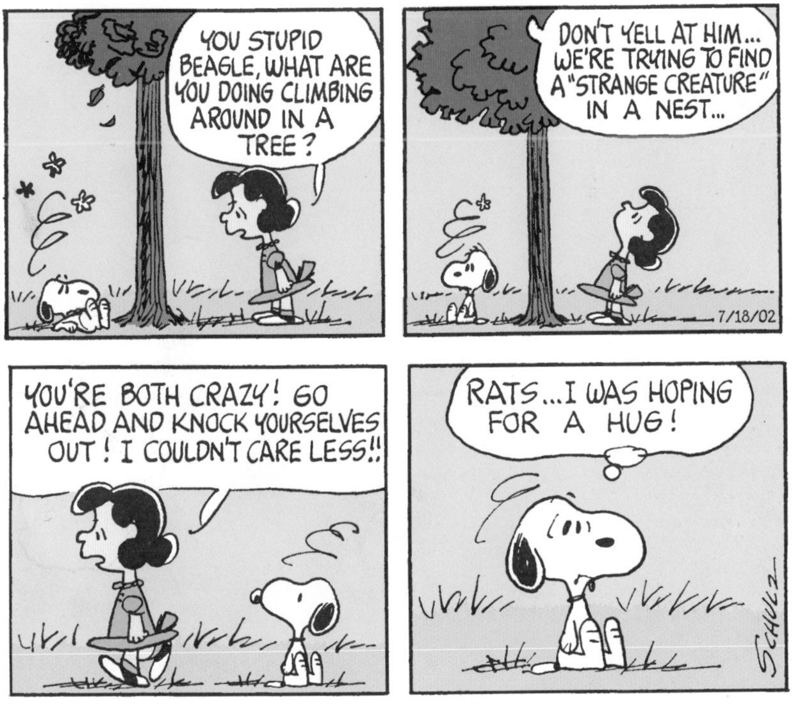
YOU STUPID BEAGLE, WHAT ARE YOU DOING CLIMBING AROUND IN A TREE?
DON'T YELL AT HIM... WE'RE TRYING TO FIND A "STRANGE CREATURE" IN A NEST...
7/18/02
YOU'RE BOTH CRAZY! GO AHEAD AND KNOCK YOURSELVES OUT! I COULDN'T CARE LESS!!
RATS... I WAS HOPING FOR A HUG!
SCHULZ

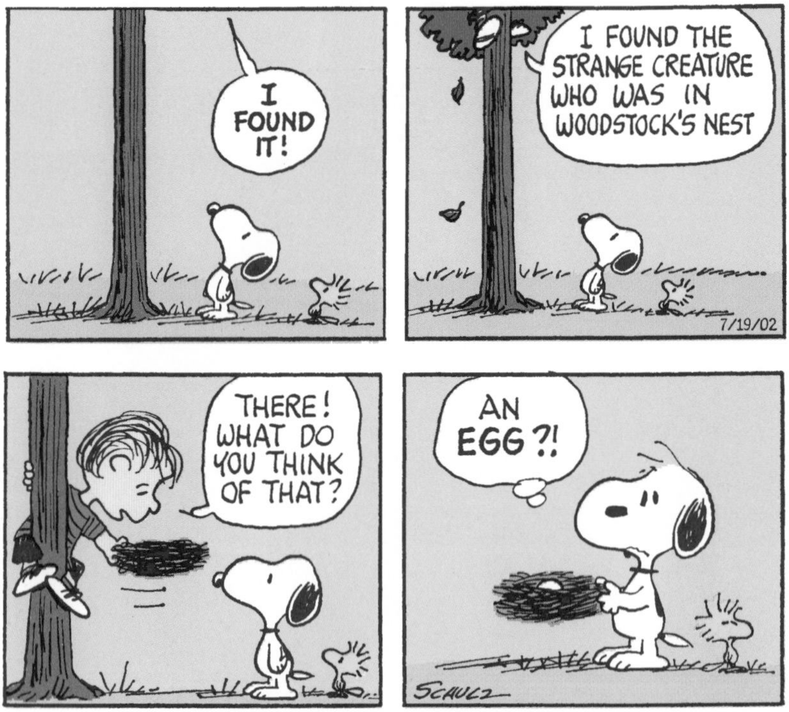
I FOUND IT!
I FOUND THE STRANGE CREATURE WHO WAS IN WOODSTOCK'S NEST
7/19/02
THERE! WHAT DO YOU THINK OF THAT?
AN EGG?!
SCHULZ

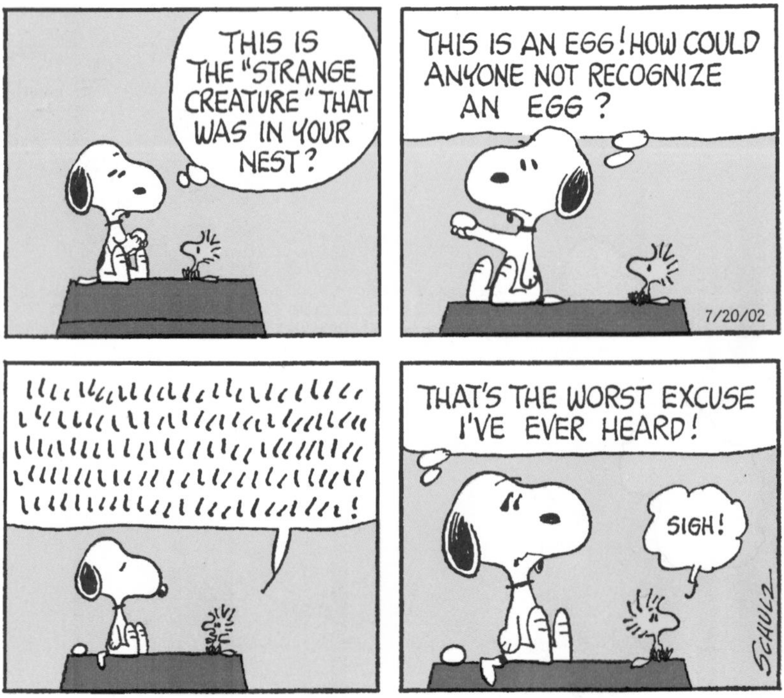
THIS IS THE "STRANGE CREATURE" THAT WAS IN YOUR NEST?
THIS IS AN EGG! HOW COULD ANYONE NOT RECOGNIZE AN EGG?
7/20/02
THAT'S THE WORST EXCUSE I'VE EVER HEARD!
SIGH!
SCHULZ

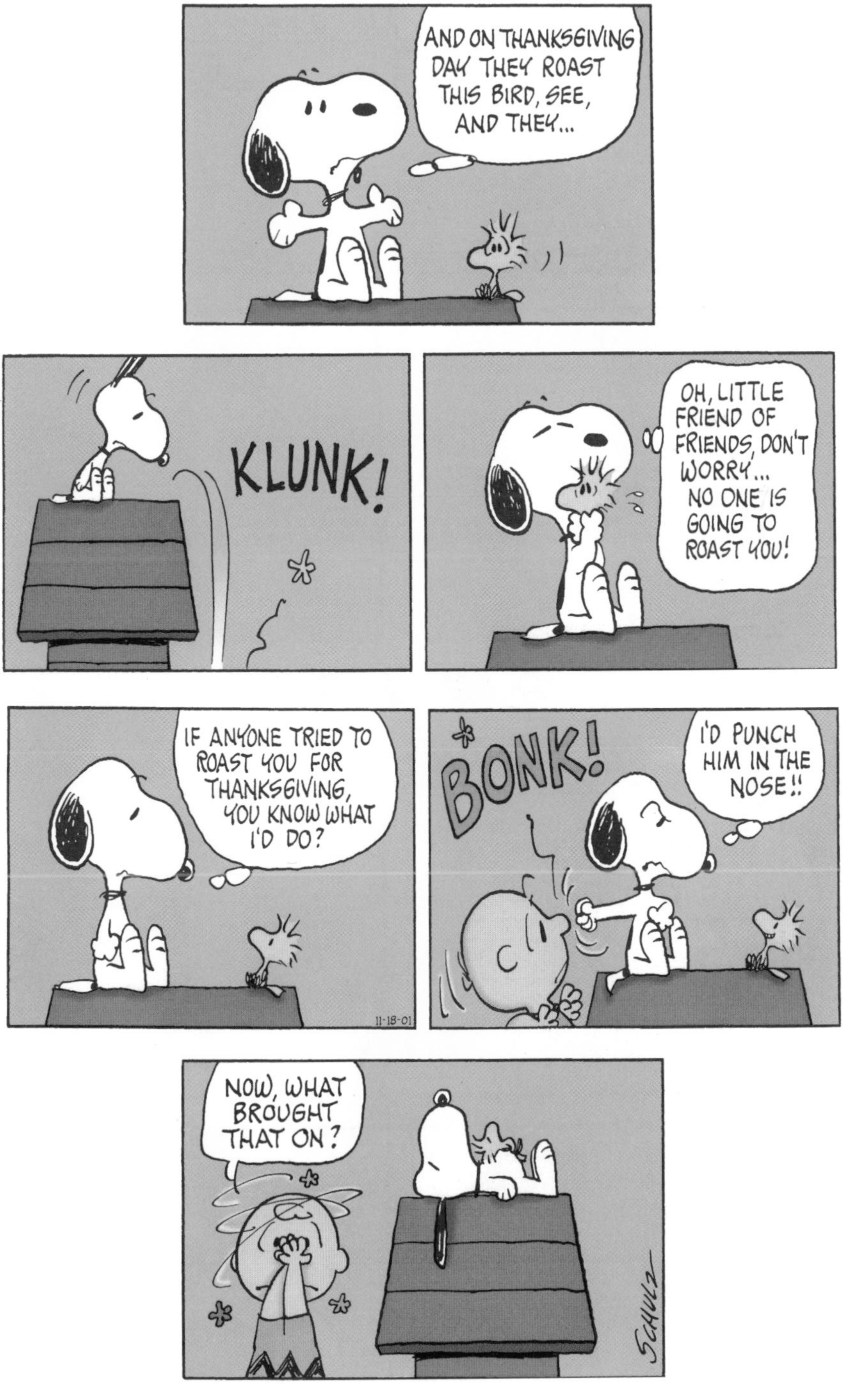
AND ON THANKSGIVING DAY THEY ROAST THIS BIRD, SEE, AND THEY...
KLUNK!
OH, LITTLE FRIEND OF FRIENDS, DON'T WORRY... NO ONE IS GOING TO ROAST YOU!
IF ANYONE TRIED TO ROAST YOU FOR THANKSGIVING, YOU KNOW WHAT I'D DO?
11-18-01
BONK!
I'D PUNCH HIM IN THE NOSE!!
NOW, WHAT BROUGHT THAT ON?
SCHULZ

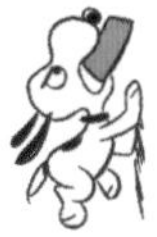

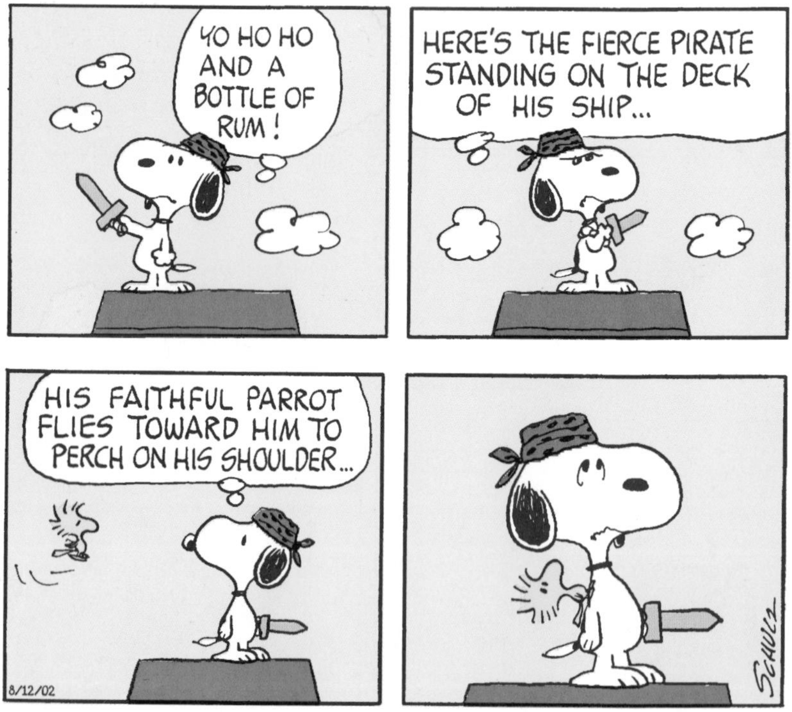
YO HO HO AND A BOTTLE OF RUM!
HERE'S THE FIERCE PIRATE STANDING ON THE DECK OF HIS SHIP...
HIS FAITHFUL PARROT FLIES TOWARD HIM TO PERCH ON HIS SHOULDER...
8/12/02
SCHULZ

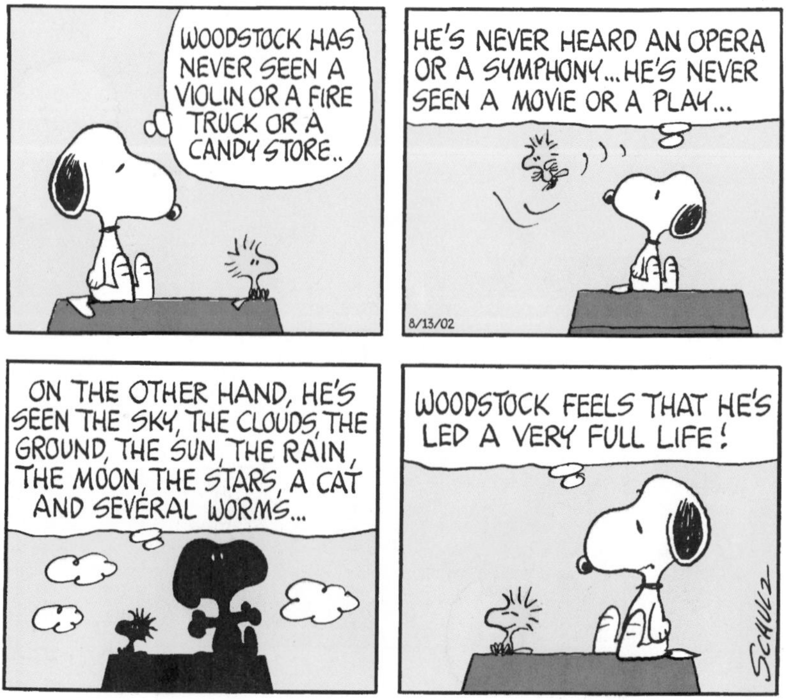
WOODSTOCK HAS NEVER SEEN A VIOLIN OR A FIRE TRUCK OR A CANDY STORE..
HE'S NEVER HEARD AN OPERA OR A SYMPHONY... HE'S NEVER SEEN A MOVIE OR A PLAY...
8/13/02
ON THE OTHER HAND, HE'S SEEN THE SKY, THE CLOUDS, THE GROUND, THE SUN, THE RAIN, THE MOON, THE STARS, A CAT AND SEVERAL WORMS...
WOODSTOCK FEELS THAT HE'S LED A VERY FULL LIFE!
SCHULZ

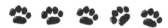

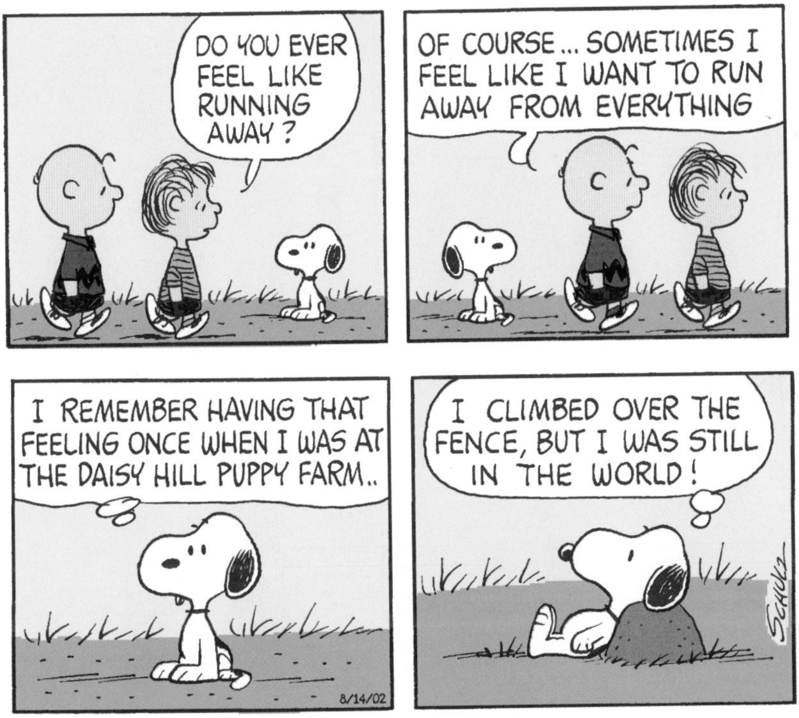
DO YOU EVER FEEL LIKE RUNNING AWAY?
OF COURSE... SOMETIMES I FEEL LIKE I WANT TO RUN AWAY FROM EVERYTHING
I REMEMBER HAVING THAT FEELING ONCE WHEN I WAS AT THE DAISY HILL PUPPY FARM..
8/14/02
I CLIMBED OVER THE FENCE, BUT I WAS STILL IN THE WORLD!
SCHULZ

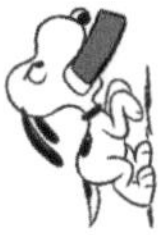

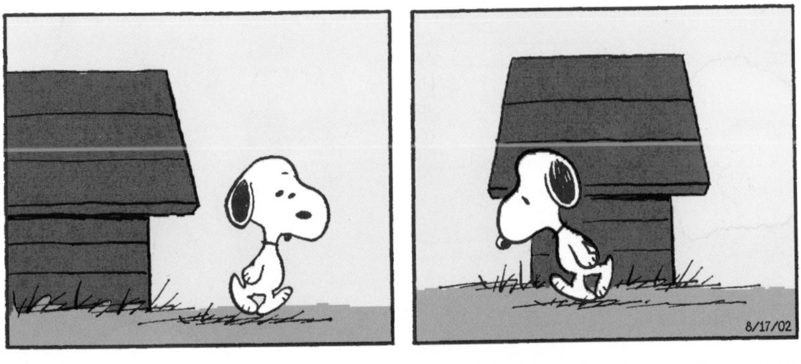
8/17/02

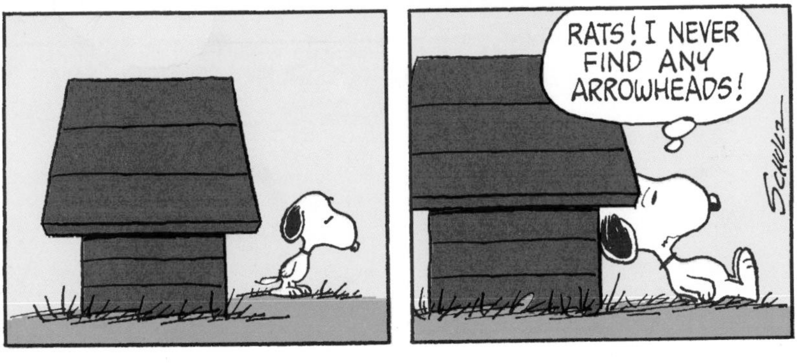
RATS! I NEVER FIND ANY ARROWHEADS!
SCHULZ

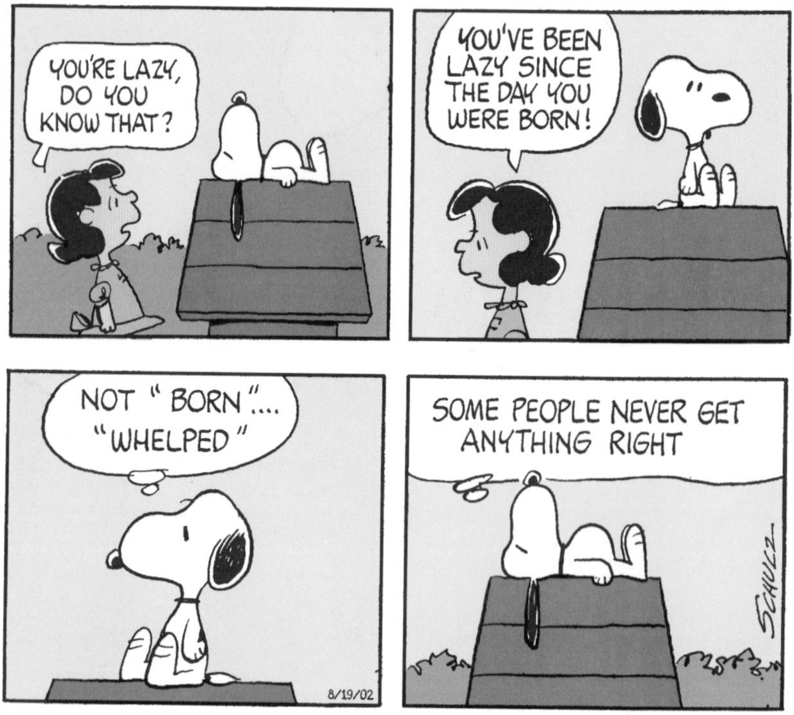
YOU'RE LAZY, DO YOU KNOW THAT?
YOU'VE BEEN LAZY SINCE THE DAY YOU WERE BORN!
NOT "BORN"... "WHELPED"
8/19/02
SOME PEOPLE NEVER GET ANYTHING RIGHT
SCHULZ

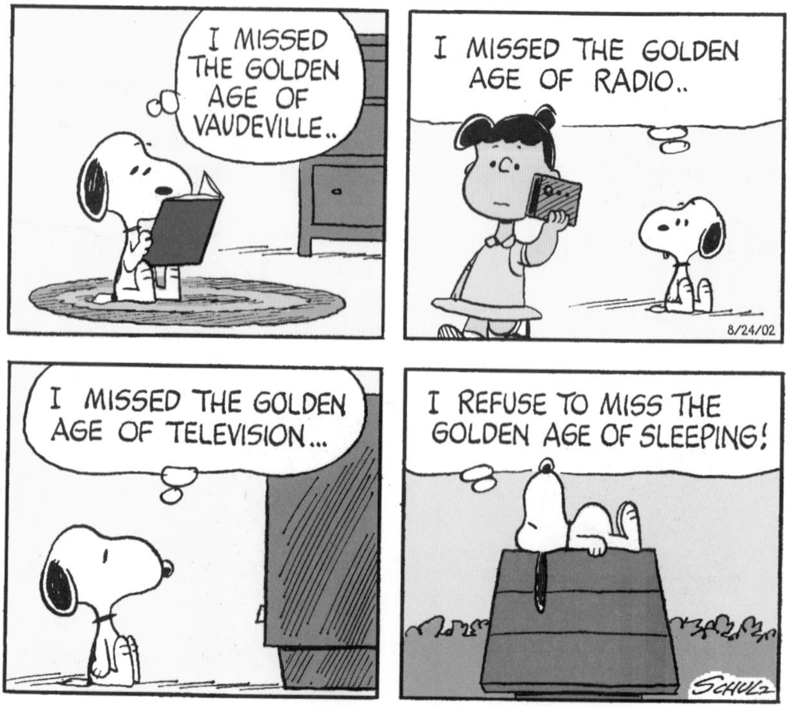
I MISSED THE GOLDEN AGE OF VAUDEVILLE..
I MISSED THE GOLDEN AGE OF RADIO..
8/24/02
I MISSED THE GOLDEN AGE OF TELEVISION...
I REFUSE TO MISS THE GOLDEN AGE OF SLEEPING!
SCHULZ

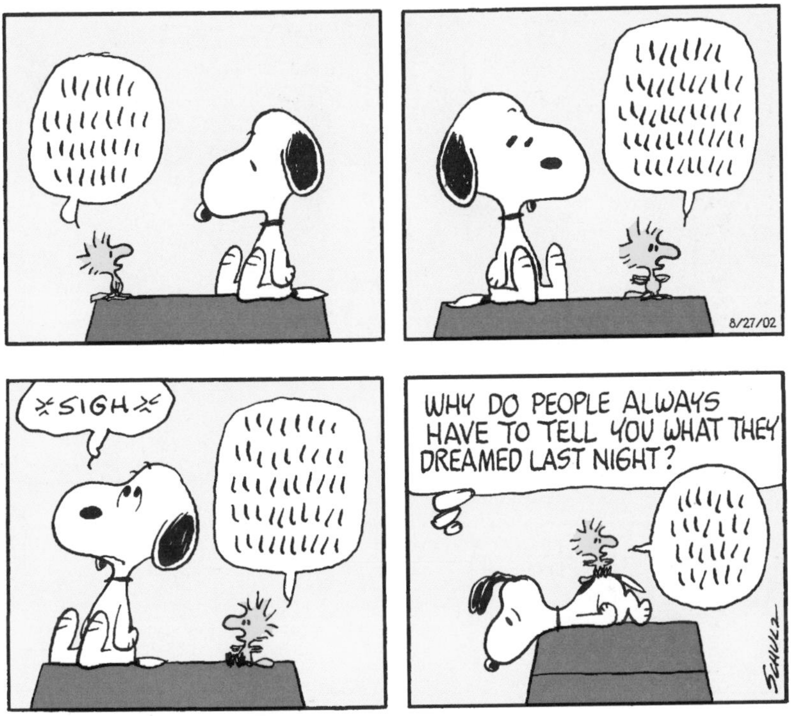
8/27/02
SIGH
WHY DO PEOPLE ALWAYS HAVE TO TELL YOU WHAT THEY DREAMED LAST NIGHT?
SCHULZ

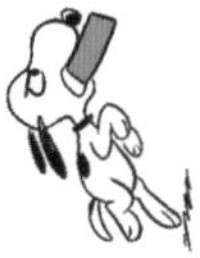

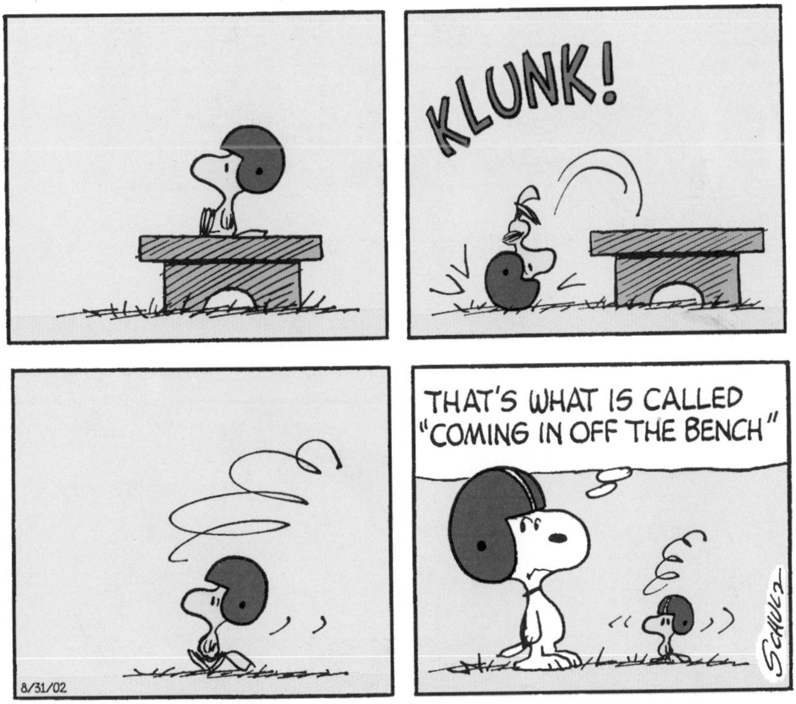
KLUNK!
8/31/02
THAT'S WHAT IS CALLED "COMING IN OFF THE BENCH"
SCHULZ

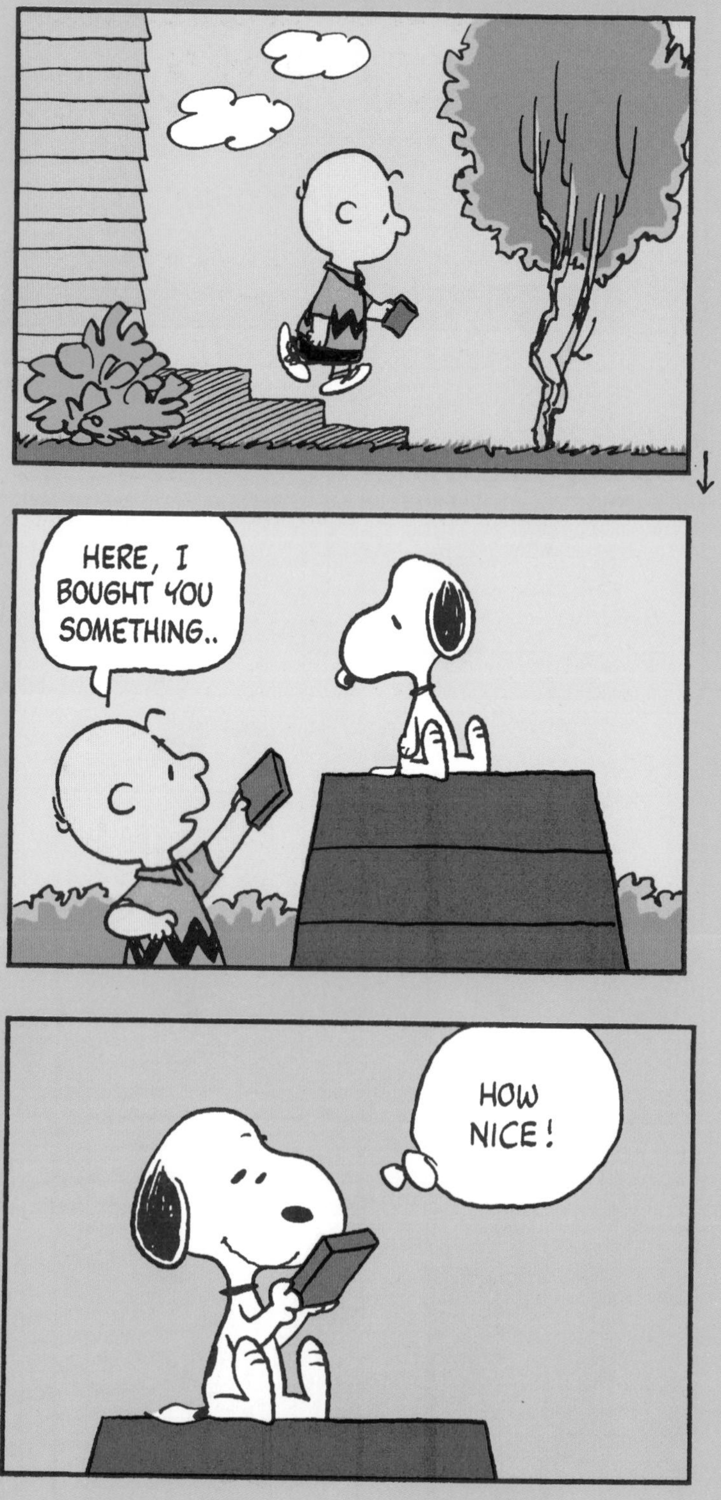
HERE, I BOUGHT YOU SOMETHING..
HOW NICE!

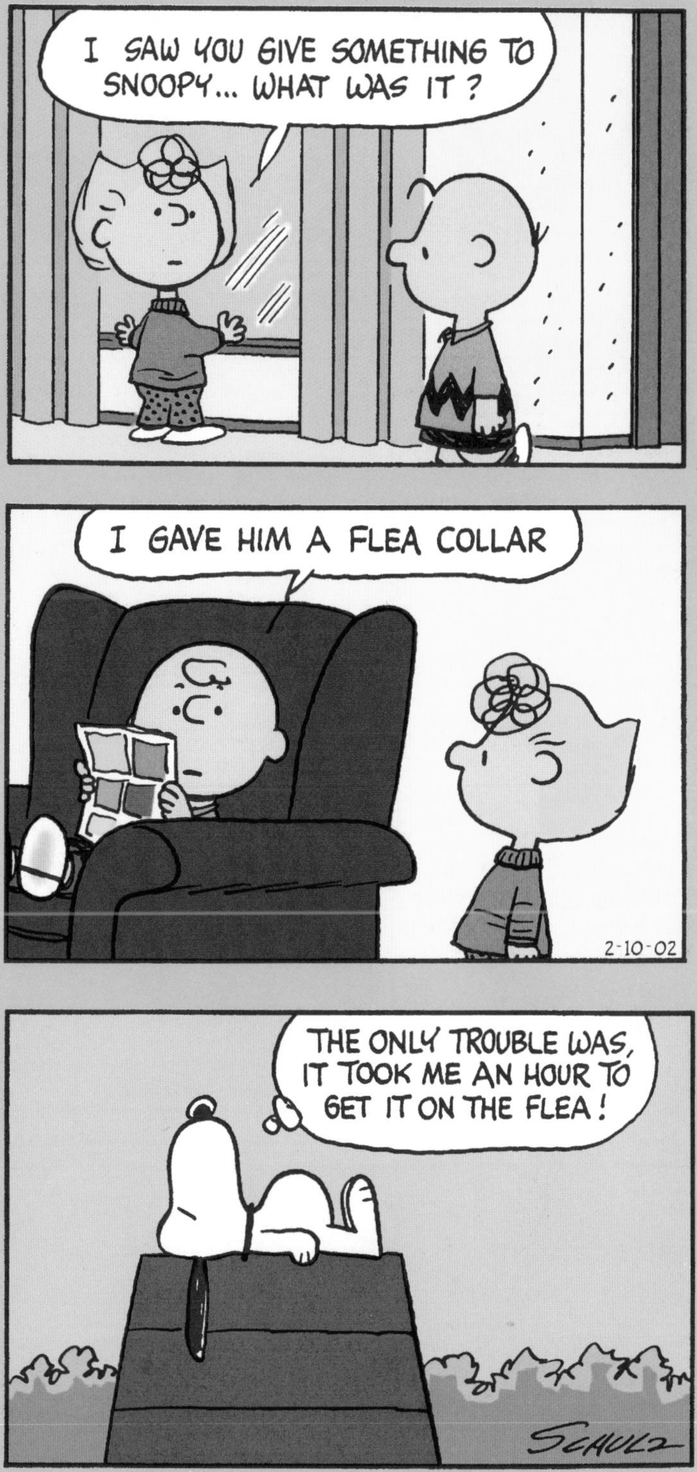
I SAW YOU GIVE SOMETHING TO SNOOPY... WHAT WAS IT ?
I GAVE HIM A FLEA COLLAR
2-10-02
THE ONLY TROUBLE WAS, IT TOOK ME AN HOUR TO GET IT ON THE FLEA !
SCHULZ

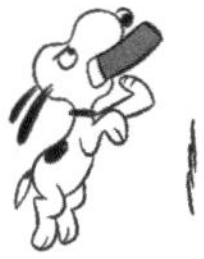

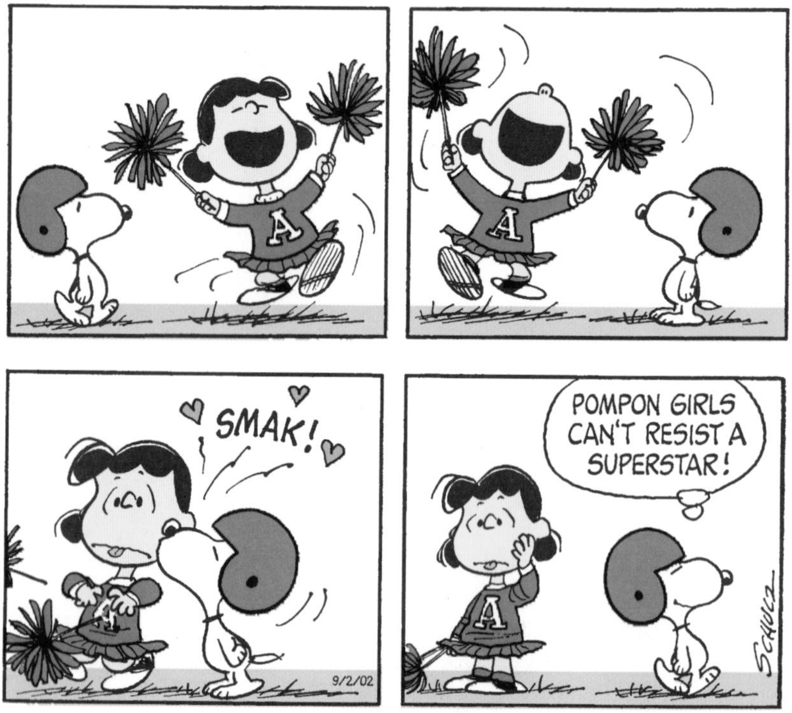
SMAK!
POMPON GIRLS CAN'T RESIST A SUPERSTAR!
9/2/02
SCHULZ

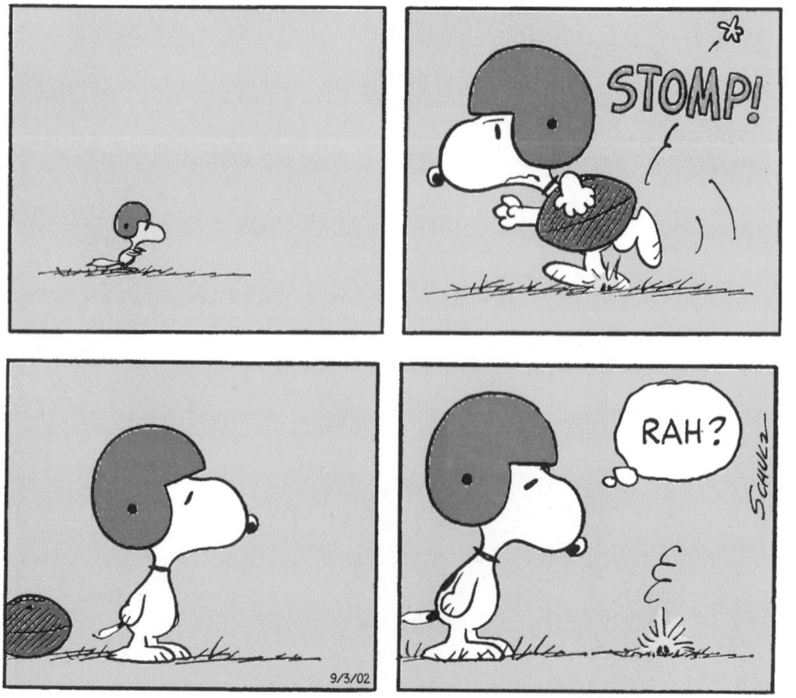
STOMP!
9/3/02
RAH?
SCHULZ

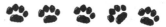

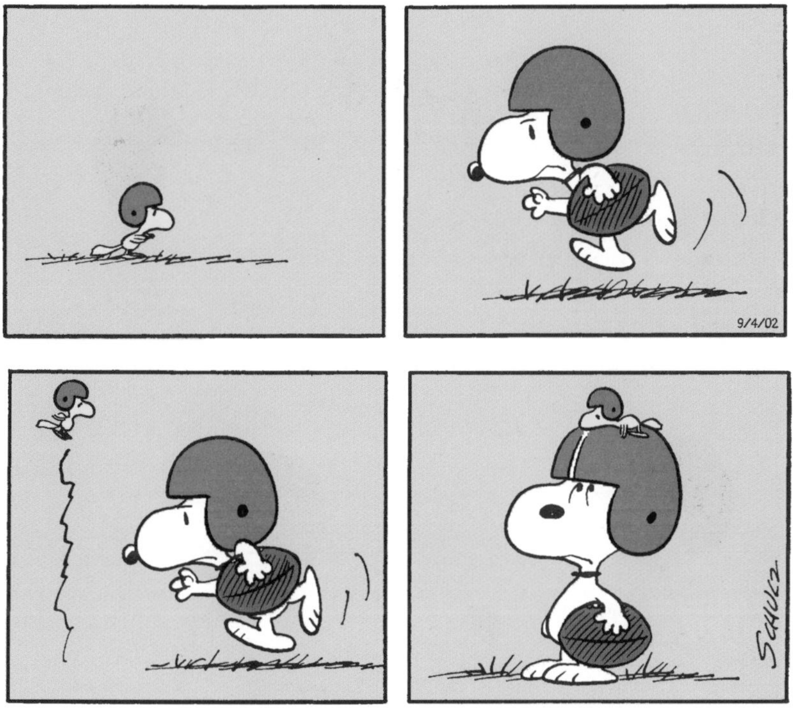
9/4/02
SCHULZ

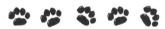

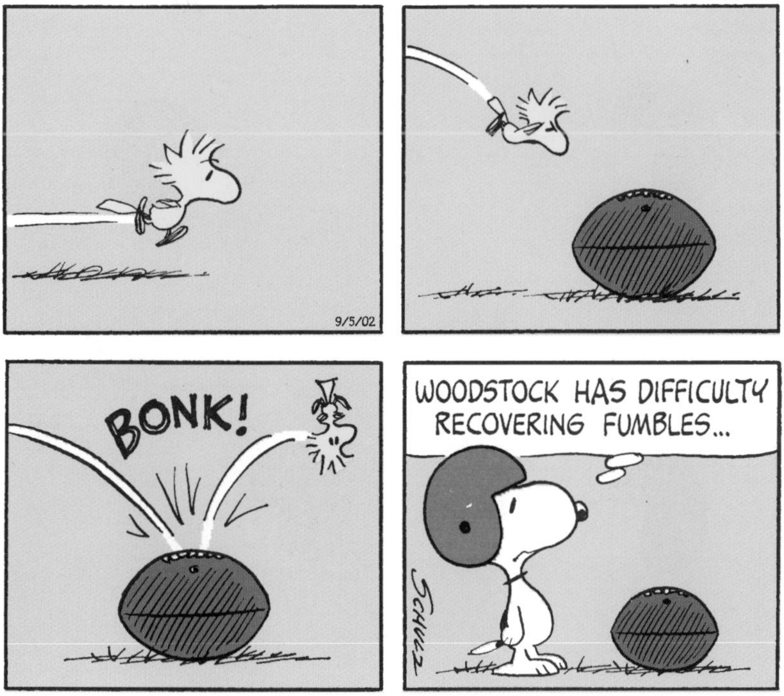
9/5/02
BONK!
WOODSTOCK HAS DIFFICULTY RECOVERING FUMBLES...
SCHULZ

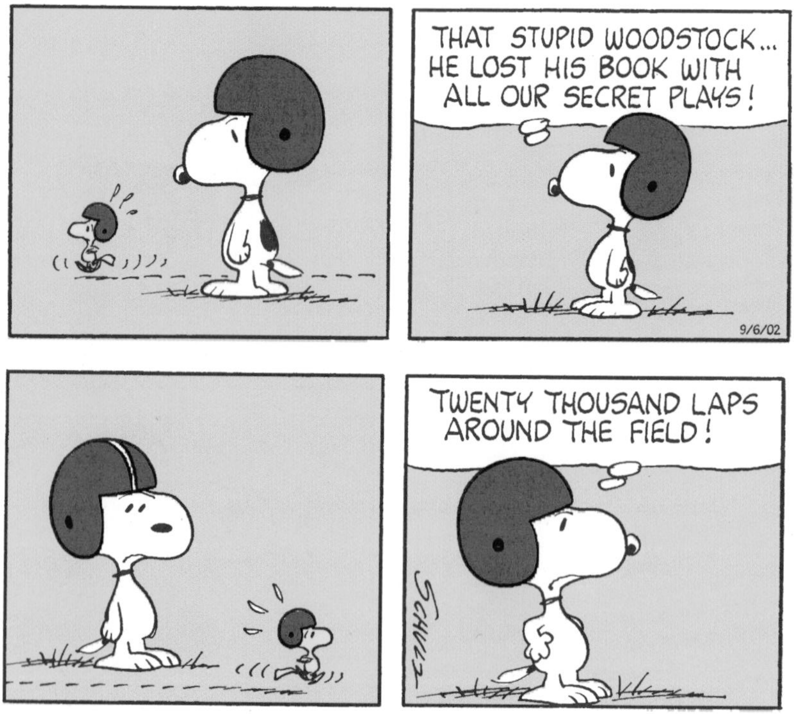
THAT STUPID WOODSTOCK... HE LOST HIS BOOK WITH ALL OUR SECRET PLAYS!
9/6/02
TWENTY THOUSAND LAPS AROUND THE FIELD!

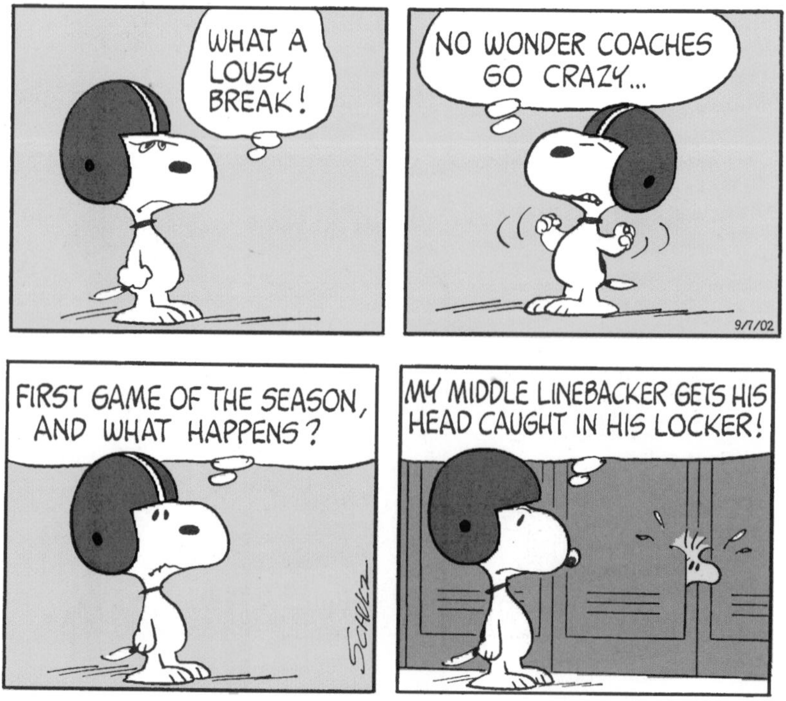
WHAT A LOUSY BREAK!
NO WONDER COACHES GO CRAZY...
9/7/02
FIRST GAME OF THE SEASON, AND WHAT HAPPENS?
MY MIDDLE LINEBACKER GETS HIS HEAD CAUGHT IN HIS LOCKER!

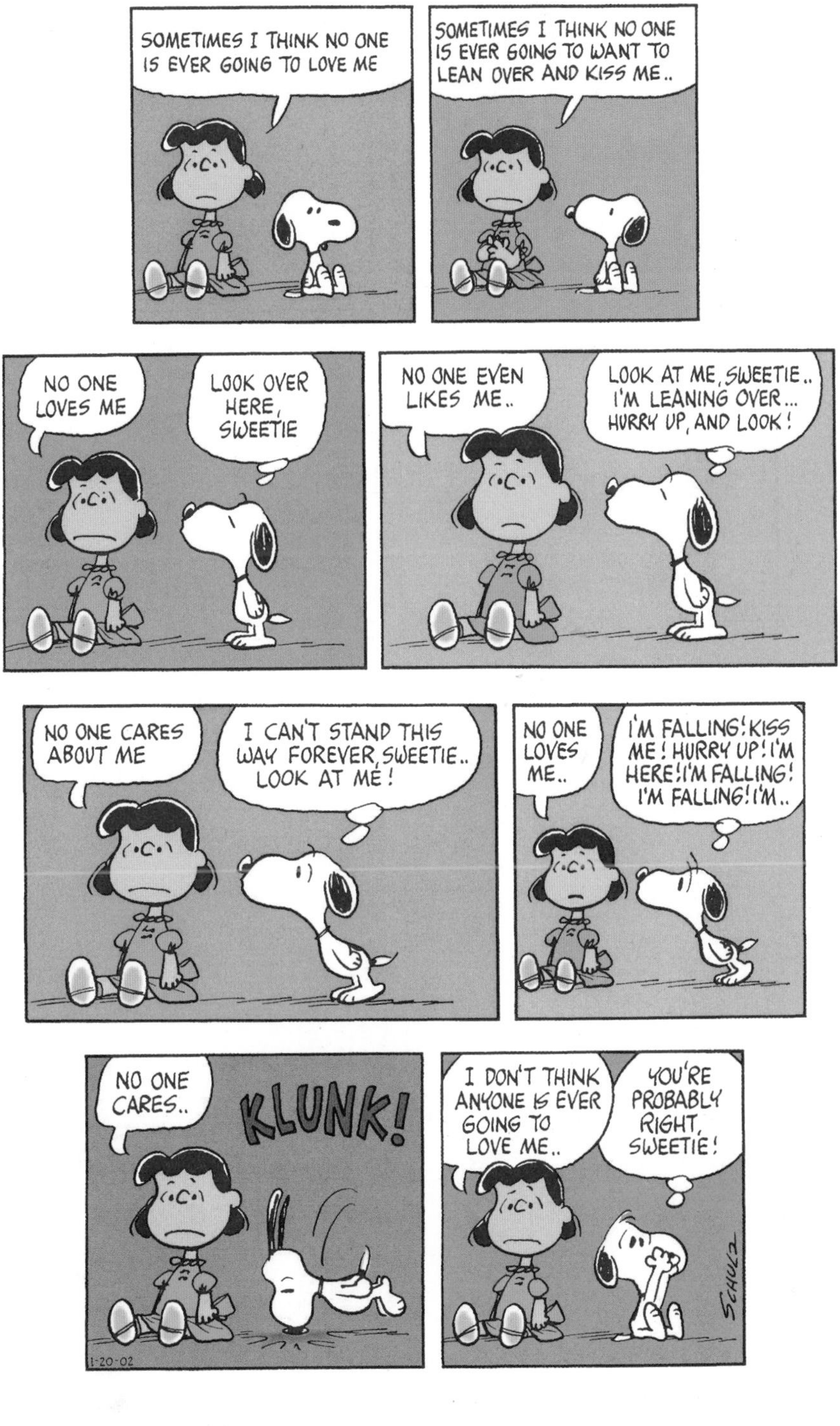
SOMETIMES I THINK NO ONE IS EVER GOING TO LOVE ME
SOMETIMES I THINK NO ONE IS EVER GOING TO WANT TO LEAN OVER AND KISS ME..
NO ONE LOVES ME
LOOK OVER HERE, SWEETIE
NO ONE EVEN LIKES ME..
LOOK AT ME, SWEETIE.. I'M LEANING OVER... HURRY UP, AND LOOK!
NO ONE CARES ABOUT ME
I CAN'T STAND THIS WAY FOREVER, SWEETIE.. LOOK AT ME!
NO ONE LOVES ME..
I'M FALLING! KISS ME! HURRY UP! I'M HERE! I'M FALLING! I'M FALLING! I'M..
NO ONE CARES..
KLUNK!
1-20-02
I DON'T THINK ANYONE IS EVER GOING TO LOVE ME..
YOU'RE PROBABLY RIGHT, SWEETIE!
SCHULZ

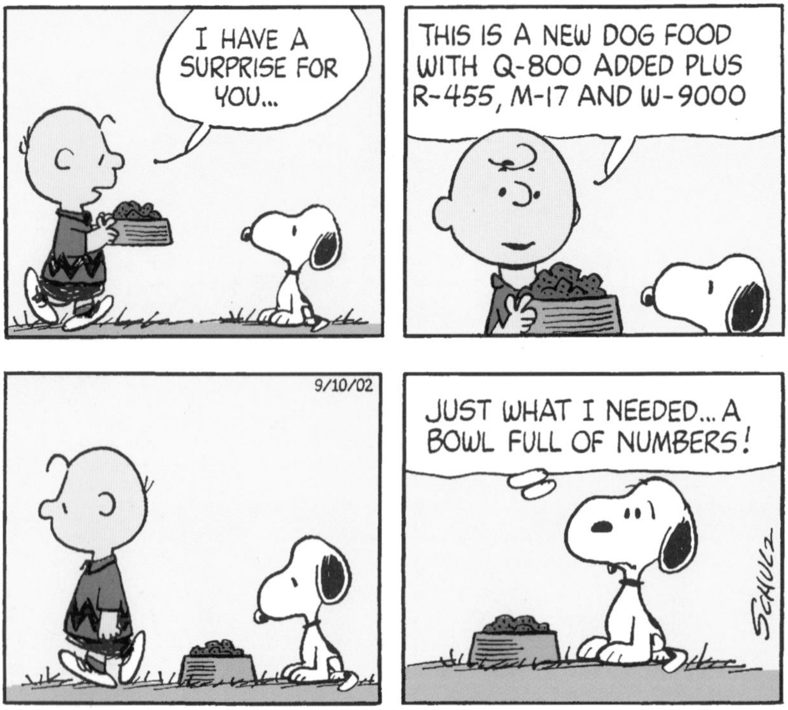
I HAVE A SURPRISE FOR YOU...
THIS IS A NEW DOG FOOD WITH Q-800 ADDED PLUS R-455, M-17 AND W-9000
9/10/02
JUST WHAT I NEEDED... A BOWL FULL OF NUMBERS!

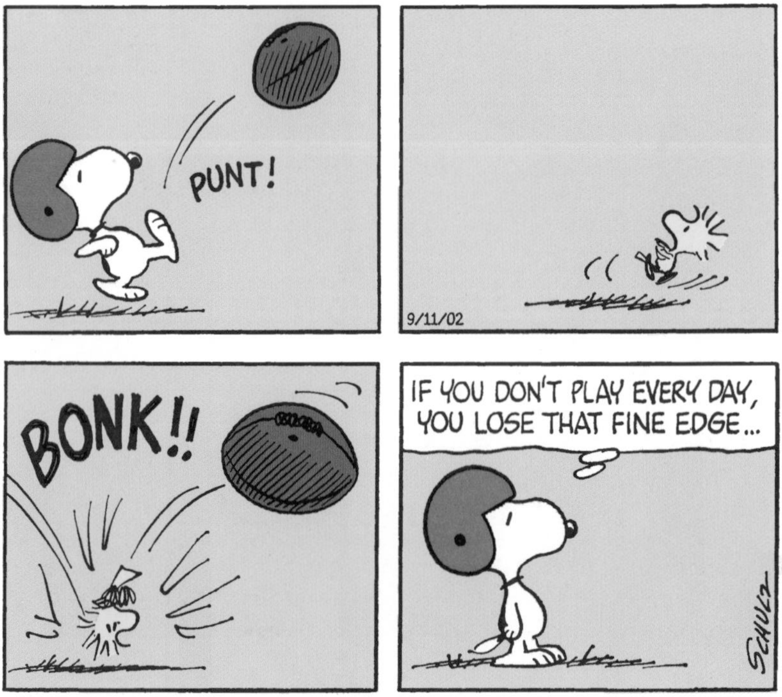
PUNT!
9/11/02
BONK!!
IF YOU DON'T PLAY EVERY DAY, YOU LOSE THAT FINE EDGE...

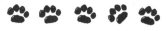

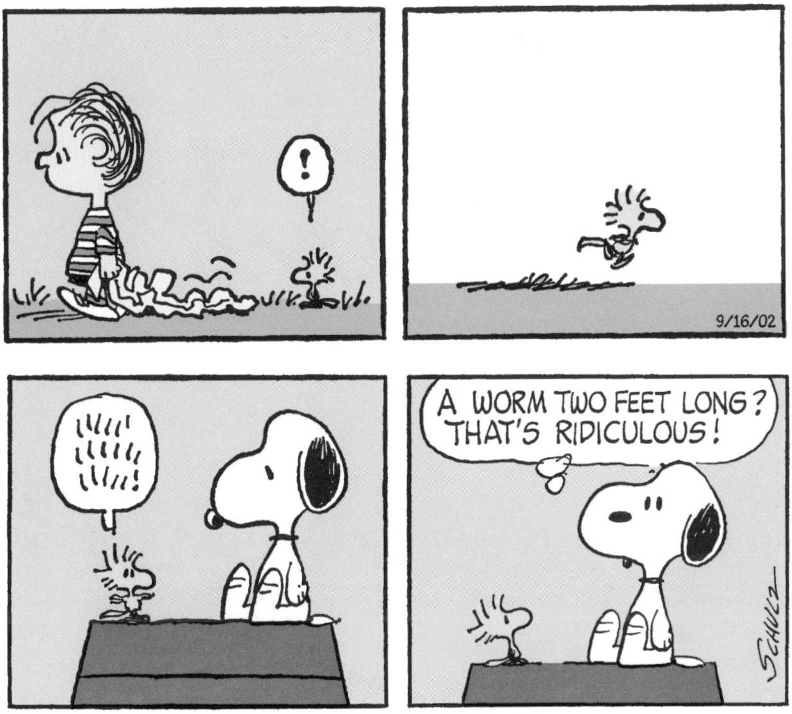
!
9/16/02
A WORM TWO FEET LONG? THAT'S RIDICULOUS!
SCHULZ

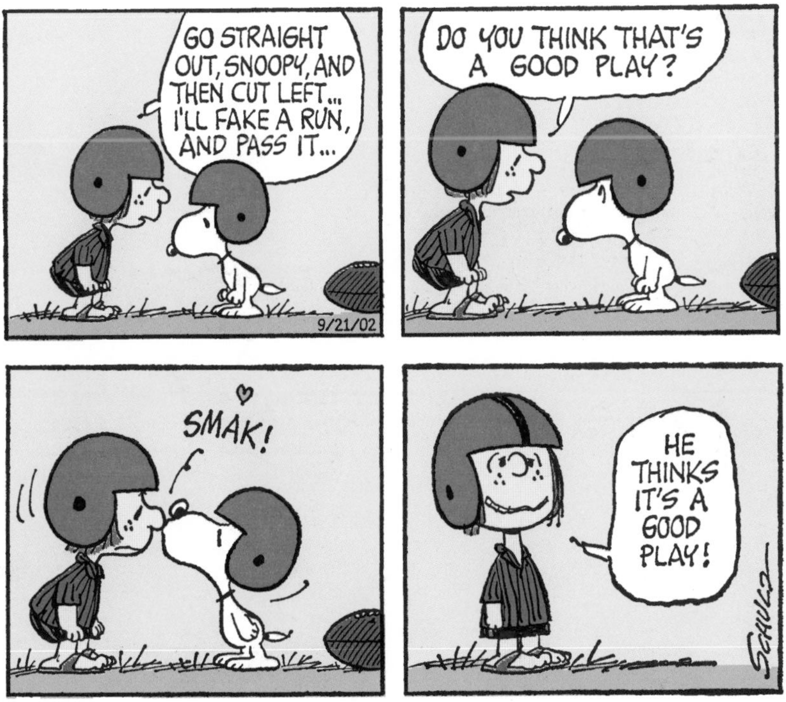
GO STRAIGHT OUT, SNOOPY, AND THEN CUT LEFT... I'LL FAKE A RUN, AND PASS IT...
9/21/02
DO YOU THINK THAT'S A GOOD PLAY?
SMAK!
HE THINKS IT'S A GOOD PLAY!
SCHULZ

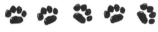

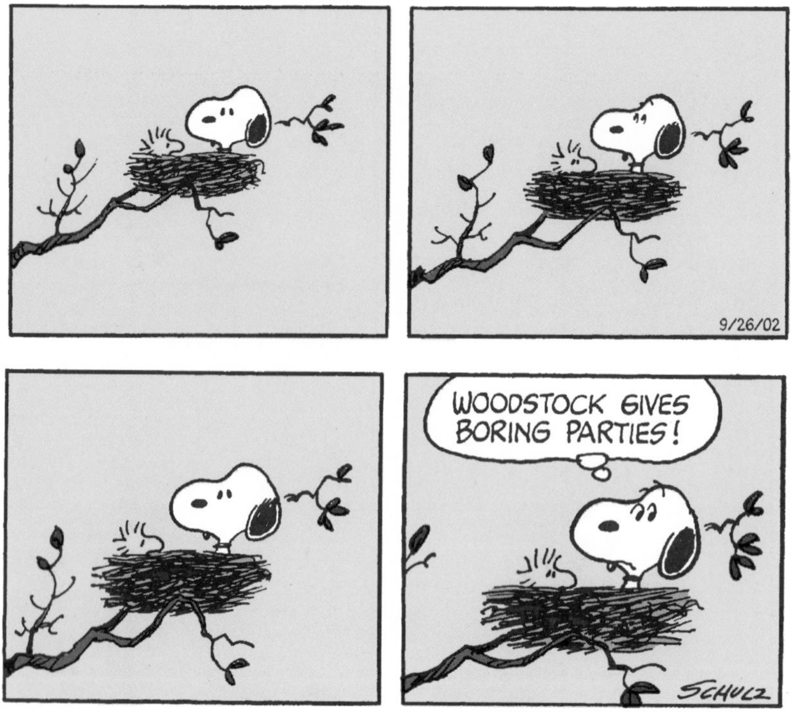
9/26/02
WOODSTOCK GIVES BORING PARTIES!
SCHULZ

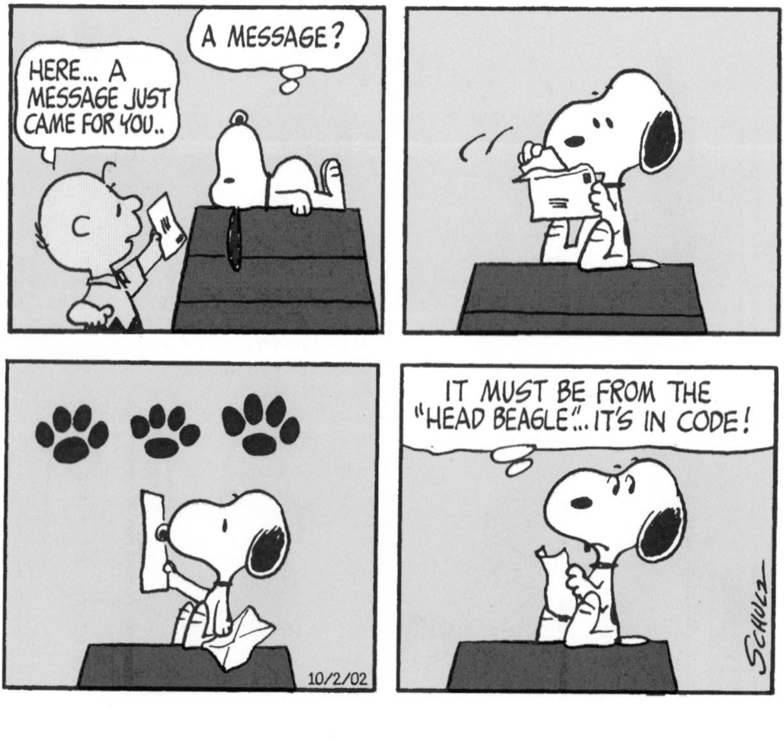
HERE... A MESSAGE JUST CAME FOR YOU..
A MESSAGE?
10/2/02
IT MUST BE FROM THE "HEAD BEAGLE"... IT'S IN CODE!
SCHULZ

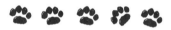

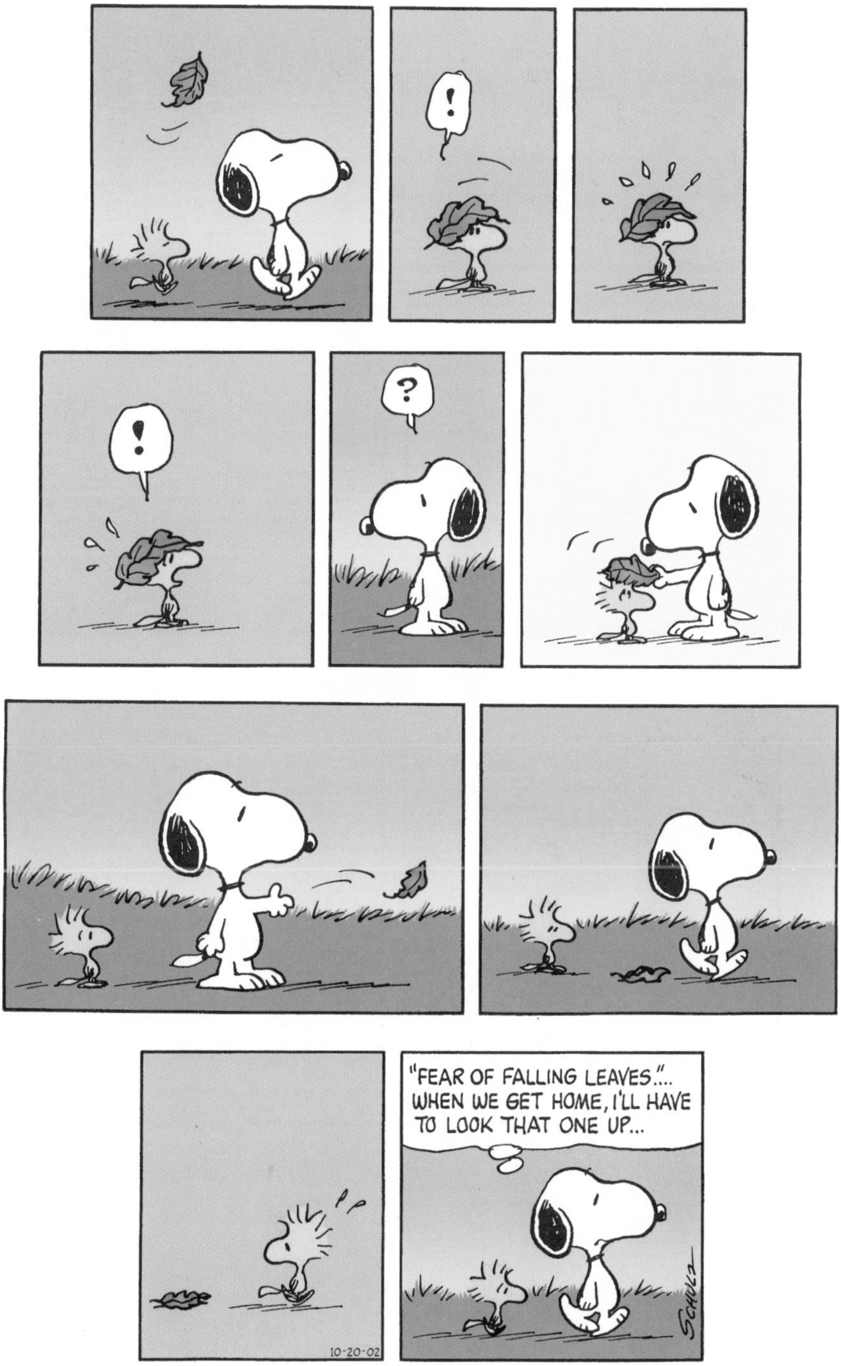
!
!
?
"FEAR OF FALLING LEAVES."... WHEN WE GET HOME, I'LL HAVE TO LOOK THAT ONE UP...
10-20-02
SCHULZ

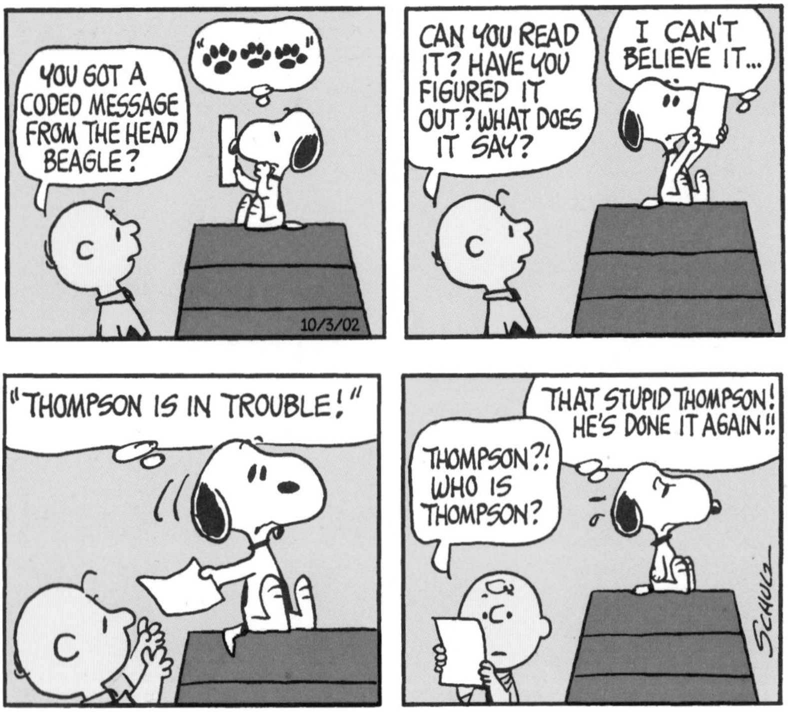
YOU GOT A CODED MESSAGE FROM THE HEAD BEAGLE?
"🐾🐾🐾"
10/3/02
CAN YOU READ IT? HAVE YOU FIGURED IT OUT? WHAT DOES IT SAY?
I CAN'T BELIEVE IT...
"THOMPSON IS IN TROUBLE!"
THOMPSON?! WHO IS THOMPSON?
THAT STUPID THOMPSON! HE'S DONE IT AGAIN!!
SCHULZ

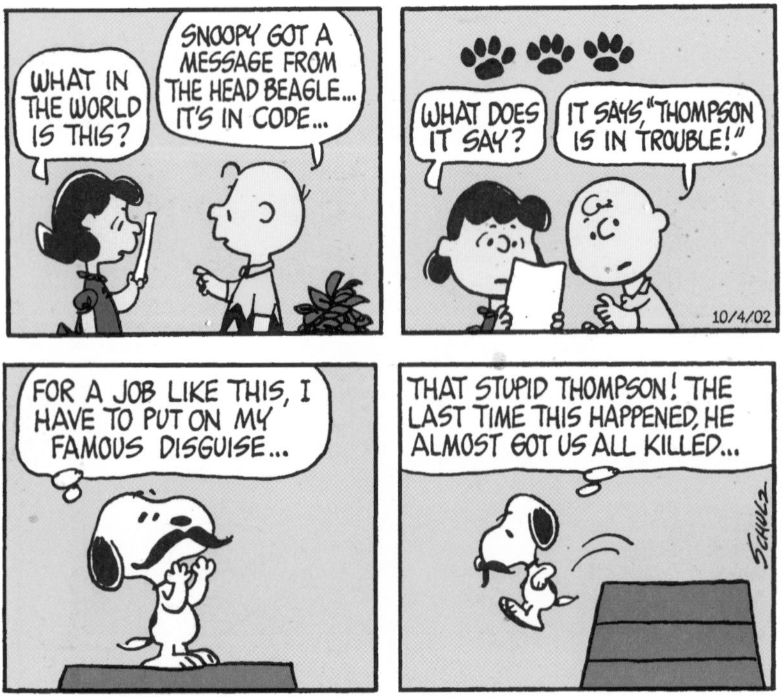
WHAT IN THE WORLD IS THIS?
SNOOPY GOT A MESSAGE FROM THE HEAD BEAGLE... IT'S IN CODE...
WHAT DOES IT SAY?
IT SAYS, "THOMPSON IS IN TROUBLE!"
10/4/02
FOR A JOB LIKE THIS, I HAVE TO PUT ON MY FAMOUS DISGUISE...
THAT STUPID THOMPSON! THE LAST TIME THIS HAPPENED, HE ALMOST GOT US ALL KILLED...
SCHULZ

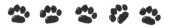

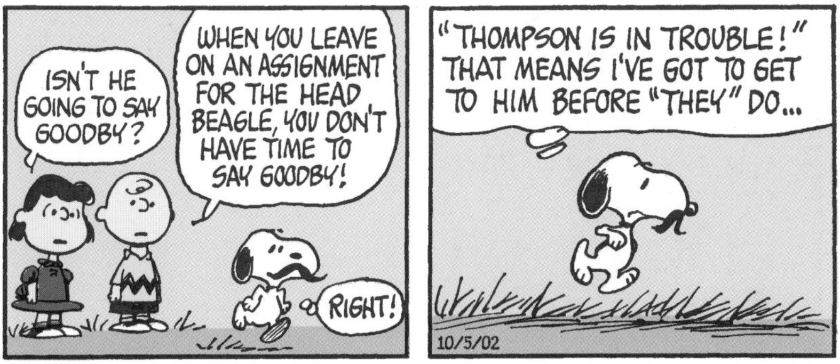
ISN'T HE GOING TO SAY GOODBY?
WHEN YOU LEAVE ON AN ASSIGNMENT FOR THE HEAD BEAGLE, YOU DON'T HAVE TIME TO SAY GOODBY!
RIGHT!
"THOMPSON IS IN TROUBLE!" THAT MEANS I'VE GOT TO GET TO HIM BEFORE "THEY" DO...
10/5/02

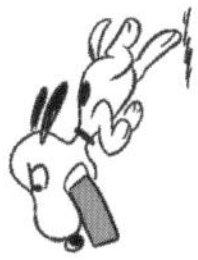

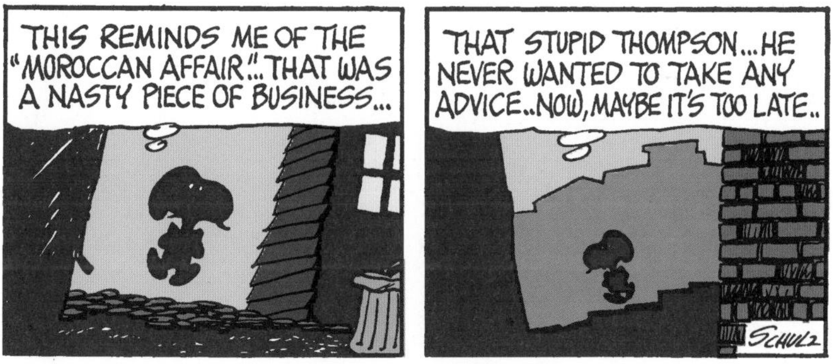
THIS REMINDS ME OF THE "MOROCCAN AFFAIR"... THAT WAS A NASTY PIECE OF BUSINESS...
THAT STUPID THOMPSON...HE NEVER WANTED TO TAKE ANY ADVICE..NOW, MAYBE IT'S TOO LATE..

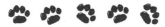

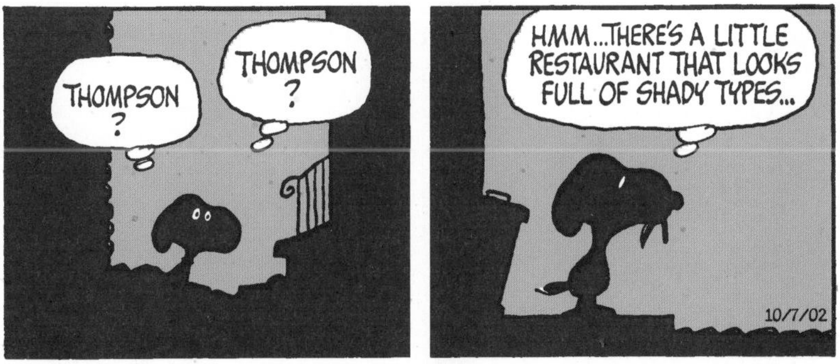
THOMPSON ?
THOMPSON ?
HMM...THERE'S A LITTLE RESTAURANT THAT LOOKS FULL OF SHADY TYPES...
10/7/02

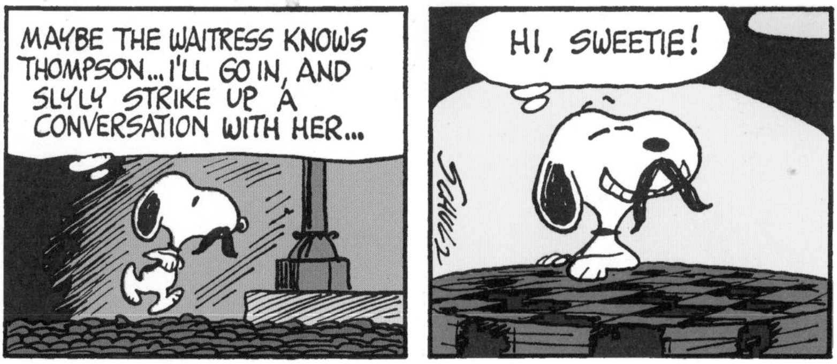
MAYBE THE WAITRESS KNOWS THOMPSON... I'LL GO IN, AND SLYLY STRIKE UP A CONVERSATION WITH HER...
HI, SWEETIE!

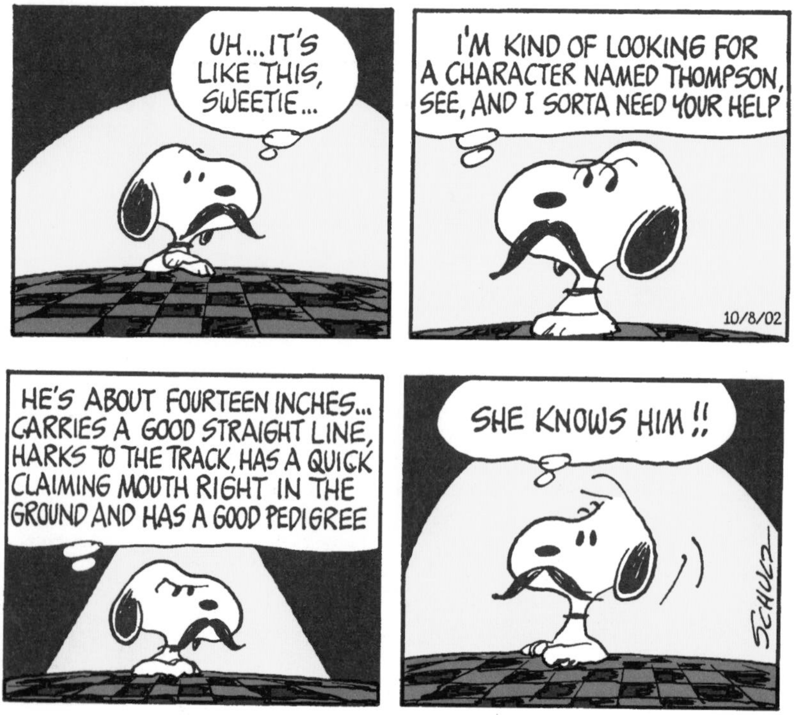

UH...IT'S LIKE THIS, SWEETIE...
I'M KIND OF LOOKING FOR A CHARACTER NAMED THOMPSON, SEE, AND I SORTA NEED YOUR HELP
10/8/02
HE'S ABOUT FOURTEEN INCHES... CARRIES A GOOD STRAIGHT LINE, HARKS TO THE TRACK, HAS A QUICK CLAIMING MOUTH RIGHT IN THE GROUND AND HAS A GOOD PEDIGREE
SHE KNOWS HIM !!
SCHULZ

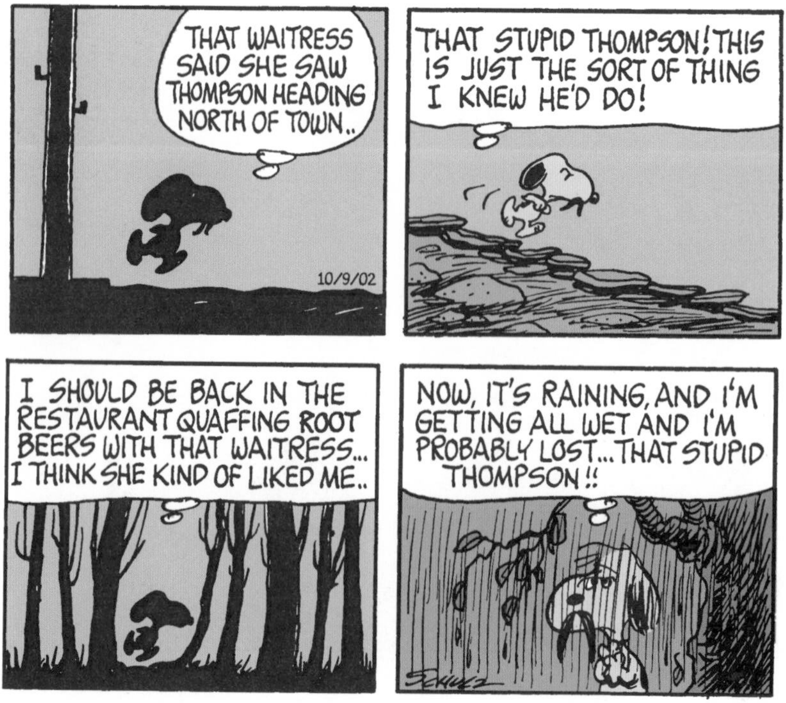

THAT WAITRESS SAID SHE SAW THOMPSON HEADING NORTH OF TOWN..
10/9/02
THAT STUPID THOMPSON! THIS IS JUST THE SORT OF THING I KNEW HE'D DO!
I SHOULD BE BACK IN THE RESTAURANT QUAFFING ROOT BEERS WITH THAT WAITRESS... I THINK SHE KIND OF LIKED ME..
NOW, IT'S RAINING, AND I'M GETTING ALL WET AND I'M PROBABLY LOST...THAT STUPID THOMPSON !!
SCHULZ

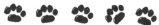

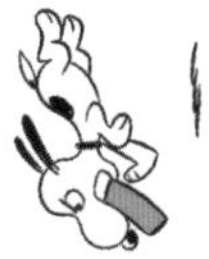

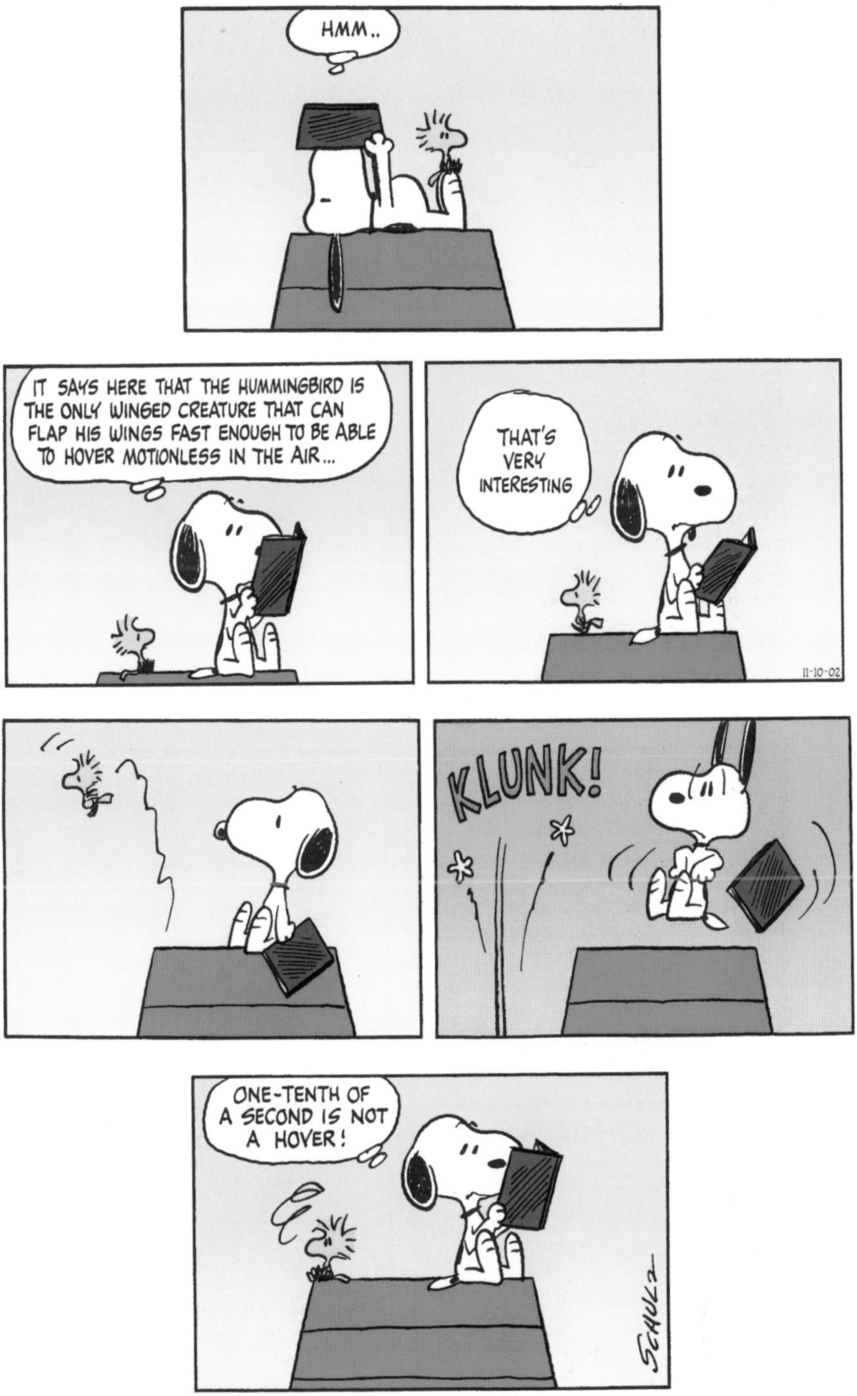
HMM..
IT SAYS HERE THAT THE HUMMINGBIRD IS THE ONLY WINGED CREATURE THAT CAN FLAP HIS WINGS FAST ENOUGH TO BE ABLE TO HOVER MOTIONLESS IN THE AIR...
THAT'S VERY INTERESTING
11-10-02
KLUNK!
ONE-TENTH OF A SECOND IS NOT A HOVER!
SCHULZ

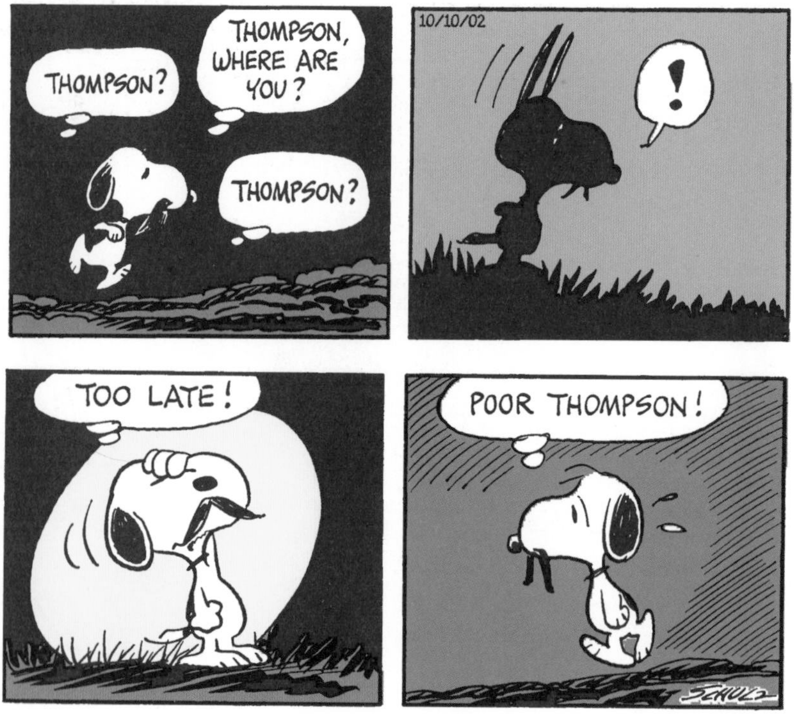
THOMPSON?
THOMPSON, WHERE ARE YOU?
THOMPSON?
10/10/02
!
TOO LATE!
POOR THOMPSON!
SCHULZ

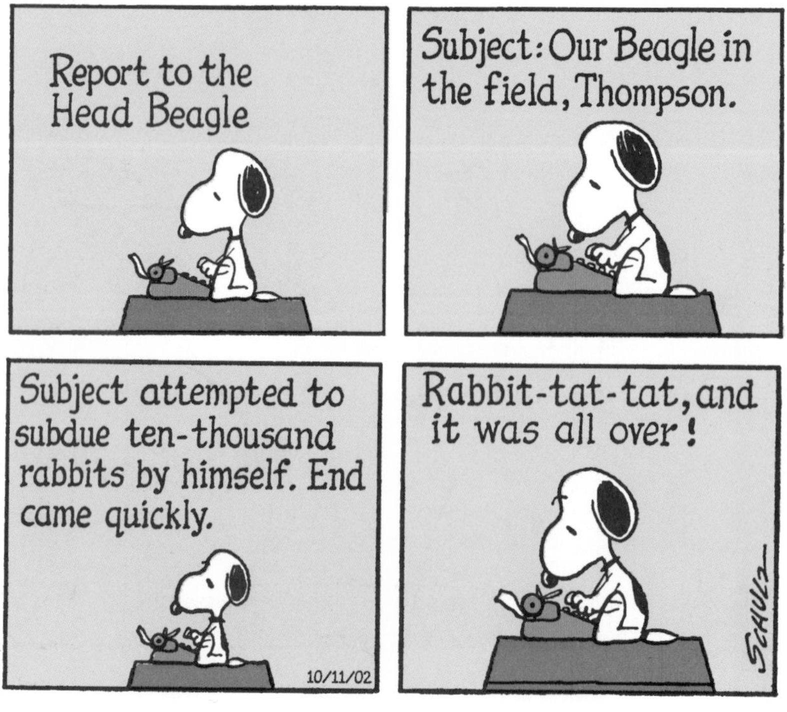
Report to the Head Beagle
Subject: Our Beagle in the field, Thompson.
Subject attempted to subdue ten-thousand rabbits by himself. End came quickly.
10/11/02
Rabbit-tat-tat, and it was all over!
SCHULZ

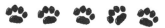

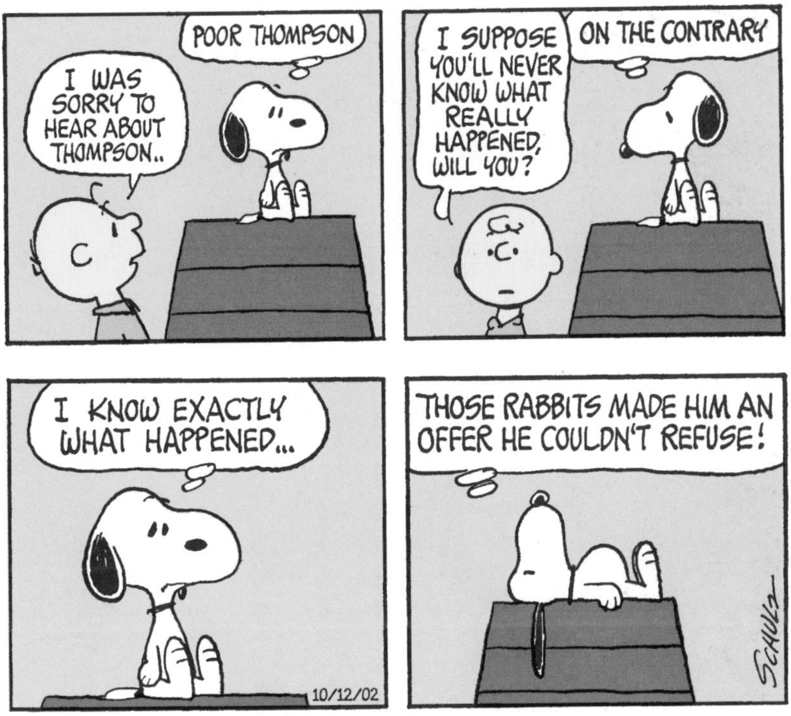
I WAS SORRY TO HEAR ABOUT THOMPSON..
POOR THOMPSON
I SUPPOSE YOU'LL NEVER KNOW WHAT REALLY HAPPENED, WILL YOU?
ON THE CONTRARY
I KNOW EXACTLY WHAT HAPPENED...
10/12/02
THOSE RABBITS MADE HIM AN OFFER HE COULDN'T REFUSE!
SCHULZ

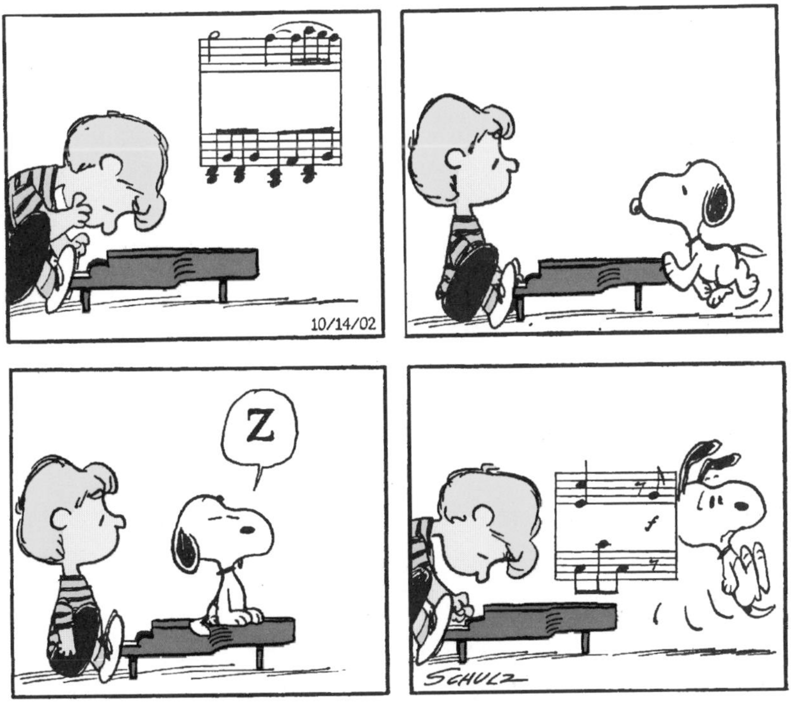
10/14/02
Z
SCHULZ

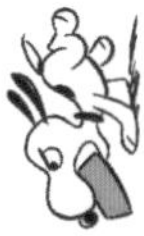

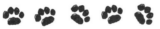

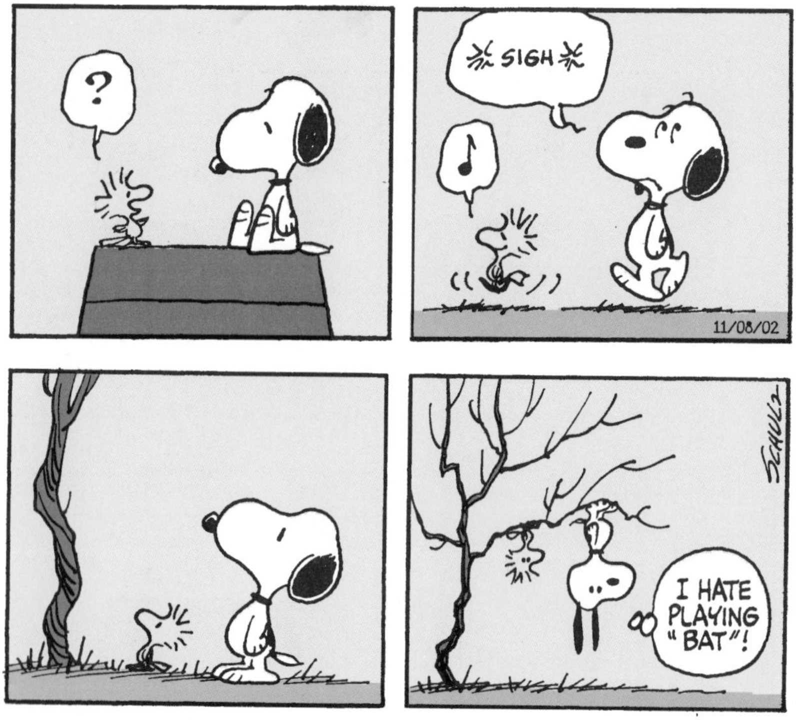
?
SIGH
11/08/02
SCHULZ
I HATE PLAYING "BAT"!

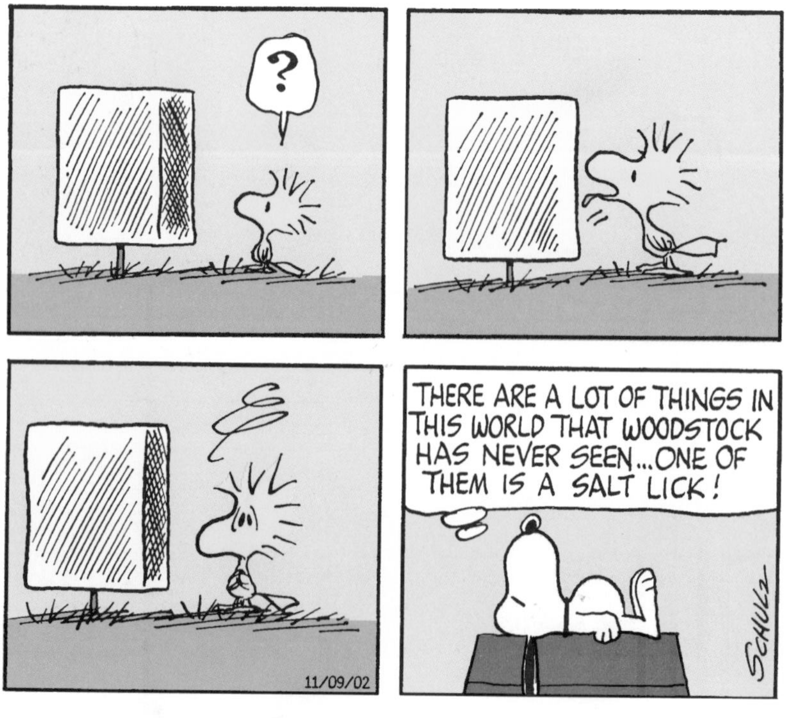
?
11/09/02
THERE ARE A LOT OF THINGS IN THIS WORLD THAT WOODSTOCK HAS NEVER SEEN...ONE OF THEM IS A SALT LICK!
SCHULZ

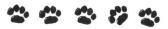

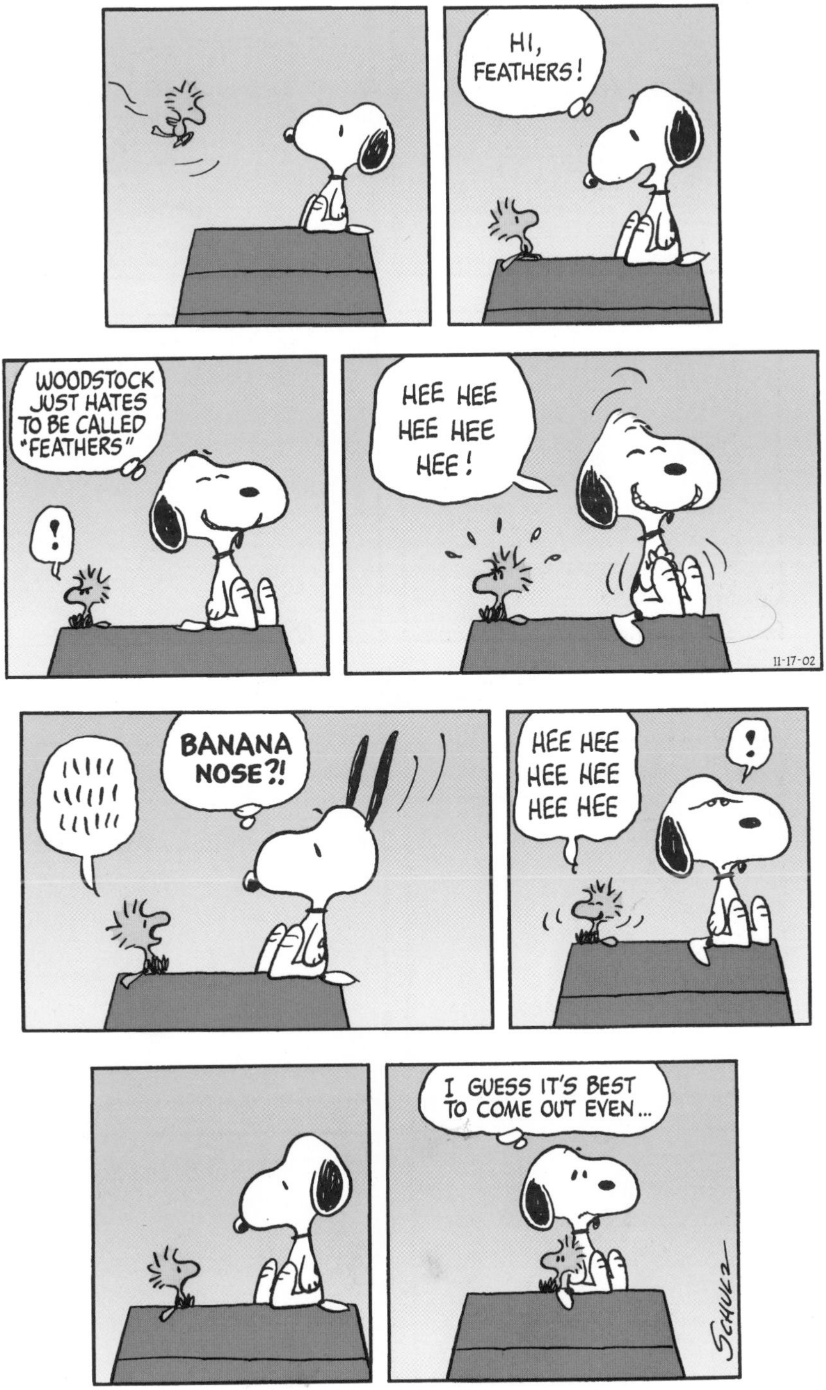

HI, FEATHERS!
WOODSTOCK JUST HATES TO BE CALLED "FEATHERS"
!
HEE HEE HEE HEE HEE!
11-17-02
BANANA NOSE?!
HEE HEE HEE HEE HEE HEE
!
I GUESS IT'S BEST TO COME OUT EVEN...
SCHULZ

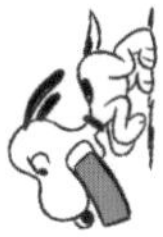

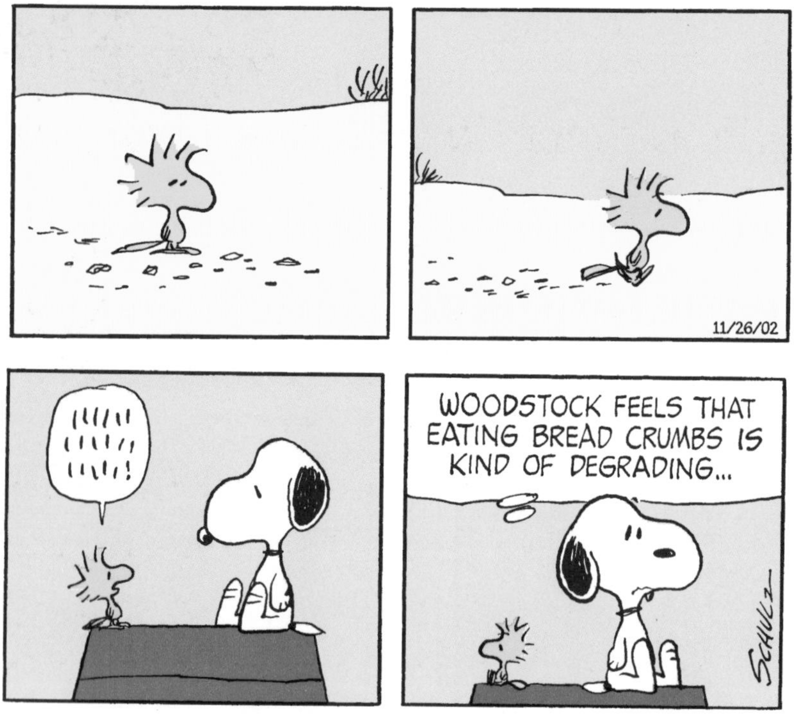
11/26/02
WOODSTOCK FEELS THAT EATING BREAD CRUMBS IS KIND OF DEGRADING...
SCHULZ

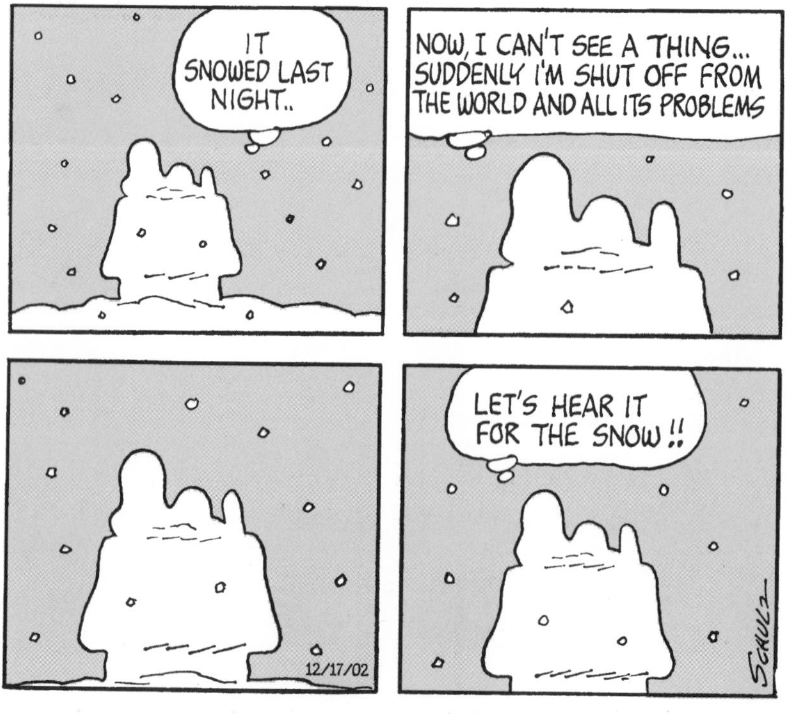
IT SNOWED LAST NIGHT..
NOW, I CAN'T SEE A THING... SUDDENLY I'M SHUT OFF FROM THE WORLD AND ALL ITS PROBLEMS
12/17/02
LET'S HEAR IT FOR THE SNOW !!
SCHULZ

In addition to all these great Snoopy cartoons, here are some cool activities and fun facts for you. Thanks to our friends at the Charles M. Schulz Museum and Research Center in Santa Rosa, California, for letting us share these with you!

M👀RE TO EXPLORE!

Make a Recycled Bird Feeder for Woodstock and His Friends

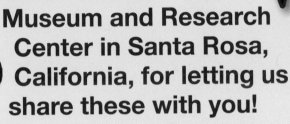

MATERIALS: empty plastic water bottle, Popsicle stick, birdseed, scissors, tape

INSTRUCTIONS:

1. Cut an opening in one side of the bottle and fill it with birdseed.

2. Decorate the bottle with paint or markers. Tape a Popsicle stick to the opening for a bird perch.

3. Tie a ribbon on top of the bottle for a hanger and hang it outside for birds to enjoy.

Make Snoopy's Dog House

MATERIALS: an 8.5 x 11 inch piece of paper, scissors, tracing paper

Start with the piece of paper. The best paper to use is colored on BOTH sides, but in the illustrations, the side of the sheet that will end up INSIDE the doghouse is white, just to make it easier to see the folds. Match corners and edges carefully and crease well.

1 Bring bottom edge to top. Crease flat.

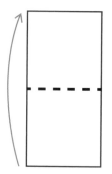

2 Rotate so open edge is at the bottom. Bring bottom edge of top layer to the top. Crease flat.

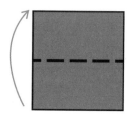

3 Turn over and repeat on other side, then rotate so open edges face down.

4 Lift the bottom edge of one side and make a fold upwards, along an imaginary line about one-half inch below the top fold.

It should look like this. ⟶

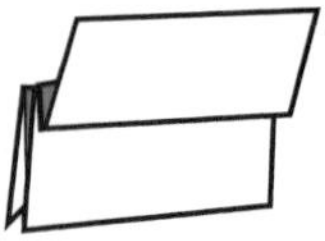

5 Turn over. Bring corners of second side up to meet corners of folded side. When pressed flat, it will crease in the right place.

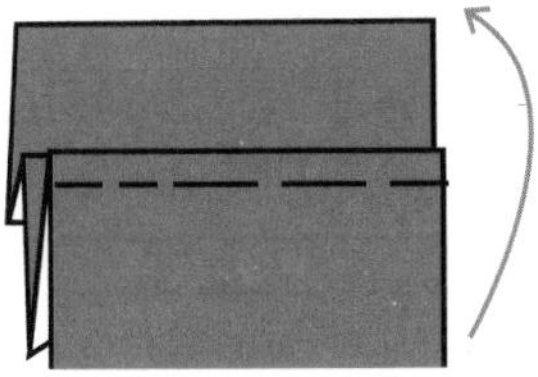

It will look like this:

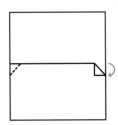

Now rotate:

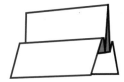

6 Lay it flat, and turn down (dog-ear) the corners of the middle fold, as squarely as you can. Crease well! Turn over and repeat.

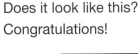

Hint: Try for *square corners* like this:

Not like this:

7 UNFOLD the corners, and poke them INSIDE the fold, along the creases you just made. Press flat.

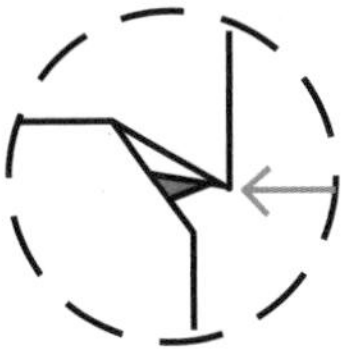

Does it look like this? Congratulations!

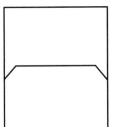

8 Fold back each edge of the top layer by opening the little corners and creasing a fold parallel to the vertical sides. Fold both edges, then turn over and repeat on other side.

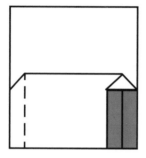

It should look like this:

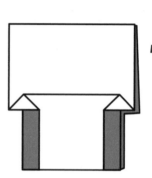

9 Re-fold the TOP of the house in the other direction, putting all your work INSIDE. Yay! A house! Now we just have to make the roof edges slant.

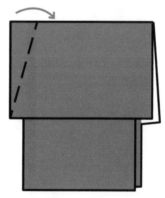

10 Fold a narrow slanted edge on each side, as shown. Crease well, unfold, and poke inside. Flatten.

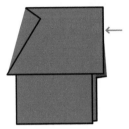

Leave room for Snoopy!

11 Open the ends a little and apply tape.

Trace the Snoopy art below, color it in, cut it out, and put Snoopy on his roof!

Charles M. Schulz and *Peanuts* Fun Facts

- Charles Schulz drew 17,897 comic strips throughout his career.
- Schulz was first published in Ripley's newspaper feature *Believe It or Not* in 1937. He was fifteen years old and the drawing was of the family dog.
- From birth, comics played a large role in Schulz's life. At just two days old, an uncle nicknamed Schulz "Sparky" after the horse Spark Plug from the *Barney Google* comic strip. And that's what he was called for the rest of his life.
- In a bit of foreshadowing, Schulz's kindergarten teacher told him, "Someday, Charles, you're going to be an artist."
- Growing up, Schulz had a black-and-white dog that later became the inspiration for Snoopy—the same dog that Schulz drew for Ripley's *Believe It or Not*. The dog's name was Spike.

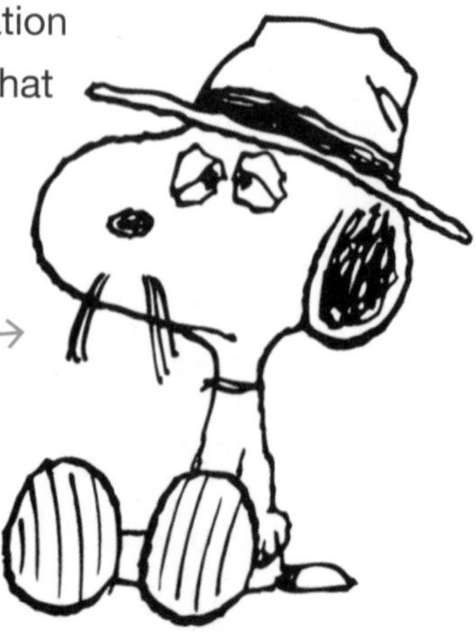

- Charles Schulz earned a star on the Hollywood Walk of Fame in 1996.

Learn How Comics Can Reflect Life

MATERIALS: blank piece of paper, pencil, markers or colored pencils

1. Make four blank cartoon panels, all the same size, on the piece of paper.
2. Look at the example below to see how Charles Schulz used his own life in his strips—even painful experiences like that of loss—and turned them into strips. Think of something that has happened to you at home or school that had a big impact on you.
3. Once you have decided on a story you want to tell, draw it in four panels. Remember, it should have a beginning, a middle, and an end.

An example from Schulz's life:

In 1966, a fire destroyed Schulz's Sebastopol studio. He translated his feelings into a strip about Snoopy's doghouse catching fire:

PEANUTS
SNIF?
I SMELL SMOKE!
SNIF SNIF
9-19
BAM! BAM!
BAM! BAM!
WHAT IN THE WORLD.....
GOOD GRIEF!
MY BOOKS! MY RECORDS! MY POOL TABLE! MY VAN GOGH!
SOB!
SCHULZ

Make a Snoopy Finger Puppet

MATERIALS: an 8.5 x 11 piece of paper, black construction paper, red or pink construction paper, scissors, tape, black marker

1 Fold paper into thirds, lengthwise.

2 Fold the paper in half by bringing one of the open ends to the other and creasing a fold in the middle.

3 Bring one of the open ends up to the middle and crease flat.

4 Turn the paper over.

5 Bring the second open end up to the middle and crease flat.

6 The finished folded square should look like an "M" or "W" when placed on its side on a flat surface.

7 Hold the square with the open ends facing you.

8 Use your thumb and index finger to gently pinch the folded points toward each other so the open ends open up.

9 Pull the two inside pages together.

10 Place a piece of tape over the middle of the inside pages.

11 Put your index finger and middle finger inside one of the pockets you have created.

12 Put your thumb inside the pocket below.

13 Close the puppet mouth by bringing your thumb to your index and middle finger. Open the puppet mouth by opening your fingers.

14 Cut out two ears from black construction paper and glue them to the face of your Snoopy.

15 Cut out one tongue from red or pink construction paper and glue it inside Snoopy's mouth.

16 Use a black marker to give Snoopy eyes.

It should look like this!

A round-headed boy named Charlie Brown, a security blanket, and a five-cent psychiatrist—just some of the classics you will find when you visit the largest collection of *Peanuts* artwork in the world. Laugh at Schulz's original comic strips, learn about the art of cartooning, and Schulz's role in its development, watch documentaries and animated *Peanuts* specials in the theater, and draw your own cartoons in the hands-on education room. The Museum features changing exhibitions, a re-creation of Schulz's art studio, outdoor gardens, holiday workshops. and special events. Take a virtual tour of the Museum at schulzmuseum.org!

CHARLES M.

SCHULZ

MUSEUM

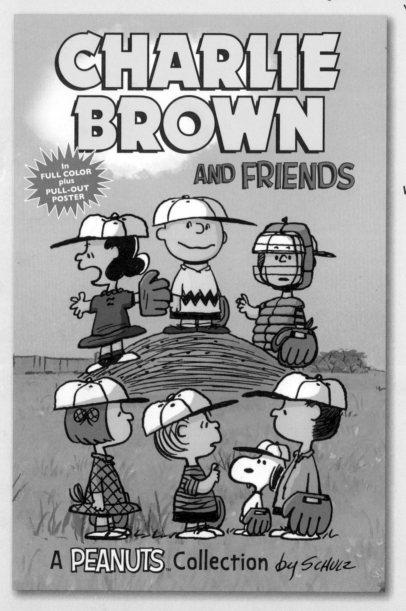